"The seamless blend of ancient Indian folklore and modern western storytelling makes this winner a standout."

—NIKKI GRIMES,

author of *Ordinary Hazards* and *Garvey's Choice*

"I felt this novel in verse in my bones. An important book; it will change how young readers see their world. And that's the best kind of book to read at any age."

—JANE YOLEN,

author of *The Devil's Arithmetic*, *Briar Rose*, and *Mapping the Bones*

"A book I wish I had growing up in the eighties!"

—VEERA HIRANANDANI,

Newbery Honor–winning author of *The Night Diary*

"This deeply memorable coming-of-age story weaves Indian mythology with the relatable modern story of Reha, as she grapples with identity, family, and what it means to truly be home."

—JOY McCULLOUGH,

author of *Blood Water Paint*; *A Field Guide to Getting Lost*; and *We Are the Ashes, We Are the Fire*

"Readers will be changed by Reha's story."

—ALA *BOOKLIST*, starred review

"A sensitive coming-of-age story with all the makings of a new middle grade classic."

—BOOKPAGE, starred review

MIRROR TO MIRROR

"A thoughtful and deeply moving story in verse."

—JACQUELINE WOODSON,

National Book Award–winning author

"A searing and poignant exploration of
sisterhood, and all of its complexities."

—JASMINE WARGA,

Newbery Honor–winning author of *Other Words for Home*

"A sensitive portrayal of sisters and music told
in lyrical free verse that sings with hope."

—MARGARITA ENGLE,

Newbery Honor–winning author of *The Surrender
Tree* and Young People's Poet Laureate Emeritus

"Deserves a place on every middle grade shelf."

—*SCHOOL LIBRARY JOURNAL*

Also by Rajani LaRocca

Red, White, and Whole
Mirror to Mirror

Midsummer's Mayhem
Much Ado About Baseball

SONA
AND THE
GOLDEN BEASTS

Rajani LaRocca

Quill Tree Books
An Imprint of HarperCollinsPublishers

Quill Tree Books is an imprint of HarperCollins Publishers.

Sona and the Golden Beasts
Copyright © 2024 by Rajani LaRocca
All rights reserved. Printed in the United States of America.
No part of this book may be used or reproduced in any manner whatsoever without written
permission except in the case of brief quotations embodied in critical articles and reviews.
For information address HarperCollins Children's Books, a division of HarperCollins
Publishers, 195 Broadway, New York, NY 10007.
www.harpercollinschildrens.com

Library of Congress Control Number: 2023937519
ISBN 978-0-06-329540-7

Map art © 2024 by Abrian Curington
Typography by Kathy H. Lam
24 25 26 27 28 LBC 5 4 3 2 1
First Edition

For those who wish they could see themselves
in the fantasy stories they love

EXCERPT FROM A LETTER FROM RAMANI, GOVERNOR OF TIR PROVINCE, TO ALDOS, MINISTER OF TRADE OF THE ROYAL ISLE OF MALECHIA

YK 503, Year 23 of the Devan Fourth Age
൧ 218 years before the Present Day ൦

I have only good news to report, Minister, and very little of concern. The golden-eared people here are welcoming and easily convinced of our good intentions. The land is fertile and rich and can support many more settlers.

Of the silks and fabrics, I have already told you. The variety of spices is beyond what we had imagined! But there is more.

This land is full of gems the likes of which we have never seen, in brilliant colors—red, blue, green, and black. The locals find them lying upon the earth, they say, and use the brightest and most pure (and most often the smallest, interestingly) in their prayers. But these people are either ignorant, lazy, or both, and do not comprehend their true value.

If this is what might be found lying upon the earth, just think what might be found by digging deeper!

Truly, I say, Devia would then herself become the glittering gem in the belt of the Malechian empire, spanning the Eight Seas!

THE NEW SONG

Devia, Year 191 of the Devan Fourth Age
꙰ 50 years before the Present Day ꙰

Come in, my friend, and rest awhile.
Sit down, I welcome you.
With open hands and honest smile,
I will sing you true.

I'll sing to you of Devia,
Our land so sweet and fair,
Our golden land of Devia,
Where music fills the air.

Some years ago, the Malechs came
With silver bright to trade
Then they saw our glittering gems
And so the Malechs stayed.

Two hundred years they have remained
Two hundred years of rule
Two hundred years they've had to leave
And so I call on you.

Now Devia has need, my friend,
Of hearts both strong and true.
Before the world comes to an end
I call, my friend, on you.

❧ 1 ❧

A Whine in the Dark

Devia, YK 721, Year 241 of the Devan Fourth Age ❧ the Present Day

Sona knew that music was forbidden, but she still heard it everywhere.

"Come on, Willa girl," she sang to the gray pony regarding her through a shaggy forelock. "Tell me what's on your mind."

The pony blinked a dark blue eye and snorted softly three times. Willa's music was gentle, but her stance told Sona she was annoyed.

"I know why you're cranky," Sona crooned, inching closer. "I haven't come to visit since breakfast, and it's almost time for dinner. Father and the boys have been in the whillet fields, and I've been busy harvesting vegetables and fruit all day." Sona held out an apple, and the pony took it in her soft mouth and started to crunch.

Sona pulled the jar of Ayah's ointment from her pocket and dabbed some on the pink sore on the pony's wide forehead. Willa nickered and leaned her head forward. Now she smelled like green herbs and fresh flowers on top of her regular pony smell of grass and hay and sweetness.

"See? It's good for you," said Sona. As she replaced the lid, she noticed the ointment was nearly gone. She'd need to ask Ayah for another jar. Ayah wouldn't like that the ointment had been used up so quickly—this was for Sona to use on her ears, since a proper Malech girl wouldn't let her ears get red and cracked in the Devan sun.

But although she was like a mother to Sona and her brothers, Ayah wasn't actually their mother. And what she didn't know wouldn't hurt her.

In the land of Devia, some thought the most important thing was the color of your ears, but Sona and Ayah knew better. Ayah had golden ears like all the Devans, and Sona didn't—just like all the Malechs. But that didn't mean she loved her ayah any less. Ayah was not a servant like those the rich Malechs living in cities hired to take care of their children; she was a friend who had stepped in to help when Sona's mother died. Ayah took care of Sona and her brothers, cooked food for the whole family, and lived in the house with them at harvest time, when they needed all the hands they could get.

Sona touched the pendant that hung around her neck, with the triangle of Malechia circumscribed by the circle of Devia, symbolizing how the two peoples could be one. She believed it. If only everyone did.

Sona put the jar of ointment in her pocket. She filled Willa's trough with hay and made sure she had enough water. As she turned to leave, a high-pitched whine pierced the air. Sona stopped short.

"What is it, girl?" Sona asked. "What's making that noise?"

Willa nickered again.

Sona listened. The horses were still out in the fields with her father and brothers. Maybe it was one of the barn cats? But Sona knew all their songs, their meows and howls and screeches. This was different. It didn't sound like a cat.

The whine was soft. It was a small creature, and it was in pain.

She tilted an ear. The sound seemed to be coming from behind Willa, who had turned broadside, almost as if to block Sona's way.

"Move, Willa. I need to see—"

"I have a right to be here!" someone bellowed from outside. "Don't touch me!"

"You're coming with us, Devan dirt!" came a deep voice.

Sona bit her lip. Trouble again, right near her farm. "Stay here," she said to Willa. "I'll be back soon."

Sona stepped out of the barn and squinted in the evening sun. She wiped her hands on her pants and raced down the field to the road. Silver peaks of helmets glinted. The soldiers might be Malechs like Sona and her family, under orders from the King of Malechia himself, but Sona couldn't stand them.

Sona drew closer. The soldiers were mounted on horses, surrounding a group of Devan farmers on foot. One of the soldiers had grabbed a Devan's arm and was twisting it cruelly.

"Let him go!" Sona cried, skidding to a stop at the edge of her family's land.

"Mind your business, girl," barked the soldier, tightening his grip so the man cried out.

"What seems to be the problem here?" came Sona's father's calm voice. She turned in relief and saw that her oldest brother, Lal, had arrived, too.

Sona took a breath and forced herself to stay quiet. The real problem was that there were too many soldiers lately, supposedly guarding gems for the King. Sona didn't care about gems. She just wanted her family and friends left in peace. But what could she do—what could anyone do against groups of armed men?

"These Devans are loitering on the King's Road," said the head soldier, still holding on to the man's arm and looking down at Father from his perch atop the horse like he was a king himself. "That Devan bandit's been sighted not far from here, and these fellows might be helping to hide him. And this one here is blatantly breaking the law."

"It's our road! Devans built it! I don't care about your stupid laws!" The Devan's voice cracked as he was almost lifted off the ground by the soldier's grip. Sona looked more carefully. The Devan seemed to be barely out of boyhood and wore his hair in a shaggy mop, completely obscuring his ears. That *was* against the law. No wonder the soldiers were angry.

The soldier reached for the sword at his side, and Sona bit her tongue to keep from crying out.

"Please, sir," said the oldest farmer, Darshan, looking up at the soldier. His hair was covered in a traditional farmer's wrap, but his golden ears were clearly visible. "No one here knows anything about the bandit Gulappan. We are just going home from work."

Father walked into the group of Devan farmers and addressed the soldier. "I'm Bar Kalpani, and this is my land." He took off his hat, showing his close-cropped hair and flesh-colored Malechian ears. "These people work the farm next door, and it's only just the end of the workday. They are on their way home to the village. These are good farmers. They help supply food for this whole region, including your regiment. If they don't get the harvest in, we'll all suffer come winter. And that one is just a boy. Please show him mercy."

The soldier thought for a moment. He nodded once at Father, then frowned with distaste as he shoved the boy away, making him stumble to the ground. He turned back to Father. "See that your farmhands follow the law, or they'll be required to do more useful service."

The land they stood on belonged to her family, but the land next door belonged to the Devans. "They're not our—" Sona began.

"Sona, hush," Father said.

The head soldier wheeled his horse, and the rest turned in a line and moved away down the road.

"Come, Raag," Darshan said as he helped the boy to his feet and put his arm around him.

Darshan turned to Father. "Thank you, Bar. We'll take this one home with us and make sure he shows up properly shorn tomorrow."

"You will not," said the boy, twisting out of Darshan's grip. "I won't be returning to this stupid farm." He turned and shot Sona and her family a look of pure loathing. "That land doesn't belong to you, no matter what you say." He took off down the road to the village in a run.

Darshan sighed. "I'm sorry for the trouble."

Father frowned. "These are difficult times, Darshan, for all of us in this corner of Devia. Apparently a new vein of black gems has been discovered in the hills not far from here."

Darshan's eyes widened. "More gems?" Devia held gems of many colors, but the black ones, the color of the Devan soil, were the rarest and the most valuable. The King and his soldiers wanted to take as many as possible to sell around the world and keep the island of Malechia the richest in the Eight Seas.

"I can see why the soldiers are concerned about Gulappan," Darshan said. Gulappan was a Devan bandit who stole gems from right under the noses of Malechian soldiers.

"Well, I know none of us is helping that bandit. Let's all go home and rest ourselves. It's important to finish the harvest soon, before the next Goldstorm comes," Father said.

The Devans said the Earth Goddess, Bhoomi, was angry that the Malechs mined her sacred gems, and Goldstorms sure felt like divine punishment. The storms covered everything in Golddust so fine and heavy that tall whillet stems snapped and whole tree limbs came down. And if you were caught outside in the middle of a Goldstorm . . . Sona shuddered at the thought. She'd seen the corpses of animals who couldn't find shelter completely buried under piles of it. After a few days, when the damage was already done, Golddust turned brown like regular dirt again, but while it was gold, it choked lungs and burned skin. The Goldstorms were getting more frequent, and now, right at harvest time, was when they were likely to start.

Father watched Darshan and the rest of the Devans start down the road, then put an arm each around Lal and Sona as they made their way back to their house. As they passed the barn, Sona pulled away. "I've got one more thing to check on. I'll be in soon to wash up for dinner."

"Another stray?" Lal smirked. At seventeen, he was as tall as Father and almost as strong, and acted like he was all grown up and knew better than everyone. "We don't have room for any more of your broken-down pets."

"They are not broken down! The cats earn their keep catching mice, the goats give us good milk, and Willa . . . well, Willa . . ."

"You might as well call her Won't," Lal said with a chuckle. "Because she won't do a thing."

"She has a right to live just as much as anything or anyone," Sona said. "She's sweet and beautiful."

"That she is, that she is," said Father, soothing. "Go on, Sona, take care of your Willa, and come in the house soon. Ayah is waiting."

Sona jogged to the barn door and listened. The horses were all in now, making their settling-down noises, their whispers of a long day done and dinner now and sleep coming soon. But underneath the nighttime melodies, Sona heard the whine again, softer than before. Like whatever creature was making it was losing the strength to even make a sound.

"Come on, Willa girl," she cajoled. "Let me see what's behind you."

Willa huffed and snorted, but she let Sona put a hand on her flank and move around her. Sona crept to the corner of the stall, where clean straw was piled. The whining grew slightly louder.

In the waning light, Sona spied a bundle of dark fur. Maybe it was another cat.

Sona hummed a soothing tune. "It's okay, little one," she murmured. "I can help."

She squatted slowly so she wouldn't scare the creature. It was small, its head tucked away in the pile of straw. Sona gingerly laid a hand on the soft fur, which rose and fell under her touch. Good. It was still breathing, whatever it was.

Sona got her hand under the creature and gently lifted. It was the size of a cat but felt heavier. It stirred and whined weakly but didn't squirm. Sona felt the lick of a warm tongue on her finger and smiled. Poor little kitty. She picked it up, cradled it close to her body, and stepped into the aisle of the barn where she could see better. She looked at the creature in her arms and gasped.

It was a wolf pup with fur as dark as the Devan soil.

It had a nasty gash on its side that was oozing blood.

And in the rays of the evening light, the tips of its ears glowed gold.

2

Swara

Sona's mind whirled. This pup was very young, probably barely weaned. Where was its mother? Her pulse quickened as she looked around, but she soon realized there couldn't be a grown wolf anywhere nearby, or the horses and Willa would be spooked. Her heartbeat steadied.

The pup looked at Sona with steady amber eyes that held no fear or malice, and Sona heard a pure, clear tone, like a perfectly struck bell. She made up her mind. This was a predator, for sure—but this was also a baby, hurt and alone and in need of help.

"Come, little one," Sona said, tucking the pup against her chest. It trembled under her fingers. "Let's get you cleaned up and fed."

Sona shook with anticipation as she walked toward the farmhouse. It was a typical Malechian structure, with a lofty, angled roof and a windmill behind it, standing tall against the darkening sky.

No matter how sweet it was now, a wolf pup would soon become dangerous, a beast that would hurt or eat chickens, lambs, even calves. Sona couldn't let her family know about it. They would make her abandon it now, which would be just as good as killing it, injured and little as it was. She would wait until it had healed and grown strong enough to hunt for itself, and then she'd release it into the wild.

Sona entered through the back door, shucked off her boots, then went straight to the washroom, where she dipped a cloth into a bucket of clean water and cleansed the pup's wound, which was long but shallow. The pup whimpered but didn't protest beyond that. Sona covered it with a dry cloth and wrapped another around the pup's torso to hold it in place. Then she poured more water into her cupped hand, and the pup lapped it up. The thirsty animal drank four handfuls of water before it seemed satisfied and looked at Sona expectantly.

Sona washed her hands with soap and water and splashed her face. She picked up the pup and brought it to her room, thankful that everyone else was already in the kitchen. She needed to feed the pup. She didn't want to leave it there, alone and hungry, so she decided to take a chance. She rummaged in a drawer for what she wanted: a big sweater, formerly Lal's, with a pocket in front, large enough to hold the pup.

"Sona, we're waiting for you," came Father's voice.

"Coming!" Sona called. She made sure the pup was safely stowed in her pocket, threw on a big wool shawl to hide it completely, and hurried to the kitchen, where delicious smells made her mouth water. There would be plenty of food to share with a tiny pup. As long as it didn't whine or bark, Sona could keep it a secret.

"Sona, pautri, sit and eat before everything gets cold," said Ayah, bringing a basket of Devan flatbread to the table and seating herself at one end. Her graying hair was gathered in a bun at the nape of her neck, and her golden ears shone in the lamplight.

"Took you long enough," said Lal, seated at Father's right at the other end of the table. "I'm starving."

"What else is new," teased Sona's second brother, Ran, who was fifteen and skinny compared to Lal's bulk. "You're always starving."

"When you grow six inches in a summer, maybe you'll understand," said Lal. "Or maybe you'll stay short forever, like those dwarf hooli fruit trees you like so much."

"I'll grow when I'm supposed to," said Ran. "If you leave any food for the rest of us."

"How is Willa doing?" asked Sona's youngest brother, Karn, just a year older than her at fourteen. He cared about animals almost as much as Sona did.

"Good," said Sona, sitting at her place between him and Ayah at the end of the table. "She's filled out so much in the three weeks she's been here." Sona had found Willa wandering in the westernmost fields of whillet, starved and bony and bleeding from her forehead, eyes rolling in fear. But she'd calmed right down at the sound of Sona's voice and gentle touch and had followed her docilely through the fields to the barn. She'd eaten from Sona's hand and stood patiently while Sona tended her wounds and groomed her, almost as if she'd grown up there. She wouldn't let any of Sona's brothers or even Father near her, though, and aside from spending her days eating fresh grass in the southern pastures, seemed quite content with staying in the barn. But last week, Willa had let Sona saddle her up and take her for a short ride.

Everyone turned toward Ayah. She lit the oil lamp in the center of the table, then poured water from her cup into her hand and sprinkled it in a circle around her plate. "For Bhoomi's bounty, we are grateful," Ayah said in her melodious voice. "Bless the land, the creatures, and the people." It was the traditional Devan way to give thanks.

"May the wind blow blessings to us all," Father responded in the Malechian way.

Everyone began serving themselves food: parathas and potatoes, black dal with spices, the last of the okra, and a salad with carrots, cucumber, and yogurt. There was a roast chicken at Father's end of the table that Ayah would not eat, but she somehow seasoned it perfectly for the rest of the family. Over the past few years, Sona had found herself not enjoying meat as much, either.

Devans believed in doing no harm—and to some, like Ayah, that extended to not eating the flesh of birds, fish, or animals. They also didn't engage in wars or armed confrontations and believed that killing a person was the most unforgivable sin of all. But Malechs had no problem killing animals, and the King of Malechia had no problem ordering the killing of people.

"Ayah, may I please have some milk?" Sona asked.

"Yes, of course, pautri," Ayah said, passing the pitcher. "We had so much today that I made extra cheese as well. We do not have to take, even from animals, when we can ask. I asked the cows, and they provided even more than I'd requested."

Ayah said something like this almost every day. Sona nodded. "Yes, Ayah. Thank you." She reached under her shawl and patted the front of her sweater, where the pup was squirming. "May I also have some of that cheese?"

Sona poured herself a cup of milk and took a sip. Then, while everyone else was preoccupied with serving themselves, she brought the cup under the table, dipped the end of a cloth napkin into it, and stuffed the napkin into her pocket, hoping it was near the pup's mouth. She was rewarded by another lick and sharp little teeth biting on the napkin and her fingers, and she had to stifle a giggle. She kept dipping and feeding the milk, and then fresh cheese, to the pup until Father said, "Sona, are you going to have some dal before Lal takes it all?"

Sona put the cup back on the table, served herself, and started eating. Everything was delicious, as usual, steaming hot and full of flavor. Ayah was the best cook in Tir Province. Father and her brothers chatted about how the harvest was going, and Sona and Ayah listened intently. The harvest would be smaller than last year's, which had been smaller than the year before. Tir Province provided food for all of Devia, and tensions were high with year after year of worsening harvests. Sona kept quiet and fed morsels of food to the pup surreptitiously.

"There were soldiers on the road today harassing Darshan and the other Devan farmers," said Father to Ayah. "Please let one of us take you if you need to go to the village. I don't trust the road right now."

Sona took a morsel of chicken and held it to her pocket.

"I have been walking that road since before you were born," Ayah said with a smile. "I can deal with soldiers. I am a Devan in Devia, and I have no fear of beast nor man."

Needlelike teeth chomped on Sona's finger. "Ah!" Sona cried as she pulled her finger away. Everyone at the table turned to stare at her.

"There was a Devan boy with Darshan's men," Sona said, rubbing her finger under the table. The skin didn't seem to be broken.

"He wore his hair covering his ears, and that's what angered the soldiers. As if they needed more to be upset about."

A shadow crossed Ayah's face. "No one should try to provoke the soldiers. Someone could get hurt."

"The soldiers are terrible," said Sona. "I wish they'd leave us all alone." She snuck another bite of chicken to the pup with the very tips of her fingers and managed not to get bitten.

"They're here to protect us," said Lal, reaching for more bread.

"They're here to protect gems on behalf of the King," said Ran. "They don't care about us. The soldiers are even more on edge because the Free Devia protests are starting up here in the country-side. And Gulappan keeps getting the best of them, so they take it out on all the other Devans."

Sona tore a piece of flatbread and had it halfway to her lap when she caught Ran looking at her with his brow furrowed. She brought the bread back up, scooped some dal, and ate. It tasted earthy and creamy and full of warm spices. Ran turned his attention back to Lal.

"The soldiers could be useful and help with the harvest instead of patrolling the road." Karn looked down at his plate. "And I've heard awful stories of villages burned, and temples sacked and ruined, their sacred gems stolen."

"That bandit. It's thieves like him that the soldiers are protecting everyone against," Lal said with his mouth full of food. "Not to mention the protestors, who cause a commotion and probably steal things, too. The soldiers are here to keep the King's peace."

Sona and Karn started to argue with Lal, but then Father said, "I'm not sure that peace is what the King wants most. Gulappan only steals from Malechs. And the protestors, although loud, have not harmed anyone or anything, as far as I know. I have a feeling that some of the soldiers are the ones doing the sacking of Devan temples."

"See? The soldiers are bad people, all of them," Sona said.

"Pautri," Ayah said, "people are not good or bad. There is both in every one of us. It is our actions that are good or bad. And we are all children of Bhoomi—Devan and Malech alike."

The pup whined. Sona jumped in her seat, then pretended to sneeze, hoping it would fool her family.

"May the wind bring you health," Father said automatically.

"Are you catching a cold, Sona?" Ayah frowned.

"Maybe," Sona said. She picked up a piece of potato, pretended to eat it, then snuck it to her lap, where the pup took it eagerly.

"The law against covering your ears is a bad law." Ran rubbed his jaw. "It's easy enough to figure out who's Devan without having to show your ears all the time."

"That's not the point," Sona said. "What's the difference whether someone is Devan or Malech?"

"That's right," Karn said. "And just because the Malechian King wants more gems, it doesn't mean he should be able to ruin Devan farmland to find them."

"I agree, but the King can do what he likes, and we can't stop him," Father said.

Karn continued: "And what about outlawing Malechs and Devans from attending school together? I'd rather go to Kanthpur than only study here."

Father shook his head. "In my day, I went to school in Kanthpur with Devans and Malechs alike. But much has changed in the last fifteen years, when King Lobh came to power."

Sona thought about all the terrible rules imposed on Devia and spoke up. "The worst thing the King has done is to outlaw music. It's like telling birds not to sing, like telling us not to hear them. Music is everywhere, whether we like it or not."

The table went silent.

Father looked behind him like someone might be listening at the window. "Sona, don't say that to anyone else. Not even your friends."

"But that law is—"

"Enough, Sona. Even as Malechs, we must be careful about some things."

"Yes, Father." Sona looked in her lap and felt the warmth of the pup cuddled against her. The clear tone filled her ears again, a song that no one else seemed to hear. An ache started behind her eyes. "May I go to my room, please? My head hurts."

"Go to your room, pautri," said Ayah. "I'll be there soon with a drink to help you feel better."

Sona walked slowly to her room, listening to the rumble of her family's conversation as they cleared the table. She wondered if they were talking about her, and how her mouth would get her in big trouble someday. Only the presence of the pup made her not turn around and insist that they listen to her. Music shouldn't be against the law. It was a part of her, a part of every creature. She heard it in the birds, fresh and free; she heard it in the land around her, generous and nourishing; and she heard it in the creatures on the farm, mild and patient. Most of all, she heard it in the animals that kept showing up on her doorstep—the ones she rescued. She patted her pocket.

Sona arrived at her room and put the pup on her bed, where it blinked at her with calm amber eyes. Sona unwrapped the bandage and examined the wound, which had stopped oozing. She took out the ointment jar and applied the very last of the ointment, then rewrapped the pup. It was a girl; what would she name it?

She heard Ayah's footstep outside her door and quickly tucked the pup under her blanket, then piled another blanket on top and whispered to the pup not to move.

Ayah opened the door. "Here, Sona, pautri," she said, handing her a steaming mug of ginger tea. "Now relax while I massage your head."

Sona sat on a stool and closed her eyes as Ayah settled herself in a chair behind her and unbraided her hair. Sona sighed as Ayah massaged her scalp with strong fingers. This must be how Willa felt when Sona brushed her.

"Your braids were too tight. Make them looser tomorrow, Sona."

"But then they sometimes come undone, and I might get in trouble."

Ayah chuckled. "A few loose hairs are nothing compared to a song, Sona."

Sona's eyes flew open, and she turned to look at Ayah. "Did you hear me?"

Ayah smiled. "Today? No. But I imagine you've been singing all day to your pony, the cats, maybe even the chickens?"

Sona nodded, a smile playing on her own mouth. "I can't help it, Ayah. But I only sing to the animals when no one else is around."

"I know, pautri, but you must be very careful. It is in your nature, as someone who loves Devia, to love music. But your father and brothers love you, and they fear what would happen if you were discovered singing. This Malechian King is too afraid of the magic of music."

"I won't ask you to sing, but will you tell me a story, Ayah?" Sona stole a glance at her bed. "About the sacred Wolf of Tir?"

Ayah's hands stilled on Sona's head. "What makes you ask for that tonight?"

Sona's heart started to speed, but she forced herself to act casual. She shrugged. "Just curious. The moon is almost full—a wolf's moon, right?"

"All right," Ayah said, resuming her massage. "But a quick story, and then you must go to bed." She took a breath and started speaking in a soft chant.

"Devia belongs to Bhoomi, now and forever," Ayah said. That was the way all Devan stories began.

"Our land, Tirna of the plains, with gems as black as earth, is guarded by Vrka, the Wolf, one of the five Golden Beasts of Devia. Vrka brings luck to farmers and promises a bountiful harvest. Where she treads with her golden paws, no blight or scavengers will ruin crops. She hears the music of the land, and her song brings rain, sunlight, and moonlight."

Sona's skin tingled.

"We strive to be as loyal as Vrka, and she rewards us with her loyalty in return. And then when Devia is at its most desperate moment, the old songs say the Sixth Beast will come and save the whole world."

Ayah gently brushed Sona's hair until it shone and settled heavily on her shoulders.

"You've told me of the Sixth Beast before. But what kind of beast is it?" Sona asked.

Ayah shook her head. "No one knows. But it is as courageous as the Tiger, as flexible as the Fish, as enduring as the Snake, as far-seeing as the Hawk, and as loyal as the Wolf."

Sona furrowed her brow. "I can't imagine an animal like that."

"Bhoomi makes all things clear in time," Ayah said. She gave Sona's shoulders one final squeeze. "Now it is time for you to finish getting ready for bed and go to sleep. You need your rest."

Sona turned around and put her hand upon Ayah's soft cheek. "Thank you for telling me more about the Wolf, Ayah. And my head feels so much better."

"You are welcome, pautri. May Bhoomi keep you safe and healthy." She laid her hand on Sona's head in a blessing.

"Ayah, I have something to tell you." Sona's heart sped up again. Surely Ayah of all people would understand how important it was to protect this gold-touched wolf pup—in honor of Vrka.

"You can tell me while I care for your ears for the night. Now, where is the jar of ointment?"

Sona took the empty jar out of her pocket. "It's finished, Ayah. I'm sorry."

Ayah inhaled sharply. "But how is this, Sona? This was brand-new from two weeks ago, and it should have lasted at least until the next new moon. You're thirteen now, almost a woman grown, and I trusted you to manage this on your own."

Sona ducked her head. "I'm sorry. I must have put on extra without thinking." She hated lying, but Ayah would get angry if she knew she'd used it all on Willa.

Ayah stood. "I must go to my house in the village to fetch more ointment for you."

"Now? But it's almost dark," Sona said. "Can't I just miss one day?" What difference could that make?

"No, Sona, this cannot wait." Ayah turned back and smiled, but a worry line appeared between her eyes. "Sona, I must tell you . . ."

"What is it, Ayah?"

Ayah stayed silent for a moment. Then she said, "Proper young Malechian ladies do not let their ears become red and cracked." She told Sona that at least three times a week! "I will go now."

"I'll wear a hat in the fields all day tomorrow." When Ayah shook her head, Sona said, "Will you at least let Lal take you to the village in the cart? Father said it's dangerous for you to be alone on the road."

"It would take the same time as walking, and Lal needs his rest. I will be fine, Sona. Don't worry about me. I will be back in the morning with a new jar, and I will be the one putting on your ointment every night from now on, so you don't use too much."

"But, Ayah—"

"No arguments, Sona. I will return with the sunrise. Now put on your nightgown, drink your tea, and go straight to sleep. We have a busy day tomorrow with the harvest. We need to finish picking and storing the vegetables."

Sona nodded. Ayah was putting herself in danger because of *her*. "I'm sorry, Ayah. I'll do as you ask. But one last thing before you go: There's a word in Old Devan you once taught me that I can't remember. It's the word for *note* or *tone*, and I can't remember what it was . . ."

"*Swara*," said Ayah. "Why, pautri?"

"No reason," Sona said quickly. "I remember liking that word, that's all."

Ayah kissed Sona on the forehead and left the room. Sona heard her speak to Father and then a few minutes later, go out the front door.

Sona pulled back her blanket. The pup, which had been asleep, opened its eyes and stretched.

"Hello, Swara," Sona said.

She slept nestled next to the pup for a few blissful hours.

Then she woke in the dark to the sound of someone banging on the front door.

ꙮ *2 years before the Present Day* ꙮ

Dear Ma,

I know I have not written in a long time—so long that you probably thought me dead. There were times in the past two years that I thought being dead would be better than what I've been doing: Digging in our precious jungles for gems. Gems that are all sent to the Malechian King to make him richer.

But as of today, I am no longer a miner in the King's service. I am sending you the money I've earned in the past two years in another way, through people I trust. I hope it will help you. I want none of it.

Yesterday, I lost my best friend, Alokh. He came from another village in Vanam and helped me get accustomed to the work when I first came here. He died in a tunnel collapse. I don't even know his mother's name, and I doubt anyone here will let her know that he is gone. To the Malechs, we are no more valuable than the shovels they give us to dig.

But I mourned my friend. And I determined that I would not spend another day here without him. Today at the end of my shift, I took a single tiny Leaf gem for myself. For the first time in two years, I did it. I am tired of working for the Malechs so they can take our sacred gems and exploit them for their own gain. I am tired of being half-starved all the time. I am tired.

So I pocketed the gem, knowing that if I were caught, they'd kill me in a moment. And that night, I ran into the jungle.

I ran for miles, deep into the trees, until I came across the ruins of a temple. It was a lonely place, abandoned and falling apart, the leaf screens rotting. The wooden bowl where a gem should be sitting was empty and forlorn. I was scared, and tired, and very hungry. But I could walk no farther, so I settled down to sleep.

I awoke with the feeling that someone was watching me.

I heard the heavy breathing of a large beast. I opened my eyes, and in the moonlight, I saw green eyes as bright as leaves glowing in the midday sun. I saw stripes of gold and black and orange. I saw Vyaghra, the Tiger, herself. Ma, she was beautiful. I was not scared. She regarded me patiently, as if she was waiting for something.

So I took the gem I'd been hiding and brought it to her. I laid it at her feet, kneeled, and bowed my head.

Ma, the Tiger opened her mouth, and I was sure she would take my life, for I was the worst kind of sinner. But instead, she breathed on me.

With that breath, she filled me with courage.

And so I am off now, heading north, looking to find people who will help me free Devia from the Malechs. Even if I perish along the way, I wanted you to know, Ma, that I am no longer craven. I am no longer subjugated. I am fierce. I am free.

I hope we meet again someday, when Devia is free, too.

3

The Hunter

Sona sat up abruptly. Her heart skittered as the banging continued. Then Father's heavy footsteps echoed down the hall and into the front room.

Swara was awake, head tilted, golden ears glinting in the moonlight spilling through the window. She growled softly, and Sona hushed her. Sona heard the door open and Father speaking to someone in a low voice. The door closed and footsteps receded toward the kitchen.

Who would Father let into the house in the middle of the night? It couldn't be Ayah, because she had a key. Was it Darshan, their farmer friend? Was there a problem in the village?

Sona slipped out of bed and willed the floorboards not to squeak. "Stay here, Swara," she murmured softly to the pup, who had stood on the bed as soon as Sona moved. The pup looked at her reproachfully but lay down, curled into a circle, and rested her face on her paws. Sona hastily threw a blanket over her.

Sona crept to her door and stepped into the hallway, shutting the door softly behind her. She was startled by the sight of Karn and Ran tiptoeing down the hall ahead of her, silhouetted in the lamplight's glow from the kitchen. Karn turned back and put a finger to his lips, as if she needed to be told to be quiet.

The three snuck down the hall to the threshold of the kitchen, where they saw Father talking to someone.

The visitor had his back to Sona and her brothers. He was large, bulkier than Lal and Father put together, and wore an enormous cape, shaggy and orange with black and gold stripes—a tiger cloak. The stranger was demolishing a plate of food like he hadn't eaten in a very long time.

"I've been tracking it for weeks," said the man in a raspy voice, pausing only to swallow. "I shot at it, and my aim was true—the great beast went down, and I finished her with my knife and took care of its offspring. I started tracking the second young one, but the trail just disappeared near the stream. Then my horse came up lame and dumped me on the ground. I believe I broke my nose." He gestured to his face and then continued: "I had to put my horse out of his misery. He's a couple of miles north of here. You can have his meat for your own."

Sona felt queasy. This man killed his own horse and was offering her family its meat? She'd rather eat rotten hooli fruit than horsemeat. She thought of Willa, and her stomach turned.

The man grunted as he scooped more food from the serving bowl onto his plate. "Glad I can't taste this Devan grub, but it feels good to be filling my belly. Yours is the only Malechian house for miles, and I didn't want to be caught in the wilderness with a Goldstorm coming. As soon as it's over I'll take one of your horses and be on my way."

Sona stifled a gasp. Take a horse? Why in the world would—

"You can take one now," said Father. "I don't think we'll see a Goldstorm until the harvest is over."

"There's one coming soon. I could smell it on the wind, before my nose was injured," said the man.

Sona's heart twinged as she thought of Ayah. Surely she had reached the village hours ago. She hoped Ayah was sleeping soundly now and wouldn't travel unless the skies were clear.

"By the way, your young ones are awake and standing in the hallway behind me."

Father squinted into the darkness of the hallway. Ran and Karn shrank back, but Sona moved forward into the kitchen, brought a fresh pitcher of water to the table, and poured Father and the stranger a cup each.

"I'm Sona Kalpani," she said. "Welcome to our home." With Ayah gone, she was the woman of the house, and it was her job to say the words and offer drink. Ayah said visitors were to be treated as honored guests. Sona tried not to wrinkle her nose at this guest's unwashed stench.

"I appreciate that, young lady," the stranger said seriously. "I am Rodh, Hunter of Malechia, demanding shelter, food, and any help I may require as is my right by the ancient laws and the will of the Wind God."

"You shall receive them all, as is fit for one who defends the Kingdom from ferocious beasts," said Father solemnly. He didn't look like he took any pleasure in the words, but he offered Rodh more bread.

There hadn't been a Hunter seen in their province since long before Sona was born. Sona and her brothers loved to hear Father tell stories of that time, but it was a shock to see a living, breathing Hunter in their midst, as if he'd been plucked from one of the old legends and plunked at their table.

Sona settled herself next to her father and peered more closely at the man before them. In the lamplight, his face looked like it was carved from stone, all crags and shadows. His nose was swollen and shifted to one side. His head was shaved and brown, his ears red and cracked, and he had an earring that held a black Earth gemstone the size of Sona's thumbnail. Sona had never seen one so big. All Malechs received a gemstone earring when they came of age, at thirteen, but Sona and the rest of her family wore tiny stones in theirs. The Hunter's eyes were pale and strangely colorless, like his soul had leaked out during his treks across Devia. Sona shivered. The eyes of the pup hiding in her bed held more warmth than those eyes could ever carry.

Ran and Karn came into the room and sat, too. Ran rubbed his eyes, but Karn watched the Hunter suspiciously. "No one's seen a wild beast around here. Whatever lives in the forest tends to stay there."

"All thanks to me and all the Hunters before me," the Hunter said. He wiped his mouth with the back of his hand, even though there was a napkin in front of him. "We have eliminated the dangerous creatures throughout Devia and have made it a land fit for civilized men and not just savages. But there is always more work to be done." He shoved what remained of his bread into his mouth and reached for another piece.

Sona bristled but kept her mouth shut. She hated it when Malechs called Devans "savages." But she had to admit that thanks to the Hunters, they all lived without fear of the ferocious beasts who had once roamed Devia, devouring animals and people alike. This was why no Malech could refuse a Hunter anything, not even if he asked for the roof over their heads or their last whillet plant. Luckily, most didn't stay for long.

It was one thing to read in *A Malechian History of Devia* about the Hunters of old, like Del the Drinker, who killed the great lion terrorizing western Van Province and then proceeded to demand one hundred flagons of beer, which she consumed over three days, and Lukstan of the Roar, who bellowed so loudly he made the Horned Snake of Khil Province shed its skin so it was more vulnerable to his attack. But it was another thing to see a Hunter in your own kitchen, eating all your food and demanding a horse.

"Where'd you face that tiger?" Lal asked from the threshold, gesturing to the cloak. He always slept like a log, but even so Sona was surprised it took him this long to wake with all the noise everyone was making.

The Hunter smiled. "Far from here, lad, in Van Province," he said. "In the jungles to the south, where it was bewitching and haunting an entire town."

"Bewitching?" Sona couldn't help asking.

The Hunter nodded. "It was getting the townspeople to come to it. Decorated it with garlands and everything, until it pounced, then mauled and ate a dozen people."

Sona recoiled in horror.

"It gave me a wound, that one did." He exposed a long, jagged scar on his forearm. "But I got the best of her in the end."

"How'd you kill it?" Lal asked, coming to sit at the table.

"I'll show you. If you'll allow me, Farmer Kalpani." The Hunter looked at Father, who nodded briefly. Then the Hunter pulled out a silver knife, curved and shining in the lamplight. "I killed that murderous tiger and her three cubs with my silver Air Blade." He caressed the handle like it was a loved one. "It's the only kind of weapon that works against the magical beasts. Regular blades just bounce off them like toys. I've got silver-tipped spears and arrows, too. Silver against their gold."

The hairs on Sona's arms stood up. "What do you mean, silver against their gold?" she asked.

A cruel smile played on the Hunter's lips. "The magical beasts are cursed, just like the dirt-loving people of this land," he said. "Gold-touched, like the storms we fear and the people who burden this country with the noise they call music."

Sona felt chilled and flushed at the same time. But she had to know. "Rodh the Hunter," she said, hoping he didn't notice the quake in her voice. "What kind of beast are you tracking now?"

"A wolf," he said, grinning like a wolf himself. "I killed a huge beast that now won't be eating your livestock." He dug in a pocket, then opened his palm to reveal four enormous canine teeth crusted with blood. Sona had to bite her tongue to keep from crying out. "I got her pup, too. But there's another. Might be touched with gold, too. Seen or heard anything like that recently? Smelled anything unusual?"

Sona's heart quailed at his penetrating gaze. This Hunter had killed the Great Wolf of Tir. And her last pup, the pup he sought, was in Sona's bedroom, not thirty feet away. Did he know? He couldn't. Could he? She couldn't move. She couldn't talk.

"There hasn't been anything unusual happening on our farm," Father said. "My daughter here loves animals, and she'd notice if any of ours were getting skittish, as they would certainly do if there were a predator about." He laid a large hand on Sona's head and glanced down at her.

Sona smiled at him gratefully.

"Attuned to animals, huh? She might become a Hunter herself someday."

The thought disgusted Sona, but she tried not to let it show on her face.

The Hunter licked his fingers and scooped another mouthful of food. "And then," he said with his mouth still full, "she might win herself something like this." He held out his left hand, where a ring holding a small but brilliant green gem sparkled on his fifth finger. It was cleverly cut so a tiny circle within the gem glowed bright in the lamplight.

"Is that a Leaf gem?" Lal cried.

"Yes indeed," said the Hunter. "Cut it right out of this great beast's heart." He patted the tiger skin on his back. "There's a gem at the heart of every magical beast, they say."

A wave of nausea and dizziness passed through Sona.

The Hunter grabbed another piece of bread and stuffed it into his mouth. "The gems over a certain size are all given to the King, of course. But since this one is so small, I got to claim it as my own."

"If the King doesn't want it, shouldn't it stay with the Devans?" Sona asked coldly. Devan temples had been destroyed for gems smaller than that one. Ayah had taught Sona that all Devan gems were sacred to Bhoomi.

"Haha, Sona, very funny," Father said. He put his arm around her and gave her a look that said *Stop talking now.*

The Hunter chuckled. But his eyes narrowed as he scrutinized Sona.

There she was, getting in trouble again for speaking her mind. Sona's father drew her close, blocking her from the Hunter's view.

"My children must sleep for another hour or so until the sun rises." Father took Sona's shoulders and nudged her toward the doorway, away from the Hunter. "They need strength to help bring in the whillet harvest before the next Goldstorm comes. Hunter Rodh, please eat your fill, and then you can rest. I'll get my children settled, and then I must run an errand."

"An errand?" Lal looked puzzled.

"I'll go, Father," Karn said. "I'm not sleepy anymore."

Father shook his head. "It must be me. Lal, you'll move into your brothers' room. The three of you rest until sunrise. I'll get Sona back to her room. She hasn't been feeling well, and I don't want her to catch a chill. Hunter Rodh, I'll be back soon. You can sleep in the last room on the left."

The Hunter barely slowed his eating but nodded as Father moved Sona down the hall with his hands on her shoulders.

What was happening?

As she was herded back to her room, Sona said a silent prayer to Bhoomi and the Wind God both that Swara wouldn't be up and pacing.

But when they got there, the pup was still under the covers, and Father had no eyes for anything but Sona. He entered the room and shut the door behind him.

"Where are you going?" Sona asked.

Father looked at her with worry in his dark eyes. "To bring Ayah back. And to warn our Devan friends to be on their best behavior, with a bloody Hunter staying with us."

It was good of Father to think of Ayah, Darshan, and the other

Devans. "You're going now, before they start walking from the village."

Father nodded. "Listen to me, Sona, my girl. You must be very careful with the Hunter in the house. Don't say anything strange, and for goodness' sake, don't sing. And until we get you Ayah's ointment, do not leave this room."

Surely Father wasn't concerned about vanity now. "Ayah is bringing more this morning. Why are you so worried?"

Father sighed. "I should have told you long ago. And I need to leave now. There's no time, not with that man in our house. And if he's right about a Goldstorm coming . . ."

"What's upsetting you, Father?"

Father took her hand in both of his. "I wanted things to remain as they've been, with all of us together and happy for as long as we could."

"Father, you're scaring me," Sona said. What could break their family apart?

Father ran a hand over his face. "There's something I must tell you." He glanced at the door. "Sit, Sona. We only have a few minutes."

Sona sat on her bed near the warm lump where Swara lay, hoping she'd stay quiet and still. She resisted the urge to put her hand under the blanket and stroke the pup's soft fur.

Father began to pace the room and spoke in a voice so low she strained toward him to hear.

"This all starts with my sister, Lia."

"Our aunt, who died in the same Goldstorm that killed Mother," said Sona. She'd heard the story so many times. It was why Goldstorms held such terror for Father. They'd lost both women of the family in a single awful night, when Sona was just an infant. She'd never known her own mother and was doubly grateful that Ayah was there to care for her.

Father nodded. "Lia was my younger sister, and like me, she loved Devia, its dark earth and harvest bounty, its cold rivers and faraway mountains. She got married right around when Karn was born." Father smiled. "She and her husband were happy—or as happy as anyone could be, during troubled times. They lived here with us, and we all worked on the farm together. Then, just when Lia was due to have a baby, a Goldstorm struck, the worst that anyone had heard of in a century." Father sighed and combed his hand through his dark hair touched with gray.

"Both Lia and my wife, Jasna, became desperately ill with Goldstorm Fever. They were burning up. They couldn't stop coughing. When it was clear that they were getting worse, Lia's husband insisted on going out into the storm to get help from the village."

Sona put her hand over her mouth. She had never heard this part of the story.

People who went out in Goldstorms never survived.

"He never returned. Both Jasna and Lia died. There was nothing I could do." Suddenly, Father looked much older.

"What happened to the baby?" Sona asked. "Was it able to be born? Did it die, too?" Sona hated the thought of her newborn cousin succumbing to Goldstorm Fever, of Father needing to mourn so many at once.

Tears welled in Father's eyes. He looked scared in a way that Sona had never seen.

"No, Sona. That baby was you."

Vyaghra, the Tiger

The Tiger is the fierce heart of the jungle.

Her song is strength, subtlety, stealth. She prowls, hunts, protects. She is the boldest mother in all of Devia. She is the fierceness of life itself, that keeps trying, that never despairs.

Her silent padding sets the beat; her breath the deepest notes; her body's sway, the melody; her growls, the harmony; her roar, the crashing crescendo.

She hears and smells the man long before she sees him. His song is muffled, disguised. He walks in time with her breath, hides his scent downwind. He is dangerous, almost as dangerous as she. He is human, she is animal. Both part of Devia, both part of Bhoomi's grace.

She does not fear him. She fears nothing, for she is Vyaghra, the Tiger. The villagers know this, leave flowers at her altar, praise the prosperity she brings.

But as she tends her cubs, the man catches her by surprise. In all her long years, this has never happened. She wounds him, but the man pulls a long claw, pierces her heart. She roars and writhes, but it is no good. The wound is mortal.

As her Devan blood drains from her, she sends thoughts to her cubs to run, to be safe.

Her heart is stilled forever.

But in her heart, there lies a seed of fierceness that may be used to mend what is broken.

4

The Truth

Sona's mind reeled. "What do you mean, it was me?"

"Quiet! We cannot be heard!" Father whispered. "I'm sorry, Sona, I should have told you years ago. It's just that I've loved you since the moment you were born as if you were my true-born daughter. You remind me of my beloved sister. And I wanted that to last a bit longer before I told you the truth."

"Why did you keep this a secret? And why tell me now?" Her father wasn't her father, her brothers weren't her brothers? Nothing made sense!

"The answer, Sona, lies here—" Father reached for her hand mirror, lovingly carved, practically the only mirror in the house. It had been her mother's—or, she should say, her aunt's.

Sona raised the mirror and looked at her face. She looked tired but normal: light brown skin and dark brown eyes, slightly upturned nose.

"Push your hair back."

Sona turned her head and tucked her hair behind her ear. Her silver earring with a tiny black gemstone sparkled in the light of her lamp. That's when she caught it. A glint of gold. She dropped the mirror on her bed like it was a hot iron—luckily, not anywhere near the sleeping pup.

"I'm *Devan*?"

"Half-Devan. This part of the country was just farmland before gems were discovered here. Devans and Malechs spent time together. Malechian and Devan children went to the same schools, and our parents worked together on shared farms. Lia met a Devan boy and they fell in love. Back then, it was unusual, but not unheard of. But shortly after Lia and her husband married, black gems were discovered nearby, the new King took over, and everything changed. Marriages between Malechs and Devans were outlawed. Farmland was divided unfairly. Lia and her husband stayed here because we could protect them."

"But . . . but half-Devans are not allowed," Sona said. There were no half-Devan children or adults in all of Tir Province, maybe in all of Devia. People said they were exiled . . . or worse.

"That's what the laws said. But I could never give you up."

"So you raised me as your daughter?" A Hunter had come to Sona's house, and her whole world was falling apart.

"You must understand." Father gripped her hands tightly. "When you were born, beautiful and strong and golden-eared, your cry like a song despite the sorrow in our house, I loved you and swore to keep you safe. Your parents were dead; it was my duty, and my great honor, to raise you. But then you sickened, too, and we almost lost you, even though the Goldstorm had ended. And then your ayah came. She is a renowned healer, and she saved you when I thought there was no hope. We've been bound together ever since by our love for you." He kissed her hands.

Sona let go of Father's hands and touched her ears gingerly. Her ears, the cream, Ayah's reaction when she realized Sona had run out. Suddenly, some things made sense. "The ointment . . ."

Father nodded. "The ointment is made specially for you. It is a healing ointment, good for all sorts of ailments. It also hides your half-Devan ears so you can live with me as my daughter, though it doesn't work on people who are fully Devan. It's what has allowed us to keep you with us, in these days of distrust and harsh laws."

Swara moved under the covers, and Sona moved to block her from Father's gaze. "But what about my Devan family?" Sona asked. "Didn't they want me?"

Father smiled sadly. "Of course they did, my girl. But according to Devan tradition and law, children stay with their mother's family. You belong here in this house, with me and your brothers."

In the silence, Sona heard a faint hum from under her blanket, and she knew Swara was listening, too.

"Lal, Ran, and Karn, do they know who I am?" Sona asked.

Father shook his head. "No one alive knows, except for Ayah, me, and now you," Father said. "It's hard to keep a secret safe among many."

Sona nodded. She was a secret! A cacophony of thoughts crashed inside her.

"And now you see why I must go and get your ayah as soon as possible," Father said. "Stay here until I return with more of Ayah's ointment. I'll say you're ill. You must *not* be discovered with golden ears. Especially not with the Hunter here."

The Hunter. The soldiers. All charged by the King of Malechia, all a threat to Sona and her family. Sona didn't want to be taken away from them, and she didn't want Father and her brothers to suffer because of her. She pulled her hair over her ears.

"I'll stay here, Father."

"I'm so sorry, Sona. I never meant to tell you like this."

When *was* he going to tell her? How could he hide such a significant part of who she was? She said, "It must have been hard to keep this secret. Because of you, I've grown up safe." She hugged Father tightly. He smelled of sandalwood soap and pipe smoke. After a few moments, she drew back and looked at him. "But I have so many questions."

"I'll answer them all, I promise, once the Hunter is gone, and we have more time." He moved to the door, then looked back at Sona. "I'll return as soon as I can. I'll ask Karn to keep an eye on the Hunter while your older brothers work in the whillet fields. Lock your door. Be careful. Be safe." Father left, closing the door softly behind him.

Once Sona had locked the door and had her room to herself, she let out the breath she'd been holding and pulled her blanket aside. Swara was lying just as Sona had left her, curled into a circle with her head on her paws, her eyes shining amber and her ears glinting gold.

"Little sister," said Sona. "Looks like we've both got something to hide from the world." Sona wished for a moment that nothing had changed, that she could just go back to being the Sona she used to be, before the truth came crashing down around her. How could she keep Swara and her family safe? How could she stay safe herself?

There was one person who would understand. Sona hoped her father would return soon with Ayah. "Ayah will know how to help us both."

EXCERPT FROM A DEVAN SONG

Devia belongs to Bhoomi, now and forever.
Devia, of five regions, five peoples, five Golden Beasts,
living in harmony with Bhoomi's creatures and each other.
Tirna of the plains, with gems as black as earth, guarded by
Vrka, the Wolf;
Vanam of the jungle, with gems as green as leaves, guarded
by Vyaghra, the Tiger;
Sindhu of the river, with gems as blue as water, guarded by
Mahseer, the Fish;
Khila of the desert, with gems as red as the sun, guarded by
Sarpa, the Snake;
and Paravat of the mountains, with gems as clear as the sky,
guarded by Shyena, the Hawk.

Four regions live on.
One does not.

Devia belongs to Bhoomi, now and forever.

5

A Clever Plan

Ayah didn't return with the dawn and neither did Father. Sona tried to read a book of Devan folktales that Ayah had given her, but she couldn't concentrate. She paced the floor until she worried that the Hunter would become suspicious. The pup peed on the floor, and Sona wiped up the mess with an old towel. Finally, she fell asleep.

Sona woke with sunlight streaming through her window and the pup snuggled under her chin. She sat up in bed and scanned the room for signs that Ayah had been there. But there was no new jar of ointment, no vase of fresh jilly flowers, only the discarded mirror on her bed just as she'd left it.

What a strange night it had been. Dinner seemed like months ago, back when she was still sure of her place in the world. Then, her biggest secret had been using all her ointment on Willa. And Swara, of course.

The thought seemed to awaken the pup, who yawned, stretched languorously, and sat up to look at Sona. "I know," Sona whispered. "I'm hungry, too."

She was about to risk venturing to the kitchen when someone knocked sharply on the door. "Sona, it's me," came Father's voice.

Finally! Sona threw the blanket over Swara again and ran to the door to let in Father and Ayah. But Father was alone.

Sona flung her arms around him in a fierce hug. "Where's Ayah? It must be ten o'clock already."

Father had deep shadows under his eyes. "It's nearly noon. Sona, Ayah was arrested last night."

"What? No!"

"She's all right, shaken but not harmed. I met Darshan on the way to the village, and he told me what happened. I saw Ayah myself. Some soldiers found her on the road alone last night and asked her all kinds of questions about that Devan bandit, who had apparently just set fire to a mining camp. When she explained that she knew nothing, they arrested her for loitering. They took her to the barracks."

"Poor Ayah. I'm so sorry, Father." Ayah had been on that road because of Sona, and the ointment they needed to keep her secret.

"I asked Darshan to keep an eye on your brothers and went to the barracks myself. It took a lot of talking and some coins changing hands, but I finally convinced them that Ayah knew nothing about any bandit and was no threat to the peace, and they needed to let her go. She's heading back to the village now and will bring your ointment soon."

"Why didn't you give Ayah a ride to the village and back?"

Father shook his head. "You know how she is—she refused, said she'd be fine walking on her own, and wanted me to get on with the harvest. Besides, I didn't dare stay away any longer with the Hunter here."

Sona nodded. She didn't like it, but he was right.

"Be patient, my girl, and all will be well. I'll go bring you some food now."

"Thank you."

Father left the room again, and Sona stood and paced. Ayah had been arrested—at her age, with no weapons or reason to be a threat. And it was all because of Sona. Thank goodness Father convinced the soldiers to let her go. But what if Ayah didn't have any more ointment at her home and had to make more from scratch? That might take hours, and then even more time for Ayah to return to the farm, and Sona knew she couldn't stay in her room until then. The pup was bound to grow restless, and Sona couldn't risk her being discovered by the Hunter.

Father returned with food but then immediately left to find her brothers in the fields, so Sona shared a quick lunch with Swara. When they were done, she picked up the pup and poked her head into the hallway. There was no one there. Sona wondered where the Hunter was. Could he still be asleep? Sona longed to stretch her legs, and she knew the pup needed to relieve herself again. Sona dressed quickly, then pulled on her boots, the big sweater, and a large jacket that had once been Ran's over everything. With sudden inspiration, she threw a soft wool scarf over her head, covering her ears, and tied it under her chin. If the Hunter found her, she could say it was to prevent a chill from making her cold worse. She reached under the jacket to stow the pup in the sweater's large pocket and snuck to the washroom at the back of the house.

There was no one there, either. Sona breathed a sigh of relief and rewashed and dressed Swara's wound, which stretched nearly the entire length of her little body. It looked like it was already starting to heal. She left the washroom through the outside door and headed straight for the barn, which she felt sure the Hunter wouldn't be interested in.

It was good to be out in the sun again. Swara squirmed in her pocket, but Sona held her and bade her to be still. She couldn't risk letting her run in the open. She reached the barn, which was empty of the horses, who were all in the field with the men. Only Willa remained, snorting softly as soon as Sona came in.

"Hello there, sweet girl," Sona crooned, reaching in her bag for a fresh hooli fruit she'd saved from lunch and offering it to the pony. Then she took a squirming, whining Swara from the sweater pocket and deposited her onto the floor, where she ran in circles before going to a corner to relieve herself.

Willa finished the fruit and nosed Sona's hand. "I'm sorry, that's all I have, but we'll get you more tonight." Sona stroked the pony, enjoying her quiet companionship. Willa's wound still looked raw. Now that she knew she couldn't use the ointment on Willa, Sona hoped Ayah would be able to devise something else to help her heal. Perhaps one day Ayah would teach Sona how to make ointments and healing teas herself.

She was half-Devan. The thought felt so strange in her head. All her life she'd been treated like a Malech, had been afforded privileges and status, had never been bothered on the road or in her home . . . and it was all because of a lie. Well, half a lie, since she was half-Malech as well. But if anyone saw her ears now, they'd see her as Devan. Or worse, half-Devan—and then she'd be exiled to some faraway place.

Guilt and worry intermingled with a lightness in her chest, like she had finally heard a song she'd been waiting for all her life. She touched the pendant that hung over her heart—her aunt's—no, her mother's—pendant. She'd been carrying something of her mother's all these years and had never known it.

Her mother had loved Devia, and Sona did, too. And her father was Devan. So Sona didn't just love Devia; she belonged to it. This explained so much! Her love of music, her ability to hear it everywhere, her bond with her animals. All the things Malechs thought about Devans—they were true about *her*. Father and her brothers would always be her family, but now there was a whole new group of people to get to know, when the time was right. Maybe they would even teach her Devan songs, the ones she knew had to be sung in secret.

But first, she had to survive this day with the Hunter in their home.

Swara tried to chew a mouthful of hay, then coughed it up almost immediately. Sona laughed.

"You'd better leave that for Willa. And—"

Sona's ears pricked up. A footstep outside the barn! She scooped up Swara and stood behind a beam in the corner of Willa's stall.

Something sniffed like a predator scenting prey. Another footstep. Another sniff.

Sona froze and barely dared to breathe. Willa stopped her chewing; she snorted and stomped a hoof.

Another step. A large silhouette stood in the opening to the barn. Sona looked around desperately. Could she make it out the back door before he came in? What if he chased her? Would it be safer to stay put?

Then: "Can I help you, Rodh the Hunter?" came Father's voice.

"Just looking around," the Hunter rasped. "If only my nose

would heal more quickly. There's something unusual about this farm."

Father laughed shortly. "Nothing more unusual than any farm trying to bring the harvest in before the next Goldstorm."

There was a brief silence.

"Of course. I don't mean to delay you," said the Hunter.

"Not at all," said Father.

More silence.

"Actually, I was looking for you. Would you come look at one of our horses? He's limping a little but doesn't seem to be in distress otherwise. You must know a great deal about horses, with all your travels."

"I'd be happy to help. Please lead the way," said the Hunter.

Their footsteps trailed away.

The Hunter *knew* there was something unusual about the farm—maybe he sensed that Swara was here, or Sona's Devan blood. He had almost discovered them both! If that had happened, the Hunter would have killed Swara, and perhaps taken Sona and Father to the soldiers. Sona's presence was endangering her family.

There was only one thing to do. "Willa, will you help me?" Sona murmured to the pony. The pony nickered, and Sona took that as a yes. Willa stood still as Sona put on a bridle and saddle. Sona tucked Swara in a saddlebag and tied the scarf more securely over her head.

All her life, she'd been helping stray animals. And now she realized with a combination of terror and joy that it was her duty as a Devan to safeguard a beast marked by Bhoomi as her own. She would protect Swara. And by taking the pup away from her family's farm, she would keep Father and her brothers safe, as well.

She would go to the village. She would tell Ayah about Swara and beg her to keep the pup safe until her wound had healed. Sona would get the jar of ointment and bring it back with her. By dinnertime, her ears would be back to normal, and she wouldn't have to hide anymore. It was a simple plan. On her way there, she had to keep her ears hidden at any cost, but everyone in these parts knew her and wouldn't think twice to see her on the road. It was only an hour by pony to the Devan village of Kanthpur, where Ayah lived. She should be able to make it back before she was missed.

Sona heard music all around her as she rode down the King's Road to the village: the insistent song of sparrows, the haunting hoot of doves, the gentle melodies of horses in the fields, and the deep hum of the very earth itself. And now that she knew the secret of her parentage, she finally understood why she heard all these things.

Sona met no one on the road and was very pleased with her plan.

She was halfway to the village when the first flakes of gold blew in from the east.

The early Malechian settlers thought they had stumbled into a land where gold literally rained from the skies, but they soon realized that the Goldstorm dust faded to its normal dark brown after a few days.

Some Devans claim that the Goldstorms arrived with the Malechs, but there are several accounts from early Malechian sailors that the Goldstorms were already happening upon their arrival.

These storms are clearly a definitive feature of the Devan weather. Luckily, while inconvenient, and occasionally harmful to wildlife, these storms are predictable and easily managed by staying indoors or seeking adequate shelter.

6

The Goldstorm

Specks of gold landed lazily on the back of Willa's pale neck and set Sona's pulse racing. She had never been outside during a Goldstorm. That was why she was still alive.

The road in front of Sona wavered and her vision started to fade. No one survived being out in the open in a Goldstorm. No one! She'd just learned that her own father had died in a storm like this while her mother succumbed to Goldstorm Fever. And now she had brought Willa and Swara with her into this danger. It was too late to turn back; it would take her as long to get home as it would to get to Kanthpur.

"Think, Sona," she said aloud. They needed to find shelter until the storm passed. But there was nothing but fields of whillet, and hooli and jojonut trees as far as the eye could see—no houses, not even a hill against which they could wait out the storm.

Sona took a breath and coughed as the air around her thickened with dust. This was not the time to panic. Maybe they could make it to the village. But she needed to try to protect the animals and herself as much as possible.

She brought Willa to a stop on the side of the road, jumped off her back, then pulled Swara from the saddlebag and stowed the pup in her sweater pocket again. She ripped her scarf in half and tied one piece loosely over Willa's nose. The pony snorted and shook her head but allowed the makeshift mask to stay. Then Sona tied the rest of the scarf over her head and across her nose and mouth, so only her eyes were exposed. Finally, she took a horse blanket in her arm, hoisted herself onto Willa's back again, then threw the blanket over herself and as much of Willa's body as she could reach. She urged Willa forward in a trot, and they kept moving toward Kanthpur.

By the time a few more minutes had passed, the flakes had picked up in pace and swirled in the air like a golden whirlpool, dazzling and deadly. Grit stung Sona's eyes. The air smelled of dirt and something sharp and caustic that made her nose run. Sona urged Willa to move faster, and the pony plodded along as the ground became covered with a deepening layer of gold.

The gold flakes settled heavily on Sona's shoulders and lap, on the scarf across her face, and she struggled to expand her chest. She cleared her inflamed throat over and over, coughed, and gasped as the dust whirled and gusted, then fell from the sky like torrential rain. She could no longer see the familiar road or landscape—only a blinding fury of gold. Sona tried to keep her head up, but found herself hunching over from the onslaught, trying desperately to clear the dust from her vision, to find a brief respite from the irritation and glare. The flakes came down even more thickly, flying sideways and even upside down, shooting upward from the ground. The skin on her hands burned as she gripped the reins.

Days from now, all the Golddust would turn brown like regular earth, but now, when it was gold, it would burn skin and make lungs feel like they were on fire.

A strange noise echoed through her, a wail on the wind that grew louder and louder until it was unbearable. She covered her ears with her hands, but the awful cacophony kept crashing against her skull. Her head was going to burst. She heard screaming and realized it was her own voice.

Sona stopped thinking about the pony and the wolf pup, Ayah and Father and her brothers on the farm, where she was going or who she was. The only thing that existed was the horrible noise like a shriek, calling and calling like a never-ending lament.

"Stop it!" Sona cried as she fell off Willa's back in a stupor. "Stop," she said as she huddled on the ground, the blanket pulled around her but still not blocking the sound. It felt like it had always been there in her head, a horrible keening, a cry of unbearable loss and pain. "Ssss . . ." she whispered as she put her head down, welcoming sleep or unconsciousness or even death if it would rid her of the din.

Sona was roused by a soothing melody, faint but distinct, and the ring of a clear bell-like note. She opened her eyes groggily and realized something was over her face. She panicked. She couldn't move. It was like a huge beast was sitting on her, pressing on her chest, her limbs. She was lying immobile in a pile of something that burned her skin. Then she recalled: she was out in the open during a Goldstorm. She had no idea what time of day it was, or whether it was even the same day, but it didn't matter. She was going to die here, just like everyone else who had ever ventured out during such a storm. Her heart stirred at the thought of Father, Lal, Ran, and Karn, of Ayah, and how devastated they'd be when they realized what had happened to her. But the Golddust pressing down on her was so heavy, and her mind was so foggy. She would give in and be left in silence forever.

But what about Willa? What about Swara?

Sona's eyes flew open, and a pair of amber eyes stared at her, eyes that shone bright in the dimness. Eyes that spoke to her without words. *Get up*, they said. Swara was under the blanket with her, and she hadn't yet surrendered to the storm.

Sona's head cleared like she'd been splashed with cold water.

She willed herself to move. First, she braced her hands on the ground. She cried out in pain from the burn of Golddust on bare skin. She pushed and struggled to sit up. The blanket covering her was heavy with dust, and it took all her strength to pull it off her shoulders. She was sitting in a large golden drift. The wind blew more dust into her face and made her scream again.

The scarf had slipped off Sona's nose and mouth, and she coughed as she swiped at her face to ease the stinging. Swara shook herself, put her paws on Sona's chest, and licked her nose. Sona smiled, and her breath came out as a rasp. She scooped up the pup, held her to her chest, and was at last able to struggle to her feet.

Willa stood patiently in front of her with the Golddust reaching halfway up her forelegs. The pony's makeshift mask had fallen off and her head was bowed, but her dark blue eyes were clear, and she snorted gently in invitation.

"Thank goodness you're okay," Sona whispered hoarsely. She stowed Swara under her jacket in her sweater pocket, retied the scarf around her face, and tried getting up onto Willa's back.

She was so tired she couldn't lift her leg high enough. She made another attempt and still couldn't get her leg over.

The Golddust continued to fall thickly, and Sona's whole body started to shake. She couldn't walk to the village in this condition. She needed Willa's strength and speed. Sona took a breath that started a bout of coughing. She hunched over and leaned on her thighs, defeated again.

She wasn't strong enough.

But the wolf pup stirred in her pocket, and Sona knew she had to keep trying until she succeeded, or pony, wolf, and girl, they would all die together. Willa looked at her and snorted again. Sona grunted in exertion as she tried to mount the pony again . . . and this time, she managed to just get her leg up and over Willa's back. Sona sat heavily in the saddle, pulled her jacket up to cover as much of her face as possible, and leaned forward.

Willa started moving. The pony went from a walk to a trot as she shook off the dust, and then, Sona was astonished to find, a fast canter. She didn't think such a tired old beast could move that quickly, especially with the Golddust so thick on the ground and in the air. Sona had never been on a boat, but she'd read stories of Malechian ships that sailed with the wind across the Eight Seas, and she imagined that it must feel something like this. She was gliding rhythmically across a landscape that sparkled. Viewed through her squinted eyes, the fields around her were covered in gold, the outlines of the grains and the trees softened. Sona coughed and struggled to breathe, and the dust stung every bit of exposed skin. She couldn't tell where the road was, but Willa seemed to know. Willa was covered in Golddust, but she didn't slow down. Sona let the pony find the way. She shut her eyes in exhaustion, held on, and hoped.

EXCERPT FROM A DEVAN SONG

Malechs in their greed want
more more more
ruining the harmony
more more more
drowning out the melody
more more more
taking what's not theirs
more more more
from the land, the sea, the world
more more more
Malechs in their greed take
more more more

When they give as much
as they take,
the Goldstorms will cease.

Until that day,
if they love what the earth gives them,
let it drown them, then
let it drown them in
more more more.

7

The Arrival

Sona opened her eyes as Willa slowed to a walk again. How far had they come? Were they anywhere near the village? Were they even still on the road? But then the outlines of the village houses appeared in the distance, with roofs rounded like the root ends of onions, so different from the sharp lines of her Malechian home. They were almost there. They might just survive after all. Tall trees had been planted as a windbreak, and once Sona entered the village itself, the pace of the gold flakes slowed down, and she could see better.

"Let's find Ayah's house," she croaked to the pony.

Sona had been to the village many times and knew that Ayah's was the largest and most central home. She was sure that anyone would allow her shelter in the middle of a Goldstorm, but she wanted Ayah. She wanted to be safe.

Willa wended her way through the empty main road of the village. There were carts and wheelbarrows abandoned on the road; it looked like the Goldstorm had taken the villagers by surprise as well. At a fork in the center of the village was a large house with a dark brown door just visible through a coating of Golddust.

Ayah's house! Sona would've cried out with joy and relief if her throat didn't burn so much.

She brought the pony right up to the door under the shelter of a canopy that covered a large front patio, meant for welcoming guests. The multicolored stone patterns were covered by drifts of Golddust. Sona climbed off Willa's back and knocked on the door. She couldn't wait to see Ayah's look of surprise followed by her bright smile, her gentle touch. She would help Sona; she always had.

When no one opened the door after a few minutes, Sona knocked again, louder this time. The wind gusted and blew the Golddust sideways against her, burning every bit of exposed skin, and Sona pulled her jacket sleeves over her hands.

Still no answer. She banged on the door and called out: "Ayah! It's me! It's Sona! Please let me in!"

No one answered. Was Ayah all right? Could she not hear Sona with the storm raging around her? Sona had made it to the village, but what would she do if Ayah wasn't home?

She would have to try another house. She forced herself away from the familiar door and looked across the street.

"I knew you'd show up eventually," came a voice from behind her.

Sona turned back to Ayah's door, which had been opened by a boy. The shaggy-haired boy, Sona realized, that Sona had seen the day before on the road in front of her farm. She felt like a lifetime had already passed since then.

"Where's Ayah?" she asked.

"*Ayah*," the boy sneered. "She's not here."

"What? Why not?"

The boy crossed his arms and gave Sona a look of disgust. "She was arrested," he said. "Coming home from your house last night."

"But she was released! Oh my goodness, is she on the road? She wouldn't go out in the middle of a Goldstorm, would she?" Sona almost collapsed at the thought of Ayah out in the storm alone, trying to get home to fetch the ointment Sona needed.

"If she's out on the road it's because of *you*," said the boy, his dark eyes flashing. "If anything happens to her, you're to blame."

Even though she'd just thought the same thing, Sona's temper flared. "Who are you to talk to me in this way?"

"I have more of a right than you to be here, Malech." He spat the word at her.

Sona thought of so many responses to this accusation: her family had lived in Devia for generations and loved it as their home; she had never been to Malechia, and never wanted to go; and she wasn't *all* Malech. All the thoughts combined in her head and made her unable to reply at all. She wanted Ayah, and she wanted this awful boy to leave her alone.

"Raag, why are you standing with the door open? Golddust will enter the house, and—oh!" Behind the boy stood a woman, her eyes wide in surprise. She was beautiful, with almond-shaped dark eyes and long black hair she wore in a thick braid that fell over her left shoulder. She was slim, dressed in cotton pants and a traditional bright, flowing Devan top. Her golden ears glinted in the lamplight inside the home. "You have arrived, and right in the middle of a Goldstorm! How—never mind. Come in," she said to Sona as she intertwined her fingers and bowed her head in greeting. "Raag, don't let our guest stand outside in this storm! She needs tending."

"But I must go look for Ayah," Sona said. She took a step back and staggered with weariness.

The woman shook her head and raised her voice to be heard over the wind. "Are you Sona? You are welcome here. Your ayah has experience with Goldstorms; she will come back when the storm is over. And she will be so relieved to see you here, unharmed. Come in and rest yourself, Sona, and I will take care of your hurts. I am Ashvi."

Sona's shoulders relaxed. The wind picked up and dust swirled around her, and she winced at the pain in her hands and face. She was exhausted, her head ached, and her ears were ringing. "My pony . . . I can't leave her out in this."

"We will take her to the barn where our animals are sheltering. It is just behind the house. Raag, please attend to the pony while I bring Sona inside. Please come in, Sona."

Raag stepped into wool boots and wrapped himself from head to toe in a thick cloak and padded gloves before coming outside. The scowl on Raag's face faded to a frown as he clucked at Willa and reached for her reins.

But Willa neighed and shied away from Raag, and no amount of encouragement from him would calm her. Her eyes rolled, and she stomped her hoof on the coated ground. Sona clutched the reins and whispered soothing nonsense to the pony in a low voice even as she struggled to stay standing herself.

Ashvi wrapped herself in protective gear and stepped outside. "Come, my beauty. You must have ridden hard to get here through the storm." She took Willa's reins from Sona, and miraculously, Willa calmed down and followed her without complaint toward the back of the house.

After Ashvi left, Sona stared awkwardly at the boy. She was covered in Golddust, her whole body ached, and Swara lay heavy and still in the pocket of her sweater.

"Well, I guess you'd better come inside," the boy said flatly. He turned and went into the house.

Sona stepped in.

"Shut that door behind you," called the boy, who had disappeared into another room. "And for the love of Bhoomi, dust yourself off, Malech, and take off your shoes. Don't be tracking Golddust through our whole house."

Sona fumed as she closed the door and dusted herself off. She shuffled to a nearby alcove and pulled off her boots. She knew not to wear shoes inside a Devan home. She wasn't clueless. And she hated the way the boy hurled the word *Malech* at her like she was a soldier come to steal something. Who were this woman and boy, and why were they in Ayah's house?

Grit and grime had worked its way into every bit of Sona's clothing, and pain flamed in every fold of skin, every muscle. She shook from exhaustion and anger. She wanted to wash. She wanted to rest. But she couldn't do either until Ayah returned. Sona was safe, but she wouldn't feel normal again until she was sure Ayah was safe, too.

EXCERPT FROM A DEVAN SONG

As Bhoomi is our mother and father,
so is Pitarau.
All good things come from Bhoomi,
and so does Pitarau.
Bhoomi has selected us,
and we choose Pitarau.

8

Pitarau

Sona stood in the entrance of Ayah's house, unsure of what to do. The boy had not told her where to go, and she didn't want to wander around on her own, even though she'd been here with Ayah and knew where everything was. And besides, she didn't want to risk Swara making a noise and alerting everyone to her existence.

She loved Ayah's house. The furniture was simple but beautiful, carved from dark wood, and adorned with shapes of the animals that were sacred to Bhoomi: tiger, wolf, fish, snake, and hawk, each enclosed by the Devan circle. The walls were made of stucco and colored in dusty jewel tones, and there were bright, round cushions everywhere, so the whole place felt inviting and warm. Except when there was a rude boy who made her feel anything but welcome.

Sona looked around quickly: the boy was nowhere to be found. She reached into her sweater pocket and felt the steady rise and fall of Swara's chest. The pup seemed to be sleeping. Sona thought Ayah would be proud of her for keeping the animal safe.

The front door opened again, and Ashvi came in, brushing Golddust off herself in the threshold before shutting the door against the wind, which had begun to howl again. She hung up her heavy shawl and removed her boots, then took a long braid of wool from the alcove and shoved it against the bottom of the door to block more dust from entering the house. She spotted Sona, and her eyebrows arched. "Did Raag not invite you in to wash and have refreshment?" When Sona shook her head, Ashvi did the same. "That boy."

"I want to wait here until Ayah returns," Sona said.

"It could be days before the storm is over. And your ayah would be upset with everyone if she finds we left you standing in the entryway like a beggar," said Ashvi. "You must let me tend your wounds, and you must rest, or you may yet fall ill. Do not worry, Sona. This is not the first time your ayah has been arrested. She always returns."

Shock coursed through Sona like a physical blow. Ayah had been arrested in the past? Before she could decide whether to ask why, Ashvi said, "Your pony is watered and fed and sheltered from the storm. I've taken care of her hurts, and she seems comfortable." She smiled. "Now it's time to care for you."

Sona followed Ashvi wordlessly to the back of the house. In the privacy of the washroom, she took off her jacket and brought Swara out of her sweater pocket. The wolf pup stood and shook herself, and Sona gave her water to drink out of her cupped hands. Swara wiggled as Sona examined her more closely, and Sona found no wound, no burn, no injury except for the shallow scratch along the pup's side.

Once Sona had washed her face, hands, and feet, the stinging from the Golddust improved a little, but painful welts persisted wherever her skin had been exposed.

"I'm putting you back in the pocket. Stay still, and I'll get us both some food," Sona said to Swara. Swara squirmed in the pocket but settled down after some pats and encouragement. Sona shook out her jacket, put it back on, and made sure her hair covered her ears before she went to the large kitchen, where Ashvi gave her a steaming cup of tea and pulled out a jar of familiar-smelling ointment.

"This will help heal the worst of these, and the others should fade with time and rest," Ashvi said. She applied the ointment to Sona's arms and hands as Raag crossed his arms and watched. Sona thought of Ayah caring for her like this, and she wondered wistfully if this was what her own mother's touch would have felt like. Ashvi hummed a tune as she worked, and Sona's skin felt soothed and cool. Was there magic in Ashvi's song? Sona hoped Ayah would return soon so she could ask her. She didn't dare ask Ashvi, friendly as she seemed, not with Raag sitting like a sulky lump and glaring at her from the other side of the round table.

But when Ashvi reached to put the ointment on Sona's face, Sona drew back. "I can do that myself," she said, pulling her hair forward so she was sure it covered her ears. Ashvi raised her eyebrows but gave Sona the jar. Sona finished applying the ointment to her face and neck, and the burning of her skin faded to a dull roar. Sona quickly smeared the ointment on her ears, asked Ashvi if she could keep the jar, and at Ashvi's nod, she pocketed it. She avoided looking at Raag.

Now that Sona was feeling more comfortable, Ashvi served her a meal of rice, vegetables, and crunchy lentil puffs. Sona asked for a shawl, saying she was still feeling chilled, and ate and drank gratefully, sneaking Swara food under the shawl. The pup ate enthusiastically, and Sona had to chew loudly and smack her lips to hide the grunts of satisfaction that Swara made.

When Sona had eaten her fill, she looked more closely at Ashvi and the boy. They were clearly related—she was likely his mother. And there was something familiar about Ashvi's face, the shape of her nose . . .

"I'm your ayah's daughter, in case you were wondering. And this is my son, Raag."

Raag gave Sona a brief sullen glance, then proceeded to stare at his teacup, which had apparently become fascinating.

"I knew Ayah had a daughter, but I didn't know you were visiting," said Sona. "She's lived alone for as long as I've known her."

Ashvi nodded. "We have lived elsewhere since before Raag was born, and only recently arrived back here in Kanthpur."

"We won't be staying long," said Raag.

"That remains to be seen," said Ashvi. She turned to Sona. "But your ayah has told me all about you."

"All . . . about me?" Sona resisted the urge to check that her ears weren't on display, that she hadn't given away her secret already.

"Yes, how she's been friends with your family for years, how she has helped to care for you since you lost your mother, how your father is good and fair to all people, Malech and Devan alike."

Swara squirmed in the pocket, and Sona quickly fed her some lentils then patted her sweater as she rocked back and forth in her seat. She needed the pup to fall asleep again. Ashvi and Raag stared.

"Oh, what delicious food. Yes, Ayah has always been wonderful to us. To me, especially." Sona leaned back again but kept her hands on her sweater.

"You should stop calling her Ayah, like that's her name," said Raag. "She's not your nursemaid servant. She deserves so much more respect than that."

"That's what she's always told me to call her," Sona retorted. "What do you call her?"

"I call her *Matrka*, since she is my grandmother," Raag said, puffing his chest out. "But to everyone here in the village, she is *Pitarau*."

Sona blinked. "I thought her name was Janaki?"

Raag laughed. "Malech, Pitarau is her title. She's the head of this village. And yet she still spends the entire harvest season living with your barbarian family. It doesn't make any sense." He glared at her again.

Sona felt heat rise in her face. Ayah was the village head? She must have many responsibilities here, especially during the harvest. How could she have kept this secret from Sona? And why *did* she spend so much time with Sona and her family? In two days, everything Sona had thought she'd known about the world had been transformed. And if Ayah didn't return, Sona would never get to ask her why there were so many secrets, would never get to tell her how much she loved her . . . and it would all be her own fault.

"Raag, stop taunting the girl." In a gentler voice she said to Sona, "If she didn't tell you, it was for a good reason."

"Yes, it was," came a voice, hoarse but instantly recognizable.

"Ayah!" Sona cried, leaping from her seat and running to the kitchen doorway, where Ayah was standing, dusty and windblown but very much alive. Sona stopped short of hugging her since she couldn't possibly keep Swara a secret then, but she put her hand on Ayah's dear, familiar face, and drank up the sight like a tonic. Ayah was back! And she was unharmed.

Ayah coughed into her sleeve. "Oh, Sona, what a shock to find you here. It's a miracle you're all right. When the soldiers finally released me, I hurried to get home. I set out on the road, but the storm came on so quickly. I found shelter in an abandoned shack until the storm lulled enough for me to return. But it's picking up again now."

"Come and refresh yourself, Ma," said Ashvi. "You must be exhausted."

"Yes, Matrka, take my seat," Raag said, standing.

"Not now, dauhitra," Ayah said with a quick smile at Raag. "Just tea, please, Ashvi. I'll wash, then take it into my room. Sona and I must speak alone, and quickly." Ayah left the kitchen and headed to the washroom.

When Ayah returned, Ashvi bowed her head and silently handed her an earthenware mug. Raag scowled at Sona as she followed Ayah out of the kitchen.

Sona had never been to Ayah's bedroom before. It was as large as Sona's parlor back home. There was a bed tucked into a corner behind a jojonut-leaf screen, but most of the room was taken up by a large circular rug with plump round cushions arranged around it, and a shelf at waist height on the wall with different colored jars and bowls. And in a place of honor on a special table was a curious object: wooden, beautifully carved with a rounded base like a gourd and a long stem and strings that stretched from one end to the other. On it was carved the sacred circle of Devia—the same symbol that made up part of Sona's pendant. Her mother Lia's pendant.

"Come, Sona, pautri, sit and talk to me." Ayah gestured to the rug.

Sona chose a deep purple cushion, the color of ripe grapes.

Ayah seated herself next to her and took her hand. "How did you manage to make it here in the midst of a Goldstorm without any help?"

"I had help," Sona said. "Willa carried me here."

Ayah tilted her head. "Your stubborn pony found a way to get you here, whole and unharmed?" She gently cupped Sona's face in her hands. "Bhoomi herself must have kept you safe."

"It wasn't that bad at first. It was hard to see, and the Golddust stung and piled up quickly. But then, something happened." Sona shuddered. "Something awful."

Ayah said nothing but looked at Sona searchingly.

"Ayah . . . I heard a cry on the wind."

Ayah's eyes widened. "Someone was hurt? And did you try to help them, and get stuck in the storm?"

Sona shook her head. "There was this terrible noise . . . and it got in my head and bounced around and got louder and louder. It overwhelmed me and hurt my head so much. And then I fell off Willa and was unconscious for I don't know how long."

Ayah covered her mouth and coughed, then wiped her eyes. "You fell off the pony in the middle of a Goldstorm, lost consciousness, and still somehow made your way here? How did you wake up?"

"I don't know," said Sona. "All of a sudden, I woke and realized where I was. And I knew Willa and . . . I knew Willa needed me, so I got up for her. And she carried me here. I wasn't sure we would make it, but Willa saved me."

Ayah raised an eyebrow like she knew Sona wasn't telling her everything, but she was willing to accept this for now. "But what would have made you leave your home in the middle of a Goldstorm?"

"Father explained who I am," Sona said. "How my real mother was his sister, and my real father . . ." She trailed off. How could she finish the sentence when she didn't even know his name?

"He came from this village," Ayah said gently. "He was a good man. He loved your mother more than anything and died trying to save her. His name was Gupil. He was my son."

FROM *A MALECHIAN HISTORY OF DEVIA*

When the early Malechian settlers first arrived, they found Devia to be a country in disarray, with weak leadership and arguing factions. Each village had its own leader, usually a woman, occasionally with a husband or brother who assisted her, and who was chosen by the villagers, rather than inheriting this position of authority. The people of the different provinces could barely communicate with one another, since they all spoke different dialects. This led to a broken system without strong, central leadership.

With the Malechian settlements came a system of Governors who enforced the laws properly and the Common Tongue that is now spoken across the Eight Seas. All of this, of course, lovingly made possible by the King of Malechia, ordained by the Wind God himself.

Without Malechian rule, Devia would have continued in its chaotic ways and would likely have destroyed itself. Instead, it is now a modern country, known throughout the world for its riches.

9

The Fever

Sona gasped. "Your son? Father didn't tell me that! That means—"

"That you are my granddaughter. Yes, Sona. That's why I call you *pautri*. That is what that word means."

Now Sona finally understood why Ayah had always been so good to her, why she'd cared for her all these years.

"Father said I grew very ill in the days after my birth, and you came and saved my life. No one ever told me, Ayah."

"My beautiful girl, I would have tried to save you, orphan that you were, even if you were not my blood, but even so, I am glad I used the amrita on you. You have brought me and the rest of your family joy from the moment you were born."

"Amrita? What is that?"

Ayah coughed into her arm, then cleared her throat. "It is the nectar of life, found in a secret place at the top of Mount Meru, all the way in Paravat, at the northern end of Devia. An ancestor of mine went there, long ago, and brought it back—just a few precious drops—and it was passed down to me by my mother, who got it from hers, and on and on for generations. One must go to that sacred place with a pure heart, it is said, and take only enough to save one person. Amrita is to be used to save another, only—never oneself. Our family had kept it for over two centuries, waiting for the moment when it was most needed. I would have used it to save your mother, had I known." Ayah sighed. "It was too late for her when I arrived. But you were still alive, fighting, and I knew I had to give it to you."

"I—I don't know what to say," Sona said. "Except thank you."

Ayah smiled and touched Sona's cheek again. "No thanks are needed, Sona. You are my only granddaughter. You have inherited your father's way with animals, and your mother's love of people, both Devan and Malech. Use these gifts, my girl. Use them to make the world better."

"I will, Ayah. I promise," Sona said, clasping her hands together and bowing in the Devan way.

Ayah continued. "And now you've met my grandson—your cousin, Raag. But I must ask you to keep this a secret for now, until he's more adjusted to life here. Can you do that, pautri?"

She wondered if Raag, who clearly despised her, would hate her more when he realized they had to share Ayah by blood, too. Or maybe he would be nicer knowing she was half-Devan? Probably nothing would make him like her. Sona thought of Father's warning about too many people knowing a secret.

"I won't tell anyone until you say it's all right. I'm so happy to see you, Ayah."

Ayah leaned over to embrace her, and Sona squeezed back, being careful to keep her belly and the pocket with Swara away.

"But why didn't you tell me the truth before now?"

Ayah sighed and started coughing again. After a few moments, she took a sip of tea. "I wanted to tell you years ago, but your father thought it would be too dangerous. When you turned thirteen, I insisted, but he was still too afraid that the rest of the world would find out, and the life he has constructed so carefully would fall apart. He is your father, and he is a Malech. But I am the head of this village, and your eldest living female relative. According to Devan tradition, I could have overruled him, but it would have hurt him. And he has had enough hurt in his life." She stroked Sona's hair and smiled sadly.

Sona nodded. Father would be so worried when he realized she wasn't in her room. She must find a way to get word to him soon.

Ayah coughed again, and this time she couldn't stop for a long time. Then she took another sip of tea and cleared her throat. "But tell me, Sona, why did you come out in the storm? That was foolish and dangerous. You could have just stayed put in your house, and no one would have known about your Devan heritage. I would have come with the ointment as soon as the Goldstorm was over. Why didn't you wait?"

"A Hunter came to our house in the middle of the night," Sona said.

"A Hunter! Has another magical animal been sighted?" Ayah's eyes widened and she put a hand on her chest. She started coughing again, deeper this time.

"Ayah, are you all right? Maybe you should rest."

But Ayah shook her head through her coughs. "Tell me more about the Hunter."

"He . . . smelled things."

Ayah raised her eyebrows.

"I know it sounds strange, but he literally sniffed and snuffled his way around our house. He *smelled* the Goldstorm coming when no one else thought it would arrive so soon. He fell off his horse and injured his nose on his most recent hunt, and I think he wasn't smelling things normally when he arrived. But he thought there was something strange about our farm. Like, maybe the animal he was hunting was with us."

Ayah had another coughing fit that took Sona's breath away, too. When Ayah finally stopped coughing, she cleared her throat and looked at Sona sharply. "Was he right, Sona?"

Sona gazed at the floor. She reached into her sweater pocket, pulled out Swara, and deposited her on Ayah's rug, where the wolf pup gazed at them both, then sat and scratched a gold-tipped ear with her hind foot.

Ayah's eyes widened. "Sona, that is a *wolf pup* with golden—" She broke off and started coughing uncontrollably.

Ayah's door burst open, and Swara darted off the rug and under Ayah's bed.

"Matrka, are you all right?" Raag asked as he rushed to her side.

But Ayah couldn't stop coughing. She wheezed and hacked and gestured, but no words came out.

"Call your mother, quickly!" Sona said.

"First help me get her in bed."

They each took one of Ayah's arms and helped her up and to her bed. She was coughing so much Sona couldn't believe she took in any air at all. When the fit started to subside, Sona tried to get Ayah to drink some of the tea, but she batted away her hand. Raag ran from the room and returned moments later with his mother.

Ashvi felt Ayah's forehead, and a shadow crossed her face. "It's Goldstorm Fever," she said.

Sona's stomach twisted. Although Goldstorm Fever usually affected the old and the young, pregnant women and the infirm, it was a threat to all, whether they were out in a storm or merely breathed Golddust from inside.

Ashvi turned to Raag. "Quickly, get a basin and fill it with boiled water from the kettle—there should be plenty left."

Raag nodded and ran out of the room.

"Sona, help me prop her against these pillows." Sona went to the other side of Ayah's bed, and together she and Ashvi helped ease Ayah back against the pillows, but even this minimal movement set off another coughing fit. Ashvi went to the table with the jars and bowls and returned with a bowl full of herbs and powders of various colors.

"This should help ease the cough."

Raag returned carrying a basin of hot water, and Ashvi poured the herbs into the basin, where they released a minty, soothing fragrance. She held the basin under Ayah's chin and tilted her face so she breathed in the steam. "Hand me that scarf," she told Sona, pointing at a piece of bright pink fabric hanging over the carved end of Ayah's bed. She draped the scarf over Ayah's head and held it over the bowl like a canopy.

She laid one hand on Ayah's chest, then reached another to Raag. Raag took her hand and reached his other toward Ayah.

"Take Sona's hand, Raag," Ashvi instructed.

Sona felt as startled as Raag looked.

"Pay attention, Malech," Raag murmured as he held out his hand. "Put your other hand on Matrka."

Raag's hand was as warm and dry as hers was cold and clammy. Sona gently laid her left hand on Ayah's arm.

Then Ashvi started to sing a song. Sona felt a thrill of excitement and alarm to see a Devan break the law against music. But who would find out, here in Ayah's house in the middle of a Goldstorm?

Sona couldn't understand the words, but a feeling of calm, of peace and restoration, came over her. Ashvi had a lovely voice, and Sona wanted her to go on singing forever. She wanted to lose herself in this song like floating down a cool, refreshing river. Ashvi repeated a phrase in Old Devan, and Raag joined in. Then, glancing at Sona to include her, she sang in the Common Tongue: *We are because you are. You are because we are. We call to you in love.* She nodded at Sona.

Sona swallowed. She was being asked to sing. By a Devan! To cast magic!

She added her voice to Ashvi's and Raag's, and it sounded coarse and tuneless compared to theirs. She heard their melody but couldn't match it. She faltered and almost stopped singing, but then she caught a glimpse of Ayah, who was smiling at her with tears in her eyes.

Ayah wanted her to sing. Sona ignored how inadequate she felt and poured her intention into the song—all her love for Ayah, her wish for her to be well—and she let the song fill her with power and lightness. A golden glow started in Ashvi's chest and spread to her arms and into the people around her. Into Sona. Into Ayah.

She was doing it! She was singing with Devans, as one of them, and was not only witnessing their magic—she was a part of it.

A few minutes later, Ashvi brought the song to a close, and the golden light faded.

"Breathe, Ma. Slowly," Ashvi whispered.

Ayah leaned lower over the bowl and inhaled. She started coughing, and Sona braced herself for another fit, but the cough tapered off quickly. Once she heard Ayah take a deep breath, Sona's own breathing eased.

Everyone stayed silent as Ayah continued to breathe in the herbed steam.

"Couldn't have done it better myself," Ayah said softly.

"It's because you taught me, Ma," Ashvi said. "You should sleep."

"I could sleep," said Ayah. "It's been a very long couple of days." She lay back against her pillows and closed her eyes. Sona gazed at the beloved lines of Ayah's face. Her hair seemed grayer than it had been just yesterday.

Ashvi felt her mother's forehead again. "The fever is down, but it may return. I hope we acted quickly enough to drive away the sickness. Can you two stay here with her while I wash this and prepare more herbs? Call me if she seems restless or starts coughing again."

Sona and Raag nodded.

"Thank you for including me in the singing," Sona said to Ashvi. "I'm honored."

Ashvi smiled. "Ma has talked about you so much—she loves you. And it's clear you love her. So your voice can help call her back from illness." She took the bowl and went to the door. "Now don't make too much noise. What she needs most right now is rest."

Ashvi left the room, and Sona sat on the bed and held Ayah's hand.

Raag went to close the door, then pulled up a stool and sat facing Sona.

"Now," he said sharply, "tell me what you're doing bringing a magical animal to our house. Where is that wolf?"

10

The Song of the Wolf

"I don't know what you're talking about," Sona said, avoiding Raag's eyes and focusing on Ayah instead.

"Fine. Be that way." Raag approached the bed and squatted down to peer under it.

Sona stood. "Wait. Don't—"

Raag lifted his head and grinned. "I thought you said you didn't know what I was talking about."

"I . . . I don't. It's just . . . don't stir up dust, not while Ayah is finally resting." Sona's cheeks burned.

Raag straightened up, empty-handed. "Come on. Let me see the creature that the Hunter wants so badly."

"So you *were* listening at the door! That's very bad manners."

"Bad manners, but effective to help me figure out what's going on when a Malech girl shows up at the door in the middle of a Goldstorm and no one will tell you anything, not even your own grandmother. It was ages before Ma let me leave the kitchen, and I only caught a little bit about the Hunter before Matrka started coughing. Was the Hunter as repulsive as the legends say?"

Sona frowned. "The legends say Hunters are heroes, but he didn't seem like a hero to me."

Raag countered: "You clearly haven't been listening to the right legends."

Sona shot him a look. "He was like . . . a predator. Someone who can't help hunting. But he enjoys it and takes grisly trophies of the beasts he kills." She cringed at the memory. "Anyway, you shouldn't eavesdrop about things that don't concern you."

Raag raised his eyebrows. "A magical animal brought to my house concerns me. It concerns everyone," he said.

"What do you mean?" Sona asked.

"Have you heard the Songs of the Beasts?"

Sona's heart sped up. "No." At Raag's sneer, she said, "After all, songs are forbidden."

Raag laughed, short and bark-like. "Spoken like a true Malech. You must follow the Malechian law, or what will happen? The King himself will come and take away your hair ribbons? You know nothing of sorrow, of sacrifice, of forever being at the mercy of someone else's cruelty."

"And you know nothing about me!" Sona cried.

Ayah moaned and shifted her head on the pillow. Sona rushed to Ayah's side and put her hand on her forehead. Her skin was still cool, at least for now.

Ayah opened her eyes and looked at Raag. "Dauhitra," she whispered.

Raag went to the other side of the bed and held Ayah's hand. "Matrka," he said. "What do you need?"

"Sing the song, dauhitra. The Song of the Wolf." Ayah stifled a cough.

Raag's jaw dropped. "Now? In front of *her*?"

Sona bit her tongue. Why did Raag still treat her as a stranger? Hadn't she just sung a Devan song and used magic to help Ayah?

"Sing it, Raag," Ayah said. Her cough started again. "She needs to understand its importance."

Raag waited until she had stopped coughing and settled back against the pillow again. "As you wish, Matrka," he said.

Raag went to the carved instrument sitting on the table. He entwined his fingers, made a short bow, and picked it up reverently. He sat on a cushion on the rug and held it with its round end resting on the ground and the long neck against his shoulder. He plucked one of its four strings.

A note rang out and filled the room with buzzing energy.

A swara, Sona thought as the sound swept over her.

And then, over the tone that continued to drone, Raag began to sing in a surprisingly sweet and tender voice:

> *Come in, my friend, and rest awhile.*
> *Sit down, I welcome you.*
> *With open hands and honest smile,*
> *I will sing you true.*
>
> *I'll sing to you of Devia,*
> *Our land so sweet and fair.*
> *Our golden land of Devia,*
> *Where music fills the air.*

The crops are growing in the fields,
The penance now is due.
And you'll soon see what friendship yields,
For I will sing you true.

The whillet stems grow tall, glow gold,
Fire red, and water blue,
The wind it whispers soft and bold,
Oh where, oh Wolf, are you?

I heard you crying at the moon,
On that last cloudless night.
The day is coming all too soon,
When we will have to fight.

The jungle's growing silently,
The river rushes through,
The day is dawning violently,
Oh where, oh Wolf, are you?

For Devia has need, my friend,
Of hearts both strong and true.
Before the world comes to an end
I call, oh Wolf, to you!

Sona looked down to find Swara sitting in front of Raag, her gold-tipped ears peaked, her head tilted. And as the last of the sound from the instrument faded, the wolf pup raised her paw and laid it on Raag's knee.

Sona started. "How—?"

The door opened, and Ashvi rushed into the room with a bowl in her hands. "Raag! What are you doing?"

Swara darted under the bed again.

Ashvi crossed the rug, set the bowl down, grabbed the instrument from Raag's hands, and placed it carefully on the table.

"Why are you singing about old legends at a time like this? And using your grandmother's tanpura?" she said to him sternly.

"But—" Raag protested.

"We have spoken of this. This is a very valuable instrument, and it must not be damaged. It belongs to the whole village."

"I know. I'm always very careful," Raag said.

"You should not be using it without permission," Ashvi said.

"It wasn't his fault. Ayah asked him to sing," Sona interrupted.

Ashvi raised her eyebrows. "Is this true, Ma?"

But Ayah's eyes were closed, and she stirred without waking. Ashvi went to her and felt her forehead again. "She needs rest." Ashvi turned to Sona. "Now show me what you've brought into our home."

Sona sighed, reached under the bed, and stood with Swara in her arms.

"Oh!" cried Ashvi.

"See, Ma? I told you there was a reason," Raag said. "Matrka knows. She asked me to sing."

Ashvi looked sharply at Sona. "How did you find this wolf?"

"She came to my barn, injured," Sona said. "And then a Hunter showed up at my house searching for a magical animal. I had to get her out of there."

Ashvi sank to a floor cushion like the strength in her legs had given out. "A *Hunter*? So nearby?"

"I can't let him have her," Sona said.

Ashvi bit her lip as she gazed at Sona and Swara. Then she glanced at Raag and her sleeping mother and stood. "While the Goldstorm rages, we will hide you. But . . . I once met a Hunter, long ago. He will stop at nothing to get this animal. We're all in terrible danger." Her hands shook as she picked up the bowl of herbs and went to Ayah's bed. "You should release that wolf into the wild, where it belongs."

"But she's just a baby. She'll die without our help," Sona said.

Ashvi began applying an herb paste to Ayah's forehead, cheeks, and neck. "You are welcome here, but that creature is not. If you insist on keeping the animal with you, then once the storm ends, you must go."

"I can't bring Swara home with the Hunter waiting there."

"Whatever you do, the creature can't stay here. You must decide what's more important to you: that animal, or people. Now please leave me alone. I must take care of my mother."

Sona's throat was tight as she picked up Swara and left the room. When she got outside Ayah's door, she found that Raag had followed her.

"Thanks for defending me in there," Raag said, looking sheepish. "Ma probably wouldn't have believed me if I'd said it."

"I just told the truth," Sona said. She squared her shoulders. "I need to convince your mother to keep Swara safe."

Raag shook his head. "You can't. She's won't budge once she's made up her mind. Trust me, I know."

"I can't abandon Swara. She'll die."

Raag put his hand on her arm and looked her in the eye. "I'll help you with the pup. She's very special, and we must protect her. I'm sorry about how I acted before."

Sona gripped Raag's arm in return. "Apology accepted." With Ayah ill, she needed an ally. "I hope Ayah recovers quickly."

"Matrka will be better soon. She is strong," Raag said.

Sona swallowed. "She's the strongest person I know." But she didn't feel sure of anything. The ghosts of her mother and father seemed to whisper in the storm outside. She had lost them both to a Goldstorm like this one. She couldn't lose Ayah, too.

Windsday, seventh day of Harvest, YK 721
ↄ *the Present Day* ↄ

Your Excellency:

I trust you are doing well during these harvest months and looking forward to the festival. I am writing to you with an update on the status of the green gems, known as "leaf" gems, in our region.

As you know, the preceding years have yielded an abundance of green gems, some of exceedingly large size. We have had to triple our mining and transport operations.

But now, I am sorry to report that the gem numbers have dwindled significantly over the past two months, despite engaging in several deep and dangerous operations. In fact, over the last week, there have been no additional gems found at all. I am not sure why this is the case after the recent boom. I have shut down the Van Province mining operations for now, and the Devan miners have already been dismissed. I believe it would be wise to transfer our Malechian miners to other provinces for the time being.

I shall remain in the region with a small group and will continue to monitor the situation here. I will apprise you immediately if more gems are found.

Yours,

Yaz Samani

11

The Throw

The Goldstorm continued to rage over the next three days. As the wind and dust swirled outside, Ayah stayed ill—feverish, wheezing, and unconscious, with only occasional moments when she opened her eyes. But even when she was awake, she was too weak to talk, and barely had the energy to take sips of water or the herbed soups and teas that Ashvi fed her, spoon by spoon.

Sona helped prepare food and herbs and spent hours singing with Ashvi and Raag over the steaming bowls that helped ease Ayah's breathing. When Sona sang, she felt a mix of joy, fear, and desperate hope. She was honored to be allowed to do her part to help her grandmother, and as she sang, she prayed to Bhoomi, to the Wind God, to whoever might be listening. But as hours and days passed, Sona's concern grew that Ayah would not get better, no matter what they tried.

Sona's stomach roiled as she thought of her father and brothers and how worried they must be about her. She wished she could get a message to them, but that was impossible while the storm lasted, and it would likely bring the Hunter right to their doorstep.

In her free moments, Sona found solace in looking after Swara. The gash on the pup's side was now almost healed, and she seemed to have suffered no lasting harm. Sona played with her on the floor, laughing when Swara tugged on a spare piece of rope, and yelping when they wrestled and the pup bit too hard, to teach the young wolf to gentle her bite. Sona taught Swara simple tricks with morsels of food, just like she and Father had done with all the farm dogs they'd had over the years. Swara proved to be a fast learner, learning "sit," "down," and "stay." When Sona praised her, Swara was so delighted that she rolled on her back and begged for belly scratches. Raag spent almost as much time with Swara as she did and taught her his own tricks. This, more than anything Raag said, convinced Sona that they might be able to be friends.

Sona hoped that seeing Swara's innocence and playfulness would make Ashvi rethink the notion of abandoning her in the wilderness. But Ashvi sighed every time she saw the wolf pup and kept warning that as soon as the storm abated, the Hunter was sure to come sniffing.

Sona bundled up for the short walk to the barn and spent time there with Raag, helping to care for Willa along with Ayah's cows, goats, sheep, and chickens. While they fed and watered the beasts and kept their stalls clean, Raag, away from Ashvi's dampening presence, filled Sona's ears with endless chatter about the sacred Devan animals and what finding Swara might mean.

"She must be one of the five magical beasts. The hawks are gone forever, but Devan legends say there's only one of each kind of sacred beast—wolf, tiger, fish, snake—per generation," he said excitedly. "But why did she come to you, and what are we supposed to do with her?"

"I'm sure Swara came to my home because it's near where the Hunter killed her mother and sibling and wounded her. But now that I understand her importance to Devia, I feel even more strongly that I can't let her fall into the Hunter's hands."

Raag nodded vigorously. "We need to get her far away from here," he said.

"*We?* Swara is my responsibility. And I'm not doing anything until Ayah tells me what's best."

"Matrka is very wise," Raag agreed. "But she can't talk right now, and I'm not sure how long it will take her to recover. Once the storm resolves, your family will come looking. And that Hunter will, too."

"Where do you think I should go?"

Raag shrugged. "I don't know. I've traveled to lots of places in Devia. Maybe I could help you find a place to keep Swara safe?"

"Why would you leave your home, your mother and grand-mother, to come with me? A few days ago, you didn't even want to let me into your house in the middle of a Goldstorm, and now you want to plan a quest with me?"

Raag looked at her and stood straighter. "The fact that Swara chose you is important. I also want to keep her safe from the Hunter. So yes, I'd go with you. And I'd be useful to you on the road. Have you even traveled outside Kanthpur before?"

The truth was, Sona had never been more than a few miles from the village. But she decided not to answer him and dabbed more ointment on Willa's forehead. She had promised Ayah she wouldn't use it on anything other than her own ears. But she had to keep trying to help Willa.

"Why are you wasting our precious ointment on that broken-down pony?"

Willa stomped a foot and tossed her head.

Sona huffed and glared at Raag. "If not for this broken-down pony, I'd be dead in the Goldstorm, and so would Swara. Willa's been hurt, too, and I'm helping her. If you don't like it, you can mind your own business."

"Fine," said Raag, holding up his hands. "You don't have to get angry." He held out a hooli fruit to Willa, who snorted again, but eventually took it from him and started crunching.

"That's a good girl," Raag said soothingly as he reached up to stroke her nose. He turned to Sona and grinned. "Now I know how to get on her good side."

Sona bundled herself up, and on the short walk back to the house, her chest tightened with worry about Ayah, her family back home, and now Willa. Why wasn't Willa's wound healing like Swara's had? Should she ask Ashvi for advice? But she was already so preoccupied caring for Ayah.

Sona made up her mind as she entered the house. Since she was going to travel, she'd need to visit the cellar storeroom to bring enough ointment to hide her ears and take care of the pony's wound.

That evening, Sona volunteered to go downstairs to gather more herbs for Ashvi. "I also need more of Ayah's ointment," she said. "Some of my burns from the Goldstorm are hurting again, and the jar you gave me the other day is almost finished."

Ashvi looked up from gathering bowls and spoons. "Of course. You can find more of the ointment on the left in the storeroom in small round jars. Take as much as you need."

"Thank you," Sona said, trying not to let her guilt show on her face.

She went alone into the cool cellar that smelled pleasantly of tulsi and chamomile, mint and marigold. There was a basin full of water, and a small fireplace with a kettle. The entire room was lined with wooden shelves, neatly labeled, with rows and rows of bottles and jars. Sona quickly found the shelf that contained numerous familiar round jars. She opened one and inhaled the scent of green herbs and flowers, of Ayah's love and the special magic that protected her. Tears started in her eyes. What if Ayah succumbed to Goldstorm Fever? How would Sona survive without her? Not just because of the ointment, but because of the wisdom and love Ayah had always showered on Sona and her family. Then Sona heard Ayah's voice, as clear as if she were in the cellar with her rather than feverish in her bed upstairs: "The past is past. Look to what can be done now."

Sona wiped her face and straightened her shoulders. What could be done now was to help Ayah recover . . . and to make plans to keep Swara safe. She recapped the jar and put it and two more into her bag. Then she looked around and gathered the herb powders and pastes that she'd seen Ashvi use to ease Ayah's breathing, and carefully carried everything upstairs.

On the fourth night of the storm, Ayah took a turn for the worse, with a dangerously high fever and agonized breathing. Ashvi spent hours at her side, singing and surrounding Ayah with a tent of herbed steam. Sona and Raag stayed nearby and helped as much as they could, singing and bringing more herbs and water. Eventually, Ashvi tried to shoo them away, telling them to rest. But neither of them could, not while Ayah was still fighting for her life.

At last, around midnight, the fever broke.

"It's been four days since you fell ill," Sona whispered. "Wake up, Ayah. Please wake up." Sona swallowed the lump in her throat. Ayah always said that tears for something that hadn't yet happened were a waste of energy. Sona stroked Swara's soft fur, and the pup blinked up at her with bright eyes.

"Wake up, Matrka," Raag said softly.

But Ayah only moaned weakly.

"The fever is gone. Why does she still sleep?" Sona asked.

"Goldstorm Fever can wreak havoc on the body," Ashvi said. "She was out in the storm for a long while and inhaled much of the Golddust. And she's not young anymore." She gently applied more herb paste to Ayah's face and neck. "I've done all I can," she said in a hoarse voice. "All we can do now is keep her warm, and hope."

"She'll return to normal soon. She must," Raag said.

Ashvi's brow furrowed. "I've never seen someone who's been unconscious for this long from Goldstorm Fever recover. Many last like this for weeks, only to perish in the end. I fear only the legendary amrita, the golden nectar of life from Bhoomi's sacred Mount Meru, can save her now. Ma had a few precious drops in her possession, years ago. But she used it to save someone and wouldn't tell me who. So there was none left—" Ashvi stopped and glanced at both kids like she only just remembered they were there. She stood and wiped her hands on a cloth. "There is no amrita here now. But Ma is strong. If anyone can defeat Goldstorm Fever, it is she." Ashvi put her hand on Raag's shoulder and looked at Sona. "It's late. You two should sleep." She smiled wearily. "I promise to call you if anything changes. I think the storm will end soon, perhaps by morning, and we'll need to prepare for the aftermath." She gave Swara a hard look.

"Could I have a few minutes alone with her?" Sona asked.

Ashvi nodded. "I'll make some tea. Raag, why don't you come and help me?"

They left the room, and Sona put her hand on Ayah's dear cheek. "Oh, Ayah. I hope you know how much you mean to me, how much I love you. I'm going to keep Swara safe because I know that's what you'd want me to do. I guess I'm going to have to figure out where to go by myself. The storm might end soon. So, for now at least, this is goodbye. But I hope we'll meet again, by Bhoomi's grace." Sona's voice cracked as she put her hand on her own heart, and then to Ayah's chest, where her heart was still beating.

Ashvi returned with two cups of tea and offered one to Sona. Sona couldn't meet her eyes, but she accepted it with thanks, then scooped up Swara and left the room.

Raag was in the hallway with his own mug of tea. "Good night," Sona murmured. He stopped and opened his mouth as if to say something. But then he seemed to think better of it, nodded, and padded toward his room.

Sona went to the small guest room where she'd spent the past few nights and grabbed the things she had put aside: a change of clothes, cheese and bread, lentil cakes and dried fruit, a water jug and a small cooking pot. The three jars of Ayah's ointment. Another pang of guilt stabbed her chest, but Sona shook it off. This was an emergency—she needed to go out in the world to save Swara, and she needed to disguise herself to do so. She threw everything into a canvas pack and strapped it over her shoulder. She patted the squirming Swara in her sweater pocket. The pup had grown so much in a few days that she barely fit anymore. If Ashvi or Raag discovered Sona leaving the house, she'd say she was collecting her clothes to wash and visiting Willa before she slept. But no one stopped her as she wrapped herself up in her jacket and a thick cloak, drew on her boots, and made her way through gusting Golddust to the barn.

Sona sat in a corner of Willa's stall with Swara's warmth against her body. She watched the storm through the barn's high window, determined to leave as soon as it let up. She dozed and dreamed that a ghostly wind blew through the walls, moaning, and that Willa nuzzled her to keep her warm.

She woke to Willa's horsey nose in her face.

"What?" Sona said blearily.

The wind blew Golddust into the barn. Dust! Her blood chilled as she realized that the barn door was open.

Sona scooped up a sleepy Swara and listened. At first, all she heard was the soft breaths of the horses and cows, the flutter of a few wings. But then she held her breath and thought she could just make out the sound of stealthy footsteps.

The Hunter was here. Now. But the Goldstorm still blew outside! How had he made it to the village? How did he know where Sona was? Willa nosed Sona gently. The other animals were quiet; had the Hunter charmed them like he'd charmed the Tiger of Van? Was the Hunter even now stalking them to aim a silver Air Blade at Swara's heart?

What was she going to do?

Sona stowed the pup in her pocket and slipped the bridle on Willa's head by touch alone. Sona threw a pad on Willa's back and felt for the saddle, which was draped across the stall wall. She put it on the pony's back as quietly as possible, and in the dim light of Golddust reflected through the high barn window, she fumbled for the buckles. She managed to get one on when she heard the footsteps grow closer. There was no mistaking it now: the Hunter was here. She tried to get the second buckle on, but the strap kept slipping away.

Hurry, Sona thought.

She finally got the second buckle on—loose, but it would have to do. She needed to lead Willa out of the stall before she could mount her and ride away. But what chance did she have against the Hunter?

Sona took a deep, quiet breath and squared her shoulders. She stopped to grab the large rock that was used to hold the stall door open. She was going to have to drop the Hunter and then run. She clutched the rock in her sweaty hand and tried to slow her racing heart.

The quiet footsteps came closer. Willa snorted, and Sona put a calming hand on her flank, then reached for her lead. In her other hand, she poised the stone. She'd only have one shot at the Hunter. She needed to get Willa out of the stall before he cornered them there, and then knock him down, or at least delay him long enough to get away.

Sona had good aim. She had experience throwing stones to startle birds away from the whillet fields, and rabbits away from their greens. She just needed to hit the Hunter hard enough that he couldn't block their way out of the barn. She led Willa out of her stall and into the center aisle. Maybe they could sneak out the back without encountering the Hunter at all?

Then Willa neighed. Loudly.

"Hush," Sona murmured.

But Willa wouldn't stop. And then, emanating from the region of her belly, she heard a whine, much stronger and louder than it had been just a few days ago. Sona rocked back and forth, praying that Swara would go back to sleep. Were the animals trying to get them caught?

The footsteps picked up in pace and weren't even trying to be quiet anymore. They drew even closer.

Sona planted her legs and bent her knees to ready herself. In the dimness of the barn, a dark silhouette loomed.

She gripped the rock hard. She didn't trust herself to hit the Hunter in the head in the dark, but his chest was a good, broad target. Sona lifted her arm and threw.

The stone hit the shadow before her with a thump. "Ow!" it said as it dropped with a thud.

She'd hit him! Sona tugged on Willa's lead, but Willa refused to budge.

"Come on, Willa girl," Sona said as she tugged again.

But Willa didn't move.

"We don't have time!" Sona whispered urgently.

"Maybe you should give her a treat?" suggested a voice from the ground.

What? "By the Wind God's sigh, Raag, you scared me to death," said Sona. "What are you doing sneaking in here in the middle of the night?"

"Technically, it's my family's barn," said Raag, still on the floor.

"I thought you were the Hunter! Did I hurt you?" Sona let go of Willa's lead and crouched over him.

Raag sat up slowly and rubbed his left shoulder. "You're a good shot. Thank Bhoomi I'm right-handed," he said.

"I was aiming for the Hunter's chest. I just wanted to knock the wind out of him so we could escape." Sona let out a breath and dropped her shoulders. "But now I guess we don't have to."

Raag stood and rotated his shoulder forward, then back. "We do have to leave now," he said. "The storm has stopped."

Sona's pulse began to hammer again. "It has?"

"Yes," Raag said. "I stayed up tonight watching. The only Golddust that's blowing is what's already on the ground. Come on, we've got to go."

Sona grabbed Willa's lead again. "Like I said, I don't need you."

"You don't even know where to go," said Raag. "The moon is out, and it's bright. I can lead us by a secret way that very few know of. A way to guarantee we won't be followed."

"I just need to travel for a few days to lose the Hunter. Then I'll return home," Sona said.

"That's not far enough," Raag said.

Sona frowned. "Then I'll go farther. I'll go . . ." Where could Sona go? Where would be far enough to keep Swara safe? What place would make sense? If only Ayah had told her. But Ayah might not tell her anything ever again. Ayah, who had loved and cared for her for years, who had saved Sona's life with amrita when she was a newborn.

Amrita. The nectar of life that Ayah had once used to heal Sona.

How could Sona not try to do the same for her?

"Mount Meru," Sona said. "To get amrita for Ayah." Now that she'd voiced the thought, she wondered why it had taken her so long to think of it.

Raag raised his eyebrows. "I'll say this much for you—you don't think small. That might be the only way to save Matrka. But do you know how to get there?"

"It's to the north," Sona said. "I know that much."

"You'll need to cross Tirna, then Sindhu, and the Great Khila Desert. You'll need to find your way through the desolate mountains of Paravat and climb Mount Meru," Raag said. "I've traveled all over Devia. I can show you the way. And somewhere on our journey, we can find a safe place to leave Swara. But we must go now. If that Hunter is as determined as you and Ma say, he's going to arrive here soon."

Sona chewed her lip. She had to admit that leaving now was a better idea than staying here and ending up the Hunter's next victim. She put her hand on Raag's arm. "Why are you doing this? Why are you helping me?"

The dim light coming through the high window glinted off of Raag's brown eyes. "We need to help Matrka in any way we can. And no matter what Ma says, I know it's my duty as a Devan to help a magical beast." He reached into his pocket and pulled something out.

"Here," he said to Willa. "Come on, girl."

Willa sniffed the hooli fruit Raag held and followed him farther toward the open door of the barn.

"So much for loyalty," Sona grumbled.

EXCERPT FROM A DEVAN SONG

Amrita, that nectar gold!
Found by a true believer,
against it, no disease can hold,
no wound, nor break, nor fever.

12

The Journey

Raag lit a lamp so they could properly bridle and saddle Willa and store their bundles in the saddlebags. Outside the barn, Sona climbed on Willa's back, and with another hooli fruit bribe, Willa consented to allow Raag to hold her lead. Then they set off into the night.

Raag was right: the storm had indeed stopped—there was no Golddust falling from the sky, although a light wind blew gusts of it around. Sona had tucked Swara into a saddlebag, and both she and Raag wore layers of clothes and scarves over their faces. The clouds had disappeared, and a full moon lit up the sky and the dazzling landscape of gold. It was beautiful, but Sona's heart quailed. She was riding away from everything she'd ever known— her home, her family. She had to leave, to save Swara. Ayah would want it this way. And just maybe, they could find the way to save Ayah, too.

"Did you leave a note for your mother, letting her know you were leaving?" Sona asked.

Raag shook his head. "The fewer people who know where we're going, the better."

"Won't she worry?"

Raag shrugged. "It's not like I haven't run away before."

Sona wondered what had made Raag run away, but she didn't know him well enough to ask.

"Besides, if Ma doesn't know, the Hunter can't force her to tell him."

Sona shivered as she thought about the Hunter who was sure to be on their trail soon, who might already be setting out from Sona's home to pursue them. His colorless eyes haunted Sona; she wondered how long it would be before his nose recovered, and she would hear his snuffling, following their scent.

Raag led them out of Kanthpur, through the trees that marked the border between the village and the neighboring farmland, then on through fields of whillet and vegetables, heading north.

"Where are we going?" Sona asked. "I mean, what's our first stop?"

"Somewhere the Hunter can't easily follow. You said he's on horseback, right?"

"Yes, he said he'd take one of our horses as soon as the Gold-storm was over. But how can we go where he can't follow us?"

"You'll see," Raag said.

"If we're doing this together, you can't keep secrets from me."

Raag looked startled. "Of course. We're going to the river—across it, in fact."

"The Risha?" That river could be reached in a few hours' walk. Sona had spent many a Harvest Festival celebrating on its banks. There was a ford where the water was shallow enough to easily cross—Swara might even be able to do it on her own.

Raag nodded. "We're crossing the Risha, but then we're going farther east, to the Genla."

"Oh." The Genla was a much larger river on the edge of Tir Province, fast-flowing and treacherous at times. "What are we doing there?"

"Crossing the river, leaving Tirna, and meeting friends in Sindhu, the riverlands," Raag said with a smile.

"That's really far away, though—at least three days' walk."

"Yes, but short of sailing away, it's the only way I know of to throw off the Hunter. The way that we're going, he can't cross the Genla on a horse—it's too deep, and the current is too swift."

"In case you haven't noticed," Sona said, "we have a pony. If a horse can't cross the river, neither can she. And don't even think of telling me to leave her behind."

"No need to leave anyone behind." Raag smiled. He stroked Willa's flank. "I have a plan. Trust me."

Why should I? Sona thought. But she didn't know the land like Raag, so she didn't have much of an alternative. She'd have to trust him for now.

After a couple of hours riding in the cool night, Sona got off and walked next to Raag to give Willa a rest. They were still in familiar territory—the farmland of Tir, with rolling hills, fields of grain, fruit trees, and woods. They stopped at a stream and drank water and shared bread, cheese, and pressed lentil cakes with Swara while Willa munched on fresh grass.

With a full belly, Swara became playful, wrestling with Sona and Raag by the light of the moon. Raag tugged at her scruff and laughed at her play growls while Sona watched them with affection. Sona couldn't abandon this sweet baby to fend for herself.

They walked a bit farther, but as the moon finally set and the night grew darker, they tied Willa to a large jojonut tree where the ground was free of Golddust. They bundled themselves in blankets and caught a little sleep, taking turns watching for pursuers.

Once the sky grew pink with the sunrise, they were up again and moving. Sona had only traveled to the Risha on the road, but Raag led them through the woods instead.

"How do you know the way so well?"

Raag gazed into the distance. "I've been traveling my whole life. We've never stayed in one place for more than half a year."

Sona had never lived anywhere other than her house, had never even set foot outside of Tir. "Why?"

"Looking for home," Raag said. Then he started walking faster, and Sona understood that the conversation was over.

They walked the whole morning through farms, fields, and forests, stopping only for short breaks to eat, drink, refill their water jugs, and let the animals rest. Swara ran alongside them on her short legs from time to time before collapsing in a heap; then they put her in a saddlebag to ride for a while. During their brief stops, Sona trained Swara with bits of food, moving past simple commands to teach her to "heel" (walk next to Sona's left leg) and "hide" (run to hide behind Willa).

Raag watched them with a furrowed brow and bemused smile. "I thought you Malechs weren't allowed to sing?"

Sona looked up from petting Swara. "What of it?"

"You sing to Swara and Willa all the time. It's a bit tuneless, but it's still a song."

Sona huffed. "I don't know—I'm just talking to them in a way that makes sense to me. It's not magical, like that song you sang to Swara at Ayah's house. That brought her right to you."

Raag raised his eyebrows but said nothing further.

That afternoon, when the Golddust had started to turn dark again, the Risha greeted Sona like a long-lost friend, sparkling and spirited. But as they approached the river, Raag grabbed her arm.

"Quick," he said as he pulled her toward a nearby copse of trees.

Soon, a score of Malechian soldiers, their tall, pointed helmets shining silver, crossed the river on horseback.

Sona made sure Swara was tucked into a saddlebag, and held Willa's lead tightly as they tried to stay hidden.

"I'm not sorry to leave Sindh behind," one soldier said to another as they reached the riverbank. "Those river rats are the worst."

His companion nodded. "Can't wait to celebrate Harvest," he said. "Let's get this bandit captured and move on to double rations and drinking ale."

"The sooner the better!"

Sona and Raag crouched behind a large shrub, barely daring to breathe. But the group of soldiers seemed endless, and they were in no hurry. Leaves tickled Sona's nose, and her foot started to fall asleep. But she didn't dare move.

Finally, the last few soldiers finished crossing the river and joined their companions on the road. After waiting for a few more minutes, Sona and Raag finally forded the river themselves.

On the other side of the Risha, they refilled their water jugs and took stock of their provisions. "We should have enough to last us three days, four if we're careful," Sona said. "And if we don't run into any more soldiers. You know, it might be better if you cut your hair, so they won't arrest you on sight."

"I'm not cutting my hair out of fear of soldiers," Raag said. "We should just keep hiding from them. At our current pace, we should reach the Genla at nightfall on our third day. You know, I was always told that Malechs were lazy and delicate. But you're a good traveler. You walk quickly, and for many hours without tiring."

"How many Malechs do you know?" Sona laughed. "I live on a farm. I'm used to hard work and long hours, especially during the harvest." She felt a pang as she thought of her father and brothers working without her and Ayah. She wondered how much of the harvest was left to bring in. Her family would surely go to Kanthpur to see whether she was with Ayah. And then they'd find Sona gone, and Ayah sick . . . or worse. But no, Sona wouldn't think of that. She had to believe that Ayah would be all right, that they would find a way to save her.

Sona had never been to the part of Tir that came after the Risha. She held Willa's lead and gave Swara a pat as she left behind the lands that she knew and stepped into the unknown.

That day and the next, Sona and Raag traveled through more farmland, fields of brilliant wildflowers, and small patches of trees. They hid from more groups of soldiers, all going from Sindh to Tir.

That night, the air grew cool enough that they risked a small fire as they made camp in a secluded area of the woods near the edge of Tir Province. They ate a meager meal, and Sona thought wistfully of Ayah's cooking and the harvest abundance that she would normally be enjoying. But she'd found some wild mint by a stream, and they'd boiled water and steeped the leaves, so they sipped tea as they watched the glowing embers of their stone-ringed campfire.

"We're lucky Malech soldiers are so loud, so we know when to hide," Raag said. "They seemed to be everywhere when Ma and I were traveling to Kanthpur."

Sona nodded. "It's good we've kept off the road. There have

been many more of them in Tir lately. Because of the black gems, and now that bandit."

Raag smirked. "They can dig for the gems, and send as many soldiers as they like, but Gulappan will still find a way to steal them and return them to the Devans. He's returned hundreds of gemstones, maybe even thousands, in every province in Devia."

"He's only one person. You make him sound like a god," Sona said.

"What do you know? He almost is." Raag leaned forward, and the embers lit his face from below, casting his eyes in shadow. "We know him as the Gray Ghost. He travels with most of his body covered up, wrapped in gray cloth, like a mourner." He pitched his voice low. "Some say that's because underneath that cloth, there's no solid body, just a whisper of a memory, because he and his whole family died at the hands of the Malechs."

A breeze blew through their camp, making the fire flare. Sona knew that Malechian soldiers could be cruel, but she hadn't heard about them killing whole families. No wonder Raag was so angry. Sona touched Swara's fur, and the pup stirred in her sleep. "I don't believe in ghosts. Do you?"

Raag shrugged. "Not really. I don't believe Gulappan is one, in any case. He's definitely a man. So many people we've met in our travels talk about him, how he tells jokes and riddles, how he laughs and eats like he'll never have another meal. I don't think that's how a ghost would act."

Sona laughed. "I've never heard of ghosts being hungry."

Raag warmed his hands over the fire. "In all the time I've traveled with Ma, I've never come across Gulappan in person. Maybe we will on this trip, though? It would be like meeting a living legend!"

Sona stared at the fire and didn't answer. She wasn't thrilled at the prospect of encountering an infamous criminal. What if he wanted them to join him in stealing gems? She hadn't known he walked around looking like a mournful ghost. . . . She wrapped herself more tightly in her blanket. "You sleep. I'll take the first watch," she said.

This part of Tir wasn't that different from the lands Sona knew, and its melodies were like home. A wood owl hooted, and something scurried in the underbrush. But Sona felt a creeping dread. She wasn't sure if she was more concerned about the Hunter or Gulappan, but she didn't want to meet either one. She kept thinking she heard a soft footstep nearby, kept looking into the shifting shadows for a glimpse of a tiger cloak, kept wondering when she'd smell the foul stench that meant the Hunter had found them. And now that Raag had told her about the Gray Ghost, she startled at every wind gust and branch rattle. She didn't want to wake Raag after moonset, but she knew that she needed her rest if they were to travel again all day.

When Raag woke her the next morning, Sona was immediately alert. "Let's hurry," she said. Raag nodded, and they packed up quickly and set off again.

They kept going, stopping only briefly, until it was almost full dark. Sona's boots were well-worn, but they began to chafe after hours on the road, and she could feel a blister forming on her left heel. Even Raag had slowed his pace, limping a little. On one of their brief stops, Sona covered their heel blisters with Ayah's ointment and dressed them in a strip of cotton cloth, which provided immediate relief. Then they kept going through the rolling hills and fields of Tir, staying off the road and alert for anyone who might try to stop them.

On the third day since they started off from Kanthpur, Willa kept tossing her head anxiously, and Swara stayed close to Sona's side. "It's okay," Sona murmured to them, even though she felt nervous herself. "We're getting away from him."

Raag stared at her with furrowed brows. "I've never heard of a Malech with your affinity for animals. Unless they were a Hunter."

Sona's skin prickled. "Well, I'm definitely not that," she said. Then she picked up her pace, and for the next several hours, they both barely had the breath to spare for talking.

Sunday, tenth day of Winter, YK 716
ᏻ *5 years before the Present Day* ᏻ

Your Excellency:

Winter greetings to you and your family. The rains are steady here, and we hope for excellent growing in the spring and through the harvest season.

I am writing on a matter of some urgency. You may be aware that the bandit Gulappan has moved from Van through Tir Province and is now roaming throughout Sindh Province. Despite our best efforts to capture him, he has managed to elude us so far. The Devans call him the Gray Ghost, as he dresses in gray clothes, and they believe he can walk through walls.

The bandit could not have accomplished any of this without significant help from the Devans. I ask for authorization to question villagers, and to search and seize gems from temples, as they are most certainly ill-gotten booty that this bandit has stolen from our miners' hard work.

Please respond as quickly as possible, and I will make sure to recover every single gem that this outlaw has illegally seized and put him in chains as well.

Yours in duty and honor,

Mor Damani

13

The River

Sona and Raag heard the Genla long before they saw it. It was twilight when they finally reached the river—wider than the Risha, and much more quick-flowing and dangerous, with rocks that jutted up like sharp teeth, hungry for wayward travelers. The water was clear and sparkled blue-green in the last rays of sunlight, and Sona heard music coming from it, a lilting melody that rose and fell.

"How in the world are we crossing that?" Sona asked as they came to a stop near the muddy bank.

"About two days' walk downstream, there is a large bridge. It's enormous—four full wagons can cross side by side!"

Sona's jaw dropped. What a bridge that must be! "But that's a long way to go. And the Hunter could easily follow us over a bridge."

Raag nodded. "That's not our path. I've got a faster way, just a couple of miles up the river. All we need are these hooli fruits"— he patted a saddlebag—"and a little luck."

They walked through the waning sunlight as the sky turned a dusty rose and the Genla rushed beside them. Devia was so big, and Sona had seen so little of it. If only they weren't in such a hurry. She tried to keep her attention on the river and not who might be already pursuing them.

Finally, Raag brought them to a stop where the river seemed quieter and curved around a bend.

"We're here," he said.

Sona looked, but she couldn't believe her eyes. "You must be joking."

An enormous beaver dam stretched before them from their shore to the far bank of the Genla.

Raag grinned. "Ma and I have crossed here before, so I know it can be done. And it's wide enough for Willa. But no adult horse rider would dare. At least, not if they're wise."

Sona blinked her eyes and looked again.

"I don't think—" Sona started. But she couldn't shake the feeling of pursuit. She swallowed. "We've run out of time. Tell me how to get Willa over."

Raag stepped onto the dam and took a hooli fruit out of his pocket. "Hold her lead, and I'll tempt her with this."

Sona began to lead Willa forward. The pony planted her feet and shook her head.

"Come on, girl, you can do it," Raag said. "Just a few steps."

But it wasn't a few steps. It was many, many steps, with a treacherous drop to the river on either side. Sona could swim, but she wasn't sure how well she would do swimming in a river this swift and wide. She doubted the pup could swim well enough, and Bhoomi only knew what Willa could do.

But the Hunter had surely left Sona's house when the Goldstorm ended. Perhaps his nose had healed enough so he could track Swara. He might even now be drawing closer. "Come on, Willa girl," Sona sang softly.

Between Sona's encouragement and Raag's promise of a treat, the pony agreed to take a step onto the dam. Two steps. "Keep going, Willa," Sona murmured.

A third step. Four. All of Willa's weight now rested on the dam. It creaked and groaned ominously. Sona held her breath. The dam didn't collapse. And so they kept going, step by step, with Raag in front and Sona coaxing Willa with Swara's head poking out of the saddlebag.

They reached the middle of the dam. Willa took a careful step, and a log broke, making her neigh. But she kept her footing and didn't fall.

Suddenly, Sona heard a melody, a tune of lightness and innocence. Sona glanced at the river to her right and saw a glint of gold.

"Raag, look," she cried.

And in the water of the Genla, darting like a fleeting bolt of joy, was a fish—its head pale gold, its body blue, long, and lithe, swimming upstream toward the dam they were standing on.

"The sacred Fish," whispered Raag, and he bent to one knee and bowed his head to the golden-headed fish. He looked back at Sona. "I thought she might be bigger, though."

Sona laughed. "That fish has to be at least as big as Willa." How could something so large swim so quickly upstream in a fast-flowing river like the Genla? Sona knew from Ayah and Raag that the Fish was one of the sacred animals of Devia, but she hadn't expected it to be so beautiful.

The Fish swam right up to the dam, stuck her head out of the water, and gazed at Sona with deep blue eyes. She seemed to be smiling, and her song filled Sona's heart with a brightness that drained her worry away.

As if in a trance, Sona held her arm out over the water.

The Fish leaped up toward Sona's hand. At its touch, all the weariness left Sona's arm.

Fast as a thought, a silver-tipped spear stabbed into the water where the Fish had just been. Sona screamed, and the Fish flipped over in midair and dove back into the water.

"Go!" Sona cried to the Fish, who clearly didn't need the instruction. It was already swimming downstream like a flash of gold and blue.

The hairs on Sona's arms stood up. She wheeled around in dread.

The Hunter had arrived at the dam.

"You have no right!" Sona cried.

The Hunter didn't spare Sona a glance as he hurled another spear at the fleeing Fish. But it landed well short and broke on a large stone jutting from the river.

"Hurry!" Sona cried to Raag as she hauled on Willa's lead.

"Ho, girl!" the Hunter shouted. "What are you doing here?"

Sona refused to look back. She didn't want to see those colorless eyes again—she would probably lose her balance and fall into the river.

They were three-fourths of the way across. They were going to make it.

"So you survived that Goldstorm after all. Your family's looking for you, girl. I told them I'd find you for them," called the Hunter.

"Keep going!" Sona whispered to Raag, who waved the hooli fruit in front of Willa's nose again.

The Hunter pointed his nose toward them and sniffed. "Why'd you run away, girl? And with a Devan boy, too. What are you hiding?"

Sona pulled on Willa's lead, urging her forward more quickly.

"I am the Hunter Rodh, ordained by the King of Malechia himself, and I command you to stop!" cried the Hunter. "It is a high crime to come between me and my prey."

Sona swallowed. Her whole body trembled. She was disobeying a direct order from a Hunter. It was against one of the most fundamental Malechian laws.

But she couldn't let the Hunter kill Swara. She nodded at Raag to keep going.

They had almost reached the far bank when Sona risked a glance back.

The Hunter was leading a dark brown horse—Cardamom, she thought, from his gait and coloring. Her family's horse. At the edge of the dam, the Hunter pulled something from behind him. Suddenly, a dark shape came flying toward Sona. Willa tossed her head, jostling Sona, and the arrow just missed Sona's arm and stuck, quivering, in the surface of the dam in front of her.

"He's shooting at us now! Hurry!" she yelled to Raag. She didn't think the Hunter would miss again.

But a cloud covered the moon, and there was no second arrow. She glanced back again—the Hunter's shadowy form was urging the reluctant Cardamom forward. She heard Cardamom neigh, then heard the crack of a whip. A whip! On her family's sweet horse!

Cardamom screamed. But he refused to step onto the dam.

The Hunter swore loudly, and finally, the horse stopped screaming. The cloud moved on, and Sona squinted in the moonlight. The Hunter was holding something to Cardamom's ear and had gotten the horse to step onto the dam.

"Keep going!" Raag cried.

Sona forced herself to turn forward. She hauled on Willa's lead and brought her the last few steps to reach the shore. "We've got to get out of here!"

"Yes, but I think I can do something first," Raag said. He put his hands together and bowed, then reached into a saddlebag and pulled out a stringed instrument, a much smaller version of what he'd played at Ayah's house.

"What are you doing?" Sona cried as Raag sat on the bank facing the dam. The Hunter was on the dam now; he was going to catch them.

"Get up on Willa and get ready to run when I tell you."

"But—"

"There's a village tucked into a curve of the river a few miles downstream. Go there and ask for Yaami and tell her you're with me. They will help you. Just get ready."

Sona climbed onto Willa's back and turned Willa parallel to the river as Raag plucked a string on the instrument and a single note rang out. And then he began to sing.

Sona couldn't understand the words, but the lyrics were made of short syllables—a work song, a song to make one try and try until the work was done. A song to make one believe one could do anything, could change the course of rivers.

And in the moonlight on the dam, she saw small dark figures

emerge and start scurrying toward the Hunter. Beavers! But they couldn't possibly do anything against a Hunter. He would kill them like he'd killed so many animals that crossed his path.

But the beavers stopped well short of reaching the Hunter; instead, they darted back into the dam and disappeared.

"Raag! Jump on! We've got to go!" Sona cried.

But Raag shook his head and kept singing.

And Sona refused to leave him at the mercy of the Hunter.

Sona counted to ten. To twenty. To fifty. The Hunter made slow but steady progress, leading Cardamom on top of the dam. He was almost halfway across.

And then, suddenly, the Hunter stumbled as the level surface of the dam in front of him broke apart.

Cardamom reared, and the reins slipped out of the Hunter's hands. The fracture grew, and the dam split, allowing the water from upstream to start flowing with a trickle that quickly became a larger stream, then even larger, as the pent-up water of the Genla broke through its chains.

Free of the Hunter's grasp, Cardamom stepped back, and finding the footing treacherous, wheeled with rolling eyes, desperate to return to safety.

The Hunter shouted at the horse, and Sona bit her tongue to stop herself from crying out. She didn't want Cardamom to fall into the river and be swept away.

Cardamom's front leg slipped into the water, and he screamed.

But then he found his footing and ran back to the far shore, kicking forcefully. Cardamom reached the opposite shore as the dam broke away completely. The dislodged piece started to float downstream with the Hunter on it, picking up pace as the full force of the river pushed against it.

The Hunter crouched on the floating piece of the dam. He took a mighty leap toward the part still attached to the shore where Raag sat.

"Raag! Get on!" Sona yelled.

Raag stopped singing. He scrambled to stand and ran toward her.

The Hunter's leap fell short, and he landed with a splash in the water, scrabbling for the edge of the dam. But the current caught him, and he roared as the Genla carried him away. "I'll find you, girl! And that demonic fish! I always get my prey!"

Sona and Raag stayed silent for a moment, listening to the Hunter's fading cries as he was swept far downstream.

"That is one crazy Malech," Raag murmured.

"We did it. We escaped him," Sona said shakily. "You were marvelous. You saved all our lives." She offered Raag a hand.

Raag grasped her hand, and she pulled him up onto Willa's back.

"You were marvelous," Raag said. "You saved that golden Fish."

Sona shook her head. "I didn't know what I was doing. I wanted . . . I felt I should hold my hand out. It was just good timing."

"I couldn't have done better if I'd sung the Song of the Fish." Raag twisted to look Sona in the eyes. "I've never, ever heard of a Malech with such a way with animals. Other than—"

"If you compare me to the Hunter again, I'll push you off this pony." Sona shoved Raag lightly.

Raag laughed. "No offense. If the Fish loves you, you're clearly something special."

Sona's face heated, and she smiled. "You're rather special your-self. Tell me, how did you do that thing with the beavers?"

Raag grinned. "I've studied hard with Matrka. There's a reason why the Malechs have outlawed music. I called down dam-nation on him."

YK 648 ✆ Year 168 of the Devan Fourth Age
✆ 73 years before the Present Day ✆

All is well, Minister, for now. The harvest is coming in, and we will have plenty to feed all of Devia, to send back to our dear Home Isle, and to trade around the world.

Mining operations are in full swing, and the gems seem inexhaustible, no matter where we delve or how deep we dig. My fellow Governors tell me the same is true in every province but Parvat—I hear it is a stark, cold place, with little to offer in the way of shelter, arable soil, or treasure. It has been abandoned by the Devans themselves, so I see no reason to waste our resources searching further.

With the huge profits from the gem mining, we have built roads, ships, and shelters for Malechs and Devans alike. The Goldstorms have been bad this year, it's true, but we shall build stronger and higher to prosper despite them.

It pains me to think what the Devans would do without us, as they are a thoroughly uncivilized people who have no centralized leadership and waste time quarreling among themselves. And then there is their insistence on clinging to their simple earth worship when we know that it is the Wind God who blows blessings to us all.

I say to you truly: not only is Devia the gem in the belt of our far-flung empire, but we are the true saviors of Devia!

Yours in loyalty and honor,

Zol Mallani

14

Disguised

It was full dark when Raag signaled to bring Willa to a halt. The children dismounted and fed and watered the animals at a small stream that spilled into the Genla.

"Here's the tricky part," Raag said.

"*Here's* the tricky part?" Sona said incredulously. Her breathing was still uneven from their close call on the dam.

"We need to get to safety in the village. We can tell the village leader, Yaami, and her people all about the Fish and the Hunter. But before we meet them, we need to disguise you a bit," Raag said.

"What? Why?"

"They're not too fond of Malechs here, so we need to make you a Devan."

Sona's skin prickled. Raag was getting rather close to the truth. Maybe she should tell him?

"Raag—"

"You're already wearing a Devan-style shirt from Ma, so that's good. Take out your earring, okay? And I have some paint here that'll make your ears as golden as any Devan's." Raag pulled a jar out of his pocket.

Sona smirked as she removed her earring and put it carefully in a secure pocket. If she hadn't used Ayah's ointment this morning, she wouldn't need any paint for her ears. "As golden as your ears? The ones you hide underneath all that hair?"

"I'm Devan through and through, whether or not my ears are visible," Raag said.

There was a quaver in Raag's voice that Sona hadn't heard before, not even when they were both so worried about Ayah, not even when they were fending off the Hunter on the dam. She meant only to tease him, not upset him.

"Never mind," said Sona. "Let's do it."

Raag opened the jar, and the contents inside glittered gold.

"That's not Golddust, is it?" Sona asked.

"It's not," said Raag. "We both know that Golddust doesn't stay golden. This is made from some special clay, and then Matrka and Ma know just how to sing so it can disguise someone."

Sona nodded and thought of the healing ointment in her pack, the one that also disguised her own ears. "But why would a Malech want to pretend to be Devan? And why would any Devans allow them to?" she asked.

Raag shrugged. "Who knows? In any case, I raided our stores before we left. Here—" He dipped his finger into the paint, which was thick like cream. "Show me your ears."

Sona pushed her hair back behind her ears. "Raag—"

"Hold still and stay quiet for a moment. Your ears move when you talk."

As Raag worked, Sona thought some more. Ayah had told her to keep her identity a secret, but how long could she keep fooling her traveling companion, the one who just saved her life? But

Raag finally seemed to like her even though he thought she was a Malech. Maybe now wasn't the time to upset their new friendship.

"There. All done. Now nothing but complete immersion in water will take that off. I need to go ahead and make sure the villagers know we're friends. Just stay here and try not to make too much noise. While I'm gone, put some of this stuff on Swara's ears to disguise the gold. She's getting too big to be carried everywhere. We're going to have to pretend she's a regular dog." He held out another jar to Sona.

"What's this?"

"Black coloring. Ma uses it to dye clothes. It should work. Here, use this cloth so your hands don't get too stained."

"You've thought of everything," Sona said, taking the piece of fabric.

"Told you I'd be helpful," Raag said. "Oh, and one more thing, Malech. We'll be speaking in the Common Tongue here, since we don't know the local dialect. But you should use the Devan words for places—*Tirna*, not *Tir*, and *Sindhu*, not *Sindh*. You Malechs want to shorten everything, as if that makes words easier to say. But in the village, you must be a Devan girl, right?"

"Right," Sona said. She swallowed. "I hope I don't make too many mistakes."

"You'll be fine," Raag said. "And I'll be there to help." Then he disappeared into the brush.

Sona applied the black dye, which was also thick and sticky, to Swara's ears. Swara squirmed and tried to turn away, but Sona held her head firmly and commanded her to stay. Eventually, she thought she had covered all the gold, and sat back to wait.

But after traveling so far so quickly, waiting was hard. Jittery energy pulsed through Sona's body. She wanted to run, to hide, to magically transport them all to Mount Meru. To get the amrita for Ayah, to find Swara a safe place to live. Had the Hunter survived his trip down the river? Sona felt in her heart that the danger was not yet past.

So she waited. And waited. After pacing back and forth for what felt like forever, she sat and put her back against a log.

Had something happened to Raag? Maybe she should go and see.

"Sona, are you there?" came a voice. That couldn't be Raag—he never called her anything but *Malech*.

"Sona? It's me, Raag. It's safe. Come out."

Sona stood, made sure Swara was tucked in tight in a bag that she put over one shoulder and across her chest, then grabbed Willa's lead and walked toward the voice. She found Raag with two Devan adults—a woman and a man—as well as a little girl who looked to be about eight years old. Well, this explained why Raag hadn't called her *Malech*.

"Welcome, Sona of Tirna," said the woman in a voice as melodic as the Genla, clasping her fingers and bowing. "I am Yaami, Pitarau of Genpur. This is my husband, Santosh, and our daughter, Revati. Raag has spoken well of you and has explained your urgent errand to help Janaki Pitarau. Welcome, friend. Welcome to Sindhu, the riverlands."

Sona clasped her hands and bowed. "I am most grateful."

Sona and Raag followed Yaami until they went up a small hill, through a gap in the trees, and down into a clearing filled with twinkling blue lights.

"Are those tiny fish, flying through the night?" Sona asked.

Yaami smiled. "They are. But they're made of glass. They are specially made for us at the Sun Temple in Bhoominath, where they have a special talent with glass. Each one contains a tiny oil lamp that burns for a very long time."

And indeed, as Sona drew closer, she saw that thin ropes had been strung around the clearing, and on each rope were dozens of small blue fish, each lit from within by a minuscule lamp. And every few feet, there was a larger golden fish among the blue. Sona reached out and touched the golden scales, which somehow felt cool and supple, like they belonged to a living fish.

"Those are in honor of Mahseer, the protector of Sindhu, the Great Fish who travels from the river to the sea and back again."

They had met her! Sona glanced at Raag, and he nodded.

"We must tell you something," Raag said. "We saw Mahseer tonight, on the Genla."

Yaami raised her eyebrows in surprise. "Mahseer doesn't usually travel on the Genla. She is too large to navigate those rocks."

Sona said, "We saw a golden-headed fish that looked as big as my pony. She was lively and swam upstream swiftly. She came up to us as we walked upon the big beaver dam."

Yaami nodded. "Ah, that must be Mahseer's young one. What great fortune! Mahseer has offspring very rarely—less than once a generation. You have brought much joy with this news. We shall celebrate tonight!"

"There's more," Raag said. "The fish was pursued by a Hunter."

Yaami's face twisted in concern. "What happened?"

"He hurled a spear at the fish, but it missed, and she escaped unharmed," Sona said. "Then he tried to capture us, saying we got between him and his prey."

Yaami's eyes blazed. "How dare he? Where is he now?"

Then Raag told them how the dam broke, and the Hunter was swept away by the river.

Yaami put her hands on the children's shoulders. "Thank you for telling me this. I will send out messengers tonight that a Hunter has come to Sindhu, and our people must be on the watch for him. If the Hunter lives, he will not rest until he has killed Mahseer. And he will bring soldiers to terrorize our villages, to steal our gems."

Sona looked anxiously at Raag. Was there no place where they could be safe from the Hunter?

Then Yaami took a deep breath. "But tonight, the Goldstorm is over, and Mahseer and her young one are safe. You are safe, and we will post guards to ensure we all remain so. Our village is well hidden, and no Malechs are allowed here. We will begin our evening meal soon," said Yaami. "We will feed your pony and let her rest. Please come and eat with us. And first, refresh yourselves."

They had come upon a village, with cozy huts lit by lanterns that glowed blue and green in the night, all clustered around a central clearing that held a large, still pool of water.

Willa let herself be led away by a young woman. Sona was taken to a bathing hut with basins of steaming water and the scent of herbed soap. In the center of the floor was a bubbling pool lit by oil lamps. Raag handed Sona something surreptitiously—the jar of gold paint for her ears, she thought—and then followed Santosh to a nearby hut.

Yaami continued, "Please soak in this bathing pool for as long as you wish. We have hot springs here, so we can easily use them for washing. There are soaps and scented oils to ease the aches from your travels. Revati will come fetch you when it's time to gather."

Sona merely nodded, too amazed for words. How many wonders there were in the world!

Once she was alone, Sona took Swara out of her bag and let her sniff at the pool. The pup wasn't interested in a bath, it seemed.

"Suit yourself." Sona laughed. She put Swara back in the bag with a knob of cheese and a piece of bread and commanded her to stay. Then she stripped down and entered the bubbling pool.

It was hot, but not too hot. Sona scrubbed herself with scented salt and herbal soap, then applied an oil whose fragrance reminded her of Ayah's hair. There was a stone bench at the edge of the pool to sit on. Sona sat, leaned back, and let the warmth of the water soak into her skin, her muscles, her heart.

She missed Ayah's fingers, massaging her scalp with love. She missed Father's rumbling laugh and Karn's quick smile. She missed Ran's jokes and Lal's strong arms hugging her. Would she ever see them again? She swiped at her face, and her tears mingled with her sweat in the heat of the pool.

Swara poked her head out of the bag, and Sona laughed again. Here was one reason she couldn't return to her family, not yet. Once she'd completed her quest, she would go home.

"THE SIXTH WILL APPEAR" (DEVAN SONG):

When Devia is in its darkest hour,
The Sixth Beast will appear.
What once was lost, it shall be found
When the Sixth appears.
What once was hurt, it shall be healed
When the Sixth appears.
Bhoomi will rejoice
When the Sixth appears.
Land, water, people, beasts
All of them will be at peace
When the Sixth appears.

15

The Water Village

Sona dressed quickly in the clean clothes from her bag and scrubbed her stinky traveling clothes and left them to dry on a rack. She had just applied the gold-colored paint to her ears when Revati knocked on the door to the hut. Sona commanded Swara to heel, and Swara came and sat by her leg.

"Ooh, hi, doggie," Revati said. "May I pet her?"

Sona nodded, grateful that Swara's black ears truly made her look like a dog. "Reach your hand out so she can sniff it first," she said. "Swara, this is a friend."

Revati held out her hand and giggled as Swara ran her snout over it and then gave it a few licks.

Then Revati brought them to Raag, who looked cleaner than she'd ever seen him, dressed in a flowing top of deep blue, his hair tamed and pushed back from his face, his golden ears shining in the moonlight.

Their next stop was to visit Willa in a small, penned area, where a friendly boy told them that she was already well taken care of. Indeed, Willa blew in Sona's ear to tell her she was safe and happy. But the sore on her forehead was still red and oozing, with white bumps on the surface. Sona dabbed some of Ayah's cream onto it again. "Heal, Willa girl," she whispered.

Sona and Raag followed Revati to a small hut reserved for guests, where they stowed the rest of their belongings. Sona took a piece of jojonut rope from her bag for Swara to chew on. Then Sona, Raag, and Swara joined the villagers outside under the stars.

They walked around more rounded huts and came to the torch-lit clearing in the center of which was a pool of water, blue and still, ringed in gray river stones. Several dozen women, men, and children sat around the pool and looked to Yaami. Instead of the long tops and snug pants of Tirna, these Sindhu villagers wore skirts, tops, and pants that were looser and moved with their every motion. And both women and men wore their hair loose, falling to their shoulders or hanging down their backs. Some had blue and green beads woven into their hair.

Yaami had changed into a bright green blouse and long blue skirt with patterns like flowing water. She wore a headband of blue and green stones; her hair fell over her shoulders and down her back in waves. She held her hands palms-up in the sign of friendship. "We welcome you, Raag and Sona, to our village, the village of Genpur, nestled between the Genla and the great Kaveri." Her eyes shone and her voice was melodic and steady.

She addressed the villagers. "Raag, we know already. But Sona is his friend, and they both come here from Tirna. They are on a noble quest to save their Pitarau. They are pursued by a Hunter and must avoid him at any cost."

The villagers looked at each other and murmured, but then they turned to Raag and Sona and nodded. They understood what was being asked of them.

Yaami continued: "The Malechs have hurt all Devans—our people, worst of all. Because of their relentless greed and quest for gems, our rivers are disrupted, with droughts and sudden floods." Her face grew grave, and her voice dropped. "The Malechs have stolen from us and from our temples, have wrecked our boats and seized cargo, have arrested, hurt, and killed. They have destroyed families." Then her voice rose, grew louder and stronger. "But they will not destroy us, our people, our country. We will continue to resist them and help those who oppose them. Forever."

"Free Devia!" someone called from the crowd.

And then they all took up the chant: "FREE DEVIA! FREE DEVIA!" The villagers cried the slogan over and over.

Sona had seen the slogan on pamphlets that blew past her home, and even scrawled in paint on the side of the soldier barracks. But she'd never heard a large group of people shout it together like this. Her heartbeat increased, swept up in their enthusiasm, but also from fear. She wanted Devia to be free from Malech rule, but where did that leave her Malechian family? Where did it leave her?

After a few minutes, Yaami raised her hand, and chanting stopped immediately. "Now is a time to rejoice. After every Goldstorm passes, we feast together. And our young guests have seen Mahseer's young one, swimming in the Genla."

A cheer went up from the villagers. Several grinned at Sona and Raag, and Revati took Sona's hand with a shy smile.

Yaami continued: "So tonight, we celebrate the young Fish as well as the passing of Bhoomi's rage, and we pray for the day the Sixth Beast arrives and everything will be set right again."

Sona knew of the Devan belief that Goldstorms were the result of Bhoomi's anger over the gem mining. And the Sixth Beast . . .

She longed to learn more. She tried to catch Raag's eye, but he was too busy greeting other kids in the village—his friends, she assumed.

"I say again: welcome again, Raag, our friend, and welcome to our home, Sona of Tirna. Eat and drink with us and seal our friendship."

"Welcome!" cried the villagers. Cups were poured for Raag and Sona, and they raised them to drink deeply. The water was cold and refreshing and soothed Sona's parched throat.

Then came a variety of delicious food—rice and bread, dal and vegetables, and a root vegetable curry that was beautifully spiced and creamy, all placed on large jojonut tree leaves that served as plates. As soon as Sona was finished with something, she was immediately served more unless she blocked her plate or raised her hand fast enough to say no. Sona ate until she could barely move, but she still found room for a luscious rice pudding dessert. She laughed with the villagers as Swara did tricks in return for treats from almost everyone in the circle. Swara eventually lay down and snuggled next to a delighted Revati.

Then came the time for storytelling. Yaami and various elders told stories that Sona had never heard—stories of the people of Sindhu and their life on the great rivers of Devia.

When there was a lull, Sona risked a question. "Do you also tell stories about the Sixth Beast of Devia, the one who is yet to come? I . . . I want to see if they're different from the ones we tell in Tirna," she explained.

"Yes," Yaami said. "I'll tell you our version of the story, and you shall tell me if there are differences." She sat straight and held her right palm up.

Santosh brought something to her, cradled in his hand like a treasure.

Yaami took it from him with a bow, and, lifting her skirts, she walked into the shallow pool and set a small blue gemstone in the center. "Gather round, everyone," she said as she walked back to dry ground.

Santosh started playing a flute, and Sona rose with everyone else to stand at the edge of the pool and join hands. The blue of the pool had turned even brighter, and, Sona realized with a shock, it no longer reflected torchlight or the gibbous moon, but seemed to glow from within.

Yaami sang in Old Devan, and Sona recognized the words— they were the same ones Ashvi sang at Ayah's bedside: *We are because you are. You are because we are. We call to you in love.*

And then Yaami started to sing a song, a song like a river, with a melody that rose and fell like the tides.

Devia had five peoples, she sang.

They flowed across the land, sang the rest of the village.

As Yaami and the villagers chanted, Sona looked into the pool and gasped. The pool glowed with a golden light—the same light that Sona had seen coming from Ashvi, Raag, and her own fingers when they had sung to Ayah.

Then there were figures moving in the pool, figures that began like shadows in the water, but then became full-color. Sona recognized the figures from Ayah's stories: they were people from the five regions of Devia, their gems, and their sacred animals.

Raag whispered the translation of Yaami's song in her ear as each group appeared in the pool: "Sindhu of the rivers, with blue Water gems, guarded by Mahseer, the Fish; Vanam of the jungle, with green Leaf gems, guarded by Vyaghra, the Tiger; Khila of the desert, with red Fire gems, guarded by Sarpa, the Snake; Tirna of the plains, with black Earth gems, guarded by Vrka, the Wolf; and Paravat of the mountains, with clear Air gems, guarded by Shyena, the Hawk."

Sona wondered if Raag was translating out of kindness or whether he was playing a part for their company, like she was with her painted ears.

Yaami continued, and Raag translated:

> *People, beasts, and gems,*
> *all sacred to the Mother,*
> *from riverlands to plains,*
> *from jungle trees to desert sand,*
> *from sea to tallest mountains,*

They flowed across the land, the village responded.

The figures moved in a complicated dance, in harmony with each other.

> *But Paravat grew too greedy,*
> *and disrupted Bhoomi's plan.*
> *And so they were punished,*
> *and banished from the land,* Yaami sang.

In the pool, one group of people—sharp-eyed, with the wind blowing in their hair, and a beautiful golden hawk with graceful wings—disappeared.

But a promise rang out, sang Yaami.

And it flowed across the land, the village responded.

A golden circle with a missing piece appeared in the pool.

In Devia's darkest hour,
the Sixth Beast shall appear,
and she will save the land, sang everyone.

And in the pool, there was an indistinct creature, blurry like it was being seen through cloudy water. Sona saw wings, and scales, and paws, and claws, and something white that she couldn't make out. But the creature remained indistinct.

The golden circle became whole.

This is our promise, called Yaami.

Let it flow across the land, sang the rest.

In the pool, the sacred circle of Devia glowed so brightly that Sona had to shield her eyes.

This is our promise,
let it flow across the land.
This is our promise,
let it flow across the land.

Ayah had never been clear about what kind of creature the Sixth Beast would be, and the pool wasn't clear about it either. When would this creature come? Sona wondered.

The villagers stayed silent as the figures in the pool faded along with the last notes of the song. Soon, the water in the pool no longer glowed gold, and reflected only moonlight and torchlight once again.

"So, Sona, was that very different from the way you sing it in Tirna?" Yaami asked.

Sona was startled out of her musing. "Uh—" she began.

"It's very similar," Raag broke in, "except we worship with a canopy of whillet leaves woven over the earth. Now that our temples have been ransacked, we worship in secret in our villages as well."

Sona gave him a grateful glance and wished that she had indeed heard Ayah sing, had seen Ayah worship in this way. "But what is the Sixth Beast?" she asked.

"Ah," Yaami said with a smile, "there is much disagreement on that. We in Sindhu believe that the Sixth Beast will swim like Mahseer, and will have scales of gold, and be flexible and fluid, like her."

"But the people of Tirna believe it will be related to Vrka the Great Wolf, and will have the same persistence and loyalty," Santosh said.

"And still others, especially the people of Vanam, believe it will be a fearsome, ferocious beast, like their Vyaghra, the Tiger," said Raag.

"If no one knows, how will we recognize it when it comes?" Sona asked.

Yaami shrugged. "An excellent question, one that we do not know the answer to at the moment. But Bhoomi makes all things plain in time."

"I think it will be a mild creature," Revati said, her high voice sweet and clear. "Bhoomi cares for the gentle and the loving, the humble and the kind. That's who will save us."

"So you think that the Sixth Beast will be some sort of furry rabbit? Surely that will strike terror into the hearts of the Malechs," came a boy's teasing voice.

Revati looked at the boy and stuck out her tongue.

But Sona smiled and put her arm around Revati. "I agree with you," she whispered in the girl's ear. She thought of Ayah and her strength. "I think gentleness and kindness might be more powerful than the most ferocious beast."

Revati snuggled close to Sona and stroked the sleeping Swara's fur.

People began leaving the group in twos and threes. After almost all the villagers had gone, Raag gave Sona a look and tilted his head. Sona picked up Swara and stood.

Yaami walked Sona and Raag to their hut. "Take good rest, my friends. For as we told Raag, in three days' time we will go by boat upstream to Bhoominath, where we are due to pick up items to trade. We will bring you with us, to set you well on your way to the mountains."

"A boat? With a pony?" Sona asked.

"Our boats are not like any you have seen," said Yaami. "They are almost like moving houses, and we transport livestock and people all the time. We will not be traveling on the Genla, with its tricky currents and sharp rocks; we will be going upstream on the Kaveri, which is wide and deep and peaceful."

"Oh, thank you," Sona said, clasping her hands and bowing in the Devan way. "How can we repay you?"

"You have already seen Mahseer's child, so that is a blessing. A young Fish has not been seen since my grandmother's mother's time. How dare that Hunter try to harm her!" Yaami clenched her fists at her side. "Is there no end to the evil that the Malechs bring?"

Sona took a step back, and her face grew hot. She understood why Raag wanted to make sure she passed as fully Devan.

Santosh laid his hand on his wife's arm. "The young Fish is safe. These children are safe. Our village is safe."

Yaami took a breath and spoke more softly. "We will help you accomplish your mission, and save Janaki Pitarau, may Bhoomi bless her. In repayment, we hope that when you return home, you will always welcome guests with as much hospitality as you have been shown tonight."

"We will certainly try," Raag said.

"But I do not know who can match the hospitality of Genpur," Sona added.

Yaami laughed. "You may not have soaking pools in Tirna, but your manners are quite lovely. Worry not, children, we have posted guards to watch. You will be safe tonight, so let no fears disturb your sleep."

Sona went with Raag and Swara to their hut feeling full and sleepy. With the Hunter far away and friends all around her, Sona tucked herself next to the pup and slept more soundly than she had in days.

FROM *A MALECHIAN HISTORY OF DEVIA*

Of the ferocious beasts of Devia, none strikes terror in the hearts of those who navigate the Devan waters and nearby seas as much as the demonic fish, blindingly gold, that haunts the waterways of Devia. It is said to feed solely on the blood of humans and makes an enormous nest in the deep with the bones of all the people she has devoured.

Once the Hunters became ordained by the King of Malechia to hunt the savage beasts, Malechs and Devans alike could once more travel the waters of Devia without fear.

EXCERPT FROM A DEVAN SONG

Where Mahseer the Great Fish goes, life blooms.
The rice fields yield plenty,
The floating tubers multiply,
The fish swim with exuberance,
The water reeds grow in abundance.
Mahseer is life,
Where she goes, all blooms.

16

The Boat

The next morning, Sona found that Genpur was even prettier in daylight, nestled between two great rivers, with round brown huts woven from water plants dotting the green land, and nets and small boats lying on the riverbanks. And everywhere there was the music of water, of life and movement, of clear streams flowing to the sea.

Swara, ravenous for food and attention and growing bigger each day, delighted in playing with the children, especially Revati. Sona taught her to come at the sound of her whistle, and she was pleased with how quickly Swara learned. Willa appeared to appreciate the rest and the abundant grass. Yaami sent out scouts and messengers, and none found any sign of the Hunter.

The two days they spent waiting to leave were peaceful, but they passed too slowly for Sona, even though she knew they would be able to go far more swiftly by boat than on foot. Worry for Ayah gnawed at Sona, and she hoped Ayah could hold on long enough for Sona and Raag to return. And Sona's chest ached with missing Father and her brothers. She wished she could get word to them, but she didn't dare ask Yaami to send a message to a Malechian family.

They awoke on the third morning to find that it had rained overnight, and the village felt fresh, with raindrops glistening on the glass fish strung throughout the area.

Sona and Raag stuffed their packs and saddlebags with dried fruit, jojonut cakes, dried lentils, and rice that Yaami gave them. Willa seemed content and Swara stalked beside them as they followed Yaami and a group of villagers for a short trek through the forest to a wide dock on the Kaveri, where they found the largest boat Sona had ever seen. If it hadn't been floating on a river, Sona wouldn't have believed it was a boat. It seemed as big as her house back home, only with two stories instead of just one.

"There are compartments in the center of the first deck," Yaami explained. "These get plenty of fresh air but are shielded from the sides so that animals are not disturbed."

Sona patted Willa. "We'll try it, girl, right?"

Willa huffed, and Sona offered her a dried hooli fruit.

That temptation got Willa off the dock and onto the deck of the boat, which was remarkably stable. She went easily into the special livestock room on the boat and was happy enough to nibble on some straw.

"How do you get such a large boat to go upstream? Even with a dozen rowers, it must be challenging," Raag said.

Yaami smiled. "I'll show you." And she led them to a large wheel at the back of the boat that would help propel it through the water. "Remember the soaking pools you bathed in? We create something like them here." She brought them to a small, hot room in the back of the boat. "We boil water and use jets of steam to move that big wheel. Sometimes we use wood as fuel, but mostly, we sing the water to a boil."

Sona's jaw dropped. This was ingenious, indeed!

"But it can take some time to get the steam going, and once we start, the boat cannot stop or change direction quickly. We have oars to help us steer and dock the ship, but this boat is not as agile as a smaller one would be. This is a boat for bulk transport, not quick maneuvering."

Soon they were moving upstream on the Kaveri at a leisurely pace. The river was calm, blue-green and clear, but Sona suspected there was a strong current underneath the surface.

All the sailors on the boat gave Sona and Raag grins and nods as they passed by, doing their work.

"They think you are heroes," Yaami said. "For helping Mahseer's child escape the Hunter the other day."

"We didn't do much," Sona said. "The young Fish is a swift swimmer."

But Yaami shook her head. "I recognize Beast Singers when I see them. Tirna is famous for them. Let me guess: You hear the songs of animals, and sing them as well?"

Sona ducked her head to hide her shock. There was a name for people who heard music like she did? How had no one told her this all her life?

Because she was a Malech, raised in a family where music was never mentioned. If only Ayah had told her the truth sooner! Then, she might have learned Old Devan, might have learned to sing the songs like Raag could. Instead, she was left with her toneless Malechian music that had no effect on beasts other than Willa and Swara, who loved her only because she'd rescued them. She glanced again at Raag, but he was looking away, into the depths of the Kaveri.

"If we are fortunate, we might catch a glimpse of Mahseer herself," said Yaami. "At harvest time, she sometimes comes to the Kaveri."

"The Malechs in Tirna say that the Great Fish is something to be feared, that it wrecks boats and devours people," Sona said.

Yaami laughed. "As someone who has met Mahseer myself, I can tell you that is not true. It's the Malechian excuse to disguise their thirst for blood. They have destroyed many ships, hurt and killed many Sindhus, ruined many lives. They . . . they killed my first husband, for nothing other than praying at a temple. They killed everyone there that day and took our sacred gems to enrich their king. I will never forget, never forgive." A shadow crossed her face. "Those of us who survived formed our secret village, our Genpur, where no Malech shall ever tread."

Sona clasped her hands to keep from checking that Raag's gold paint still marked her ears. She remembered that just a few days ago she'd almost blurted that not all Malechs were bad; little consolation that would have been to a woman whose husband had been murdered by Malechs. Father had been right about Sona needing to hold her tongue. She must continue to be careful.

"But Mahseer promises life, not death. Seeing her is a blessing," Yaami continued. "Watch the waters, hope, and do not worry."

Raag came to stand next to Sona. "Again, you've been listening to the wrong legends," he murmured so only she could hear.

Sona held her retort back with great difficulty. She scowled and turned away from him.

"Does Mahseer lay her eggs on the riverbank?" she asked Yaami.

"Mahseer gives birth to a live fish," Yaami answered. "The songs say that sometimes they are golden, like the one you saw, and sometimes they are the blue of the Kaveri itself. But there has not been a young fish in several generations. I have never seen one myself, although I've been blessed enough to see Mahseer twice before in my life."

They traveled through the afternoon, and Sona could barely believe they were on a boat, so smoothly and quickly did they move. The sun sparkled on the surface of the water, making droplets dance, and Sona gave thanks to Bhoomi for the beautiful country they lived in, a country she was now able to see so much more of.

And then she heard it again. A melody of exultation. A song full of the joy of being alive.

"Look!" Sona said.

Swimming next to the boat was the slender gold-and-blue fish they had seen the night before.

"The child!" Yaami said, her face lighting up. "Mahseer will not be far. Let us sing her song," she called to her fellow villagers.

And Yaami and the villagers sang:

> *Come in, my friend, and rest awhile,*
> *Sit down, I welcome you.*
> *With open hands and honest smile,*
> *I will sing you true.*
>
> *I'll sing to you of Devia,*
> *Our land so sweet and fair,*
> *Our golden land of Devia,*
> *Where music fills the air.*

Yaami raised her voice and sang:

> *The fish are swimming in the streams,*
> *The penance now is due.*
> *You'll see the meaning of your dreams,*
> *For I will sing you true.*

Then Raag joined in:

> *The mountain waters run down hills*
> *To form our rivers blue,*
> *The wind it travels where it will,*
> *Oh where, oh Fish, are you?*
>
> *Your golden scales shine without mark,*
> *Blue eyes, a welcome sight.*
> *Your light contrasting with the dark*
> *That we all have to fight.*

Sona heard something in the water ahead of them—a powerful song of water and wind and sun and swimming, of wisdom that flowed like the strongest current.

And swimming next to her child was Mahseer, as long as the boat they were riding on, with golden scales that blazed bright. A single flick of her mighty tail sent her speeding ahead of the boat, and her baby hastened to keep up. Mother and child, they danced in the water in harmony.

Raag raised his voice above the others to sing:

The forest's growing silently,
The river rushes through,
The day is dawning violently,
Oh where, oh Fish, are you?

For Devia has need, my friend,
Of hearts both strong and true.
Before the world comes to an end
I call, oh Fish, to you!

Leaping out of the water came Mahseer, the Fish, her golden scales shining almost too brightly to bear. Sona was mesmerized watching the Fish and her child playing as everyone on the boat applauded in joy and amazement.

The young fish leaped out of the water, and Sona held out her hand, just as she had on the dam the night before. The young fish touched Sona's hand then swam back to join her mother.

Yaami beamed at them. "You have been blessed by Mahseer and her child," she said. "You bring great pride and blessings to our people."

The minutes sped by as they approached a bend in the river and the boat took a wide curve to navigate it.

The young fish darted into the shallows near the bank, then turned back to face its mother.

Suddenly, a silver-tipped spear pierced the young fish's body. Ribbons of red streamed from her as she sank to the riverbed below.

"No!" Sona cried.

Mahseer dove to follow her child as shouts erupted on the Genpur boat.

Raag grabbed Sona's arm. "Look," he said.

Sona's blood froze. The Hunter was standing on the prow of a small Malechian boat with another spear already poised. Sona's mouth went dry. There were dozens of small Malechian boats with soldiers manning the oars—all between the Devans and the eastern shore of the river.

"I will free Devia from these ferocious beasts!" cried the Hunter. "Do not try to hide them from me!"

At his signal, some of the Malechian soldiers dropped their oars and began shooting arrows at the Devans on the Genpur boat. One Devan cried out as he was speared through the shoulder. He dropped to the deck.

"Stop!" Sona shouted. "We are unarmed!"

But no one was listening. Arrows flew again, and Raag pushed Sona down to make her duck below the railing of the boat. "Stay low," he said. "I'll return in a moment."

"Raag!" Sona called. She didn't know what to think. How could the soldiers shoot at people who had no weapons?

Yaami yelled to the captain of the boat, who issued orders to the other Devans. Some of the sailors, ducking to avoid arrows, started passing objects around. Sona felt something pressed into her hand and looked down to find a piece of polished glass shaped like a golden fish. What was she supposed to do with this?

Something flashed. Sona closed her eyes instinctively, then opened them a crack. The Devans were holding up their fish prisms, and they were flashing in the sunlight . . . right into the eyes of the Hunter and the soldiers in their boats.

Raag came up next to Sona. "Swara's fine. She's in the stall with Willa," he murmured as he held up his fish prism.

"Thank Bhoomi," Sona said as she held up her own. How could Raag think so swiftly when she was nearly paralyzed by fear?

Then splashes of water and gold-tinged steam started rising from the river near the Malechian boats. Stationed along the railings were more Devan sailors, singing a fast-paced song and directing their hands at the water near the Malechian boats. Steam rose, the soldiers yelled, and some dropped their bows.

"Do not relent! We must succeed in our quest!" cried the Hunter.

A soldier near him gave a signal, and more arrows came flying toward Sona's boat. More Devans were struck, including the ones casting the water spells.

Without the sailors generating steam, their boat was slowing. Light flickered and flashed off the mirrors. Steam and water filled the air. Arrows flew. Devans cried out as they were hit; one fell into the river.

Then Sona heard a mighty splash behind her and turned to see Mahseer return alone from her dive to the deep of the river.

Her child was gone.

Sona grabbed Raag and pulled him to the western side of the boat, where Mahseer swam. "Go, Mahseer, swim away," Sona pleaded.

"Please, save yourself," Raag called.

But the Great Fish stayed even with the boat, easily keeping pace with them. She clearly had no intention of leaving.

Sona knew the Hunter would not give up until he had murdered her, like he had murdered her child.

"Raag, can you do something? Can you make her go away?"

Raag shook his head. "I know of no such song. Besides, Mahseer follows her own free will. Every beast does."

Sona had to find a way to help. She handed her glass fish to Raag. "I'm going in. I must warn her."

"Sona, don't!" Raag cried.

"Come with me," Sona said.

But Raag stepped back, shaking his head.

Sona climbed up on the rail of the boat and paused. For a moment, she worried that the Fish would hurt her, like she'd been taught. Like all Malechs believed. She gave Raag a look.

Then she took a breath and dove into the river.

The water was cold and clear, and Sona swam to Mahseer. The Fish was majestic, her scales as bright as the sun, her eyes as blue as the ocean. She was a force of nature come to life.

Sona didn't know what to do. She only knew that she had to convince the Fish to leave and save herself. She had to make her understand. Mahseer turned toward Sona and opened her mouth as if to speak.

Sona flinched. But then she listened to the part of herself that knew that Mahseer meant no harm, that even in the face of her devastating loss, she would not hurt Sona.

The Fish came closer and closer. And Sona held her palm out, just as Yaami had done before the pool in the village.

The Fish touched her mouth to Sona's hand, and it felt refreshing, life-giving. In Sona's hand, Mahseer placed what appeared to be a shining drop of water, blue as the river, small but precious. The Fish moved away and looked at Sona with a bright eye, and Sona closed her hand on the drop of water. She bowed, touched by Mahseer's attention and her deep sorrow for the young fish's death. Then she put her hand into her pocket as if to keep the drop there forever.

Then Mahseer turned, pushing Sona with her tail, and Sona suddenly felt herself lifted . . . onto Mahseer's back. Mahseer swam, and Sona held on as they raced through the water. She was startled, but then realized why—they had drifted downstream, nowhere near the Genpur boat. Sona marveled at how peaceful it was in the water, where she could no longer hear the shouts of the people above. Mahseer slowed and swam closer to the surface as she brought Sona to the western side of the Genpur boat. Sona let go of the Fish, and Mahseer dove deeper.

She watched Mahseer dart under the boat. Would she swim away? Sona hoped with her whole heart she would. But she had run out of air and tried to get to the surface—only to find her foot tangled in something.

A water weed had wrapped itself around Sona's ankle. She reached to tug at it, but it was too strong to tear.

Sona thrashed and pulled desperately, and finally broke free. She swam up, her lungs bursting.

She broke the surface but only managed a gasp before she was hit in the face by a wave and sank under again. The water was roiling from the wakes of all the boats in the river.

She came up again and managed another brief gasp before going under. She was pulled downstream.

Keep going, she told herself. She could make it. She swam until her lungs and every muscle in her body were burning.

Sona surfaced again, and saw Raag standing at the rail of the boat, looking ready to jump in.

"Grab this!" He tossed a rope out to her.

Sona just managed to grab it. She held on and kicked as Raag pulled her in. She reached the side of the boat and it rocked, making her bang her knees against its side several times. But she didn't let go. She pretended she was climbing to the loft in her barn, scrambling up after her brothers. Finally, she seized the railing, hauled herself over, and toppled onto the boat's deck.

"Are you crazy? I thought we'd lost you," Raag murmured as he threw her a large blanket.

Sona lay in a puddle and tried to catch her breath.

Suddenly, the boat churned through the water faster than it had gone all day. How were they picking up speed?

And Sona understood. The Fish was pushing the boat from underwater, pushing it like Sona had pushed toy boats in the Risha when she was little. Mahseer gave a last mighty shove, and the boat sped upstream, away from the Hunter and the soldiers, out of arrow range, finally. Many of the Devan sailors were wounded and bleeding, but everyone looked back as the enormous Fish grew smaller.

Even then, Mahseer didn't swim away. Sona felt like she was in slow motion, watching events unfurl in front of her like a story whose ending was already known.

"Don't." Sona's teeth chattered as she pleaded with the Fish in a whisper. "Raag! What is she doing?"

Raag said nothing as he stared behind them. They were already so far away; there was nothing to do but watch.

The soldiers shot arrows at the Fish, but they bounced off her harmlessly. Mahseer undulated her powerful body. With each slap of her tail, Malechian boats broke apart. The Kaveri became littered with the wreckage, with soldiers foundering in the water, trying to swim to shore. Mahseer kept churning the water, and more boats were destroyed until there was only one left: the one with the Hunter.

And Mahseer leaped out of the water, her golden scales glinting, and reared up, up, up, facing the Hunter, as if she would swallow him whole. She opened her mouth wide, wide, impossibly wide, and lunged for the Hunter.

But he was ready. Faster than thought, he lifted his spear, its silver tip glowing bright, and hurled it into the open mouth of the Great Fish.

"NO!" Sona screamed. Water splashed, blood spurted, and the Fish landed with a great crash on the eastern bank of the Kaveri, staining it dark. Mahseer flopped and flailed desperately. And then she went still.

Sona reeled with grief and rage. So much beauty, destroyed in a few moments.

There was no sign of the Hunter. *Please be dead*, Sona thought. *Please be dead, you evil man.*

Their boat churned upstream through the water, and the river flowed along as if the Great Fish and her child had not been murdered right before them.

Something stirred on the bank next to the body of the Fish. Sona leaned over the rail, trying to see.

The Hunter staggered to his feet. He took a curved, wicked knife and gutted the Fish. He plunged his fist into the gore and pulled something out with a horrible grin on his face.

As their boat sped farther upstream, the Hunter held his bloody fist in front of him. "Where is it?" he bellowed. "WHERE IS IT?"

Mahseer, the Fish

The Fish is fluidity and flow. Her song is of formlessness, of flexibility. Her music moves like a current, ebbs and flows like the tides, murmurs like waves upon a shore, echoes like the silence of the deep.

Just as water goes from sky to river to ocean and back to sky, she knows that life is a circle. That the world repeats, over and over, with life and death and life again. That all deeds and misdeeds will be answered.

When her child is taken from her, her grief and rage are endless as the sea.

Before her own life ends, she sees a chance to leave a drop of water that will become a trickle, that will become a flood, a river, an ocean—an ocean of justice, of peace, of life. In Bhoomi's name, she gives it.

That drop is hope.

The Fish's life ends, and the Kaveri water flows, taking her song and her Devan blood with it.

17

Aftermath

The Genpur boat crept on, gliding toward the next upstream village. Even those who weren't injured physically were overcome with grief at the death of Mahseer and her child. Grown men and women huddled together, weeping; others stared at the suddenly peaceful river in shock. Sona watched the river and the shore, certain they would be followed, but there were no Malechs in sight. Numb and despairing, she wandered the boat, trying to find something to do to ease the horror in her heart.

She found Raag helping to tend the wounded. Some held arrows still while they were carefully cut and pulled out, while others attended to the wounds themselves. Two of their company had gone overboard, and it was unclear whether they'd been too injured to reach the shore. Sona ran to grab a jar of Ayah's ointment. She asked Raag to tear cloth into strips to cover wounds and tied more strips firmly so that bleeding was staunched.

"You know something of the healing arts, I see," Yaami said.

"I learned from—from Janaki Pitarau," Sona said, grateful for all the times she had watched and learned from Ayah tending to her own hurts, to those of her family and the local farmers.

When they were faced with a particularly deep or dangerous wound, Sona and Raag tried to sing the healing song that Ashvi had sung over Ayah, but it didn't appear to work—there was no flow of golden light, no feeling that any magic was taking place.

Raag frowned. "Maybe it only works on dry land. Or maybe we're too tired."

"Or maybe we're not doing it right," Sona muttered.

A couple of hours later, the boat docked at another village. And lying on the riverbank in plain sight were half a dozen blue gemstones—Water gems.

"It's good we can save these from the Malechs. These will grace temples, villages, and homes," Yaami said as she gathered the gems with Devans from the boat and the village.

"I've traveled throughout Devia, but I've never seen this many in one place just lying upon the ground," Raag said softly.

"They say this was the way the gems were always found, before the Malechs came," Yaami said. "These are Mahseer's last gift to us."

This reminded Sona of something, but the thought flowed away like water.

They stayed at the village only long enough to leave the more seriously wounded sailors, and to ask that messengers be sent throughout Sindhu regarding the Hunter, the lost villagers, and Mahseer.

As Sona dressed in robes of mourning gray, as she helped drape the boat in swathes of it, she realized that the Hunter killed not only people and creatures; he killed the true memory of them, too. She imagined him telling lies about the Devans, how they had acted against the Hunter's orders and deserved to be punished, and about how Mahseer was a ferocious, destructive people-killer who had to be destroyed for the protection of Malechs and Devans alike. And in Malechia and other faraway places, people would believe him. But now that she'd seen it with her own eyes, Sona knew that the Hunter's desire to kill was for his own pleasure, that he didn't do it to help anyone else, and gave no thought at all to the lives he destroyed. He had killed innocent Devans; he killed the Tiger and her cubs; he killed Mahseer and her child; and he had killed Swara's mother, the Wolf.

Sona would never let him kill Swara.

When they were on their way again, Sona drew Raag into the stall with the animals. Willa nickered gently in greeting, and Swara wagged her whole body, beside herself with happiness.

Sona stroked Willa's nose, then bent to scratch Swara under the chin. Then she stood again and faced Raag as guilt settled heavily in her chest. "It's our fault—the attack on the boat, and Mahseer's death," she said.

"That's not true," Raag said with a short shake of his head.

"The Hunter was pursuing us, and that's why he was on the river when the Fish appeared. That's why he found Mahseer and her child."

Raag shook his head again. "He didn't know we were on this boat. I have to believe he would have called out to you if he'd seen you."

"But then how did he find Mahseer?"

"I think he was tracking her. He's after all the sacred beasts, right? And he'd already found her child. Remember, he was surprised to see us on the dam several days ago."

"Maybe you're right." Sona took a shuddering breath. "I didn't think I could hate the Hunter more than I already did."

"Where is that Sixth Beast, the one that's supposed to save us all? I can't imagine things could get any worse than they are right now." Raag clenched his hands so tightly his knuckles turned white. Swara whined and licked his fists until he let go.

Willa snorted, and Sona sat heavily on the floor. "I agree. But could any Beast escape the Hunter if the Tiger, the Fish, and the Wolf could not?" She put her arms around Swara.

"If only we could do something to rid us of that Hunter and his cronies," Raag said, throwing himself on the floor across from her.

"Even Yaami and a boatful of adults couldn't stop them. How could those soldiers shoot at us, even though we were unarmed? I thought the arrests in Tirna were bad, but this is much worse."

"You grew up safe and sound on your farm with your Malechian family," Raag said bitterly. "Do you know what it's like to be treated like you're lower than the lowest insect, like your life is worth nothing? This is what it is to be Devan. This is what Malechs do to us. My mother and I have traveled through all of Devia, searching for safety and never finding it. This is why I wish we could be rid of all the Malechs."

Sona swallowed, embarrassed. She truly didn't know what it was like to be a Devan. She only knew how her family treated their Devan neighbors. She thought things were good enough, when they clearly were not. Now she wondered what else she didn't know. "But why did you need to travel? Couldn't you have stayed in Kanthpur with your grandmother?" she asked.

Raag stayed silent for a moment. "Never mind," he said with a dark look.

Sona opened her mouth to tell him he could trust her. But if she wasn't willing to share her secrets, then it wasn't fair to press him for his.

They continued upriver for two more days and nights, stopping only briefly at other Sindhu villages. And then, on the third day's journey upstream, Sona began to feel uneasy. She heard a faint voice in the wind, bereft and ominous. She found Yaami in the front of the boat.

"Where's the next village?" Sona asked.

"At the speed we're going, Adapal is just another half an hour or so upstream," Yaami said. "But we are well provisioned and should make it to Bhoominath by the end of the day."

"We need to dock now. There's a Goldstorm coming."

Yaami furrowed her brow. "But the harvest is just about over, and the time for Goldstorms is almost past."

Sona swallowed hard. "There's . . . there's something in the air, something I felt just a couple of weeks ago, when we had a terrible storm in Tirna. We don't want to be on the water if a Goldstorm comes, right?" Sona rubbed her temples, which were starting to ache.

"It would be dangerous to be on the water during a Goldstorm. But are you sure? If we stop now, it will take a long time to get to this speed again," Yaami said.

Raag came up to them. It was clear from his furrowed brow that he had overheard the conversation. Sona almost told him not to bother arguing with her, but the pressure in her head was increasing.

"Believe her," Raag said to Yaami. "You know Mahseer favored her. She also survived a Goldstorm on her own."

Sona couldn't believe he believed her!

Yaami pursed her lips. "I'll tell the captain."

The crew greeted the news with raised eyebrows and muttered

discussions, but they docked at Adapal, where Yaami informed the village leaders that they should ready themselves for a Goldstorm.

Everyone on the boat was assigned a spot to wait out the storm, and Sona and Raag returned to Willa and Swara in their stall. They threw a blanket over Willa and covered the open parts of the stall with sheets to prevent the Golddust from gusting in.

"I've made Swara a cozy bed for when the storm comes," Raag said. "For now, let's let her run around and work off some of her energy."

"Thank you for backing me up about the Goldstorm."

Raag shrugged. "You're the only one I've met in person who's been out in a full-fledged Goldstorm and lived to tell the tale. I wonder, though . . . why do you have these abilities, Malech? Sensing Goldstorms, and making friends with Beasts?"

Sona cleared her throat. "My family has lived here a long time. And I love Devia with my whole heart. So maybe that's it?" It was a poor explanation, and Sona knew it.

Silence stretched between them. Sona bit her lip as Raag stared at her. She resisted the urge to cover her ears.

Eventually, Raag let out a breath. "Fine. You keep your secrets and I'll keep mine."

Sona wished she could unburden herself to someone who had saved her life twice already. But she had promised Ayah. She again wondered briefly what Raag was hiding. "Let's finish getting ready for the storm," she said.

As the morning progressed without a single flake of gold, Sona began to worry that her instinct had been wrong, that she'd delayed their arrival in Bhoominath for nothing. But every time she thought that, she heard the echo of a wail on the wind, and knew they were right to stay put.

Eventually, the residents of the Adapal grew impatient and sent their boats out on the river to carry goods downstream.

As the last boat left, Yaami came to where Sona and Raag were sitting with the animals.

"I'm sorry," said Sona. "I know we're delaying your arrival in Bhoominath to pick up your cargo."

Yaami shrugged. "If this storm doesn't come, we'll have wasted almost an entire day for nothing. But I can't risk our boat out in a Goldstorm. Those Malechs and their greed ruin everything. I hate the very thought of them."

Sona winced at the pain in her head and the venom in Yaami's voice. Would she hate Sona's family? Would she hate Sona, too, if she knew who she was? "I . . . I think it's coming soon," Sona said, closing her eyes.

"We'll see," said Yaami, squinting into the sky. "If not, we'll be heading out again before the sun sets."

The storm arrived after the midday meal. And even though they were safe and sheltered, Sona cringed from the noise on the wind, the keening, the cry that was suffused with sorrow and rage. She sat in the corner of the room, braced her back against the wall, and covered herself with a blanket.

When she finally fell into a fitful sleep, Sona dreamed that she stood with the heart of the Great Fish, bloody and still beating, in her hands.

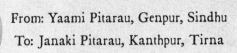

From: Yaami Pitarau, Genpur, Sindhu
To: Janaki Pitarau, Kanthpur, Tirna

Moonsday, tenth day of Growing, in the Year 229
of the Fourth Age
ᔆᕵ 12 years before the Present Day ᔆᕵ

In Bhoomi's name I greet you, Janaki Pitarau.

These years have been difficult for all of us in Tirna and in Sindhu. But I cannot agree with your exhortation to protect the families with mixed Devan and Malechian blood. While I do not support turning them over to the Malechs to be put to whatever cruel uses they have devised, I believe the best solution is to help these families relocate to a different part of the world. The prospect of mixed children is horrendous to contemplate, for to which society would they belong?

I know this is not the answer you hoped for, but I must do what is right for my people. I may be open to discussing further at some point when tensions have eased, but for now I must focus on keeping my people safe.

Yours respectfully,

Yaami Pitarau

18

Bhoominath

Swara was licking Sona's face.

"What is it?" Sona asked groggily.

"We're here, Malech," Raag said. "At Bhoominath."

With no Devans around, that name was back. Sona's heart sank. Whatever time they'd spent together helping each other, Raag still saw her as a Malech.

"Already?"

"The storm ended in the middle of the night, and Yaami got us moving right away," Raag said.

Sona sat up from where she'd been sprawled on the floor. Every muscle in her body was stiff. Willa stuck her horsey nose in her face and snorted gently. "Is everyone okay?" Sona asked.

"Yes, thank Bhoomi," Raag said. "Are *you* okay? I couldn't wake you up, no matter what I tried. Swara nearly lost her mind, and even Willa looked unsettled."

Swara whined and climbed into Sona's lap, and Willa stomped a hoof.

Although the day was warm, Sona shivered. "I had nightmares.

I heard a terrible voice on the wind, and I thought my head would burst from it. Didn't you hear it?"

Raag shook his head. He held out a water jug and a plate of food. "You'll feel better after some grub. Here." He turned to leave and then looked back. "And don't forget your ears before you come out."

As Sona gratefully ate the curry and rice and drank the whole jug of water, she felt the boat slow and come to a stop. She applied the gold paint to her ears, then went out on the deck and saw that they were moving slowly through a river of gold to an enormous dock at the base of a huge city.

"Welcome to Bhoominath, the City of Five," Raag said. "It's called that for its five great gates, and the five peoples of Devia who come here from all corners of the country. We're fortunate that Yaami let us come by boat, for it would have taken us weeks to get here on foot."

Sona looked back to the Kaveri, where other boats were slowly making their way toward Bhoominath. "So, no sign of the Hunter or the soldiers who were with him?"

"None. I hope they all got caught in the Goldstorm. They deserve it," Raag said.

Sona hugged herself as she remembered the Malechs firing arrows at unarmed Devans, and Mahseer speared with the silver-tipped weapon. The Hunter, cutting out her heart. "Yes," Sona agreed. "They do."

Yaami joined them at the front of the boat. "Put aside your worries for now, children. For the moment at least, the horror is over. Thank you both," she said, clasping their shoulders. "You helped save our boat and our people. I hope the Adapal village boats are all right—they were laden with cargo that they could not afford to lose."

"It was our honor to help in any way we could," Raag said, clasping his hands and bowing.

"We only did what any good people would do," Sona said, bowing in turn.

Yaami went to find the captain as they pulled into the dock. Sona stayed with Raag and marveled at the riverfront. She had never seen so many people in one place. It teemed with women, men, and children, all dashing around busily. The remnants of Golddust were being swept into the river by a large team of workers. Even Raag looked impressed.

"I thought you'd been here before?" Sona asked.

"Yes, but I've never come here by boat," Raag said, his eyes on the busy dock. "I'd almost forgotten how amazing it is to be here. Sona, you can buy anything here. Absolutely anything."

"If only we had something to buy things with," Sona joked.

"We can still dream," Raag said. "And look."

Sona thought wistfully of her brothers, who loved going to Kanthpur, tiny as it was compared to this place. Karn would want to find the nearest library and read every book he could find . . . no more waiting for the book wagon, which came only irregularly to their remote farm. Ran would love to haggle in a huge market. And Lal would likely eat everything in sight! And Father . . . well, Father would put his arm around Sona and encourage her to explore all the wonders of the city.

"We will leave you here," Yaami said. "In Bhoominath, we will take on cargo and go downstream again, to home. We must continue to spread the news of Mahseer and pray to Bhoomi that another Great Fish will once again grace our rivers."

"Is there hope of that?" Sona asked.

Yaami smiled wistfully. "There is always hope. Bhoomi, like most mothers, is forgiving, and wants the best for all her children. And her children are all the creatures on this earth."

Sona felt a pang as she was reminded of Ayah. They had to find a way to save her. And in the meantime, Sona couldn't forget all that Ayah had tried to teach her. "Janaki Pitarau taught me . . . that we are all Bhoomi's children, Devan and Malech alike," Sona said tentatively.

Yaami frowned and crossed her arms. "You say this even after witnessing firsthand their cruelty, their savagery? Malechs do not behave like Bhoomi's children. We must free Devia and drive the Malech barbarians away."

Sona glanced at Raag, who shook his head slightly. *Don't ruin this with your big mouth*, his look seemed to say.

"Janaki Pitarau always includes Malechs in her prayers," Sona said stubbornly. She was grateful Yaami thought of her as Devan. But she knew there were good Malechs—she was raised by and with them. "She says there is good and bad in all people, that we all have to choose. I pray that the Malechs learn that their actions are wrong."

Yaami grimaced. "The Malechs always choose badly, and they never learn."

Sona held her breath as Raag gritted his teeth.

Then Yaami let out a breath and shook her head. "I'm glad you have both benefited from Janaki Pitarau's wisdom, even if I do not agree. And you are too young, perhaps, to see the world as it truly is."

Sona bristled, but Raag stomped on her foot before she could say anything else.

Yaami inhaled and smoothed her expression. "Before we part, I would like to give you some things to help you in your quest, which is noble and good," she said in a calmer tone.

"You've already done so much for us," Sona protested.

"We would never have made it this far without your help," Raag agreed.

"And you have done much for us in turn," Yaami said, smiling at them both. "You are fine young Devans, and I'm honored to know you."

Sona bit the inside of her mouth. If only Yaami knew the truth! She felt Raag stiffen beside her.

"So quickly, now, take our gifts with no argument," Yaami said.

She gave them food—rice, lentils, vegetables, and fruit—enough to last for weeks, several water jugs filled with fresh Kaveri water, and a small bag, made of woven blue cloth and decorated with blue and green beads, that clearly held coins.

"We cannot take money from you," Sona said. If Yaami knew she was giving it to a half-Malech girl, what would she think?

Raag raised his eyebrows at Sona as if to say, *Why are you arguing with her?*

But Yaami wouldn't hear of it. "It's not that much. You must take it," she said, pressing the bag into Sona's hands.

Raag clasped his hands together and bowed. "In Bhoomi's name, we thank you."

"In Bhoomi's name, thank you," Sona echoed as she bowed herself.

Sona and Raag tucked everything into Willa's saddlebags and their own packs.

"We will miss you, Raag and Sona," Yaami said as she led them on the ramp off the boat. "I wish you good fortune on your quest, and hope that someday, you will return to our village. While you are here in Bhoominath, I would recommend that you seek lodging at the Great Temple. There, as Devan travelers, you will be able to keep your animals safe. Tonight, there will be feasting, for it is the day of the Harvest Festival."

The Harvest Festival! But Sona had never celebrated one without Father and her brothers. Without Ayah. She didn't think she had the heart to do so now, when they didn't know where she was or whether she was even alive.

Yaami continued: "We will finish our business in the city and return home as quickly as possible to assess the damage from the Goldstorm and assure our loved ones that we are all right. We still mourn, but you are both young and should enjoy yourselves tonight. I hope you will be able to find passage across the desert on a Sun Ship soon."

"Farewell, Yaami Pitarau," Raag said.

"Thank you once again," Sona added.

Yaami embraced them both. "Be careful, young ones," she whispered into their hair. "May Bhoomi bless you and help you, and may you find friends wherever you go. And may any Malech who wishes you evil meet a terrible fate."

And so Sona and Raag took their leave of the people of the riverlands and made their way into the city of Bhoominath.

"This way," Raag said, pointing. Sona could see a large golden dome towering above the city buildings.

They passed through crowded streets paved with white stones and filled with harvest bounty from Tirna, brilliant fabrics from Khila, spices and herbs from Vanam, and mats and blankets from Sindhu, as well as other goods from across the Eight Seas that Sona had never seen before. This included toys that moved and talked on their own, gigantic books with arcane knowledge, and elixirs that promised to do everything from increasing strength to untangling hair. Sona gawked.

"It's something else, isn't it? But don't buy anything on the main road—the stores here exist just to part tourists from their money."

"Thanks for the warning," Sona said with a giggle.

As they passed spire-topped temples and multicolored buildings in the vibrant tones that Ayah had in her house, no one spared Willa a second glance, but many stared at Swara, who stalked next to Sona like a shaggy shadow. Sona looked nervously at Swara's ears, but there was no hint of gold. In such a short time, they had lost their puppy floppiness, though, and stood straight and peaked on Swara's head. She looked like the young wolf that she was. Sona needed to think of how to disguise her better.

A Devan girl who looked to be around their age, dressed in a swirl of colors bright as a lilah bird, approached them. "Kind sir, kind mistress, would you like to eat at the best restaurant in Bhoominath?" she asked.

"We can hardly afford the best restaurant here." Raag laughed. "We are but humble travelers."

"Then come for the storytelling," the girl said, undeterred and grinning. "The water is free, and so are the tales. Maybe you'll hear something worth your while."

"Maybe later," Sona said. "First we must get ourselves and our beasts settled."

The girl bowed, then looked her up and down. "If you're looking to earn a coin or two, there might be a job to be had as well."

Raag laughed again. "First you invite us for food, then for stories, and now you offer a job?"

"Anything you need, you can find at the World's End," the girl said. "When you come, just ask for me, Purvi, and I'll make sure you're taken care of." She winked, and then took off in a swirl of color.

"That girl has a lot of confidence," Sona said, watching the girl again as she walked up to another group of visitors. "It makes me want to visit the World's End, wherever that is."

"Maybe we will," Raag said. "But our first stop is the Great Temple."

The Humble Guest, A Folktale of Tirna

One day, a poor farming family heard a knock on their door just as they were about to begin their meager dinner.

When the wife of the family answered the door, she found an old woman wearing threadbare clothes. "Mistress, I am hungry," the old woman said. "Will you feed me? I've been refused at every door tonight."

And because the farmwife knew what it was to be hungry and weary, she invited the old woman in to rest and eat. She brought clean water and soap and helped the old woman wash her hands and feet. And then she brought their guest to the dinner table with her husband and little daughter and gave her the seat of honor.

The farmers offered the serving bowl first to their guest as was the custom.

"I have not eaten in so many days," said the old woman, whose hand shook as she took the serving spoon.

"Please eat as much as you want," the wife said.

The old woman served herself half of what was in the serving bowl.

The husband and wife shared a look, for the harvest had not been good, their dinner was small, and they also were hungry, for they had not eaten all day. Their good milk cow had sickened and died, and they had saved the last of her milk for their little daughter.

"Oh, but I am so hungry I fear this will not be enough," said the old woman in a quaking voice.

"Then please take more," said the farmhusband.

And the old woman served herself the rest of the food from the bowl.

As their visitor scooped food and lifted it to her mouth, the little girl spoke up. "Stop, oh, honored guest."

The old woman looked at the girl. "What is it, young mistress?"

The little girl stood and held up her milk cup with the very last milk they had on the farm.

"You must drink this milk as well," said the girl as she brought the cup to their guest.

The old woman smiled as she took the cup and drank it all down in one gulp. She finished all the food on the plate and thanked the family for their hospitality.

The family drank to their visitor's health with plain water, for that was all they had left.

At the end of the meal, the visitor rose. She was transformed into a beautiful woman with golden eyes, a striped dress of black, green, blue, red, and white, and a small instrument she wore in her jeweled belt.

The family bowed to the ground in front of the Goddess Bhoomi.

"You went hungry yourself in order to feed a stranger in need," Bhoomi said. "For that, I bless you. Your crops will be plentiful during your life and those of your children, and their children. Your fruit trees will bear for many years. And your beasts will live long, healthy lives."

"We only had one beast, and she died today, oh great Goddess," said the little girl.

"Look again," said Bhoomi with a smile. She raised her horn and played a song of prosperity.

The family ran to their barn, where their cow was alive again, awake and eating peacefully.

When they went back inside their home, their table was full, and the Goddess was gone, leaving behind only the echo of her music.

19

The Water Drop

When they arrived at the Great Temple of Bhoomi, Sona gawked again. She had only ever been to the ruins of Kanthpur Earth Temple with Ayah—a simple wooden structure surrounding a central clearing. This temple was massive, with a large stone entrance carved with artwork representing all five peoples of Devia—a circle with five wedges, each with the color and Beast of a different region. Under a soaring filigree dome of sparkling gold glass was a large central courtyard with altars to five aspects of Bhoomi, including, Sona noted, an altar to the Air God.

"Why is that here?" Sona whispered to Raag.

"The Air God of Paravat is son to Bhoomi, like the Sun God, and just as the River, Grassland, and Leaf Goddesses are her daughters," Raag whispered back. "But there are no Air gems, so there is no active worship."

Sona stared at the empty altar to the Air God, the temple of the lost people of Paravat. She wondered why they had disappeared.

"Let me do the talking, okay?" Raag said, and Sona nodded.

He went up to a priestess wearing the black and gold of the Earth Temple and said, "Holy priestess, my sister and I are on a quest to save our Pitarau and seek shelter and food for ourselves and our pony and dog. Will you help us?"

"Of course, young ones, you are to be commended. Bhoomi wants us to welcome all travelers. Please, come and rest yourselves. We happen to have one shelter left that you can share with your beasts. It will cost four pennies per night."

"Thank you, holy one." Raag handed over the pennies and bowed, and Sona bowed as well.

The stall where they put Willa had plenty of fresh hay and water. Sona brushed Willa and made sure she was settled, then took Swara to the other end of the room, which had two plain but clean floor mats and a large jug of water. The children and Swara ate lunch, and then Sona practiced teaching Swara to "go home," which meant jumping into the open saddlebag sitting on the floor.

"Good girl," she said, giving Swara another small treat.

Then Raag practiced with her. "Clever girl," he said, and Swara flattened her ears and rolled on her back for scratches.

"She's a faster learner than any dog we ever had," Sona said. "And she's so beautiful." She scratched the pup under the chin.

"She knows it, too." Raag laughed. "I bet she's happy to walk on dry land again—I know I am. But now I think we should explore the city. Are you ready?"

The children and Swara went to the grand market in the center of the city, where Sona spent a penny on rock sugar candy flavored with pomegranate from Vanam. Raag bought fried dough dripping with honey and shared it with Sona. Even after they let Swara lick their hands, they were still extremely sticky.

The afternoon was hot, so they found a public wading pool

with a central fountain covered in blue mosaic tiles. They rolled up their pants and stepped into the cool water. As they sat at the edge of the pool, Raag said, "Before we return to the temple for the Harvest celebrations, we should visit the edge of the desert, where the Sun Ships are."

"I'm excited to see the Sun Ships," Sona said. "How do ships travel over a desert?"

"I've never sailed on one," Raag said. "But I think they somehow power their ships with sunlight, like the Sindhu people use water and steam to power theirs. I don't know how expensive it is to travel on one, though."

"Yaami helped us for free, but what if a Sun Ship trip is more than we can afford?" Sona asked.

"We'll have to find a way. We must get passage across the Khila Desert. It stands between us and the amrita for Matrka."

On the northern edge of Bhoominath, the Great Khila Desert radiated like an oven. The stone city streets faded into an expanse of yellow sand, and the air wavered with heat.

"How can this be here, when just on the other side of the city is the Kaveri?" Sona asked.

"Who can understand how Bhoomi designs the world?" Raag said. "All its tributaries start as springs in the mountains, but they run underground or on the edges of this mass of land."

"And yet there are people who live there? People who weave beautiful cloth and trade it here?" Sona had seen the work of the Khilan artisans, who made clothing as vibrant as a desert sunrise.

"There are villages in the desert, but they are all near the rivers, and it would take weeks to go that way," Raag said. "But the quickest way to Mount Meru is straight across Khila, and some Sun

Ships go that way. We need to travel with those who know the way, or we risk being lost in the sands forever."

They arrived at the edge of the desert, where several people stood next to narrow ships with pointed prows and enormous black sails. Most were bound for Khilan villages on the outskirts of the desert; only a few small ships would go straight across to the mountains.

"Two thousand coins," said the first Sun Ship captain, who had leathery skin and a scarf tied around her head.

That's ridiculous, Sona thought. That was ten times what anyone she'd ever known made in a year.

"Although if you're willing to help do some of the work, we might be able to discount it a bit." The Sun Ship captain eyed Raag dubiously.

"We are both strong," Raag said. "And we know how to work hard."

Sona nodded, but she didn't like the way the woman stared at her. She looked over the ship, which was small and very narrow, with a sharply curving hull. "Where would we put our pony?"

The woman cackled, showing rotten teeth. "Pony? You'd best sell it here, girl, if you're going to the cursed mountains to seek your fortune. A pony won't last long over there. It would likely end up a meal for Sarpa."

Sona wanted to give the woman a piece of her mind, but Raag pulled her away. "Thank you," he said to the captain. "We'll be back at sunrise if we're interested."

"We're not going without Willa," Sona said as they walked away. "And who is Sarpa?"

"The Great Snake that lives in the Khila," Raag said. "Let's keep asking."

They visited four other captains, who said they would charge between two thousand five hundred and an astounding six thousand coins to cross the desert. But none of them would take on a pony.

"It would only slow us down," said one man with nut-brown skin and brilliant green eyes.

"It would require too much water," said a woman who wore a hooded robe that kept her face in shadow.

"We'd end up eating it," said a Malechian captain with strangely sharp canine teeth.

After these not very promising exchanges, they returned to the city and headed back toward the Great Temple.

"Maybe we can convince the captain of that first Sun Ship to take us on as workers," Raag said.

"But what about Willa?"

Raag glanced at Sona, then quickly looked away. "It might be kinder to sell her to someone here," Raag said. "The desert and mountains are no place for a pony. She'll be happier in Sindhu or Tirna."

"She trusts me to take care of her. I won't abandon her to some stranger who might beat her or work her to death."

"If you care about Matrka—"

"You know I do! I'm here, aren't I?"

"Lower your voice. Okay, since you care about Matrka, you know we need to get to Mount Meru as quickly as possible. And this is the fastest way."

"There must be another way. There just must be," Sona insisted.

But she had to admit that she couldn't think of one, either.

∽ ∽ ∽

On the way back to the temple, Sona spent a few pennies on a long, colorful dress from Khila, with reds, oranges, and purples swirled like the setting sun. Raag bought a neck scarf with the same colors. They went to their room and checked on Willa, who was chewing hay happily.

Sona held out a hooli fruit, and Willa took it with what looked like a smile. "Good girl, Willa," Sona murmured. She wouldn't leave her behind. She couldn't.

As soon as they entered their own room, Swara ran to a corner, pounced on something furry, and proceeded to throw it up in the air. It fell back down, and she started chewing on it with crunching noises.

"What is that?" Raag asked.

Sona checked. "Ugh. Swara caught a rat."

Raag gagged. "No way. We can't let her have it, can we?"

Sona shrugged. "She'd be learning to stalk prey from her mother, so I guess this is normal?"

"You're supposed to be a Devan," Raag said. "Vegetarian, right?"

"I'm a vegetarian now," Sona said. "I can't force Swara to be one, too. Haven't you ever had a pet dog or cat?"

Raag shook his head. "We were always traveling."

"Swara is a beast, so she follows her instincts when she's hungry," Sona said.

Raag shook his head. "Just keep her disgusting meal away from me."

After finishing the rat, bones and all, Swara took a big drink of water and then curled up in the corner and promptly fell asleep.

Sona and Raag took turns going to the bathing houses. Sona gazed at the round bathing tub she was about to step into and remembered the hot pool she'd used in Sindhu. She stripped, scrubbed her used clothes in a small washbasin, squeezed out the water, then hung them on a rack to dry while she bathed. She scrubbed herself for a few minutes in the cold water of the tub, rinsed off, and put on her new dress. She slathered Raag's gold paint on her ears. As Sona gathered her washed clothes, something fell out of her pants and onto the floor. She picked up the small object. It was a stone.

No, a gem.

Sona's breath caught. She looked around; there was no one nearby. She quickly tucked the gem into a pocket and left the bathing room. As Sona passed the sacred circle of Devia in the center of the temple courtyard, she remembered something.

She arrived at their room vibrating with excitement. "Raag," Sona said. "Why do you think the Hunter was so upset after he killed Mahseer?"

Raag shrugged. "He cut her wide open like he was searching for something, but I can't imagine what that might be."

"I think . . ." Sona pitched her voice to a whisper. "I think he was looking for a gem."

Raag frowned. "A gem? Inside a fish?"

Sona swallowed and nodded. "Yes. When he was at my house, the Hunter said that when he killed the Tiger and her cubs, he found a Leaf gem embedded in its heart! Maybe that's what he expected with the Fish, too?"

Raag's eyes widened. "I've never heard of that. Are you sure the Hunter has a Leaf gem?"

"Yes. It was very small, and set in a ring, but it was definitely a Leaf gem. And it had a circle that seemed to float inside it. It reminded me of this." Sona pulled out her mother's necklace. "And the same circle is in the center of the temple here. But that circle is a Devan symbol, right? Like the triangle is a symbol of the sails of Malechia. I wondered why the Hunter would have that circle carved into a gem."

Raag shook his head. "What's making you think of this now?"

Sona clutched her hand in her pocket. "I have something to show you," she said.

She opened her palm. In it sat a tiny but brilliant blue gem with a circle floating in its center—the water drop that Mahseer had given her.

"I think the Hunter was looking for this in Mahseer's heart," Sona said. "But she had already given it to me when I went into the water. No one needs to kill sacred animals for sacred gems." Sona smiled as she thought of Ayah. "We do not have to take," she said, "when we can ask."

"You know what this means?" Raag said, his eyes sparking with excitement.

"What?"

"It's even more urgent that we cross the Khila Desert quickly."

20

The Harvest Festival

"Let's go to the gem district," Raag said.

"You can't be saying that we should sell Mahseer's gift," Sona said, clutching the gem.

"No, no, of course not. But the merchants there should be able to tell if it's unique," Raag said.

"We're going to show it to Malechian merchants?"

"We can go and say we're looking to buy something like it. We can pretend we're the servants of a rich Malech. Come on, we've got time before the celebration tonight."

Sona was still dubious. "But how does this get us closer to getting on a Sun Ship?"

"Simple," Raag said with an exasperated look. "If there are many like it, we can just sell it and buy our fare for a Sun Ship and be on our way tomorrow."

"But Mahseer gave us this gem," Sona said. "I can't help but think it's special."

"Let's find out for sure, then," Raag replied. "If it's unique, we take it with us and find some other way across the desert. Maybe it's magical?"

Sona still didn't think they should sell the gem, but she could see there was no point in arguing now. Raag was determined.

Sona tied the gem tightly in a strip of cloth around her waist, then paced the room while Raag bathed. He came back in fresh clothing and with his colorful Khilan scarf around his neck. "Let's hurry," he said.

They tied up both animals in the room, and Sona told Swara to stay. Then they set off into the city once more. They wove their way through crowded streets full of people rushing about getting ready for the Harvest Festival and arrived only slightly out of breath at what Raag knew to be the entrance to the gem district, where precious stones from Devia and across the world were bought and sold. There were four soldiers guarding the street—grim and humorless, standing stiffly with their hands on their swords.

Sona straightened her back and forced herself to swing her arms loosely, like she knew where she was going and what she was doing.

"What business have you here, Devans?" said one guard gruffly.

"We are here on an errand for our master, Lord Parvani of Tir, shopping for a gem for his wife," Raag lied smoothly. He brought out their small blue bag of money, jingled it briefly, then paid the soldier a coin.

"Very well then, off with you," said the guard, pocketing the coin.

Once they were out of earshot, Sona whispered, "Why did you pay him?"

Raag raised one eyebrow. "It's the way things are done here in Bhoominath. Especially among the Malechs."

Raag took them off the main road to a gem merchant who had

a line out his door. The man was tall, thin, and hunched over, with only a few wisps of gray hair left on his head. Two large gems, one black and one red, dangled from his ears. "What do you need, urchins," he said in an uninterested voice.

Sona trembled as Raag spoke up. "We are servants of Lord Parvani of Tir, looking for a special gem for his wife on her name day."

"What price range?" the man said, peering at them over a pair of small glasses.

"He's looking for something specific," Raag said. "A small gem, but with a curious marking . . . a Water gem with some sort of circle in it."

The man looked at Raag sharply. "A circular marking in the center of a small Water gem, you say?"

"Yes," Raag said as Sona's heart started to gallop.

"We have no such things here," the man said coldly. "We only have the finest gems, and certainly none with flaws. Now begone." He waved his hand in dismissal.

Sona and Raag visited three more stores, but no one had heard of such a gem. But at the last store they visited, Sona had the strange feeling that the merchant was expecting them. The merchant, whose ears and fingers glittered with many different colored gems, sat them on a fancy divan and gave them weak tea before telling them he didn't have such a stone, but he could try getting one, and it would cost fifty thousand coins to buy it.

Sona's mouth went dry.

"Fifty thousand coins? Lord Parvani will want to know why," Raag said, wiping his hands on his pants.

"No one's ever seen a gem like that," the merchant said. "But there are rumors of one existing. The Devans have a legend about it being magical." He tittered into his soft hand.

"Thank you," Sona said as she stood. "Let's get out of here," she whispered, pulling on Raag's hand.

"Tell Lord Parvani that he should come himself next time," the merchant called as they left the store. "Even if he trusted you with his money, you couldn't buy a gem and walk out. I don't know what the laws are like in Tir, but in Bhoominath it's against the law for any Devan, even a servant, to be found holding a gem."

Once they were outside the store, Sona hauled on Raag's arm. "This was a mistake."

"We found our answer, though," Raag murmured as he let himself be pulled along. "There's nothing like that gem in the world."

Sona dragged Raag back toward the Great Temple, glancing around frequently to make sure they weren't followed. After they left the district, Raag finally pulled his arm away. "Calm down. We're fine."

"It was a bad idea," Sona said. "That last one knew we were coming."

"Of course he didn't. Don't be ridiculous," Raag said. "Now we know exactly how valuable the gem is."

"We already knew that because Mahseer gave it to us," Sona said. "And we're still no closer to getting across the desert."

On their way back to the Great Temple, Sona saw a different side of the city, away from the main thoroughfares that drew tourists. Children in rags slunk through alleys like stray cats. Mothers with babies on their hips begged for food.

Raag saw where her gaze had gone. "The Malechs force the Devan merchants to pay unfairly high taxes. And if they refuse, they put them out of business," Raag said. "And they make sure all the high-paying jobs go to Malechs only. They might be worse here than in the countryside, if that's possible."

A flash of color caught Sona's eyes again. "Interested in that meal now?" Purvi asked.

Sona smiled. "Not tonight, but we thank you."

"But you should come to the Harvest Festival at the Great Temple tonight," Raag said. "There will be free food for all there."

Purvi gave a mock bow. "I know that. I am a Guardian of Bhoominath! I have many sisters and brothers, and I help feed them all."

Sona smiled. "Here, then. Take this as thanks for doing such an excellent job helping those children." And she handed Purvi a penny.

The girl bowed deeply. "Many thanks, kind mistress. And if you ever need anything at all, do come see me at the World's End." She gave Sona a small piece of paper, which Sona stowed in a pocket. They had to save every coin for their journey, but maybe they'd visit the World's End for storytelling one night.

Purvi left them, and Raag wouldn't stop talking about the Sun Ships all the way back to their room at the Great Temple. "There's no way around it, Malech. We need to get across the desert to get the amrita. And we need to do it as soon as possible. Not to mention the fact that we need to bring Swara with us."

"I always thought we'd bring Swara with us, since she's still just a pup," Sona said. "But now you're saying we need to?"

Raag tugged on his shaggy hair and began to pace. "I don't

know," he said. "I don't know all the legends. But I can't help feeling that bringing a sacred animal with us might help us get the amrita." He pointed at Swara, who was gnawing on a piece of rope and looking quite dog-like. "We must get the next Sun Ship leaving for the mountains."

Sona shook her head. "We don't have the money. And I won't leave Willa, and none of those ships would take her."

Raag opened his mouth, but then seemed to change his mind about what he was going to say. "Maybe there'll be a new ship tomorrow, one that will take Willa, too, and we can work our way across the desert." He tugged at Sona's arm. "Come on, it's time to go to the Harvest Festival. There will be so much free food, and dancing, too."

"Maybe you should go without me," Sona said. She didn't feel like celebrating now, after spending all afternoon dealing with the avaricious merchants.

"Not a chance," Raag said. "I'm sure the Tirna Harvest celebration is wonderful, but you've never experienced anything like what they do here in Bhoominath. I've only been here for Harvest once, and I'll never forget it. The animals will be fine, I promise."

Eventually, Sona agreed. She carefully rewrapped the Water gem from Mahseer in a cloth and tied it across her chest, near her heart. She followed Raag out into the temple courtyard, where a huge crowd had gathered—Devans, Malechs, and, from their odd clothes, people from other parts of the Eight Seas, travelers who would all celebrate the Harvest together. There were flamethrowers from Khila, water dancers from Sindhu, mask makers from Vanam, and, Sona realized with a thump of her heart, earth dancers from Tirna. She joined hands with Raag and dozens of other people and danced around in a circle, tapping wooden sticks and dancing to the tunes she'd grown up with, tunes Ayah had sung to her from when she was a baby. At Harvest, this much music was allowed. Sona missed her family so much her chest hurt.

For this night, Sona could put aside all her secrets and her worry, her fatigue and her desperate hope. She could just be a girl, twirling and whirling in a dance, celebrating the harvest. A harvest that wasn't as bountiful as in the past, but was precious, nonetheless. She was grateful to Bhoomi for the food she provided, and for the fact that they had made it this far with both beloved animals.

Raag seemed happy to just be a Devan boy, dancing and clapping with everyone, even as he kept a close eye on Sona and made sure she enjoyed herself. Raag was constantly by her side to bring her another cup of fruit juice, or a star cake to eat, and he often grabbed her hand and twirled her into a dance. His knowledge of many Devan dialects came in handy, and he introduced Sona to all kinds of people. Whatever their disagreements, Sona felt they were finally becoming friends.

There was one man who remained wrapped in faded traveling clothes, his head hooded and shadowed. He stood outside the main crowd, smoking a pipe. Sona caught a whiff; it was a type of smoking plant Father enjoyed, and it reminded her even more of home. She eyed him warily, but he never came close to her or Raag, and soon she forgot about him.

Sona danced barefoot on the earth, as all the Devans did. After all the time on the water, it felt good to be connected to the soil again. Though she was dancing on the border of Sindhu and Khila, she sent her thoughts far away to her family in Tirna, to her father and brothers and Ayah, hoping they were celebrating, too, and somehow knew she was all right.

Around midnight, Sona noticed a commotion near the food stalls and went there with Raag to investigate.

"Help," cried a Khilan cook, holding up a large wooden spoon. "There's a wolf in here!"

Sona gave Raag a look and hurried to the back of the stall, where Swara was gobbling flatbreads out of a pan on the floor and growling at anyone who came near her.

"Swara!" Sona called. "Heel! NOW."

Swara stuck her ears against her head and tucked her tail as she ran to Sona's side. "I'm so sorry," Sona said. "My dog is normally well-behaved."

"There wasn't much food left, as it's the end of the night," said the stall owner. "But she gave us quite a scare."

"I'm so sorry," Sona said. "Should—should we pay you?"

The stall owner shook her head. "Don't worry. As I said, the evening is just about done, and we were going to donate that food to the temple anyway. I was just worried that soon your dog would want to eat us."

"Thank you," Raag said. "We apologize again."

Sona smelled the familiar smoking plant again and scanned the area quickly, but the hooded man was nowhere to be found. She held on to Swara's scruff and went back with Raag to their room.

"Bad girl!" Sona scolded Swara when they got back. "You need to stay here while we're away. How did you slip your rope?" Swara looked appropriately mortified, rolling on her back to show her belly.

After a moment, Sona relented. "Okay, Swara. But you can't go stealing food."

"We need to get out of here," Raag said. "There are too many temptations for her."

"I know," Sona replied shortly. But she still couldn't imagine going anywhere without Willa.

After a day full of new sights, strange encounters, and celebration, Sona was exhausted. She unbound the gem from her chest, wrapped it carefully again, and buried it deep in her pack, which she left within arm's reach of her sleeping mat. Then she fell asleep before her head hit the mat.

She dreamed that they were walking through the desert, following a thin red line that moved this way and that. Then the line grew thicker and raised itself off the desert floor to become a snake with eyes made of glowing red Fire gems. The snake swayed back and forth, and Sona felt herself swaying too, struggling to stay awake while the snake danced. She knew, somehow, that she must remain awake, but her eyes felt too heavy, and she had to close them.

Sona woke to the sound of Willa neighing. She sat up in a cold sweat, panic filling her veins. Her pack was still next to her, just as she'd left it.

"Raag?" she said. "Did you have a strange dream, too?"

There was no answer. Willa continued to neigh.

Groggily, Sona got to her feet and squinted in the dim moonlight. Willa snorted and stomped her foot. "What is it, Willa girl?" Sona whispered.

She went to the pony, who shook her head and neighed again. "What's bothering you? We both need our sleep."

She stroked the pony's nose and forehead. The open sore was now crusted with a scab. Willa calmed down at her touch but looked at her with wide eyes.

"What's gotten into you? Calm down, now, there's a good girl," Sona said soothingly.

"How about you, Swara? Are you restless, too?" Sona went to the corner of the room where Swara had fallen asleep.

But the wolf pup wasn't there.

In a panic, Sona raced to the other mat, where Raag slept. "Raag, Swara is missing," she whispered. "Wake up!"

Her heart stuttered. She was talking to a blanket.

Raag was gone, too.

EXCERPT FROM "WE GIVE THANKS" (DEVAN SONG)

The Harvest Star, it shines tonight,
Over fields so bountiful.
The Harvest Moon, it lights the night,
Embracing friends so plentiful.
So we give thanks tonight.

For whillet, rice, and hooli fruit,
Lentil, bean, and golden jute,
For leaf and flower and sturdy root,
We give thanks tonight.

Thanks to Bhoomi, loving mother,
Thanks for sisters and for brothers,
Our greatest treasure is each other.
We give thanks tonight.

21

Betrayed

Raag's pack was gone, too. *Raag, what have you done?* Sona thought in a panic. She lit a lamp, then dumped the contents of her pack on the floor. She frantically searched, but it was clear that the Water gem that Mahseer had given them was gone—Raag had taken it as she slept. Sona ran to Willa's saddlebag and pulled out the pouch of coins that Yaami had given them. It was still more than half-full. So Raag hadn't taken their money. But he had taken the gem and Swara.

How long had he been gone? Would he try to sell the gem first, or go straight to the Sun Ships? Sona couldn't guess wrong, or she'd lose Swara forever. *Think, Sona.*

Sona decided to go straight to the Sun Ships, for who knew whether the gem district stores were even open at this hour? She figured it would be advantageous to appear to be a Malech, especially in the middle of the night, so she dressed in her light brown Malechian traveling clothes and put in her earring with the tiny Earth gem. She pulled out Ayah's ointment and smeared it on her ears, and the scent of herbs and flowers brought her back to Ayah and her sayings: "Might does not make right, Sona. Right makes right."

Sona braided her hair quickly, then threw on her boots, saddled up Willa, and led the pony out of the stall. The moon hung low in the sky, and she could tell that sunrise wasn't far away. She ground her teeth and hoped she could catch Raag in time.

To get to the Sun Ships, she had to go to the northern edge of Bhoominath. The streets right around the temple were empty and silent, but the ones farther away, near the taverns, were still full of revelers, and Sona had to make her way around them, pulling Willa as she went. Finally, she came to quiet streets again, with nothing but the clip-clop of Willa's hooves and her own rapid breathing echoing in the night. She had to find Swara. She just had to. She couldn't let Raag take her away. How could he steal off into the night like a thief? How could he kidnap Swara? How could he take the gem that Mahseer had given her? Worst of all, how could he abandon her? She had thought they were finally friends. But maybe that had been his plan all along. She should have known when he kept suggesting leaving Willa behind that he wouldn't wait for her.

Sona rushed through the city and soon broke into a sweat. The ships wouldn't leave before sunrise, would they? Sona hoped she was retracing her steps from the day before correctly. At one point, she thought she saw a shadow peel away from the side of a building, but she didn't wait to see who or what it was; she just hurried along, letting starlight and the quarter moon light her way.

She could smell the heat of the desert before she could see it. Just one more street, around a block of warehouses, and she would find the Sun Ships.

"Halt. Who goes there?" a rough voice called.

Argh, Sona thought. She knew where she was: the entrance to the gem district.

"Hello, guardian of the King," Sona said in her best Malechian drawl. "I am here to deliver goods to my father, who will set out on a Sun Ship at dawn."

The soldier was wearing a pointed silver helmet and kept his bejeweled hand on his sword as he leaned forward and held a torch in front of him to illuminate Sona's face. "Your father, huh? Turn your head, girl."

Sona dutifully turned her head to show her ears and her earring. She sent a swift prayer to both Bhoomi and the Wind God that she'd applied Ayah's ointment correctly in her haste. She held her breath as the soldier looked at her.

"Fine," he said, and held out a hand.

What was that about?

"Sunrise is coming," said the soldier, shoving his hand in front of her.

"Oh," said Sona, finally understanding. "Yes. And a fine Harvest night it's been." She dug in her pocket and gave him a coin.

"Off with you, then," the soldier said finally. As if she had been the one delaying him!

Sona gave a quick bob of her head, and Willa snorted as they walked away quickly. "No kidding, Willa," Sona said under her breath.

She arrived at the Sun Ship port and looked for the first captain they had met with, the woman with the cracked skin and head scarf. "Have you seen my—my servant?" Sona asked.

"Gone missing, has he?" The woman cackled. "Sure he was

your servant, missy? Sure it weren't no . . . lover's quarrel?" She raised her eyebrows and showed off a mouth full of rotten teeth.

"I'm sure," Sona said coldly. For Bhoomi's sake, he was her cousin! "Are you sure he isn't with you?"

"Nah, he's not. I'd sure remember a skinny boy with two thousand coins, wouldn't I?"

Sona's shoulders drooped. If he wasn't with this woman's caravan, he wasn't likely to be with any of the more expensive ones. And she definitely wasn't going to mention a valuable gem. But she had to keep looking. Sona went to each of the other captains as the sky began to lighten with the dawn.

Each of them said that Raag had not joined them.

Where was he? He had to be in one of the Sun Ships—Sona knew it. He would have been arrested if he'd been discovered in the gem district carrying a gem.

As the sun started to peek over the horizon, Sona realized that Raag might have tried a different way to get on a Sun Ship without losing the Water gem or being able to pay.

"We're about to leave, and I already told you he weren't here, girl. Are you accusing me of hiding that boy?" said the scarf-wearing, gap-toothed woman.

Sona took a breath. "No, Captain. But he really wanted to go, even though he didn't have the money. I think he might have stowed away."

Something leaped from the back of the ship and landed with a huge splash of sand.

"Swara!" Sona called. "Swara!" She whistled for the wolf.

Swara howled as she ran toward Sona. "Awoo! Awoo-woo-woo!"

Another figure jumped off the ship.

"Tan!" the captain cried. "Grab him!" Her eyes grew narrow and dangerous. "I hate stowaways. But I love the coins they get me when I turn 'em in to the authorities," she said to Sona.

Sona clutched Willa's lead as Swara ran the rest of the way to her, whining and wagging. She had a scarf tied around her neck— Raag's scarf from the night before. Thankfully, her ears were still black, and the scarf made her look more like a pet and less like a predator. Sona grabbed her scruff and let her lick her face.

"Nice dog you got there, missy," said the captain. "I'll pay you good coin for her."

"Not for sale," Sona said shortly.

Tan pulled an unresisting Raag by the arm. "We didn't have to search for him. He were already off the ship," Tan said. Raag hung his head.

Sona glared at Raag. "How could you?" she cried.

Raag wouldn't meet her eyes.

The captain whistled loudly, and two Malechian guards ambled over.

"This one was aiming to stow away," said the woman. "Now take him and do what you will. But first, give me my bounty."

One of the guards pressed something into her hand. "He's scrawny, but we'll find some work for him to do," he said with a leer.

Raag looked up with panic in his eyes. "I didn't actually stow away," he protested. "I changed my mind and got off the ship."

"That don't matter. You was on my ship without my say-so, and now you must pay the price."

"Wait! Please, wait!" Raag struggled, but the guards held him tight in their massive arms.

"Don't struggle, it'll just make things harder," said one guard.

Sona was furious at Raag, but she didn't really want the guards to take him away and do Bhoomi knew what to him. "I'll take this servant home, and my father will punish him," Sona said as confidently as she could.

"I don't know where you come from, bumpkin," said the guard, "but that's not how we do things here in the city."

Raag gave Sona a pleading look.

"Could I give you something that might change your mind?" she asked the guard.

"Not unless you got a gemstone, little lady," the guard sneered.

"I . . . my father might be able to get one," Sona stammered.

"Well then, go see your daddy, and come to the Eastern Jail," he said. "Make it nice-sized, though, and ask for the head guard, Denny."

"All right," Sona said.

"Wait!" Raag cried. "Can I apologize to my mistress, first?"

"All right, little man, go ahead," said the guard. "But if you try to run, things won't go well for you," he added darkly.

"I'm sorry." Raag took both of Sona's hands in his. "I shouldn't have run away like that. You were right, and I was wrong." He glanced at Swara. "But I really did change my mind before it was too late."

"How nice of you," Sona said coldly. "Now I would like nothing better than to forget you."

"I hope you find it in your heart to forgive me," Raag said. "I gave you my scarf to remember me by." He dropped his head, turned around, and held out his wrists to the soldiers, who tied them together.

Sona called Swara to heel. Then without a backward glance, she took Willa's lead and started walking back toward the city.

FROM *A MALECHIAN HISTORY OF DEVIA*

Bhoominath, the greatest city in all of Devia, is a wonder that all should experience at least once. Known as the City of Five for its five gates and welcoming of those from all five regions of Devia, it is a place of culture, learning, and tradition.

It is the only city in which Devan music is allowed, limited to the temples and during the Harvest Festival, which is known across the Eight Seas as one of the most exciting and beautiful celebrations in the world.

It is also the home of the famous Sun Ships, fueled by Devan Sun Singers and special black sails that allow the ships to cross the Great Khila Desert quickly. These ships were once outlawed by the Malechian King, but once it became clear how much of an advantage they provided in transporting soldiers, weapons, and gems across the desert, they were allowed to resume their voyages under tightly controlled conditions. The captains of these ships are thoroughly vetted by Malechia and are considered employees of the Malechian government.

22

Jail

Sona kept her back straight as she walked away with the animals. But once she was out of sight of the Sun Ships, she took the first opportunity to stop in an alley. She leaned against the side of a building and took deep breaths to try to calm herself.

Sona crouched down and touched her forehead to Swara's, then pulled back to look her in the eyes. Swara gazed back with her amber ones, and Sona once again heard the clear, bell-like tone that told her, more than anything she could see, that Swara was fine. "Oh, Swara," she said as the pup licked her face over and over, "thank goodness you aren't taking off across the desert without me."

Sona fed Swara a treat for being so good, and then took a hooli fruit out of a saddlebag and gave it to Willa, who nickered appreciatively. "You woke me and let me know they were gone, Willa. Thank you."

But now what should she do?

Raag had taken the Water gem from her. Now those guards were going to take it away from him, and then he was going to be in even bigger trouble than he was for stowing away on a Sun Ship! How could he be so foolish? And he'd acted so weird just before he was taken away, like he was actually a contrite servant, instead of a scheming cousin who had tried to leave her behind. Well, he didn't know he was her cousin, but he was still scheming.

Wait. What did he say? *I gave you my scarf to remember me by.*

Sona asked Swara to sit, then she knelt and untied Raag's scarf from around Swara's neck. She held it in her hand and felt a small, hard something like a pebble rolled up in the scarf. She carefully unrolled it.

And there, sparkling in the rays of the morning sun, was the Water gem. The circle inside it seemed to pulse gently.

Sona looked around quickly, pocketed the stone, then retied the scarf around Swara's neck. She heaved a sigh of relief. Raag may have betrayed her, but at least he had thought quickly and saved the gem from the soldiers.

Now what?

Raag had taken Swara and the gem to try to go to Mount Meru and get the amrita for Ayah on his own. He hadn't treated Sona like a family member, a friend, or even a halfway decent acquaintance. Instead, once they'd disagreed he'd taken the first opportunity to leave her behind. By rights, she should let him rot in that Malechian prison and find her own way to the mountains.

But Raag had helped her when he hadn't needed to, had led her across Tirna and then through Sindhu. He'd saved her life twice already, at the dam and in the Kaveri, pulling her up onto the boat. And without Raag's friendship with Yaami, they wouldn't have a gem or any coins at all. Besides, she couldn't leave him at the mercy of the Malechs—Bhoomi only knew what they'd do to him.

Raag had betrayed her. But she couldn't abandon him.

"There's nothing to do but try to get him back," she murmured to the animals. "So to the jail we will go."

She lifted Swara into a saddlebag and led Willa to the eastern end of the city as the sun climbed the sky in a swathe of pink. The city was waking up, and Sona's mouth watered at the smell of bread baking. A dairy cart rolled down the main street, and servants and restaurant owners stopped to buy fresh milk, cream, and cheese. Sona's stomach rumbled, but she didn't have time to eat.

After asking several people, Sona finally found the Eastern Jail—a squat, square building, crumbling at the corners, painted a murky brown in contrast to the colorful buildings around it. A grim-faced guard stood at the entrance. "What's your business?" he asked.

"I've come to see my servant, and free him if I can," Sona said, pushing her hair behind her ears so it was clear that she was a Malech.

"You can leave your pony over there." He nodded at a fence to the side of the building with posts for tying up horses.

Sona went to the fence and hesitated; she didn't want to leave the animals out here on their own. But she had no choice.

"Willa girl, listen carefully. Stay here," she whispered.

Willa looked at her with a dark blue eye, twitched her ear, and nickered.

She looked at Swara in the saddlebag and told the pup to stay. Swara closed her eyes like she might fall asleep.

Sona reached into her pocket and kept her hand there. She went to the front door of the jail, nodded to the guard at the door, and strode inside.

A guard was sitting behind a wooden desk. He had his helmet

off; his head was shaved, and his ears were cracked and red. He appraised her with dark eyes.

"Are you the head guard, sir? Is your name Denny?" Sona asked politely.

"It is, young lady. How can I help you?"

"I'm here to retrieve my servant," Sona said. "He was arrested trying to stow away on a Sun Ship this morning." And on the desk, she poured out all the coins she had, and dropped the empty blue bag as well.

"I see," said the guard. He scooped all the coins into the bag, then pocketed it. "Unfortunately, though, I can't release him."

"But you just took my money!" Sona exclaimed.

Denny looked at the empty desk. "I don't see any money."

"But—"

The guard shook his head. "Too bad I can't free him. A good servant is truly a *gem*, huh?" He gave her a knowing look.

Sona's shoulders drooped. There was no way she was giving the Water gem to this corrupt oaf—not when Mahseer had given it to her, and it appeared to be the only one like it in the world.

"Whatever you want to do, better do it quick," the guard said under his breath. "The wagon of prisoners leaves for the mines in an hour."

Sona's stomach sank to her feet. She wandered in a daze out to Willa and Swara.

She'd just handed over all her money.

Raag was in danger of being sent to mine gems Bhoomi knew where.

And she knew no one in Bhoominath.

What was she going to do?

She leaned her head against Willa's warm flank and touched Swara's sleepy head. A faint melody floated to her, a song of hope, of faithfulness.

She eyed the swirl of color in the scarf on Swara's neck and inhaled sharply.

She had to ask for help. It might not work, but it was the only option she could think of.

"Well, girls," she whispered as she led Willa away. "Looks like we need to visit the World's End."

FREE DEVIA!

We must work TOGETHER to free ourselves from our OPPRESSORS!

The Malechian rule must END!

Come to a meeting with inspiring leaders who will help us STOP this invasion NOW!

Time: The second night after Harvest, at midnight

Place: Follow the signs! If you don't know them, you aren't meant to know!

FREE DEVIA!

23

The Gambit

Sona pulled Willa along and asked the first merchant she could find—a Devan man selling vegetables out of a cart. "Can you tell me where to find the World's End? It's a restaurant, I think," she said.

"Yes, mistress," the man said, eyeing her Malechian outfit and ears. "It's on Dusk Street, near the desert. Go down River Street, here, and then make a right at the marble store." He indicated the way.

"Thank you," Sona said.

"Would you like some vegetables? They're the freshest in Bhoominath, brought here straight from Tirna."

"Sorry," Sona said, thinking wistfully of her own family's harvest. "May Bhoomi bless your day," she added as she pulled Willa along and ambled down the street as quickly as possible.

She arrived at a store selling various types of colored marble from all over Devia and then turned right as the vegetable seller had instructed her. Dusk Street was narrow and old, twisting this way and that and lined with cracked, ancient-looking cobblestones.

After walking for quite a while, Sona glimpsed the desert ahead. Where was this restaurant? Most of the places she saw on the street appeared to be either private residences or abandoned storefronts.

Then Sona came to a large wooden door. She thought she could just make out the words *World's End* above it in faded paint of an indistinct color. She knocked, and the door was opened by a burly Malech with a shaved head and three earrings in each ear.

"Oh," Sona said in surprise.

"Can I help you?" he asked in a gruff voice. "We're not open yet."

"Is—is this the World's End?" Sona asked.

He studied her for a moment without any expression on his face. "What's it to you?"

"I'm looking for Purvi," Sona said. "She said I should come here if I needed something."

"Purvi? How do you know her?" The man seemed to grow even larger and fill the doorway.

"I'm a friend. I need her help," Sona said. "Please."

"What's your name?"

"Sona. But she doesn't know it."

"But you're her friend, you say?" The man raised an eyebrow and made to close the door.

"Please," Sona pleaded. "She said to come to her if I needed anything. Wait!" Sona dug in her pocket and found the piece of paper that Purvi had given her. When she pulled it out, she saw that all that was on it was a symbol: a triangle circumscribed by a circle.

The same symbol that was on her pendant. Her mother Lia's pendant.

How was that possible?

The man considered her for a beat longer. "Fine. Stay here."

He shut the door in her face.

"Some restaurant," Sona whispered to herself. "Very welcoming."

Willa snorted.

A few minutes later, the man returned with Purvi, who looked at Sona cautiously. "Do I know you?" she asked Sona.

"Purvi, I'm Sona. You saw me and my . . . traveling companion on the streets of Bhoominath twice."

"I don't remember you," Purvi said.

"I was with my friend. He's a boy. You must remember our pony. See?" She gestured at Willa. "You saw us in the city center, and then outside the gem district, remember?"

"Maybe. Anyone can come and eat here, but why did you ask for me?"

"My friend is in trouble. You told us to come and ask for you if we needed anything."

Purvi laughed. "I meant anything to *eat*." She looked around. "That's what we offer here. But the restaurant isn't open now."

Sona touched her ears. Of course! Purvi thought she was a Malechian girl. "Don't you remember me? And . . . and my dog?" She pulled Swara out of the saddlebag and placed her on the ground, where the wolf shook herself.

"Oh yes, I remember the dog," Purvi said. She stared at Sona and furrowed her brow. "You look different."

Sona smiled nervously. "My friend . . . he's in jail. We need help from a Guardian of Bhoominath."

Purvi tilted her head.

Sona decided to take a risk. She pulled her pendant out of her shirt. "See?"

Purvi straightened up. "So you believe, as well. Come inside with me," she said. "You can bring the dog. Lars, please wait with the pony."

Willa whinnied as if she understood and wasn't excited about the notion.

"I can tie her up here. You don't need to do anything," Sona said to Lars as she hitched Willa to a pole.

Sona motioned Swara to her side and then followed Purvi inside.

Just inside the door, Sona was surprised to find a large restaurant with waitstaff running around. "We're preparing for lunch service in a few hours," Purvi said.

She led Sona and Swara to what appeared to be a storage room, filled with bags and jars of everything from rice to flour to lentils. She closed the door behind her. "Now we have some privacy. Tell me what's happened."

Sona told Purvi how Raag was in the Eastern Jail and would be shipped off to a mine within an hour.

By the time she finished talking, Purvi was smiling. "Eastern Jail? We're in luck, then. All we need is a distraction."

"Lucky? And what do you mean, distraction?"

Purvi thought for a moment. "I think I can . . . but he's about to leave." She stood. "Wait here."

"Wait—"

But Purvi had already left the room.

Sona tried to calm her nerves by petting Swara, who leaned toward her and closed her eyes.

After what seemed like a very long wait, Purvi returned wearing faded rags instead of her bright dress. "We have a plan," she said. "Come, we should leave now."

"Where are we going?" Sona asked as she hurried along with Swara at her side.

"To the Eastern Jail, of course," Purvi said.

Sona untied Willa, and then she and Purvi hurried through the streets. There were more people bustling about, and Sona ground her teeth every time they had to stop and let someone else pass. What if they were too late? She was angry with Raag, but she didn't want him to be lost in some mining operation for the rest of his life. How could they do that to someone without even pretending to have a trial?

Of course. He was Devan, so it didn't matter.

When they arrived at the square where the jail was located, Purvi said, "Stay in this alley with the animals. If you come in again with me, the head guard will be suspicious."

"What are you going to do?" Sona asked.

"I'm going to run in there and tell them that Gulappan is robbing the Western Jail."

"Will that work?" Sona asked.

Purvi nodded.

"But won't they leave a guard behind? And what will happen when they get there and find that Gulappan is nowhere to be found? Won't you get in trouble?"

Purvi smiled. "They will leave a guard behind—I'm counting on it. And don't worry. Gulappan *is* robbing the Western Jail."

Sona gaped at her.

"Stay here, and don't be seen. I'll signal to you when all is clear." Purvi pulled at her hair and made it look more mussed. She reached to the ground and smeared some dirt on her face.

Sona stepped back into the alley and watched as Purvi ran to the jail. She held her breath as Purvi shouted something at the guard at the door, then went inside with him.

A few minutes later, she was flabbergasted as a dozen Malechian guards ran out of the building and took off down a road away from her. Purvi raced after them as they disappeared out of sight. But then a few minutes later, she sprinted back into the square and right to Sona.

"Come," she beckoned. "We must do this quickly."

Sona hurried to the jail and hitched Willa to the fence.

She went inside with Swara and Purvi, and stopped short at seeing a Malechian soldier, the one who had been at the door when she had visited earlier in the day, standing at the desk holding a prisoner's arm.

"I got him," said the guard. "You sure this is the one? Says his name's Raag, but he doesn't fit your description."

Purvi glanced at the prisoner and let out a low whistle. "Well, he certainly looks different, but yes, I think it's him. We're getting the others out, too, right?"

The guard nodded and handed Purvi a set of keys.

"What is happening here? How are you agreeing to this?" Sona sputtered.

The guard considered her and looked pointedly at her ears. "Takes one to know one, right?"

Sona had no idea what the man was talking about. Then he brought forth the prisoner, and Sona was stunned into silence.

She barely recognized the boy dragged before her. His lower lip was swollen and bleeding. His head was shorn brutally, nearly shaved, so much of his pale scalp was showing.

And his ears had not a hint of gold.

"That's him, right?" Purvi asked briskly.

Sona nodded mutely, and Purvi clapped her hands once. "Quickly," she said. "Take him and go."

"But what about you, and the other prisoners?" Sona asked.

"We'll take care of that." Purvi nodded at the guard.

"You *will*?"

"We'll let the rest of the Devans out, and then Purvi here will knock me on the head with my own stick," the guard said. "Make it look good, though, kid, or I'll get in trouble."

"Don't worry," Purvi said with a grin. "I'm good with a stick."

"But—"

"Enough with the questions. You must leave now," the guard said. He extended his hand. "I'm Ven."

Sona grasped it by instinct. Why was he helping them?

"I'm Sona."

The guard leaned toward her to whisper in her ear. "Free Devia."

Sona gawked at him, but then Purvi started pushing them toward a side door. "Go! Get far away from here. And if you want to talk more, come to the World's End tonight. I can get you jobs to earn back some of those coins you lost."

Sona nodded and grabbed Raag's arm. She didn't say anything until she'd gotten to Willa, brought the whole group to a quiet alley, and tied a bandage around Raag's head to disguise his ears.

She helped Raag get up on Willa's back, checked that Swara was still in a saddlebag, then swung herself up behind him. She clucked at Willa and headed back toward the Great Temple.

Bhoomi only knew what she should do with Raag now.

EXCERPT FROM A LETTER FROM THE KING OF THE ROYAL ISLE OF MALECHIA TO ALL GOVERNORS OF THE DEVAN COLONIES

Wanderday, sixth day of harvest, YK 707
ℰ Year 227 of the Devan Fourth Age ℰ
ℰ 14 years before the Present Day ℰ

It is hereby decreed by His Majesty, the King, that henceforth no matrimonial union between Malechs and Devans shall be permitted. Any children of such unions are deemed unsuitable and must be banished or sent to work camps so they may be properly utilized by society.

Any Devan or Malech found to be in violation of this decree must be punished in the strictest manner possible, so as to prevent the intermingling of Malechian blood with those of inferiors.

24

Some Truths

The streets of Bhoominath were even more crowded at mid-day. Willa carried them slowly through crowds of Devans and Malechs, adults and schoolchildren, merchants hawking goods, horses, dogs, and even a flock of goats. Now that Raag was safe, all Sona could think of was the secrets he'd kept, and how after his talk of friendship and trust, he'd decided to abandon her in a strange city.

How had Raag disguised himself as a Malech? She had never seen him use Ayah's ointment on his ears . . . and wasn't it only supposed to work on half-Devans, like her? She sniffed him—he smelled like boy sweat mixed with the sharp tang of blood, not herbs and flowers.

Sona was so distracted that she barely touched Willa's lead, but luckily, Willa found her way back to the Great Temple without needing much direction. When they finally reached the temple, Sona took them back to their old room. But everything looked different now in the face of Raag's betrayal.

After getting Willa unsaddled and fed, Sona turned to Raag.

"Let's see your face." She washed her hands, then took water and soap and cleaned the cut on his lip efficiently. He barely flinched.

"Any other wounds?"

Raag silently showed her a long scratch on his forearm, which she washed, and a bruise blooming purple on his ribs.

Sona fished in her pack and used Ayah's ointment on all Raag's wounds. After a few minutes, the tension in his shoulders eased.

"Better?" Sona asked as Swara watched them both.

Raag nodded, not meeting her eyes.

"So, do you have anything to say to me?" Sona asked.

Raag hung his head.

"Well? You're always talking. Where are your words now?"

Raag turned away and hunched over, shrinking into himself.

"You need to answer! You abandoned me—after all we've been through together! And Swara isn't yours to take wherever you please! Who are you to do such a horrible thing?" Sona cried.

"I'm no one," Raag said in a hoarse voice. "I belong nowhere. I want to pretend that I'm a hero. But actually, I'm an abomination." He pointed at his ears. "See?"

Sona sat next to him. When an animal was skittish, it was often better not to make direct eye contact. "You're not," she said. "You're your mother's son and Ayah's grandson. But who is your father?"

Raag shook his head miserably. "Some Malech. Ma never even told me his name. Once . . . once she let slip that he'd been killed. Murdered by another Malech." He swallowed. "So I've never had a father. We've spent my whole life traveling from village to city to village, hiding who I am. But people always find out." He swiped at his face. "If we're lucky, they tell us to go. If we're unlucky, they try to have us arrested, or worse. Many times, we've left before anyone could discover what I am. That's what happened in Yaami's village, and that's why she's still friendly to me. She shouldn't be, though. I keep calling you Malech, but I'm the Malech. I hate Malechs. But that's what I am."

Angry tears squeezed out of Raag's eyes. "I shouldn't have taken Swara—I know that. But I just wanted to get her to Mount Meru. I convinced myself it was the only way to get amrita for Matrka, and that finding another way would delay us too much. I want to save her, my grandmother, my Pitarau . . . I wanted to be a hero, like the Devan heroes I've heard about all my life. It was stupid, I know. But I wanted to prove to myself that no matter who my father was, no matter what I look like, I'm Devan." He swiped at his face and finally turned to look at Sona with red eyes. "I know you've been lying, too. But that was no excuse for me to take Swara and leave you behind."

Sona looked at him carefully. "What do you mean?"

"I told you that the gold paint washes off with full immersion, and you were underwater with Mahseer." Raag pointed at Sona's ear. "That was when I realized that you're Devan."

"Raag—"

"Why didn't you just tell me?" He dropped his head, then snapped it up to look at her. "But how were you living with a Malech family? Are they secretly Devan, too?"

"No. I can explain. Ayah made me promise not to tell you—"

"Matrka? What does this have to do with her?" He furrowed his brow.

"Raag, I didn't know myself, not until the day I left my home and the Goldstorm came. Ayah is my grandmother." She gestured between them. "We're cousins."

He shook his head. "There's no way," he said. "Matrka had only one other child, and my uncle died in a Goldstorm. He had no children."

"Please. Let me explain." And she told him all she had learned from her father and Ayah.

By the end of Sona's speech, Raag had slumped back against the wall of the room, staring into nothing.

"Matrka is your grandmother, too," he said.

"Yes. She thought it might upset you if you knew."

"Upset me?" Raag started to snicker, then laugh. His laughter took on a hysterical quality, and he held his hands over his face as tears streamed down. Still, he kept laughing, and Sona became alarmed that he'd lost his mind.

Raag's laughter finally quieted and ended in a hiccup. "We're cousins," he said finally.

Sona glanced at him out of the corner of her eye. "Yes."

"What a pair we are: you look like a Devan and live with the Malechs, while I look like a Malech and live with Devans. But why did Matrka trust you with the truth, and not me?"

Sona shrugged. "Maybe she wanted you to learn to like me for myself, and not just because we're related?"

Raag thought for several long moments. Finally, he nodded.

"Yeah, that sounds like Matrka—trying to influence people without them realizing it. At least now your abilities with animals make much more sense. I knew no Malech could ever do what you do."

"You didn't care for me at all until you found out how special Swara is. Did that make you feel better sneaking off across the desert without me?" Sona asked.

At that, Raag's face turned pink again. "I realized how wrong I was and tried to get off the ship, but it was too late."

Sona huffed. "Oh, I'm sure."

Raag sniffed. "It's the truth. I just—I just wanted to do something legendary and be a hero. But then I realized that betraying a friend is something a hero would never do."

Silence stretched between them again.

Raag let out a big breath. "I'm sorry. Can you forgive me?"

Sona pursed her lips. All these days, she'd known Raag was her cousin and tried to get him to be her friend. But could she ever trust him again?

Swara whined and began to lick Raag's hand. From across the room, Willa whinnied. Sona heard the gentle melody again, heard the clear tone.

Sona let out a breath. "Well, Swara forgives you."

Raag put his arm around the wolf. Hope leaped in his eyes. "Thank you."

"I didn't say that *I* forgive you."

"Oh." Raag straightened up with his arm still on Swara. "I'll never let you down again, I promise."

Sona sighed and shook her head.

Raag turned to look in Sona's eyes. "I'm sorry for everything, Sona. I've resented you for living in your happy farmhouse with your dad and brothers who love you. For having a home, a place you never needed to run from. For being Matrka's favorite, even when I thought you were a Malech. And for somehow having such a way with animals, more than I ever could."

"But your singing!" Sona said. "You charmed Swara to come right up to you! You asked those beavers to destroy their own dam, and they did it. I'd never be able to do that. I just trained Swara and Willa like I would any dog or pony. There's no magic in that."

"There is," Raag said. He scratched Swara under the chin, and she kicked her leg. "They love you. Swara wouldn't stop whining when we got to the Sun Ship and she realized you weren't coming. If I hadn't already changed my mind, she would have given me away. You love these two, and they love you back. And Mahseer chose you to give the gem to, not me. I can sing to the animals, but you can *hear* them."

Sona shrugged. "Yes, but that's not unusual among Devans, right?"

"Beast Singers are supposed to be able to hear the animals," Raag said. "But I can't. Stupid ears." Again, he pointed at his ears. "You're the Beast Singer."

"I'm no Beast Singer," Sona said. "I can barely carry a tune, and I don't know Old Devan. That's it!" She stood. "We're each *half* a Beast Singer. I can hear them, and you can sing to them."

Raag stood as well. "You're right. So . . ."

Sona let out a breath. "I suppose we have to be a team. To keep Swara safe. To save Ayah. We're both her grandchildren, after all. Agreed?" She held out her hand.

"Agreed." Raag took Sona's hand and shook it once, firmly. Then he held her hand in both of his. "I'm sorry, Sona—for so many things. Not the least of which is that I never should have called you Malech."

Sona put her free hand on top of his. "We're both Devan and Malech. Maybe we can be the best of both."

They hugged for a moment. They were the same height. But

unlike her brothers, Raag was bony. She could feel all his ribs through his thin shirt. He had never had a home, had felt alone for his entire life. Sona squeezed her cousin once, then stepped back.

"I'm amazed you didn't let me rot in jail," Raag said. "You were furious—quite rightfully—when I last saw you."

"I couldn't let them send you off to some mine forever," Sona said.

"I'm more grateful than I can say. But how did you manage to get me out?"

"Well, I started by bribing the head guard."

Raag raised his eyebrows. "You did?"

Sona nodded. "I gave him our money. *All* our money. But he said I needed to bring him a gem."

Raag gasped. "You didn't."

"I couldn't give him something so priceless! It's safe and sound. But I was desperate. So I ran to Purvi to ask for her help. I didn't know what else to do."

Raag gave a low whistle. "Well, you clearly made the right decision. That guard Ven was some surprise, huh? I guess there are some good Malechs. Besides you, of course, Malech."

Sona gave him a look. "*This* is how you thank me?"

Raag shook his head and looked at her earnestly. "I'll never forget that you came back for me. No more lies, no more secrets. We really are a team now."

"Willa included?"

Raag laughed. "Willa included." He turned to the pony, hand over heart. "I'm sorry, Willa."

Willa snorted and munched on another mouthful of hay.

"Okay, then. Now we've got to find our way across Khila without a Sun Ship," Sona said.

"It won't be easy," Raag said. "But we will find a way. I know it."

"We need information," Sona said.

"We do." Raag had a gleam in his eye. "So does that mean . . ."

Sona nodded. "Looks like we're both going to the World's End tonight."

MALECHIAN SAYING:

Fortune favors the strong.

DEVAN SAYING:

Kindness and compassion are more precious than jewels or gold.

25

World's End

After digging deep in their packs, Sona and Raag found nine pennies in total and gave four to the temple attendant for another night's stay. They munched on provisions from their saddlebags while they made plans for the rest of the day. They decided to go to the World's End at nightfall, when they'd be less likely to be discovered by any guards. After a long nap, they spent the afternoon training the animals, walking Willa around the temple, and having Swara jump in and out of the saddlebag. The wolf pup had grown enormously, and bright intelligence shone from her amber eyes. Sona used the last of their black dye on Swara's ears.

"Do you think Purvi will be able to help us cross the desert without a Sun Ship?" Sona asked.

"It sounds like she's well-connected, so I hope so," Raag said. "And I like the idea of working there tonight to get a few extra coins."

"I don't know anything about working in a restaurant," Sona said.

"It can't be that different from working on a farm," Raag said. "I've been on restaurant staff in various towns and villages. Just do what I do and listen." He brought out the gold paint. "Tonight, we'll be Devan kids. Remember, no Malechian haughtiness."

Sona snickered. "I'll put it away for tonight."

They covered Raag's severe haircut with a scarf in the style of a Tirna farmer's head wrap. Sona took out her earring and braided her hair in the style of Tirna, with two braids tied at each end so they nestled along the back of her head. They put on their worn Devan traveling clothes and applied Ayah's gold paint to each other's ears.

They asked for paper and a pen at the temple so Sona could write a quick letter to her family, letting them know she was alive and safe, at least for the moment. She didn't tell them where she was or where she intended to go, but said she hoped to see them again soon. She sealed the letter and brought it to a mail office, where she was able to send it for another penny.

"I hope it doesn't make them worry more," she said.

"I'm sure they'll be relieved to know you're all right," Raag said.

"Want to write to your mother?"

But Raag just shook his head and clenched his jaw.

Sona wondered how Raag could let his mother worry about her only son. But she didn't push Raag any further.

They fed and watered Willa and Swara and left them tied at their shelter at the Great Temple. As the sunset cooled the sky and the city, Sona led Raag to Dusk Street and knocked on the wooden door again. A familiar face greeted them.

"Hello again, Lars," Sona said.

The man lifted an eyebrow. "I like your look better tonight." Then he considered Raag. "This the one you were so worried about?"

"My cousin," Sona said.

"Purvi's waiting for you," Lars said as he opened the door wide. "Go back to the kitchen."

The World's End was oddly twisty, with more corners than flat walls. Even though the sun had barely set, it seemed darker inside than out, lit with lamps and torches that cast dramatic shadows on the walls. The biggest feature on the first floor was a huge counter in the shape of a circle from which all kinds of interesting drinks were served. Some smoked, some bubbled, and a few of the glasses held liquids that seemed to be on fire.

"Charming," Raag said.

"Let's find Purvi quickly." Sona took his arm and led him toward the smell of good food.

Purvi, dressed in another swirl of colors, was talking to a cluster of waitstaff in the kitchen. "If someone doesn't tip you, let me know," she instructed. "And if they tip too much, let me know that, too. Remember: keep your ears open and your mouths closed. All right then, off you go."

Sona waited for the others to leave before she and Raag came forward.

Purvi smiled as she looked at Raag. "You look much better than you did earlier today."

"Thanks to Sona. And you." Raag clasped his hands and bowed.

"So then, friends. Are you ready to help the cause?" Purvi asked.

"We want to hear what you have to say. But we'd like to tell you some things, too." Sona looked around warily. "Can we go somewhere more private?"

Purvi nodded, then led them to a back room, threadbare but clean. "You're from Tirna, then?"

Sona nodded, and Raag added, "Kanthpur."

"I believe things in Tirna have become more difficult recently, since black gems were discovered there again?"

"Yes," Sona said. "More miners. More protests and arrests."

"Soldiers have been pouring in from both Vanam and Sindhu," Raag said.

Purvi nodded and pitched her voice low. "This is the home of the Free Devia movement. We help those in need, and we strike blows against Malechian rule. Our goal is to make Devia so bothersome to the Malechian government that they finally leave this country to those of us, Devans and Malechs, who wish to live in harmony."

"We admire what you're doing," Raag said. "But how do you know you can trust us with this information?"

Purvi smiled. "We know you're part of us."

Sona shook her head. "Although I believe in what you're doing, I've never done anything for Free Devia. I only came to you for help, and you gave it willingly."

Purvi turned her head and showed them one golden ear. "You're both like us, literally." She turned her head to the other side.

Her other ear had no gold at all.

Sona's eyes grew wide. "You're . . ."

"Devan and Malechian. Outlawed. Like both of you, correct?"

"Oh," Raag said, stunned. "I never knew there were more of us still left in Devia."

"There's a big group of us here in Bhoominath. Kids, teens, adults. And many others, Devan and Malech, who are sympathetic to our cause. Some have lost spouses and children. Some just think that of all the horrible things the Malechs have done, outlawing mixed marriages and children is the worst. We can't allow them to outlaw love. That's why Lars and Ven the soldier joined us. As you know, they're both Malechian, and they've been very useful to us. So, no matter why you both came to Bhoominath, you can have a home here, and useful work, if you want."

"We could . . . stay here?" Raag asked in a dazed voice.

Purvi nodded. "Not *here*, as this really is a restaurant, but there is an empty warehouse nearby, and that's where we house newcomers until we find better housing. It's where I live. And I help run this place. Technically, it belongs to Lars, because only Malechs can own businesses in Bhoominath now. But in reality, it belongs to all of us—and we use the information we gather and the money we make to further the cause. So, I ask you: Will you join us? We're having a big meeting tomorrow night to make plans for the weeks ahead."

Sona knew what her answer was. She still had a job to do, to save Ayah. She needed to get to Mount Meru, one way or another. And she was bringing Willa and Swara with her and protecting them for as long as she could.

But she waited for Raag to answer first. After all, this was what he'd been searching for all his life: a home. A place where people knew who he was, and accepted him, maybe even valued him more, because of his background.

"Thank you, Purvi, but we have another mission," Raag said.

He flashed Sona a grin, and she couldn't help grinning back.

Purvi raised her eyebrows. "I can't say I'm not disappointed. You're both clever. And that pony and your dog could help us, as well. What is your mission, may I ask? Maybe after you've completed it, you could return here?"

Sona explained their quest to Mount Meru, and Raag added

details. After Purvi had listened to their story, she gave a low whistle. "So you need to find a way to cross the Khila quickly with a pony and a dog? And not on a Sun Ship?"

Sona nodded. "Is there a way?"

Purvi shrugged. "I've heard rumors from time to time, but nothing specific. But then, I've never needed to cross the Khila and go to the mountains." She shook her head. "Many have tried to cross the desert on their own. Most change their minds quickly or aren't heard from again."

Sona glanced at Raag, who'd gone pale. "But there must be some way," he said.

"If there is, someone here might know. We attract an interesting clientele, and information gathering is one of our specialties."

"Who should we talk to?" Sona asked.

"I don't know who, but I do know where to send you," Purvi said. "Paravat."

But that's where we're trying to go—to the mountains of Paravat, all the way across the Khila Desert, Sona thought.

At Sona's and Raag's confused expressions, Purvi added, "Paravat is upstairs, on the top floor of the restaurant." She raised an eyebrow.

"Okay . . ." Raag said.

"You can be waitstaff tonight. We can pay you twenty pennies each, plus any tips you collect, plus dinner. But you'll be working hard. You'll bring food and drinks to the tables. You'll wipe down tables when people clear out. And you'll listen." Purvi winked. "Especially to the ones who are doing more drinking than eating."

"Okay," Sona said. "We can do that."

"And if you don't find what you're looking for tonight, you can come back tomorrow, and try again," Purvi said. "And maybe do a side job or two for me."

Raag glanced at Sona, who nodded. "Fair enough," he said.

"There are five sections in the restaurant, named after the five provinces of Devia," Purvi said as she led them up three flights of rickety stairs. "All the people who don't want to be seen go upstairs," she whispered. "It's the best place to eavesdrop. It will mean going up and down a lot, but it will be worth it."

The top level was even darker than the floors below, and it smelled of herb smoke and alcohol.

"Hey, Jilly," Purvi said to a young Devan woman wearing an apron. "This is Sona and Raag, both new tonight."

"Oh, good," said Jilly. "We need the help. We're already full up here." She pointed to the tables in the small room. "Sona, the back three tables are one through three—you can take those. Raag can have four through six, and I'll take seven through ten. Make sure everyone pays up front, or you'll never get 'em to pay at the end, when they're good and drunk."

Sona and Raag were given aprons and towels, then they went to take care of their customers.

After three hours, Sona understood why Raag had compared waiting on tables to working on a farm: it was hard work, and she broke a sweat early on, running up and down the stairs bringing food and drink to the customers. She dealt with many beast-like, obstinate people, who ate and drank vast quantities. And although some might have found the job boring, Sona found it entertaining. There were farmers from Tirna, boat people from Sindhu, Khilan Sun Ship workers, and even some spice merchants wearing the green of Vanam. There were Malechian soldiers and people from elsewhere in the Eight Seas. They talked of their journeys, their quests for gems, and their loved ones. There were endless fascinating conversations, but none about crossing the desert.

And then there was a conversation between two Devan women—one from Vanam and one from Sindhu—that piqued Sona's interest.

"The green gems are gone," said the woman from Vanam. "They seem to have dried up completely. They've moved all the miners out, sent them to Tirna. And the children are suffering with a mysterious illness."

"Well," said the woman from Sindhu, pitching her voice to a whisper. Sona leaned over the table to pick up an empty glass, then wiped the spot. "There's been no more Water gems seen in Sindhu since several days ago, when . . . well, you know the tragedy that occurred. So many more soldiers have been sent our way, and now they'll start digging our riverbanks again. But I doubt they'll find more gems. They took our Mahseer, and Mahseer took the gems away. And now there is a wasting illness ravaging the children, Devan and Malechian alike—perhaps it has spread from Vanam. Is there no end to the troubles in Devia?"

"Girl," came a deep voice from table two, where a man sat all alone.

Sona startled, straightened up, and moved closer to his table.

The man wore dark clothes and a hood that kept his face shadowed. He removed a pipe from his mouth and exhaled a puff of familiar-smelling smoke. "I'd like a fire feni," he said.

Sona held out her hand. "That'll be five pennies," she said.

"Here. Pay for my whole evening with this." He put something in Sona's hand.

It was a pouch of coins. The blue woven pouch of coins that

Sona had given to Denny in the Eastern Jail to get Raag out. She was sure of it. She could picture Yaami handing it to her. Sona bit her tongue to keep from crying out.

"I heard an interesting story playing cards with some guards from the Eastern Jail this evening. A story about two kids who showed up in Bhoominath, looking to cross the Khila," he said in a gravelly voice. "But one got in trouble, and the other tried to bail him out of jail with this. And then there was a very suspicious jail break. Know anything about it?"

Sona swallowed and stood up straight, hoping that disguised the sudden trembling in her limbs. "I'll bring this down to the bartender. You can use it as your tab all night. I'll be right back with your fire feni." She backed away from the man, accidentally bumping someone.

"Watch it," whispered Raag. "You almost knocked me over."

"Come with me," Sona said. "I need to talk to you, *now*."

Raag followed her downstairs to the bar.

"I need to talk to Purvi," Sona said to the bartender, a slender young Malechian man.

"She's out," the bartender said. "What do you need?"

Sona bit her lip. "Is Lars here?"

"He's out, too. What is it?"

Sona handed him the bag of coins. "The man at table two upstairs wants to start a tab. He—he asked for a fire feni."

"Nice," said the bartender. He took the bag and counted the coins, then turned to make the drink.

"What's wrong?" Raag whispered.

"That man upstairs—I think I've seen him before. He told me

he won that bag of coins off a guard from the Eastern Jail tonight. A guard who told him about two kids looking to cross the desert. It's our pouch. Raag, *he knows who we are*! We've got to get out of here!"

Raag nodded. "We've been here long enough. I've found out how we can cross Khila. It won't be easy, but there's a way."

"Up you go," the bartender interrupted, handing Sona a flaming drink.

Sona took it carefully and turned toward the stairs.

"Meet me in the back alley in five minutes," Raag whispered. He headed for the kitchen with a stack of empty plates.

Back upstairs, Sona placed the drink in front of the shadowy man. "Can I get you something to eat, sir?" she asked.

"I'll be fine with this for a while," the man said in a hoarse whisper. "But I have some questions for you."

"I—I need to go downstairs to bring up my next order," Sona said.

"All right, but when you get a moment, we should talk. I'll wait all night, if needed," said the man. He clasped his hands; they were large and covered in scars.

Sona did her best not to run down the stairs. She took an empty tray and hurried to the kitchen. Purvi was still nowhere in sight, and Sona couldn't stand the thought of staying in the World's End for one more minute. She found a back door that opened onto an alley and stepped out into the night.

The alley was pitch-black and reeked of refuse. "Raag?" Sona whispered. "Are you there? We must go."

She was met with silence.

Sona leaned against the wall of the building, glad to have escaped the shadowy man. Raag had to be coming out any minute.

She heard a noise and turned her head.

A large hand covered Sona's mouth. Cold metal pressed against her neck.

"Don't make a sound, girl," the Hunter whispered in her ear.

Firday, first day of autumn, YK 721

Dear Father,

I wanted to write to tell you that I'm all right. I'm far from home, hoping to bring something back that can help Ayah recover from Goldstorm Fever. I'm sorry I can't say more than that.

I had to leave suddenly for a very important reason—I can't tell you more about that, either. But I think you would be proud of me, and I know Ayah would be.

I miss you, Lal, Ran, and Karn very much, and I can't wait to see you all again. I don't know when that will be, but I hope that time is not too far away. In the meantime, my thoughts are with you. I hope the harvest went well, and that you celebrated all your hard work at the festival.

With love,
Your daughter, Sona

26

Captured

Sona struggled in vain against her bonds. She was blindfolded, her mouth full of the taste of the dirty rag used to gag her. Her arms were tied behind her back as she sat with something hard behind her. A warm wind blew sand that tickled her arms and face.

"You're a difficult one to pin down, girl," came the Hunter's sinister voice. He removed the gag, and a shiver shook Sona.

"Let me go!" she cried, twisting her wrists and trying to free them. But it was no good; they were tied too tightly, and twisting only made the ropes bite more. "Help! Help me!" Sona cried.

A finger touched her hand gently. Raag was here, too, on the other side of the post behind her. At least she wasn't alone. But how could they escape?

"You can yell as much as you want; no one can hear you out here," said the Hunter. "You needn't remain tied up," he said in a less forceful tone. "Just answer my questions, and I'll let you go."

"Mmph mmph mmph!" Raag cried next to her.

"Ungag and untie him, and I'll talk," Sona said. "For that matter, take off our blindfolds."

"So much concern for a boy who's been leading you into danger for weeks," the Hunter said. "But I am not unkind."

Sona felt fumbling at the back of her head. The cloth over her eyes was removed, and she blinked to clear her vision. It was still nighttime, and all she could see around her was moonlit desert sand. How far were they from Bhoominath?

She felt Raag's warmth behind her and craned her neck to glimpse him out of the corner of her eye. "What do you want to know?" she asked the Hunter.

"Why did you leave your home in the middle of a Goldstorm?" the Hunter asked. His unearthly eyes shone weirdly in the moonlight, and his nose was no longer swollen, but was still bent to the side.

"The weather was fine when I left," Sona said.

"That's not an answer. Why did you leave during the harvest when your family needed you at home? Your father was quite concerned."

Sona's heart quailed. Father must have been so worried and upset. "I never wanted him to worry."

"And yet you left. I ask for the final time: Why? Tell me the truth. I command you—"

"Don't start that Hunter of Malechia stuff again. She's no wild animal," Raag cut in.

"Quiet, Devan dirt, or I'll gag you again," said the Hunter. "This is your last chance, girl. Why did you leave your home? Do not lie; I will know. And then I will need to punish the boy for it. No matter what paint you've used on your ears, I know that you are a Malech, and he is a Devan, and he must suffer for your inability to tell the truth."

Sona thought furiously. "I was worried," she said. "About my ayah. She hadn't returned home."

Silence. Did he believe her? It was true, but not the complete truth.

"Your ayah? A servant?"

Raag stiffened next to her, but Sona spoke before he could get himself in more trouble. "She's not a servant. She's my friend. And I learned that soldiers had detained her the night before."

"Was she engaging in traitorous acts? Was she helping that ridiculous outlaw?"

"No! She was just going home, and the soldiers arrested her for no reason. But then they let her go, because they knew she had done nothing wrong."

"Then why did you not just wait for her, girl?"

That was a good question. This time, she could tell the truth, almost.

"She is older," Sona said, her voice softening. "And I was worried. So I took my pony and thought I'd bring her back with me, so she didn't have to walk."

"I see," said the Hunter. "And you made it to the village when the Goldstorm hit and had to shelter there."

Sona kept her face carefully blank.

"Then why didn't you return home after the Goldstorm ended? Your family went to the village, but they said you were not there."

Why did the Hunter insist on asking all these questions? "I . . ."

"Her ayah is my grandmother," Raag cut in. "Sona stayed with us. But my grandmother became very sick with Goldstorm Fever.

That's why we left together. We are trying to find a medicine here in Bhoominath to cure her."

Sona felt a sudden surge of gratefulness for Raag. He was certainly better than she was at making up things in the moment.

The Hunter started laughing. "You children came all the way here to find a magic potion to cure an old Devan woman of Goldstorm Fever? Hahahahaha!" He started to wheeze, and it was some moments before he was able to talk again.

"Tell me what you're really doing," the Hunter said in a voice dripping with venom.

"That's the truth," Sona said. It was part of the truth, at least.

"That's a lie." He opened his palm, and Sona squinted at it. "Then what, girl, were you doing with this?"

On his palm lay a Water gem. The Water gem that Mahseer had given her. Sona inhaled sharply.

"We found it," Raag said. "It was lying on a riverbank on the Kaveri a few days ago."

"It is *mine*," the Hunter seethed. "I slew the ferocious Fish and its demonic child, and this is my bounty."

"I thought the gems belonged to the King," Sona said.

"All of them but these," the Hunter rasped. He closed his fist over the gem. "These are my prizes, along with the pieces of the beasts." He pulled his shirt down to reveal a collar made of golden fish scales, and Sona had to fight a wave of nausea. Beautiful Mahseer, displayed like a trophy.

"You had no right to kill her!" Raag shouted. "Mahseer was gentle and generous. She brought prosperity to Sindhu."

"Do not recount your stupid myths to me," the Hunter said.

"I know my duty, ordained by the King. And you two were foolish enough to ask the gem merchants about this one. When I heard the rumors that someone was asking about this gem, I knew it must be here in Bhoominath."

Sona refrained from telling Raag *I told you so*. But she thought it with all her might.

The Hunter continued. "But you, girl, you seem to have an affinity for these beasts."

Sona swallowed. "I don't know what you're talking about."

The Hunter pocketed the gem. "Your father said you had some ability with animals. Now I see it's true—you know how to find them, or you know how to bring them to you. Join me, girl, and I will teach you how to hunt them. Come with me on my quest, and you will be Hunter after me."

Sona fought the bile that rose in her throat. "Never," she ground out.

"That woman is just a servant. Your family can get another. Abandon this foolish notion. If you come with me, I will leave your Devan friend alone."

Sona tried to swallow, but her throat was too dry. "And if I refuse?"

The Hunter shrugged. "Then I must follow the law. You, a Malechian fugitive holding a Devan gem without leave, must be turned over to the authorities."

Sona raised her chin. "Fine, then. Take us to the jail." Sona hoped it would be the Eastern Jail, and maybe Ven would help them again.

The Hunter smiled in the moonlight. "Oh, no, this boy will

not be going to jail. The sentence for a Devan found to be illegally holding gems may be carried out by any of the King's representatives immediately. That sentence is death."

Sona's breath hitched. She extended her fingers to touch Raag's hand.

"Go ahead, oh great Hunter. This just proves what you are: a murderer," Raag said.

FROM *A MALECHIAN HISTORY OF DEVIA*

What are the origins of the heroic Hunters of Devia?

These highly trained soldiers were first ordained over two hundred years ago, when the Malechs arrived in Devia and realized that dangerous wild beasts endangered Malechs and Devans alike. The King called for a search for those with strength, endurance, and a special way with animals to be trained in stalking and destroying very unique quarry.

Since that time, the Hunters have been given free rein and resources to move about Devia at will, keeping the land safe for all.

27

The Hooded Man

The Hunter reached for the silver Air Blade at his belt.

"No!" Sona cried. "I'll go with you. Don't hurt him!"

"Sona, don't!"

"Hush!"

Sona couldn't let the Hunter kill her cousin in cold blood. She thought of Willa and Swara, back at the temple. She would go with the horrible Hunter if he let Raag go free. Then Raag could keep the animals safe. She knew he would. And he would find his way to Mount Meru, with or without Sona.

The Hunter smiled as he walked toward them with his Air Blade drawn. Was he going to kill them both anyway?

"Please," Sona said. "Don't hurt us. I'll go with you, I promise."

The Hunter reached down with his knife and cut the bonds tying Sona's wrists. "Good. You have bought this boy his life. Come, girl, let's go. We will take a Sun Ship across the desert and find the home of the Great Horned Snake, which has terrorized Khil for too long. You shall help me track it."

He grabbed Sona's wrist roughly and started leading her away.

"Wait! What about my friend? Let him go!"

"I said I'd spare him. I never said I'd free him," the Hunter said dismissively. "He can figure out how to get himself out of those bonds. Come, girl. Dawn is coming, and the Sun Ships will not wait."

"He's tied too tightly!" Sona struggled against the Hunter, but his grip was too strong.

"You'll learn the ways of the wild with me, girl. Animals either adapt, or they die."

"He's not an animal! He's a boy!"

"He's a Devan," said the Hunter, as if that was the same thing.

Raag struggled against his bonds, but Sona knew he'd never be able to break them.

"Please," Sona begged. "Please set him free." She blinked furiously as unasked-for tears stung her eyes.

The Hunter yanked her so hard she stumbled and nearly fell. "Shut your mouth, girl. We do not weep, and we do not beg."

"You are leaving him here to die."

"Only if he's not clever or strong enough to get free," the Hunter replied. "Now come quickly." He tugged her again, and Sona was pulled along.

Suddenly, a tall figure appeared behind the Hunter. There was a thud, and the Hunter's hand let go as he dropped to the ground with a splash of sand.

"Free your friend," whispered the man, who was wearing gray robes with a hood.

He held out a wooden handle to Sona. She took it by instinct before she realized it was a knife. Sona ran to Raag and cut the ropes tying his wrists.

"Now what? Who's that?" Raag whispered, rubbing his wrists and standing up stiffly.

"He's been following us," Sona said. "I'm almost certain that was who I was running away from in the tavern last night."

The hooded man took the silver Air Blade knife off the Hunter's belt.

"Get ready to run," Sona whispered to Raag.

Their rescuer hunched over the unconscious Hunter and pushed his head to the side to expose his neck. He held the Air Blade to the Hunter's skin.

Sona gasped. Was he going to kill the Hunter in cold blood?

The man paused. Sona held her breath. She didn't want to look, but she couldn't tear her eyes away.

The man glanced back at them. Then he pulled out the Hunter's necklace with the Wolf's teeth and held it, the ties fastening the Tiger cloak around the Hunter's neck, and the golden collar made of Mahseer's scales. The Air Blade flashed as he made a slash.

A moment later, he held up the cloak, collar, and long white teeth to the children. "The murderer of these beasts does not deserve to hold these as trophies," he said. He stuffed the Tiger cloak inside his pack and pocketed the teeth and collar.

Then he brought out rope from his pack and bound the Hunter's wrists and ankles. Once that was done, he searched the Hunter's pockets, taking items out and putting them in his own pockets.

"Ah," he said, reaching down to take the Hunter's earring. "Another precious item he has no right to." He turned to the children. "Help me tie him to the post."

Sona looked at Raag, who shrugged. "He did want to leave me in the same situation," he said.

They tugged on the Hunter, who was even heavier than Sona had imagined he'd be. There was a large bloody lump blooming on the back of his head, but he was breathing. They sat him up and tied him around his chest to the post that they'd just been hitched to.

"Shouldn't we turn him in to the authorities?" Sona asked.

The man gave a short laugh. "And who would the Malechian guards believe—three Devans, two of them children, or one of their own, *a man ordained by the King himself*? There is no justice here, not for Devans."

"He has a point," Raag said.

The man tugged on his knots. "We're giving him the same odds he gave your friend here. Better, since he's a mighty Hunter and this one is only on the edge of manhood."

The man took the Hunter's pack and went through every pocket and compartment, dumping things on the ground as he was done with them. He took out a small bag of coins and at least six silver spear tips and stuck them in his own pack. Then he picked up the Hunter's empty pack and threw it into the desert.

Finally satisfied, the man clapped his hands. "Come, my friends. Let's go somewhere less desolate, and let's eat and drink while we introduce ourselves. I've been looking for you for quite some time."

Sona gripped Raag's hand. "Why should we go anywhere with you?"

"We'll be in a public place. You can leave anytime. I'll tell you everything once we get away from here. But in the meantime, here's a sign of my good faith. Hold out your hand."

The man deposited Mahseer's gem in Sona's open palm. She looked at Raag, and he nodded.

Sona's stomach rumbled. They had completely missed dinner

the night before. "Did you say something about food?" she said as she stuck the gem in her pocket.

The eastern horizon was just turning pink when they entered Bhoominath once again.

"Can we head toward the southern part of town, near the Great Temple?" Sona asked, thinking of Willa and Swara, who would be up and hungry soon.

"The place I want to take you is in that part of town, as it happens," the man said.

He took them to a large café overlooking the Kaveri, decorated in blues and greens. "A table on the terrace, if you please, Shilpa," he told the hostess, who nodded and took them to a quiet spot with no other diners nearby. Sona looked at the river and felt like she had traveled across the country again.

Once seated, the man ordered tea, omelets, and toast for all of them, then waited for Shilpa to walk away before turning to Sona and Raag. "Now for our introductions." He pulled down his hood to reveal a handsome face that was crisscrossed with lines and puckered skin like he had been burned. But his brown eyes danced, and his smile flickered like a flame.

"You're the Gray Ghost, aren't you?" Raag asked. Sona was startled, but then she looked at the man again and wondered how she had missed it—his clothes were all gray, like he was in mourning.

The man grinned. "Some call me by that name, it's true." He held out his hands palms up, in the sign of friendship. "But you can call me Gulappan."

Raag's face lit up. "I'm Raag, and this is Sona. We're—"

"On an important mission," Sona said. "Thanks for the rescue, but we should be going. After we eat," she added. The smells in the restaurant were too good to pass up.

Gulappan nodded. "I, too, am on an important mission, and I think we can help each other."

Sona regarded him warily. The tea and food arrived, and the children spent a few minutes drinking and eating ravenously. Gulappan noticed and called Shilpa over to order more of everything. But Sona wasn't going to be fooled into trusting the wrong person, no matter how good the food and drink were.

"I am friends with Yaami, and she told me of your mission to find amrita to save Janaki Pitarau," Gulappan said. "And Purvi told me the same. I want to help you."

"Why?" Sona asked as Raag said, "Yes!" Sona gave Raag a look, but he only had eyes for the bandit.

"Janaki Pitarau is well-known among all Devans. We need a leader like her."

"You know her?" Sona asked.

Gulappan's eyes were distant as he looked past them, out the window to the south where Tirna lay. "I know all the village leaders. Especially in Tirna, where I come from."

"So she still lives?" Sona asked.

"Yes." Gulappan looked from Sona to Raag. "Janaki Pitarau is still unconscious, still sick with Goldstorm Fever, but she lives. At least, that's what I heard when I was in Tirna five days ago."

Sona breathed again. "But really, you expect us to believe that you're dropping everything to help two children save an old woman? No matter how important she is to her village, that's hard to accept."

"Sona!" Raag scolded.

But Gulappan only laughed again. "You are right, Sona. I want to help you also because our paths go together. I, too, am going to Mount Meru. But I need your help."

"Of course!" Raag said immediately.

"What kind of help?" Sona asked. This man made her nervous. He knew too much already.

"I'm tracking the sacred beasts of Devia," Gulappan said.

"Then you're no better than that Hunter," Sona said as Raag shook his head at her.

Gulappan held his hands up. "Not to kill them."

"To do what, then?" Sona asked. Who was this man and what did he want?

"To save Devia. To drive away the Malechs, once and for all."

DEVAN SAYING:

Never trust one who does not sing.

MALECHIAN SAYING:

When a Devan plucks a string, watch out!

28

The Prophecy

"That gem I returned to you is the key. Well, it's part of the key. I'm asking you to help me to collect as many as we can," Gulappan said.

"Why?" Sona asked. "What are you going to do with them? They're small, so I don't think they're as valuable as the other gems you've stolen."

Raag kicked her under the table.

"What? He's a thief, everyone knows that," Sona said. She tore another piece of vegetable omelet, dipped it in chutney, and put it in her mouth along with a bite of toast. The creamy, tangy, spicy flavors made her think of Ayah's cooking.

"Fair enough." Gulappan laughed. Then he lowered his voice. "But the gems with the sacred circle of Devia in them are more valuable than any others in the world. Sacred gems, if you will."

Sona gave Raag a look that said *I told you so.* Then she turned back to Gulappan. "Aren't you supposed to return gems to Devan temples?" She drank another sip of divinely strong, divinely sweet tea. It was on the verge of being too hot—just the way she liked it.

"Actually, I am returning them to a temple—*the* temple, the first temple in all of Devia. That happens to be at the top of Mount Meru. *When a true child of Devia brings the sacred gems to Bhoomi's Crown, then Devia shall be healed*," he whispered.

"What is Bhoomi's Crown?" Raag asked, pushing his empty plate away and slurping his tea luxuriously.

"They say there is a Crown of earth in a special chamber in Mount Meru where the sacred gems had always been housed. When the Malechs came"—he spat the word like it tasted bad—"the great heroes Asha and Ajit—"

"I love them! I want to be like Ajit," Raag said, clasping his hands and bouncing in his seat like a small child.

Gulappan grinned. "Me, too. After the Malechs came, Asha and Ajit took the sacred gems out of the Crown and dispersed them for safekeeping. I think Asha and Ajit somehow put the sacred gems into the sacred beasts," Gulappan said.

Sona held her breath. This made sense to her.

Gulappan continued. "And our friend"—he tilted his head toward the desert, where they'd left the Hunter—"has been systematically hunting down and killing not only the sacred beasts, but their offspring as well. Something that no one has ever done in the history of Devia."

"You sound impressed," Sona said.

The bandit shook his head. "I'm not. The Hunter's actions have been savage, ruthless. He deserves to rot on that post."

Sona didn't know what to say. She agreed with him—what the Hunter did was horrifying. But she didn't believe in killing anyone—beasts or people—and she hoped they hadn't indirectly caused the Hunter's death. If all life was sacred, that had to mean *all* life, even if a person made terrible choices.

"In any case, I heard rumors that the Hunter went wild looking for something after he killed Mahseer. So I went to investigate, and helped Yaami get many of the other Water gems back to Sindhu temples. But I suspected the Hunter was looking for something specific, something more valuable than all the Water gems in the world."

Raag opened his mouth, but Sona silenced him with a glare.

Gulappan glanced back and forth between them. "There's been something strange going on in the last several months, since the Great Tiger of Vanam and her cubs were murdered. More Gold-storms, more unrest."

Sona and Raag both nodded.

Gulappan went on. "I think that the Hunter is collecting the sacred gems for some nefarious purpose. Perhaps, if he keeps them all himself, he will make sure that Devia is never free of the Malechs."

Sona took another sip of tea. "I'm not so sure about that. From what he told us, he thinks of the gems as personal trophies, proof that he vanquished the beasts by himself. He doesn't believe in legends or prophecies. At least, not Devan ones."

"I understand," Gulappan said. "But just because *he* doesn't believe them doesn't mean they aren't real. No matter what, we cannot let him collect all the sacred gems. Even if he holds on to them and doesn't destroy them, that takes away our ability to save Devia and rid ourselves of the cursed Malechs. If the gems never make it to Bhoomi's Crown, Devia cannot be saved."

"We have to stop him! Free Devia!" Raag cried. The effect was less dramatic when he stuffed an entire piece of toast into his mouth.

Sona chewed her lip. It was great to talk about saving Devia, but did that also have to mean hating all Malechs, including her family? They were good people and hadn't done anything wrong. "How does this relate to the Sixth Beast coming? Isn't that what's supposed to save Devia?"

Gulappan shook his head. "I don't know. Maybe putting all the sacred gems in Bhoomi's Crown will call the Sixth Beast? But whatever we do, we need to keep these jewels out of Malechian hands. We need to gather them ourselves."

"I heard something else last night, before the Hunter kidnapped us. There are no more Leaf gems in Vanam," Sona said.

Raag stared at her. "Truly?"

Sona nodded. "I overheard two Devans last night saying they've dried up. That's why the Malechs sent more miners and soldiers into Tirna."

Gulappan rubbed his chin. "I have also heard this. Also, there seem to be no more Water gems in Sindhu."

"Is it because both the Tiger and the Fish are dead?" Sona asked.

"I think so," Gulappan said. "But maybe not, because the Wolf is dead—that grisly necklace the Hunter made proved it—but there are still plenty of Earth gems in Tirna."

Sona glanced at Raag and was glad to see he wasn't going to tell Gulappan about Swara. At least not yet.

"How did you know we had the Water gem?" Raag asked with his mouth full of toast again. "And how did you find us?"

Gulappan poured them all more tea. "Yaami told me that Mahseer and her child favored you, and you were there when Mahseer was killed. Since the Hunter obviously didn't have the sacred gem—he was screaming about it in front of everyone—and neither did anyone else, I thought maybe you had found it. So I came to Bhoominath looking for you. I tried to talk to you a couple of times, at the Harvest Festival and again at the World's End, but I must have seemed too suspicious. When I realized Sona wasn't coming back upstairs, I went downstairs and found you had disappeared. It wasn't easy to find your trail, but I managed to follow it into the desert." He again spread his hands in the sign of friendship. "So here we are."

Sona finished her food and sat back with her cup of tea. "Here we are," she echoed. "But how do you intend to get the gems—by killing the sacred beasts? You might as well be the Hunter."

Gulappan shook his head. *"We do not have to take, when we can ask."*

Sona sat up straighter and peered at him.

"Legend says that even the sacred beasts can be charmed with music. I believe that when sung to correctly by someone who loves Devia—a Beast Singer—the animals would give up the gems without having to be killed."

Sona looked at Raag. Gulappan was right, and they knew it. "Why do you need us, then?"

The bandit looked at them both. "I was once a Beast Singer. I can still hear them. But alas, my voice was damaged in a terrible Goldstorm, years ago." He touched scarred fingers to his throat. "I cannot sing. So I am seeking someone who can help me track the beasts and sing to them."

"And what makes you think we can do that?" Sona asked. This man knew or guessed everything about them!

"So suspicious for such a young person," Gulappan said. "Yaami told me that you travel with a very well-behaved pony and a large dog that obeys your every command. She said that Mahseer and her child blessed you both. And she heard this boy sing." He put his hand on Raag's shoulder. "He has a voice bestowed by Bhoomi herself."

Raag actually blushed. His smile was wider than Sona had ever seen it.

"Yaami shouldn't have told you anything about us! It's none of your business!" Sona said fiercely.

"Come on, Sona. He's a friend. Otherwise, Yaami would never have told him anything," Raag said.

"Fine. But how are you helping us?" Sona still didn't know what to make of this man who had blown into their lives like a Goldstorm.

"He already helped us. He saved us from the Hunter, didn't he?"

"Yes," Sona said reluctantly. "But that doesn't mean—"

"And he already gave us back the Water gem," Raag said.

"True," Sona said. But it still didn't mean his intentions were good.

"I can lead you across Khila to Mount Meru," Gulappan said. "And I can help you find Sarpa, the Great Snake, along the way."

Sona shook her head. "Who says we want to find her?"

"But we need to," Raag said. "We need to get the Fire gem and bring it to Mount Meru."

"Now you're going on about these gems, too? We're trying to save Ay—Janaki Pitarau," Sona said. "I don't think we can save the whole country."

"That's just it," Gulappan said. He entwined his fingers and rested his chin on them. "What if we could? I can help us find the path, and defend you—from the Hunter, or any other Malechs who get in the way. You know my skills in traveling across Devia. We will get to Mount Meru together, I promise. We will obtain the amrita for Janaki Pitarau, and we will restore as many sacred gems as possible to Bhoomi's Crown."

Sona leaned over to whisper in Raag's ear. He thought for a moment, then nodded.

"Okay," Sona said to Gulappan. "We have one more test for you. If you pass it, we can work together. If you don't, you must promise to let us go on our own, and not to interfere with what we're doing."

"It's a deal," Gulappan said. "I promise." He clasped his hands together and bowed his head.

Sona stood. "Come on, then."

Outside the restaurant, Gulappan was swarmed by a group of skinny children. Gulappan handed out rolls of flatbread wrapped around omelets, plus pennies for each of the kids. "Go and eat, little birds, and share with your friends," he said to them.

"The Gray Ghost! The Gray Ghost!" the children shouted.

"See? He's a hero," Raag murmured to Sona.

"He knows how to act like one," Sona whispered back. "But is he really?"

Gulappan laughed. "Enough, my friends, before soldiers come to investigate and fine us for holding a parade! Off you go now, and I will see you soon!"

"Come along, children," came another voice. "Hello, Sona and Raag. I see you have finally met our mutual friend."

To Sona's shock, Purvi strode toward them. She went to Gulappan and whispered in his ear, but Gulappan shook his head, indicated Sona and Raag, and whispered something back to her. A brief expression of dismay crossed Purvi's face, but then she wiped that away and plastered on a smile.

"I will see you when you return from your quest," Purvi said. She bowed to the three of them, then led the children away.

"They are orphans," Gulappan said. "Children orphaned by Malech cruelty. Purvi helps find them a place to live, and Shilpa makes sure they're fed. And we all find them ways to help our movement."

"See?" Raag whispered.

Sona nodded reluctantly. If Purvi trusted this man, she supposed she could, too.

The sun was well up in the sky by the time Sona got to Willa and Swara, and she felt guilty that she'd been stuffing herself when her animal friends hadn't yet had breakfast. Willa nickered and stomped her foot, but Sona made it up to her with a fresh hooli fruit she'd asked Gulappan to buy at a stand along the way. Willa ate it in three bites and looked to her for more, but Sona laughed and scooped hay for her and poured fresh water into her trough.

For Swara, she had ordered more of what they'd eaten at the restaurant, and the young wolf, who seemed even bigger after their brief absence, devoured the food but still looked hungry. Sona also gave her three dried lentil cakes and a large bowl of water, which Swara dispatched quickly. Then she pranced about, clearly wanting to play.

After some wrestling and play-biting, Swara sat and looked at Sona expectantly. She was ready for an adventure, she seemed to say.

Sona made sure Swara's ears were still completely black. Sona might be beginning to trust Gulappan, but she couldn't trust him with all their secrets—not just yet. Then she called for Raag and Gulappan. "We're ready," she said.

When Gulappan came to the stall and saw Swara, his face split into a delighted grin. He immediately sank down to one knee. "Hello there, my friend," he said, pitching his voice high and not looking directly at Swara. He held out his knuckles.

Sona held her breath as Swara approached Gulappan slowly, ears alert and tail stiff, a growl reverberating through her chest. Swara sniffed Gulappan's knuckles, then walked behind him and sniffed his bottom, to Sona's embarrassment and Raag's glee. She circled around and came to a stop in front of him as he remained kneeling. Then she reared back and put her paws on his shoulders. Sona's breath hitched. She wasn't sure she trusted Gulappan, but she still didn't want to see him mauled in front of her.

But then the wolf pup licked Gulappan's entire face, and he started laughing. "Oh, what a good girl you are."

After a few minutes, Sona pushed Swara down. "That's enough," she said. "We know you like him."

Willa wasn't as easy to charm. She shied away from Gulappan and kept stomping her feet. But then he offered her another hooli fruit, and she deigned to take it from him.

"Thanks for the tip, Raag," Gulappan murmured as Sona shook her head and laughed.

Finally, Gulappan turned to Sona and Raag. "Did I pass the test?"

"Yes," Sona said begrudgingly.

"So let's get across that desert," Raag said excitedly.

Gulappan nodded his head and clapped his hands once. "Absolutely. We don't have any time to waste. Let's go find that Snake."

29

Temple of the Sun

The travelers decided to leave at sundown, when the desert would be cooler. The rest of the day was spent gathering supplies that Gulappan paid for—extra jugs for water, linen cloth to keep the sun off them all, blankets, and a tarp for shelter.

"Are you bringing a horse?" Sona asked Gulappan as they walked through the crowded marketplace, which was full of merchants and shoppers haggling.

He shook his head. "I fear this will be too difficult a journey for a large beast. But your petite pony seems to be made of hardy stuff, and she will help us carry our supplies." He reached a hand to Willa, but she shied away. "Besides, I don't have enough coin for a horse, or a pony, or even a pack mule."

"How do you travel across Devia so quickly, then?"

Gulappan smiled at her, and the lines on his face creased. "I can walk quickly, and far. And I've made friends across the land. If I need to get somewhere more rapidly than my legs can carry me, I can usually get someone to give me a ride."

"Have you ever crossed the Khila Desert, then?" Raag asked.

"Yes, but never on foot. I've worked on Sun Ships going from

Bhoominath to some of the desert villages, and once even as far as the mountains. But Sun Ships are expensive and cannot carry our pony. And our mission is secret. We must travel across the desert on foot."

"Last night I overheard a group of Devans say you're supposed to follow a red line to cross the desert in the fastest way," Raag said.

Gulappan nodded. "Yes, I've heard of it, too. But I've never seen the red line, nor met anyone who's traveled it."

"We'll find it and get to the mountains," Raag said confidently.

"What are the mountains like?" Sona asked.

Gulappan frowned. "Aside from rare outposts of fortune-seekers in the foothills, there's nothing in the mountains for anyone. They are truly desolate. But now we have a reason to go there."

"How are we going to find a place in the mountains that no one has seen in decades, maybe centuries?" Sona asked.

"We'll make it, I'm sure. Now we're with Gulappan, the Gray Ghost, hero of Devia!" Raag said.

Sona looked around, worried that soldiers would come running, but no one on the streets of Bhoominath seemed to care.

Gulappan laughed heartily. "Thank you for the flattery, my friend. But I'm no hero—just a Devan trying to do what's right. And together, we will succeed. Now." He clapped his scarred hands. "Like I said, I have heard of the red line running from the eastern gate of Bhoominath that leads across the desert, but I have never seen it myself. Shall we see what wisdom we may find from the priestesses at the Sun Temple, the traditional Khilan place of worship? It is near the eastern gate, so we can leave directly from there."

"Great idea," Raag said.

"One more thing," Sona said. "I've been wondering how you

plan on getting an Air gem, since they haven't been seen in centuries, and the hawks of Paravat have disappeared?"

Gulappan nodded. "That is a good question. One that I don't have an answer to."

"Then your plan isn't a real plan," Sona said indignantly. "Surely, you're supposed to bring *all* the sacred stones to Mount Meru. You can't just take part of a prophecy and expect it to work."

"Sona . . ." Raag began.

"She's right, Raag," Gulappan said. "But I'm not ignoring the prophecy. I'm just doing what I can do, while I can do it. You have the Water gem. I have the Earth gem."

Raag looked puzzled, but Sona nodded.

Gulappan continued. "We are seeking the Fire gem. The rest, we'll have to figure out. But even if it takes years, I am determined to bring all the sacred stones to Mount Meru. I'm willing to give my life trying to do this. I cannot sit idly by while the Malechs destroy our country. Returning stolen gems to Devan temples is not enough, not when Goldstorms rage through our lands, farmland yields less food, the courses of rivers and tides are changed, and our people suffer under the Malechian yoke. We cannot continue to live our lives like sheep. We cannot continue to accept injustice. We must *act*. Devia must be free."

Sona was taken aback. She wasn't used to adults speaking like this. But she had to admit that Gulappan was right—something had to change. "Okay," Sona said finally.

Gulappan continued: "I thought the Hunter had the Leaf and Earth gems, but I only found the Earth gem, in his earring."

Raag responded, "Oh, but that's not the—"

Sona shushed him with a look. Let Gulappan think that the Hunter was wearing the Wolf's Earth gem in his ear. Eventually, he'd look more closely and realize he had only a regular gem, but right now, she didn't want him asking too many questions about where the sacred Earth gem was hiding. It took all her willpower not to look at Swara, who strode beside her like a large, furry shadow. The Hunter had not killed the Wolf's last pup, so the Earth gem was still safe.

Then she remembered something.

"Oh my goodness!" Sona gasped and clapped a hand to her forehead. "I know where the Leaf gem is. In the Hunter's ring!"

"What? Are you sure?" Gulappan asked.

Sona nodded. "I saw him just before the last Goldstorm in Tirna. The Leaf gem is in a ring on his left little finger." Sona swallowed. "He said he'd cut it out of the Tiger's heart."

"I can't believe I missed that," Gulappan said with a frown.

Sona shook her head. "I can't believe I didn't remember it at the time."

"There was rather a lot going on," Raag said.

Gulappan scratched his head. "So, Sona, your wish has come true. It looks like I must go check on our friend in the desert after all."

"We'll go with you," Sona said quickly as Raag raised his eyebrows.

"I could skip seeing him," Raag whispered to Sona. "We barely escaped last time."

"What's to stop him from taking the Leaf gem and taking off?" Sona whispered back.

"You should eat, drink, and gather the rest of the items for the journey tonight," Gulappan said, handing them a small bag of coins. "I'll meet you at the Sun Temple at sunset, after I've taken the Leaf gem from the Hunter."

Sona looked at Gulappan seriously. "If the Hunter refuses to give it to you, will you kill him?"

Gulappan put his hand over his heart and bowed his head. "I won't kill the Hunter," he said. "Not unless I have to."

He took off before Sona could say anything more.

After buying the rest of their items and eating a quick dinner, the children headed east, winding their way through the city, and Sona found herself feeling wistful. "I'll really miss Bhoominath," she confided to Raag.

"Maybe, once we're done with our quest, we'll come back," Raag said. She could tell he was tempted by the life that Purvi had offered them.

"If our families let us," Sona said. "I'm sure Ayah will have some choice words for us about how we ran all over the world."

Raag laughed. "I would *love* to hear Matrka scold us."

"It would mean she was back to normal," Sona agreed.

It was not difficult to find the Sun Temple, which was an enormous open-air pavilion surrounded by spires of multicolored glass that reflected a rainbow of colors.

They approached the circular entrance, which was made of red and orange glass in the shape of the sun's corona.

"Welcome, friends," said the priestess at the door, who wore robes of scarlet and purple. "Our sunset worship is about to begin. Please, come in. There is a place inside for your beasts."

Sure enough, there was a shady area just inside the entrance where Willa could munch hay to her heart's content and Swara could be made to stay put. Sona gave Swara a piece of twine and commanded her to stay. The wolf pup looked at her longingly, but then curled up and started to chew.

"Might we talk to the head priestess about an important matter?" Raag asked a priestess who looked barely older than they were.

"Not now, I'm afraid," she said, not breaking stride. "The sun is setting in a few minutes, and she cannot be late for the prayers."

Raag bowed his head.

"What do we do now?" Sona asked.

"I'm not that familiar with Sun Temple rituals," he said. "But I don't think we need to do much but watch and listen respectfully. Then we can see if we can talk to the head priestess."

Sona and Raag went to the entrance of the circular central courtyard, where they removed their shoes, then washed their faces, hands, and feet. They entered the courtyard, where a few dozen Devans were seated around what looked like a large map of Devia on the ground. Sona gasped; the map was a mosaic of colored glass, and each region of Devia shone with its traditional colors: Vanam in green, Tirna in black, Sindhu in blue, Khila in red, and Paravat with clear glass. Surrounding the entire map, also in mosaic glass, was a depiction of the long, long body of a golden snake—the Sarpa. Its red mosaic eyes glittered, and Sona felt a chill despite the heat of the evening.

"Welcome, friends, to our sunset worship," said a priestess who looked to be about Ayah's age, still tall and unbent. She placed a red Fire gem in a small cup in the center of the map, then went back to the edge of the circle and joined hands with the priestesses to either side of her, who held their free hands out. Soon all the worshippers were linked.

We are because you are. You are because we are. We call to you in love, the priestess sang in Old Devan. The worshippers repeated after her. Everyone's hands glowed gold, and the golden light spread to form a sphere around them. Then the head priestess began chanting, and although Sona didn't understand most of the words, she understood their meaning: how the sun was part of Bhoomi's creation, how the sun's light and heat made life possible. The other priestesses held mirrors so that the light of the setting sun illuminated the map from the west to the east, bathing everything in a multicolored brilliance. Sona closed her eyes and allowed herself to relax for a moment, savoring the music and letting the golden sound fill her with strength. They would reach Mount Meru, she thought, and would get the amrita to save Ayah's life. They would find a place for Swara to be safe. And maybe, just maybe, they could help save all of Devia. Hope flickered like a flame in her heart.

"Sona!" Raag whispered in her ear. "Look! Do you see it, too?"

Sona opened her eyes and blinked. "See what?" she asked.

"I don't want to point," Raag said out of the corner of his mouth. "Look at Bhoominath on the map. Do you see the red line running across the Khila?"

Sona stared.

On the mosaic map, a red line of light went from the eastern end of Bhoominath north to the mountains. Three-fourths of the way between the city and the mountains, the line lit up a piece of green glass.

"The line goes kind of northeast," Raag whispered.

"Yes," Sona breathed. "But why is that piece in between green?"

"Because," came a familiar voice beside her, "that's an oasis." Gulappan's smile made his face look handsome and young. "That's how we will survive the desert."

30

Deserted

The prayer ended, and Sona, Raag, and Gulappan sought the head priestess.

"Ah, the red line," she said. "We have all seen it, but few have walked it." The wrinkles around her eyes creased as she looked into the eastern horizon.

"I can see why," Gulappan said.

"Our songs say that it is a holy path, one that only those with pure hearts and pure purpose should try, because those who seek evil will find it. Sarpa sees all, knows all."

Sona looked at Raag and raised her eyebrows.

"And if you are blessed enough to see Sarpa, beware her horn," the priestess continued.

Sona thought this was quite alarming, but Raag seemed impressed.

"Is there anything else you can tell us?" Gulappan asked.

"Only that when all seems lost, one must follow the red line with one's heart. I have not walked the path myself, but my grandmother did when she was young, and lived to tell the tale. She never forgot that journey and devoted herself to Sarpa for the rest of her life."

"One more question, holy priestess," Sona said. "Have you heard anything about the Sixth Beast?"

"Ah, yes," said the priestess. "It appears that things are indeed at their worst. So where, we ask, is the Sixth Beast that is supposed to save us all? Some believe it will be the fiercest beast in the Eight Seas and will drive all the Malechs away. All we know about the Sixth Beast is a name from some of the oldest legends: Ekashaggra. No one knows what manner of beast that might be. But there is a description of the person who will call the Sixth Beast."

Sona blinked. "There is?"

The priestess nodded. "Yes, my child. The legend is this:

> *The savior of Devia who will call the Sixth Beast*
> *Hears, and also sings*
> *Betrays, and also keeps faithful*
> *Despairs, and also hopes*
> *Blames, and also forgives*
> *Hates, and also loves*
> *Is of Devia, and is also a stranger.*"

Sona thought this made no sense at all, and it appeared that Raag agreed with her, judging from the bewildered expression on his face.

"Thank you, holy priestess." Gulappan bowed and handed her a small bag of coins. "Please take this and use it as you will to continue the worship here, and to help the poor of the city."

The priestess bowed in return. "May Bhoomi bless you on your journey, wherever it may take you."

Sona and Raag brought Gulappan to where Willa and Swara were waiting.

"That was some advice," Raag said. "I doubt it could be any vaguer."

"Well, we know that we're approaching this journey with pure hearts and pure intentions," Sona said.

"Certainly," Gulappan said.

"Do *all* our thoughts have to be pure? Say, if I were to tease one of you while on this trek . . ." Raag grinned.

"For Bhoomi's sake, Raag, stop it! This is serious business." Sona gave him a shove. She turned to Gulappan with her burning question. "Did you get it?" Sona asked, searching his face. "Is—is the Hunter still alive?"

Gulappan's shoulders sank, and he shook his head. "Worst of all worlds, Sona," he said. "No . . . and yes."

Sona clapped a hand to her mouth.

"So you saw him? Did you fight?" Raag asked.

Gulappan shook his head again. "I went to where we'd left him, but there was nothing there but pieces of cut rope. I don't know whether the Hunter had help, but he was nowhere to be found, and neither was his ring. I asked around the city at healers and restaurants, but no one had seen him. It's like he's the ghost instead of me."

Sona chewed her lip. "I should have remembered when you rescued us—then we'd have the gem already. I'm sorry."

But Gulappan only laughed. "That was a chaotic moment. You barely knew me. We'll get the Fire gem, and then we'll track him down somehow."

Sona shuddered. She didn't want to see the Hunter ever again.

The sky was turning dark blue when they reached the eastern

gate of Bhoominath. "Take a good long drink at the fountain, and let's fill all our water jugs completely," Gulappan instructed. "And then wrap yourselves well in the linen. Desert nights can be very cold."

When everyone, including the animals, had had their fill, they stepped out of the city gate and turned their faces north to the desert.

"I don't know what the scale was for that map, but we need to head slightly northeast to reach the oasis," Sona said as they stepped out onto the sand.

"How will we know which way to go?" Raag asked.

Gulappan pointed to an enormous star hanging low in the sky like a beacon. "See that bright star?"

"Yes," Sona and Raag said.

"That's the Hawk, the star of Paravat," Gulappan said. "It will always take you north."

Sona looked at the familiar star rising in the sky. "The Malechs call it the Wind God's Lantern," she said softly. "At least, that's what I heard."

Gulappan looked at her thoughtfully for a moment before he turned his face to the north again.

They estimated the correct angle and strode along in silence. They walked on through the dark desert night and did not stop to rest until dawn colored the sky again.

Sona was gently shaken awake. "We'd better get going," Gulappan said, his face in shadow above her. "It's still cool now, but we'd better make more progress before the sun gets much higher."

"Yes, that makes sense," Sona said blearily. The sky was bright blue, and based on the sun's position, Sona could tell it was already midmorning. She drank a few swallows of water and ducked her head out of the linen tarp they'd slept under. She made sure Willa and Swara had something to eat and drink, checked Swara's ears, and was relieved to see they were still black. Once they'd packed up, she munched on a lentil cake as they prepared to go north again. Then she stopped.

"How do we know which way to go without the W—the Hawk to guide us?" Sona asked. She spun around, making herself dizzy. "I can't even see Bhoominath anymore." All around her was sand and more sand, dunes, and sky. For a moment, Sona felt like she was drowning in sand. Her breath caught in her throat.

"I made a mark in the sand last night, and I placed my pack so it's pointing in the right direction," Gulappan said, putting a hand on her shoulder. He went to his pack, hefted it onto his shoulder, and pointed. "That way."

"See? Told you we should trust him," Raag said. "He's pretty useful as a guide."

"I'll congratulate you when we get to that oasis," Sona said.

But after four more hours of walking, all they saw was more sand, more dunes, more sky. The sun beat down upon them mercilessly, and the children's steps slowed. Willa hung her head, and Swara panted.

"The animals need rest and water." Sona used the end of the white linen wrapped around her head to blot her face. "So do I."

Gulappan drew an arrow in the sand with his foot. "Let's set up the tarp again."

They set up their tarp and threw themselves under it, out of the sun. At first, they did nothing but drink water—although it was hot, and hardly refreshing.

"Are we sure we're going in the right direction?" Raag asked.

"It was our best guess based on the map," Sona said. "We all agreed on the direction when we set out."

"I thought we would have reached the oasis by now," Raag replied.

"If you think you can do better, be my guest," Sona retorted. Now on top of being hot, thirsty, and tired, she was annoyed.

"Let's not criticize each other," Gulappan said mildly. "We have plenty of water. Let's save our energy for the walking."

"Fine." Raag turned away from Sona and crossed his arms.

"Fine." Sona turned away from Raag and crossed her arms.

"Well, at least we can agree that we are all fine," Gulappan said.

There was a pause. Then all three burst out laughing.

They rested under the tarp for the hottest part of the day, and then set out again when the sun sank lower in the sky. But it was still hot, and no matter how much they tried to conserve their water, they found that they were going through it at an alarming rate. Sona didn't want to eat—it just made her thirstier—but Gulappan encouraged both children to put more than water in their bellies. "We need to keep our strength up," he said.

Sona had a fleeting thought about what might happen if they ran out of water, but she quickly put it out of her mind.

Other than plodding along more slowly than usual, Willa seemed to be all right, but Swara suffered more than any of them, dragging behind them with her tongue lolling on the second day of their journey. Having a black fur coat had to make it unbearable for her. After another midday rest, she took one step out from under the tarp and yelped.

"Poor Swara," Sona said. "Her tender paws!"

"Should we put her in a saddlebag?" Raag asked.

"But that would tire Willa even more. And I'm not sure Swara will fit anymore," Sona said.

Ultimately, they decided to tie pieces of tough canvas over Swara's paws. Although she tried to chew them off at first, when she started walking again and found that they helped, she left them alone.

When night came and the Hawk rose in the sky, they realized they'd been going too far to the east.

"Should we go straight north a while?" Sona asked.

"Then we might overshoot," Raag replied.

"I'm not asking you," Sona said.

"Because you have so much experience in a desert. Or traveling anywhere," Raag said.

"Children, stop," Gulappan said. "Let me think."

Sona started to chew her lip, but then stopped because it hurt too much.

"Let's go straight north for a few hours," Gulappan said. "Hopefully that will make up for getting off course."

They walked through the night, eventually adjusting their direction to a few degrees east of due north. They stopped to rest again, exhausted and aching for water, when the sun started to rise.

Raag drank an entire water jug and fell asleep immediately.

Sona drank a swallow of water and shared some with Swara and Willa. "We have to get there soon, right?" she whispered to Gulappan.

"I hope so, Sona," he said, staring into endless dunes. "Because we're almost out of water."

Sona pushed down the panic that rose in her throat.

After a few hours' sleep, they packed up and started walking again.

"Look!" Raag called suddenly. "Water! Grass!"

Sona squinted, but she couldn't see anything but sand. She tried to pick up her pace, but she couldn't catch Raag, who had broken into a halting run.

"Raag!" Gulappan called. "You're going the wrong way!"

"There's water," Raag repeated. "It's the oasis."

Sona tried to follow, but Gulappan held her back. "Wait, Sona. Don't exhaust yourself until we're sure."

So the rest of the party stayed put and watched Raag as he ran toward nothing.

After another minute, Gulappan called, "Raag! Come back! It's not real."

Ahead of them, Raag staggered to a halt, then dropped to his knees.

He stayed hunched over for a few more moments, and Sona started toward him, but Gulappan put a hot hand on her arm. "Don't waste your energy," he said. "See? He's already coming back."

Raag stumbled slowly back to them. When he finally reached them, he was making noises like he was crying, but there were no tears on his face. "It seemed so real," he said.

"It's a mirage," Gulappan said softly. "I've heard that the Khila does this to many travelers. We cannot believe our eyes unless all three of us see an oasis at the same time."

Together, they made their way slowly northeast, or at least as close to northeast as they could estimate. Twice more, one of them saw green land, and once, even a pool of water. But they made no more stops because the others did not see the same things.

Finally, they were too exhausted to continue. Humans and animals alike were listless and glassy-eyed. They set up the tarp again and rested, unable to talk or even think straight.

"Have some water." Gulappan passed Sona and Raag a jug each. Sona drained the last bit of her jug as Gulappan offered the animals water as well.

"You haven't had any," Sona said.

"I'm all right," Gulappan said.

But he was bigger and probably needed more water, not less, Sona thought.

They stayed under the tarp until the sun went down.

"Can I have some more water?" Raag asked as they prepared for another trek.

"I'm sorry, Raag," Gulappan said. "We've had the last of it."

As they stumbled through the sand in the deepening darkness, Sona knew one thing: they would either find the oasis at last before the sun rose, or they would all die. It was them against the Great Khila Desert, and from the way it seemed now, the desert was likely to win.

DEVAN SAYING:

Sometimes the Snake sheds the skin of tragedy to reveal good fortune.

Sometimes, good fortune is discarded, leaving tragedy in its wake.

The Snake weathers both, and endures.

31

The Red Line

As Sona stumbled through the night with the Wind God's Lantern in front of her, she knew it would be her last night in the Khila Desert—one way or another.

They were wandering in the dark. There was no red line, and there probably was no oasis. Whatever legends were believed in the Sun Temple didn't apply to them. They were never going to make it to Mount Meru. Ayah would die. And Sona's father and brothers would never know what had happened to her.

They were sunburned and blistered. Their lips were painfully cracked. Everything was covered in a film of sand that left them constantly itching. And burning in Sona's mind every moment was her all-consuming thirst.

As Sona looked at the pony and wolf plodding next to her, too tired to even lift their heads, she knew she had brought them to their deaths, too. Her breath caught in her throat, and she stuttered to a halt.

Willa and Swara stopped. The pup sat and tilted her head at

Sona, like she was about to teach her a new trick, like Sona could somehow save her.

Listen to your heart, Sona, pautri, Sona heard Ayah's voice saying in her mind. *It will not lead you astray.*

Then Sona heard the same gentle music, the same clear tone that she'd heard the first time she saw Swara. She gasped. *"Listen. That's it!"* she cried in a hoarse voice.

Gulappan looked back. "Hold, Raag," he said as he walked back to Sona.

"Just a little farther, Sona," he whispered when he reached her. "Don't stop now."

"We're doing this wrong," Sona said, her tongue thick in her mouth. "We've been relying on what we saw in the temple, and guiding our steps based on a star."

"What else are we supposed to do? We're following the red line we saw in the temple mosaic." Raag had come back to join them.

"Bhoomi's magic is all about music," Sona said. "We're supposed to *hear* our way forward."

Gulappan stared at her for a moment. "You might have something there," he said.

"Well? Do you hear anything?" Raag asked. "I don't."

Sona listened. She heard a breeze blowing sand, a gentle snort from Willa, Swara's panting, and the labored breaths of her two human companions. "Not anything unusual," Sona admitted.

"This is a waste of time," Raag said. "We should keep going."

"But we're lost!" Sona said. "We need to make sure we're on the right path, or we won't last another day."

"Fair enough," Gulappan said. "But how do we find the right path if we can't see it and we can't hear it?"

"Just a moment. Let me think." Sona's brain felt as slow and labored as her footsteps. What was she missing?

Raag crossed his arms but stayed silent.

Sona didn't know how to listen for a line or a path. But she did know how to listen for an animal.

"That's it!" she cried. "Raag, you need to sing."

Raag shook his head like she had hit him. "Sing?"

Sona nodded. "Something to do with the Snake, Raag. Please."

Raag looked at Gulappan, who shrugged his shoulders. "It certainly can't hurt."

Sona tried to hide her annoyance that her ideas were considered useless to Raag unless Gulappan approved them. Since when had he become the leader of this expedition?

Raag huffed like he couldn't believe they were asking him to sing. Sona's throat was parched, and she knew it couldn't be easy for Raag.

"Please, let's just try," she said softly. "And besides, I'd love to hear you sing again, before we reach the end of this journey."

Raag nodded wearily. "Let me sit."

They didn't bother to bring out the tarp, but they took out their sleeping mats and arranged them like a carpet. Raag pulled his tanpura out of his pack and sat down with his legs crossed and back straight. He plucked one string, and the sound reverberated. Sona was transported back to the first time she'd heard Raag sing, sitting in Ayah's bedroom, with Swara hiding.

"Sing the Song of the Snake, Raag."

Raag nodded and held out his hands to Sona and Gulappan, who grasped them. Then he began to sing:

Come in, my friend, and rest awhile,
Sit down, I welcome you.
With open hands and honest smile,
I will sing you true.

I'll sing to you of Devia,
Our land so sweet and fair,
Our golden land of Devia,
Where music fills the air.

The sun is glowing in the sky,
Earth black, and water blue,
And freedom-seeking people cry
Oh where, oh Snake, are you?

I heard you singing to the sand,
And trembled at your might.
The time is coming in our land
When we will have to fight.

The desert beckons silently
The river rushes through,
The day is dawning violently,
Oh where, oh Snake, are you?

For Devia has need, my friend
Of hearts both strong and true.
Before the world comes to an end
I call, oh Snake, to you!

Raag's voice was hoarse, but still beautiful. Even if this didn't work, Sona was happy to lie down and fall asleep forever now that she'd heard him sing again. Her cousin truly did have a voice blessed by Bhoomi. The travelers sat in the desert night and breathed.

And then, Sona heard it—faint, but real as the night around her. A sinuous song, a song of baking in the sun and cooling in the dark. A song of endurance. All the hairs on Sona's arms stood on end. Swara peaked her ears, and Willa stomped her foot.

"Do you hear it?" Sona asked Raag and Gulappan, who shook their heads.

She stood and pointed her face toward where the song seemed to come from.

"There's a red line of sound that leads across the sand," she said.

"How can sound be red?" Raag asked. "What does that mean?"

But Gulappan shook his head. "It doesn't matter. I believe she knows the path, however that may be. Lead us, Sona."

"This way," she said.

They walked all night. Sona followed the line and had no doubt she was taking them the right way, for the song grew clearer and louder and somehow *redder* as they traveled farther. At one point, Gulappan grasped her hand, his skin as rough as the outside of a jojonut. "I hear it too now, Sona," he whispered hoarsely. "You've done it."

As the sun peeked over the horizon, draping the sky in pink, Sona looked ahead and saw the most welcome sight imaginable: a swathe of green, with trees and, miraculously, water.

She turned to Raag and Gulappan. "Do you see it?" she asked in a creaky voice.

She knew it was true and not a mirage, but it was still reassuring to see her companions nod. They walked, and the green did not disappear, but grew larger and more detailed. It was real.

They had found the oasis at last.

They would not die, alone and forgotten, in the Khila Desert. Sona was buoyed by a relief so fierce it seemed to make her float.

It felt like hours before they finally stepped on soft grass. They walked as if in a dream toward the sound of rushing water, and they soon saw a small stream. Willa and Swara ran to it in a burst of energy and plunged their heads in to drink.

The humans were not far behind. Sona stumbled to the edge of the stream, dropped to her knees, and stuck in her cupped hands, shaking with fatigue. The water was clear and cold, and she felt refreshed even before she brought her hands to her lips and drank.

Raag lay down and stuck his face in the water.

"Slowly, children," Gulappan said beside them. "Do not drink too quickly, or you will vomit. Small sips."

It was hard to do, given how parched they were. But Ayah had once told Sona the same thing when she was recovering from a vomiting illness. She took small sips, and elbowed Raag to listen, too.

They followed the stream until it widened and became deeper. There, they set up their tarp again, under a type of leafy green tree that Sona had never seen before, and waded into the stream. In the center, the water came up to their waists, and they all ducked their heads under gloriously. Willa walked in until her belly was wet, and Sona took a jug and poured water over her, helping to cool her off completely.

Swara swam in the stream in a dignified doggie paddle, and Sona laughed to see her at ease again. She worried briefly about the black dye wearing off, but she couldn't prevent the wolf from swimming after the ordeal they'd all been through.

"Thank you, Sona," Gulappan said, clasping his hands and bowing, his face dripping with water. "You saved all our lives."

"Yes," Raag said. "Thank you. I'm sorry I was such a pain. But I won't forget what you've done." He bowed to her.

"At least not until next time," Sona said. "I believe I've now saved your life three times, while you've only saved mine twice." She laughed and splashed him.

Raag splashed her back, then threw water at Gulappan. Swara joined in the fun, and they spent the next ten minutes splashing and shaking with laughter. Sona had never loved water this much. How had she taken it for granted for all the years she'd been alive, including and especially when she traveled through Sindhu?

After everyone had emerged from the stream, cool and refreshed, they all suddenly realized how hungry they were. Willa tore up mouthfuls of grass, and Sona broke out more dried fruit and lentil cakes.

Gulappan asked the children to gather dried leaves and wood, and then started a cook fire, ringed by river stones. He filled their small, blackened pot with water and added rice, dried lentils, and some green herbs he'd found growing next to the stream. Soon, they feasted, and Sona thought she had never tasted anything better. Everyone, including Swara, had two large helpings, and Gulappan added more to the pot for later.

Hydrated and full for the first time in days, they all fell asleep under the tarp as the marvelous stream sang its song.

FROM *A MALECHIAN HISTORY OF DEVIA*

The Snake of Khil is one of the most dreaded creatures in all of Devia. It can grow to massive proportions and strike fear into the hearts of the bravest men. Its attacks are many-fold: its venomous bite, its destructive tail, and its terrifying horn. The Snake travels throughout the Khil Desert, stalking travelers and treasure-seekers, leaving fear and death in its wake. No matter how many times it has been struck down, another—or perhaps the same Snake, according to the Devans of the area—always rises.

32

The Snake

They slept all day and only woke as the sun began to set. Gulappan rekindled the fire, and they ate and drank more before falling asleep yet again. Swara cuddled against Sona's belly like she had when Sona first found her, even though she was now bigger than the largest dog Sona had ever seen.

At dawn the next day, Sona found Gulappan repacking his bag. "We should find Sarpa today if we can," he said.

Sona nodded, but a chill crawled up her spine. It was one thing to care for a baby like Swara, and to meet majestic Mahseer in the water. Did she really want to meet the Great Snake of Khila? But Raag and Gulappan were determined that they needed to ask the Snake for her Fire gem before they went to Mount Meru, and they needed Sona to lead them to the creature. Sona was willing to go along, at least for now, because she needed Raag's and Gulappan's help for the rest of the journey. She only hoped that Sarpa was half as friendly as Mahseer had been.

Sona listened for the Snake's song again, and she heard it, not very far away. A song that twisted this way and that, that made her want to dance, to take hands with the others and make them dance as well. But Sona contented herself with striding in time as they moved through the oasis. Along the way, they found some hooli and jojonut trees, and they picked and ate as much of the fruit as they could, and then packed more to enjoy later.

The music led them to a clearing in the trees, carpeted with short plants that had golden leaves and brilliant red flowers. A delicious fruity aroma wafted to them.

"So beautiful," Raag said. "I could stay here all day."

"It's lovely here," Sona said. She glanced around them. "But I think the Snake is nearby, so that may not be the best idea."

"Sarpa will know we are friends," Raag said confidently. "Just like Mahseer."

They walked through the golden-leaved plants slowly and came to a stop in the center of the clearing, where a cluster of three gray rocks stood. Each was about Swara's height and nearly as long, looking like pieces of sculpture. Swara took a sniff and then moved away, uninterested.

"How do you think these got here?" Raag asked. "They look almost decorative, like in a museum."

Sona laughed. "We are a long way from any civilization. And who would haul these rocks across the Khila?"

"You're right," Raag said with a snicker.

"Do you hear that? It sounds like water rushing, but we're not near the stream. I wonder if there's a waterfall nearby," Gulappan said.

"I hear it," Raag agreed. "I'd love to take another dip. I can't get over how curious these rocks are. Where do you think they came from?" He reached out and touched one of the stones.

The stone split.

Swara took off, running out of the golden clearing.

Willa tossed her head, yanked the lead out of Sona's hand, and did the same.

From the opening in the rock—which was clearly not a rock at all—came a snake's head that was easily as big as Raag's own head.

A scream stuck in Sona's throat.

The snake had golden eyes and a large white bump between them. Its skin was bright red, and its forked tongue flickered, tasting the air in front of it. Raag staggered back.

Gulappan looked over Sona's shoulder, and the blood drained from his face. "Quick, Raag, start singing."

Raag continued to face the red snake in front of him, which was emerging from the rock-like egg and proving to be larger than he was. But Sona turned around to see what Gulappan was talking about, and her mouth went as dry as the Khila Desert. Her heart hammered, and she could barely draw breath.

An enormous golden snake with a large white horn in the center of its forehead and eyes that glowed like red gems was slithering toward them. The Snake's head was as big as Swara's entire body, and there was no telling how long her serpentine body stretched.

"Sarpa," Sona breathed as the Snake circled round and round and round them, round and round and round her eggs. This was not a gentle creature, like Mahseer. And Sarpa had caught them right near her eggs.

Once she had completely encircled them, the Snake gazed at them with unblinking red eyes and began to sway back and forth. From the Snake came music—but not the red line of mysterious music that had led Sona to the oasis. This was a different tune, hopeful, a promise of good things to come. And as the Snake swayed, Sona wanted to sway herself, wanted to move closer to the huge head, the darting tongue. She would pledge herself to Sarpa, would do whatever Sarpa wanted of her. All her fears were forgotten.

But the Snake was not looking at Sona. Sarpa was looking at Raag, so close to one of her children. Fast as a flick of its tongue, the young red snake slithered past Raag, over the coils of Sarpa's body, and out of the clearing.

Sona wished the Snake would look at her, would bless her with attention.

Another tune competed with Sarpa's song—that same reassuring melody she'd heard before, punctuated by a clear ringing tone.

Swara. Sona shook her head. What was she doing? She had been entranced by the Snake, but now she realized their danger.

"Raag! Hurry!" Sona cried.

Gulappan shook his head, snapping out of his own trance.

But Raag just looked dreamily at the serpent as her head drew closer and closer to him.

"Raag! The song!" Gulappan yelled.

But Raag didn't sing. Didn't blink. He was still mesmerized by the Snake, just as she had been moments ago. If only he could hear Swara like she could.

"Raag! Wake up!" Sona called.

Then Sarpa's song changed yet again—to a melody that made Sona stand up taller, that made her want to run, to climb, to prove herself a hero. She could do anything; she could save all of Devia. The Snake moved sinuously, and the music filled the clearing. Raag straightened up and put his hand on his heart. Sarpa, the Snake, was here, and all the humans began to sway in time with her song.

Another egg cracked, and another enormous baby snake, this one gold, slithered away.

The Snake kept singing. Sona, Gulappan, and Raag kept swaying. Sona knew they were all going to fulfill their destiny, and Sarpa would be so pleased with them.

Sarpa brought her head down, down, down toward Raag again. She opened her mouth, displaying enormous yellow fangs. Raag reached up as if to touch the Snake.

Once again, a different song filled Sona's ears. A bright note struck. *Wake up*, it said.

Sona's head cleared again. She gasped at what she saw and broke out in a cold sweat.

Sarpa wouldn't hurt Raag, would she? But Sona couldn't risk it.

She tried to pull Raag away, but he wouldn't budge. He kept swaying in time with the Snake, staying eye to eye.

The Snake opened her mouth wider, wide enough to swallow Raag whole. Sona called his name, kept yanking on his arm, but she couldn't move him.

A yell came from behind them.

And the Snake turned around, fast as a thought, and sped away from the clearing.

33

Mayhem and Murder

Raag rubbed his eyes as if waking from sleep. "What happened?" he asked.

The Hunter appeared at the edge of the clearing. "You conniving thief!"

Gulappan drew the Hunter's own silver Air Blade. "Children," he said calmly, "get out of here now."

"Not a chance," Sona said.

"We're a team," Raag said, taking her hand.

"Stay back, then," Gulappan said. "And get ready to run."

Sona and Raag turned to stand in front of the last egg as Gulappan and the Hunter approached each other warily.

"I'm taking back what's mine, criminal!" the Hunter cried. "And then I'll take your life!"

Gulappan shifted on his feet, never taking his eyes off the Hunter's face. "Come and get it."

The Hunter howled as the men charged. Sona and Raag held each other's sweaty hands as they stood powerless in front of the last unhatched egg.

"The Gray Ghost will beat him," Raag said with a conviction that Sona wished she shared.

The clash of metal on metal echoed in the clearing. Gulappan was quick, but the Hunter matched him in speed, despite being larger and heavier.

"Ooh!" Sona said as Gulappan dodged a knife thrust to his throat.

"Get him!" Raag cried.

Gulappan was holding the Hunter at bay, dodging and blocking blows, but not quite able to land his own.

Then the Hunter dropped low, and Gulappan doubled over. "Aaaaah!" He grabbed his leg, and blood welled through his fingers.

The two men wrestled on the ground, grunting and swearing. Gulappan punched the Hunter's face, then groaned as the Hunter kneed him in the belly. They rolled over again, their bodies caked with blood and dirt.

The Hunter sprang up with the Air Blade in his hand. He smiled, showing bloodstained teeth. "Finally," he said.

Sona's blood froze as he turned to look at her.

Something large moved in the ground cover near the edge of the clearing. Sunlight bounced briefly off scales. The Hunter turned his head, sniffed, and took off out of the clearing and into the trees.

The children rushed to Gulappan, who was lying facedown on the ground.

"Gulappan!" Sona cried.

"Please don't be dead," Raag pleaded.

They turned the bandit over. He groaned. Blood flowed from a deep wound in his thigh. His entire pant leg was soaked.

"Quick," Sona said to Raag as she put pressure on the wound. "Take off your head wrap."

He took it off quickly and handed it to her.

Sona wrapped the material around Gulappan's thigh above the cut. She tied a knot and pulled it tight, then secured it with a second knot. She ripped off the end, put it over the wound, and made a makeshift bandage. "Keep pressure on it," she told Raag.

She looked Gulappan over for any more injuries and found nothing but scratches and bruises.

"Gulappan? Can you talk?" she asked.

"I can," he said faintly.

"Does anything else hurt?"

"Only my pride," Gulappan said with a shaky laugh. "I'm ashamed of how quickly he disarmed me."

"He's a Hunter," Raag said. "It's what he does."

"Where is he?" Gulappan said.

"He ran off," Sona said. "After the snakes."

Gulappan tried to rise, but then groaned and sank back down.

"Try to stay still for now," Sona said. "We'll keep a lookout for him."

Eventually, the bleeding slowed down enough that Sona was able to release the tourniquet.

"That was fast thinking," Raag said. "How'd you learn to do that?"

"Ay—Janaki Pitarau showed me, on the farm, when one of the farmers fell and sliced his leg. She showed me what to do, and I never forgot." Sona whistled for Swara. A few minutes later, she came running, with Willa in tow.

"Now let's get this bandage more secure. I can't do much more while the Hunter is still out there."

They helped Gulappan hobble to the edge of the clearing and propped him up against a jojonut tree. Sona plucked some large leaves from the tree and wrapped them around Gulappan's leg, securing them with linen strips from her pack.

"You need to save yourself," Gulappan said, gritting his teeth as she tied her last knot. "Take Raag and Willa and Swara. Get away from this place. I will guard the last egg and follow as soon as I can."

"No," Sona said. "We're allies."

Raag nodded. "We came all this way together, and we won't leave you now."

"The Hunter will return soon," Gulappan said. His hands curled into fists. "And I'm in no condition to fight."

"So we'll fight him," Sona said. She grabbed a large rock from the ground and looked around for the Hunter.

"Not me," Gulappan said. "Guard that egg."

Raag shook his head. "But—"

"He cares the most about that egg. I'm just a bonus," Gulappan said.

"Okay," Sona said, running to stand in front of the egg.

Raag raced to join her and faced the opposite direction, looking through the trees. "We won't let him get it."

"I know this man from long ago, in Tirna. He made my life hell. He will not stop."

"You know him?" Sona asked.

But she got no answer, because at that moment the Hunter returned to the clearing, breathing hard. He held a straight knife in his left hand, and his curved silver Air Blade in his right, and both were covered in blood. "Move aside, children. Do not come between a Hunter and his prey," he said in a sinister drawl.

"You don't have to do this," Sona said.

Swara left Gulappan's side and loped to join Sona.

The Hunter flashed another bloody grin. "I end ferocious beasts before they can cause harm." He leaned over, spat out a mouthful of blood, and held up his Air Blade. "I have you to thank, girl. I knew if I followed you, I'd find the Snake. I finished both those baby snakes, and I struck the mother as well, but then she slithered away. But she'll return to guard her last egg."

He limped as he stalked slowly toward Sona. Raag had moved right next to her. Swara crouched low, and her growl filled the clearing.

"Nice big dog you got there," the Hunter said. He sniffed. "At least part wolf. It doesn't have to die. Just let me get at that infernal egg."

"Not a chance," Sona said, trying to hide the trembling in her body.

"You've got the instinct, girl," the Hunter said, stalking closer, moving from side to side erratically as Swara followed him with her eyes. "You're tenacious. And you have talent with animals. You just need to put it to good use. The offer still stands. Come with me and let me train you."

"I have no interest in killing, and I would never go anywhere with you," Sona said, raising her chin.

"But you would travel with a notorious thief, who betrays everyone and everything?" the Hunter hissed. "He acts high and mighty, but he's killed plenty. You know he got a bunch of Devans killed, back in Bhoominath?"

"Stop your lies," Gulappan cried. He tried to rise, but then fell again, cursing.

"I do not lie, thief," the Hunter said. "There was some sort of

Free Devia meeting held a few nights ago. The authorities learned it would be held in an abandoned warehouse. This great bandit was supposed to be there, but he didn't show. There was a fire." He paused. "Many Devans did not manage to get away."

"No!" Sona cried.

"Liar!" Raag yelled hoarsely.

Gulappan tried to stand, and again fell. His leg was bleeding through the bandages.

"You know I speak the truth. Their deaths are on you, thief. If you had been the leader they thought you were, perhaps you would have been captured, and they would have been spared."

"I have no illusions about Malechian mercy," Gulappan muttered.

Sona couldn't stop shaking. Was Purvi lost, along with all those other children—the children like her and Raag? All in the name of the Malechian King? How many more had to die before Devia was free? Was freedom truly possible? She looked to the sky, blue and blank. Where was the Sixth Beast? When would it come, if not now?

"How did you find us?" Perhaps if Sona kept him talking, they could find some way to subdue him. They had no weapons, but she had a sturdy stone in her hand, and she knew how to throw it.

Halfway across the clearing, the Hunter stopped and sniffed the air. "I've got your scent, girl. I can track you across the whole world."

Goose bumps erupted on Sona's arms.

"She's not your prey!" Raag shouted.

Swara took off toward the Hunter like a bolt of darkness.

"Swara, no!" Sona cried.

But the Hunter was ready. In a split second, he threw the knife in his left hand.

Sona screamed. She had made this happen. She didn't know how she could bear it if Swara died.

But the knife bounced off Swara, and she continued toward the Hunter, unharmed and undeterred.

"*What?*" the Hunter cried.

"You missed!" Raag yelled.

But Sona realized what had just happened. The Hunter hadn't missed.

And he knew it, too.

"Aha!" he cried. "The missing wolf pup. How she's grown." He smiled and lifted his silver Air Blade knife, curved and cruel, and squared off again as Swara closed the distance between them. Sona's blood erupted.

"No!"

Suddenly, the Hunter was knocked on his side. The Air Blade flew from his grip.

"What happened?" Raag asked.

"Willa!" Sona cried.

The pony jumped over the discarded Air Blade and herded Swara toward Gulappan, out of range of a thrown knife, then farther into the trees.

"Even trained your pony, huh? Clever girl," the Hunter said as he reached for his Air Blade and started limping toward Sona and Raag. "But not clever enough to distract me. Now all the questions are answered. This is why you left the house. Not some Devan woman. It was the wolf. That's the scent I've been tracking you with. No worries—I'll kill that wolf after I've taken care of this egg."

Sona stood shoulder to shoulder with Raag and raised her chin again. "You don't have to do this. Sarpa sees all, and she will punish you when she returns."

"I'm ordained by—"

"The King of Malechia, yeah, yeah," Raag said. "We've heard that enough. So you're the King's trained attack dog. Is that supposed to impress us?"

"Quiet, idiot boy. Get out of the way or beware the consequences."

Sona set her stance and took aim. The Hunter was close enough that Sona could see his eerie eyes, his crooked nose, his cruel mouth.

"Raag, go," Sona whispered.

"No chance," he whispered back. "You're not facing him alone."

"He won't hurt me," Sona said.

"We have no weapons," Raag said out loud to the Hunter. "Go ahead and kill us like you killed those poor children back in Bhoominath. You're already cursed forever."

"Shut your mouth, Devan!" the Hunter screamed.

Sona stepped in front of Raag. If the Hunter wanted to hurt him, he'd have to go through her.

Sunlight glinted off the silver Air Blade as the Hunter ran the last few yards to the children. Gulappan was screaming something and trying to crawl across the clearing.

Sona threw her stone. She hit the Hunter square in the chest, but he shrugged off the blow like it was a child's toy. He kept coming. Growls filled the clearing, and out of the corner of her eye, Sona saw Swara return from the woods and streak toward her. But the Hunter had almost reached them. Sona closed her eyes and waited for the blow to fall.

Suddenly, music filled the air.

Sona opened her eyes. The Hunter was standing in front of her, Air Blade raised.

He was frozen. His eyes were wide and staring.

"Raag, are you okay?" she whispered.

"Y-yes," Raag said. "What happened?"

The music continued, and Sona turned around.

It was Sarpa, the Snake. She had a terrible belly wound, but her whole body swayed with her song. Her eyes were focused entirely on the Hunter. The Snake drew closer and closer, dancing and weaving. The Hunter's eyes were glazed, and he moved his head from side to side in time with the Snake.

Sona grabbed Raag's hand and pulled him away, toward where Gulappan was kneeling on the ground. Swara ran next to them like a shadow.

The Hunter stood in front of the Snake, unable to look away from her.

The Snake drew herself up, up, up, red eyes locked on the Hunter. Then she moved her head down, down, down. Her mouth opened slowly, so slowly. Wider. Even wider.

The Hunter stayed still, mesmerized.

This was what the Snake had done to Raag. Sona almost couldn't bear to watch.

The Snake bared her fangs with a hissing noise.

The Hunter blinked. He screamed.

He moved his Air Blade, still raised in his hand, and brought it down upon the Snake's white horn.

The horn snapped off and fell, shattering into pieces as it hit the ground.

The Snake's music stopped. The wound left behind on her head poured blood on serpent and man alike.

Sarpa lunged. She sank her fangs into the Hunter's chest just as the Hunter plunged his Air Blade through her heart.

Sona screamed. The world seemed to freeze, and a buzzing filled her ears.

The Hunter fell back with the force of the Snake's bite. And Sarpa did as well, her enormous body falling, falling to land on her own egg with a horrendous cracking sound.

Silence filled the glade for several long moments.

Sona ran to where the Hunter lay. He had two enormous holes in his chest, oozing venom and blood. Sona sobbed in horror but couldn't bring herself to touch him.

The Hunter laid an icy hand on her arm. "It's too late for me," he rasped. "Don't trust him."

Sona glanced at Raag, who had gone to help the Snake, and shook her head. "S-s-save your breath."

"Not the boy. The thief," the Hunter panted. "He lies. He's consumed with b-bitterness."

Sona shook her head again.

The Hunter's body trembled. His breaths grew shallower. "You would have made a good Hunter," he said.

Sona's face twisted in disgust.

"Here," the Hunter said. "Take it." With shaking hands, he removed the ring with the Leaf gem and held it out to her.

"Why?" Sona asked.

"Don't let him have it," the Hunter said. He held out the ring again. "Take it."

Sona took the ring. The Hunter's eyes lost their desperate look.

"I love this country," he said so softly that Sona had to lean closer. "I served it in the way I thought best."

And with that, the Hunter closed his eyes and spoke no more. His chest didn't rise again.

"You were wrong," she said. "You were wrong." She bowed her head and felt oddly empty. While the Hunter had spent his life doing terrible things, watching a person die was still horrific.

"Sona!" Raag called. "The Snake!"

Sona rushed to Raag's side. Sarpa was lying on her back, her crushed egg below her. Her eyes' brilliance dwindled like a dying flame. Her tongue flickered once, and Sona reached out to touch her.

"Be careful," Raag said, his voice shaking. "I . . . I've been singing to her, trying to keep her calm, but I don't know if she'll lash out in her pain."

"She's dying. I think she finally understands we're trying to help," Sona said.

She reached out to touch the Snake's head. Her scales were soft and smooth. "I'm sorry," she whispered. "I'm so sorry we couldn't save you."

The Snake's eyes glowed brighter just a moment, like coals at the heart of a fire. She opened her mouth.

"Careful," Raag said.

"She's trying to tell us something," Sona said. "Or give us something." She reached into the Snake's mouth, and her hand closed around something small and hard.

The light went out of the Snake's eyes as Sona pulled out the Fire gem.

Sarpa, the Snake

The Snake is sinuous, supple, shifting. Just as seasons move and years pass and sun and wind and water come and go, she sheds her skin to grow. She knows that all life is about change.

Her music varies with her mood and her audience. She never stays still, always playing and dancing and compelling and being compelled. Sometimes she squeezes, sometimes she strikes. Sometimes she tastes, sometimes she swallows whole. Through the centuries, she is always transforming.

Her young, barely hatched, are cut down before her, and her rage burns like the desert sun. She has lived so long, and the wound she sustains means that her final transformation has come.

She inflicts a hurt as deadly as the one she receives. Before her own life ends, she sees a chance to leave a drop of blood that will cause a shift, a seed that will change the world, from which blessings and peace will emerge. In Bhoomi's name, she gives it.

That drop is renewal.

The Snake's life ends, and the desert sun beats upon her as her song and her Devan blood fade.

34

The Cave

The glade was suddenly dotted with a dozen Fire gems, glistening like tears of the sun.

Sona trembled.

"Are you all right?" Raag asked.

Sona looked at the Snake's body. Her knees gave way, and she collapsed to the ground. "Th-th-this is s-s-so awful," she said.

"Come here, both of you," Gulappan said. He was kneeling in the grass, and he had his arms open, like her own father used to when she was little and had hurt herself in some small way.

Sona and Raag ran to him, and he embraced them. His arms were strong, and his heartbeat steady as he held them. Sona leaned on him. She laid her head against his shoulder and let the tears flow for the horror they'd just experienced, for what they'd heard about the Devans back in Bhoominath.

"You both did so well," Gulappan said in a choked voice. "As courageous as any ancient Devan heroes."

They might have stayed that way for a few moments, or a few hours—Sona couldn't tell. Eventually, her shaking lessened, and she drew away and wiped her face on her sleeve.

"Why don't you go to the stream and clean off," Raag said, drying his own tears. "I'll pick up the Fire gems in the meantime."

"Leave them," Gulappan said, grimacing. "No Malechs will find them out here."

Sona stood, then sat back down, unsure of what to do. She felt disconnected from everything, like she was trapped in some strange dream.

"Go on, Sona," Gulappan said softly. "This has been a terrible day, but we are alive. We are safe. Take Swara with you and start to wash away the fear and sadness."

Sona's shaking returned as she stowed the Fire gem in her pack and grabbed some soap and a change of clothes from Willa's saddlebags. She called Swara to her side and laid her hand on the wolf's warm fur as they walked the short distance to the stream. She stripped off her bloody clothing and stepped into the cool, refreshing water.

Was it just three days ago that they had seen Purvi and the other children, happy and fluttering like birds, proclaiming themselves the "Guardians of Bhoominath"? Was it just yesterday that they had finished crossing the desert? Was it just this morning that the Snake and her young ones were alive and well? Was it just a few hours ago that they thought they'd outrun the Hunter?

Sona scrubbed and scrubbed at her face and hands, but she couldn't scrub away the image of the Hunter plunging his blade into the Snake, couldn't stop seeing the Snake biting into the Hunter's chest, couldn't stop hearing the sound of the Snake falling to her death, crushing her last egg beneath her. She couldn't stop seeing Purvi's colorful dress, her bright smile. What was the point of coming all this way if she couldn't save Devan children, couldn't save the sacred animals, Bhoomi's chosen ones? How could she even dream that she could save Ayah after the many ways in which she'd failed? Why were some fated to die so horribly, while she still lived? She started to tremble again.

Swara whined and pressed herself against her, and the wolf's warmth seeped into Sona's skin even in the cool water. Swara looked up at Sona, and Sona heard the bell-like tone again. "You're still here, though, girl, aren't you?" Sona said. She knelt in the stream to hug the young wolf, whose heart she could feel beating, whose presence helped ease some of the dread and guilt from Sona's chest.

Eventually, her shaking stopped. She finished washing and hurried to dry herself and put on clothes. Swara shook herself, sprinkling Sona with droplets, and Sona couldn't help smiling. The black dye had worn off, and Swara's ears shone gold in the sunlight. There was no mistaking what she was now: the Wolf. The last sacred animal remaining in Devia.

Sona arrived back at the glade to find Raag and Gulappan speaking to each other softly.

"You go clean up now," Sona said. "I'll re-dress Gulappan's wound."

As she brought fresh water and soap to Gulappan, he said, "Thank you, Sona, for saving me again. For saving us all." He was even paler than before, and his face was drawn in pain.

"No thanks needed," Sona said. "You did quite a lot of saving yourself." She removed the makeshift dressing and examined the wound, which was still oozing. "This is going to hurt, but I need to do it."

Gulappan nodded. He gritted his teeth and grunted while Sona cleaned the deep cut with soap and rinsed it. She applied Ayah's ointment, and Gulappan was able to relax a little. "Is that—"

"Janaki Pitarau's special ointment," Sona said with a smile. "The best in the world, as far as I'm concerned." She tore clean strips of linen and bandaged the wound again. "There. I wish I had a needle and thread—I've seen Janaki close deep wounds like that—but that's the best I can do for now."

"Sona," Gulappan said. "I'm sorry."

Sona shook her head. "About what?"

Gulappan gripped her arm. "I wasn't a good enough fighter to defeat Rodh, the Hunter. I couldn't save the Snake. I've failed you all—you, Raag, the animals. Purvi and the children back in Bhoominath." His eyes were bleak.

Sona turned his head so he had to look at her. "You saved us," she said. "You saved us from the Hunter in Bhoominath, and got us through the desert, and took the brunt of the Hunter's attack here. We owe you our lives."

Gulappan glanced at the Hunter's still body. "For all his talk of virtue, he was an awful man. Full of Malechian self-righteousness, rigidity, and selfishness. He was the worst type of soldier, carrying out grim orders with pleasure, and without mercy. It was disgusting. He used his strength and talents not to help those in need, but to take as much as he could for his King." His mouth twisted. "What did he say to you, at the end?"

"He told me not to trust you, but I told him to save his breath."

Gulappan barked a laugh, but then grimaced in pain.

"He gave me his ring, the one with the Leaf gem." Sona pulled it out to show him.

"Well." Gulappan twisted to sit up, groaning. "At least he did one thing right in his miserable life."

"Was he . . ." Sona paused, not sure if she wanted to continue. "Was he truly a soldier in Tirna?"

Gulappan nodded. "When I lived in Tirna, Rodh was a soldier in the Malechian army, and his ambition made him do terrible things. When the law was passed outlawing intermarriage and the children of those unions, he led the hunt for those innocents. He killed them, Devan and Malech alike. He used those successes to become promoted to Hunter." His face grew even more grim, and the Golddust scars stood out more prominently.

A chill crawled up Sona's spine. Her own parents might have been the Hunter's victims, if the Goldstorm hadn't killed them first.

"Give me his Air Blade, will you?" Gulappan asked. "It might come in handy if I need to defend us."

It pained Sona to think about anyone wielding that dreadful blade. But she did as Gulappan asked, cleaned the dreadful weapon, and helped him sheathe the blade at his belt just as Raag returned from the stream.

They discussed what to do with the body of the Snake, since it was too enormous to even consider moving to bury.

So the three covered themselves in Gulappan's gray robes and stood over the body of Sarpa, with Gulappan leaning on Sona and Raag. They sprinkled the Snake's body with earth and sang:

> *To Bhoomi you go, to Bhoomi you go,*
> *She has loved from the start,*
> *She will love till the end,*
> *To Bhoomi we go, to Bhoomi we go.*

And they shed tears for Sarpa the Snake, for her children, and for all of Devia, who would miss them.

Sona glanced at the Hunter's body. "As a Malech, the Hunter would prefer to be left in the open air, not buried in the earth."

Gulappan gave her a curious look.

"I for one don't care what his wishes would be," Raag said. "But we can't lift him, anyway."

Sona went to where the Hunter lay, still and cold. She hated what he had done, how bent on pursuing and slaughtering Bhoomi's sacred animals he had become, how determined he was to destroy anyone and anything in his way. And if he had indeed hunted down families and children, he was the worst kind of Malech. But he was still a person. So Sona cleaned the blood and dirt from his face and limbs and laid a knife, his weapon of choice, over his heart. Then she blew her breath over his face in the Malechian way, and murmured, "May the Wind God blow you home, and may you find peace there."

She returned to Raag and Gulappan. Raag shook his head, but Gulappan gave her a brief nod. At least one of them understood.

The travelers decided they would cross the remaining stretch of desert that evening, so while they were still in the oasis, they refilled all their water jugs and gathered as much fruit, fresh herbs, and dried wood as they could fit in Willa's saddlebags.

Sona and Raag argued with Gulappan, insisting that he ride Willa for the desert journey. "You've lost too much blood," Raag said.

"I can walk," he protested.

"We don't want you slowing us down," Sona said.

"Fair enough then," Gulappan said. But he needed both

children's help to get up on Willa's back, and he looked so exhausted that Sona worried for him. How would he survive the trek to the mountain . . . and then the farther trek *up* the mountain?

Looking north, they started toward the mountains as the sun sank below the horizon. And this time, they could follow the Hawk, or, as Sona still couldn't help thinking of it, the Wind God's Lantern, straight on into the mountains.

At one point, Raag went ahead with Swara, and Gulappan called Sona to him. "How did you get the gem from the Snake?" he asked. "I didn't hear you sing, but it's possible that I missed it."

"I didn't sing," Sona said. "Sarpa was dying. I think she finally understood we were friends and gave it to us freely."

Gulappan grimaced as he shifted in the saddle, and Sona noted that his wound was oozing again.

"Let me tend to that."

Gulappan shook his head. "I'm fine. Let's get to the mountains. You are truly remarkable, Sona."

This sounded a lot like what the Hunter had told her. Sona smiled sadly. "We still have far to go. And we never hear of all the people who tried and failed."

"You will not fail," Gulappan said. He gripped her hand. "I know it."

Sona shrugged. "We'll see." It was hard to keep hoping. But she had to keep going forward. She had to keep trying.

They walked along in silence for a while. Then Gulappan said, "I saw something strange."

"What?" Sona asked.

Gulappan looked ahead at where Raag was racing Swara in the light of a crescent moon. "Raag took off his head wrap. And . . .

his ears were not golden. And Swara, when you returned from washing in the stream . . . I thought I was seeing things, but her ears *are* golden."

Sona sighed. She might as well tell him the truth. "The Hunter killed Swara's mother and sibling before he showed up at my house. I've been trying to keep Swara safe from him since I left my home at harvest time. That Earth gem in the Hunter's earring wasn't the sacred gem. It's still hidden. Inside Swara, because she is the last child of the Wolf left alive."

Gulappan raised his eyebrows, then frowned in concentration.

"And as for Raag . . ." Sona glanced at Raag, running ahead in the moonlight with Swara. His secret was not hers to tell. "You should talk to him yourself. But for now, you should rest," she said. "You can sleep—Willa won't let you fall."

A few minutes later, Sona was happy to see Gulappan close his eyes.

After walking all night, the travelers found themselves almost at the foothills of the mountains as dawn came again. Sona and Raag helped Gulappan off Willa's back and settled him back to sleep on a mat as they set up the tarp around him.

"Time to bring out the blankets," Raag said, shivering in the cool wind that blew over the desert.

Sona and Raag laid their mats on either side of Gulappan, and Swara snuggled next to Sona.

"At least we don't have to worry about the Hunter," Raag said.

"Yes," Sona said. No matter what happened, Swara was safe from him. When they got home, Sona could let Swara go.

As the sun rose and started across the sky, Sona stayed awake and stared out at the desert, turning from gray to pink to gold.

Sona woke Raag and Gulappan at noon. "You both need to eat," she told them.

Raag ate eagerly, but Sona didn't like the way Gulappan only picked at his food. He drank an entire jug of water, though, so that satisfied Sona for the moment.

When they reached the foothills of the mountains, they looked up to the tallest mountain in the range—Mount Meru. They saw that it would be slow going, up and down through rough terrain. Gulappan refused to ride on Willa, saying it would sap her strength. So they let Swara lead the way, and she seemed to understand what was being asked of her, finding paths that were the least steep and wide enough for Willa.

There was no wildlife in the mountains. No birdsong, no melody from the land. It was completely desolate.

Gulappan was dragging. His leg began to bleed again, and his limp grew worse.

"You must ride," Sona said.

He shook his head, and Sona shared a worried look with Raag.

After a few hours climbing, they seemed to have made barely any progress. Gulappan lagged too far behind, and Sona called a halt. They ate in the cooling afternoon, and Sona again noted that Gulappan barely touched his food. When she handed him a water jug, she brushed his hand and found that it was burning up.

"You have a fever," she said. "You need to rest now."

"Maybe just for a few minutes," Gulappan said, shivering. But he fell asleep for more than an hour before Sona and Raag had the heart to wake him again. They told him he needed to ride, and this time he didn't have the strength to object.

"We need to find better shelter before night falls," Sona murmured to Raag.

As dusk stained the sky purple and Gulappan could barely stay upright in the saddle, they found a small cave, tucked into the mountainside and sheltered from the wind. Raag and Swara went in first to make sure there was nothing lurking inside.

"All clear," Raag said, and Sona led Willa inside with Gulappan swaying and barely conscious on her back.

"Quickly, let's get a fire going and water boiling," she instructed Raag. He started a fire and set a pot of water to boil while Sona covered Gulappan in blankets. She rolled up his pant leg and gasped. The whole leg was swollen and hot to the touch. The deep cut had turned an angry red and leaked foul-smelling pus. And the redness was spreading upward, toward Gulappan's heart.

Sona let the water boil, then put some in another bowl to cool. She took warm water and soap and cleaned the wound, wiping away pus and blood as Gulappan moaned. Next, she took more of Ayah's healing ointment and spread it on the wound and over the entire leg, wrapping everything in jojonut leaves. She made a tea of tulsi and chamomile and fed it to Gulappan, sip by sip, until at last he seemed more comfortable and fell asleep again.

"I don't know what else to do," Sona said. "But I don't think this will be enough. We need help. But this seems like the last place in Devia that we'll get it."

"His face looks as gray as his clothes," Raag said.

The children fed and watered the animals, then ate their own meal. But Sona didn't taste anything; she was too consumed with worry. "We can't lose him."

"He's the Gray Ghost," Raag said. "He will rise again." But there was a tremor in his voice.

"Let's sing to keep the darkness away," Sona suggested. "Something lighthearted—like a Harvest song." As the fire crackled, she sang softly:

> *Over the ground the moon is glowing,*
> *In the barn, the cow is lowing,*
> *And to the lands we all are going,*
> *On this Harvest night.*

Raag smiled and replied:

> *In the field, the crops are growing,*
> *In the yard, the horse is blowing,*
> *The earth, her bounty she is showing,*
> *On this Harvest night.*

And they sang together:

> *We are thankful for each other,*
> *All are sisters, all are brothers,*
> *Showing love for one another*
> *On this Harvest night.*

Willa snuffled nearby, and Swara rested her head on Sona's leg. Sona reached for Raag's hand and held it tight as they sang the refrain again.

"I'm sorry," Gulappan murmured. "I let you down."

"Don't start that again. We'd never have made it this far without you," Sona said. But when she looked at Gulappan, his eyes were still closed, and he shifted his head from side to side.

"He's dreaming," Raag said.

"I'm sorry! I let you down. I lost you. I lost you both," Gulappan said, writhing in his bed. "The Goldstorm took you both. It's the Malechs' fault. And mine."

"He's delirious." Sona stood and felt Gulappan's arm. "He's burning up again." She took a cloth, dipped it in cool water, and leaned over to wipe his forehead.

Gulappan opened his eyes and looked at Sona blearily. He caught her pendant, hanging down in front of him. "Lia," he said. "I thought I'd never see you again. I'm so sorry. So, so sorry about you and the babe. I tried. But it wasn't enough."

Sona dropped the cloth and stood quickly. It couldn't be!

"Lia! Come back, Lia, don't leave me. Soon the babe will be born, and we'll leave this place."

Sona's heart beat so hard she was sure it would leave her chest.

"What is it?" Raag asked.

"I love you, Lia," Gulappan murmured, his eyes closed. "And I love our babe."

Sona put her hands over her face. But then she looked at Gulappan again, looked past the gray clothes and the scars that covered him.

"I think," she said as she grasped the pendant, her mother Lia's pendant, over her heart, "I think that he's my father."

DEVAN SAYING:

Music and community can heal all hurts.

35

We Call to You in Love

"What?" Raag cried. "Your father . . . but . . . how?"

Sona pulled on her braids. "He just talked about someone he loved named Lia—that's my mother, the sister of Bar Kalpani, the man who raised me. She was married to Ayah's son, Gupil."

"But my uncle died in a Goldstorm," Raag said.

"What if he didn't die? What if he lived, but was scarred—from the storm itself, and from losing his wife and child? What if Gupil didn't die that night, but became someone else?"

"Gupil . . . Gulappan," Raag said.

Sona nodded. "He recognized this." She held out her pendant. "My mother's pendant. He might have even given it to her. I think . . . I think he made it the symbol of the Free Devia movement because of her. Because of our family." She sank back down and put the wet cloth on Gulappan's forehead again, but he didn't stir. "I can't lose him now, not when I've only just found him."

Raag stood. "We've got to find a healer."

"Where are you going?" Sona asked. "These mountains are deserted—that's what everyone's said."

"There *has* to be someone here!" Raag insisted. "Or maybe the Sixth Beast can heal him. What if it's already here? I'll go and look." He went to where they'd left their boots and started to pull them on.

"You can't go wandering in the mountains in the dark! You'll risk breaking your leg. Or your neck."

"What do you expect me to do? He's your father, and my uncle. He needs help!"

"I know!" Sona cried. "Just . . . I can't lose you, too." She went to him and held both his hands.

Raag squeezed back. "But we have to do something," he said. "And you can't go because you need to care for him. I know nothing about healing."

"I'm going to try to get his fever down again," Sona said. "If he's not better in the morning, you can go look for someone to help. You can even take Willa. But for now, please stay."

After a moment, Raag loosed a breath and nodded. "What can I do tonight, then?"

"Just stay with us," Sona said. She reheated the tea she'd made for Gulappan and wiped his face and neck with cool water. And as she worked, Raag sang snatches of work songs, of children's rhymes, of funny tunes to keep them all company. Gulappan seemed to rest more easily as Raag's voice filled the small cave. Willa snorted as if in agreement, and Swara howled once, high and clear. The fever broke, and Gulappan fell into what appeared to be a real sleep.

The children bedded down with Swara between them as Willa dozed in a corner.

In the morning, Gulappan's fever had returned, and he moaned and raved in restless dreams. "Purvi," he said. "All the little birds. Forgive me."

Raag saddled Willa, and she miraculously agreed to let him get up on her back.

"Don't be gone too long," Sona said. "If you can't find anyone by midday, turn around. I don't want you spending the night out there alone."

"If there's any help out there, I will return with it as soon as I can," Raag said. "I promise."

She gave his hand one last squeeze. Swara whined as the boy and pony set off farther into the mountains.

Sona scratched her behind her ears. "Don't worry, girl. They'll be back soon."

Sona returned to caring for Gulappan and managed to get his fever down again. He was almost lucid for a short while, but Sona held her questions back, as she didn't want him to waste his energy on speaking. She got him to eat some thin lentil soup, although she still had to feed it to him.

But at midday, Gulappan's fever rose again, and he became delirious. His wound still oozed pus, his leg was still hot and angry looking, and the redness had spread even higher. Sona applied more of Ayah's healing ointment on his wound and realized that they would soon run out.

"Lia! Lia, run away with me," Gulappan said, tossing his head back and forth. "Let's go across the sea to someplace where no one cares who we are and where we're from. Lia! Lia, I'll save you! I promise, Lia. I'll be back soon. Ma will help—I know she will. No matter how against this marriage she was, she will not let you die.

Hang on, my love. Our babe will be born, and we will live our life together, no matter what the laws say."

A dull headache worked its way behind Sona's eyes as she put cool cloths on Gulappan's head and neck. Swara paced anxiously at the entrance to the cave, whining.

"Stop it, Swara. Crying won't make them appear sooner," Sona snapped.

Swara stopped for a moment, then resumed pacing and whining. Sona held herself back from scolding the wolf again. Sona couldn't blame her; she couldn't wait to see Raag and Willa again, too.

Suddenly, Swara let out a loud whine, and Sona looked up eagerly.

But Raag's head was down as he led Willa into the cave. "Got more firewood," he said listlessly as he unloaded a bundle near a wall. He unsaddled Willa and brushed her in silence, then gave her water and food.

"I take it you didn't find anyone?" Sona asked as she passed him a lentil cake and a jug of water.

Raag shook his head. "There's no one out there," he said.

Sona chewed her lip. "We'll find a way to get Gulappan through tonight, and maybe tomorrow we can go looking again."

"I don't think so," Raag said. "There's a Goldstorm starting."

And Sona understood her headache wasn't just from staying hunched over and worrying about Gulappan.

"Can you help me put a blanket up to keep the Golddust out of here? That's the last thing we need," Sona said.

They tied a rope to some rocky outcroppings on either side of the cave entrance and slung Willa's horse blanket over it to prevent large gusts of Golddust from blowing in. Sona looked out to the bleak landscape, where gold flakes were falling rapidly, and her head pulsed and ached.

"Now we need to make more tea and try to get his fever down," she said.

"Take a break and eat. I can boil water," Raag said.

Sona sipped water and nibbled on a lentil cake, but it tasted like ash. She couldn't lose her father—her real father, who had risked his life trying to save her and her mother—so soon after finding him. And how in the world were they going to get to the top of a mountain without his knowledge and strength? Everything seemed as empty as these wretched mountains.

But Willa snuffled into her ear, and Swara leaned against Sona, chasing away her dark thoughts for a moment. "Yes, girls," she said. "There is still work to be done."

She showed Raag how to make the tea, steeping tulsi and chamomile and mint. He reheated the thin lentil soup as well. Raag was good at this work—probably from his years of helping his mother.

"How come you aren't a healer, like your mother?" Sona asked.

Raag shrugged. "I was never that interested. I always loved working with animals—the ones on farms, of course, but also the ones in the wild. I once charmed a leopard and got it to let me touch its paw! But you've been the one charming all the magical beasts we've encountered."

Sona shook her head. "We're a team, each half of a Beast Singer."

"But Sarpa—"

"Let's not argue. Let's see if we can wake Gulappan and get him to drink this tea and eat something."

But Gulappan was burning up, and they could not rouse him,

no matter what they tried. He was limp as flatbread dough; his breathing was rapid and shallow, his pulse thready.

Sona thought of Gulappan's smile the morning they ate at Shilpa's restaurant, the way he kept Raag and her from arguing in the desert, his laughter as they splashed in the oasis. Her chest hurt. Her eyes stung.

After coming all the way to the foot of Mount Meru, they were going to lose him.

The Goldstorm howled outside, and Sona heard a fell voice on the wind, a voice full of loss and sorrow. Her head felt like it was going to burst. A wave of nausea washed over her, and her eyelids became heavy. But she couldn't sleep, not while her father was ill and needed her.

"Help me, Swara," she said. Swara had helped her during the Goldstorm back in Tirna, and on the boat with Yaami.

Willa tossed her mane, and Swara raised her head and looked at Sona. Sona heard a gentle, comforting melody, and a bright note like a bell, and her head cleared a bit. She bent to wipe Gulappan's forehead again.

"Come on, Gulappan, wake up," Raag said softly. "We need you. Come back to us."

Sona remembered saying the same thing at Ayah's bedside. She made up her mind. "Raag, we need to use magic to heal him."

Raag shook his head. "I told you I don't know any healing magic."

"But you know the melody your mother sang that time, when we all sang to Ayah, right?"

Raag shrugged. "I think so?"

"All Devan worship starts with the same phrases: *We are*

because you are. You are because we are. We call to you in love. Let's sing those phrases to that tune. Let's try to use the gems and see if they can do something outside of Bhoomi's Crown. It can't make things worse, can it?"

Raag blew a breath out. "It's certainly worth a try."

Sona took the Leaf, Water, and Fire gems and arranged them around Gulappan. She put Swara at his feet, and she and Raag sat on either side of him. Raag plucked a string on his tanpura, and they each laid a hand on Gulappan's injured leg. Then they joined their free hands together.

We are because you are, they sang. Sona wouldn't exist without this man, her father.

You are because we are. They would bring him back, would help him live a long life. Together, she hoped.

We call to you in love. They were bonded to him by blood and affection, and were calling him back from illness, from despair, from death. They were calling him back to be with the living. With them.

They sang over and over. Swara laid her head on Gulappan's foot, and Sona smiled. They kept singing. Willa came over from her place in the corner and rested her head on Sona's shoulder, like she was trying to help, too. Through their singing, Sona heard the familiar gentle melody and the bright bell note, and they kept the wailing of the Goldstorm away.

Sona's voice grew hoarse, but she didn't stop singing, and neither did Raag.

We are because you are. You are because we are. We call to you in love, they sang. The storm raged outside, but inside the cave, the air rang with tenderness and hope.

From: The Honorable Alt Somani, Governor of Sindh Province
To: Tal, Lord Malady, Chief Minister to the King of Malechia

Moonday, first day of growing, YK 707
ღ Year 227 of the Devan Fourth Age ღ
ღ 14 years before the Present Day ღ

High Minister:

I must urgently warn you of trouble brewing here in Sindh. The Devans here have become obstinate and dangerous, and despite their unyielding commitment to nonviolence, their control of water transport will bring our trade to a grinding halt.

They have no weapons, but in groups, they wield magic with as much force as any Air Blade. And the key to their strength, their magic, and indeed, their history—is music.

I exhort you, Minister, to speak with the King. Outlaw music, and we shall have these Devan rebels by the throat.

Yours in duty and honor,

Alt Somani

36

The Path

Sona shoved the wolf's snout out of her face. "Swara, stop!" she giggled. Then she remembered where they were and what they were doing, and she sat up suddenly, bumping her head against Swara's. The wolf stumbled back and sat.

Sona stretched her stiff neck. She had fallen asleep next to Gulappan on the hard dirt floor. The fire had died down to embers, and Sona couldn't tell if it was still night or day because of the blanket blocking the cave entrance. Raag was sleeping soundly on the bandit's other side. Sona felt Gulappan's skin—it was cool. Too cool? Had he succumbed to the infection during the night? Panic flared in her chest.

Calm down, Sona, pautri, came Ayah's voice in her head. *Do what you know how to do.* Sona swallowed and took several deep breaths. She felt Gulappan's neck for his pulse. There it was— strong and steady. She put her ear near his nose—he was breathing! Relief coursed through her like a sweet melody.

She pulled the blanket off Gulappan's injured leg and found that it was still red, but perhaps a little less red than the night before. And the wound, although still angry looking, was no longer leaking pus. That had to be a good sign.

She watched his scarred face while he slept. Did her nose look a little like his? Her hair was the same shade of dark brown. Her mouth, she thought, must resemble her mother Lia's.

Sona stood and added more wood to the fire, then put water on to boil. She went to Raag and shook him gently. "Our singing worked!"

Raag sat up and rubbed his eyes. "It did?"

Sona dropped to her knees, grabbed Raag's shoulders, and hugged him tight. "We did it!" she cried. "He's not well, but he's definitely less sick."

"Can I get a hug, too?" Gulappan's voice floated from next to them. "And I could eat something, if there's anything to be had."

Sona and Raag helped him sit up. Then they hugged him for a long time, until Swara whined and claimed him for her own kisses.

"Do you remember anything?" Sona asked.

"The last I remember, I was riding Willa in the foothills," Gulappan said. "How long have we been here in this cave?"

"Two days," Sona said. "You were very ill."

Raag whispered to her, "Aren't you going to tell him?"

"I will," Sona whispered back. "Let's get him completely well first."

The Goldstorm lasted two more days. While Gulappan didn't recover instantly, he did make progress each day. His fever came and went, but it was never so high that he became delirious again. After one day, he insisted on hobbling around the cave to try to get his stamina back. Sona only let him do so for a short while before she made him sit and rest his leg on his pack. She scraped the bottom of the jar of Ayah's ointment, applying the last of it, and eventually, the wound lost the stink of infection, and the redness began to recede. But the one thing that Sona would not budge on was that she and Raag sang over Gulappan each night. At first, he seemed embarrassed, then moved beyond words. He held their hands as they sang, and Swara nestled her head on his chest and wouldn't move.

On the morning of the third day, they could finally see a blue sky peeking through at the edges of the blanket at the cave entrance. Raag jumped up and started pulling on boots and layers of clothing. "I'm getting more firewood. And Willa and I found a stream on our last trek, so I'll bring back fresh water, as well."

"I can come with you," Sona said.

"No, you should stay . . . and talk," Raag said, leaning his head toward Gulappan.

It might be easier to tell Gulappan what she'd learned if they were alone. "Don't be long, please," Sona said.

"Just long enough," Raag whispered as he pulled aside the blanket and led Willa outside.

Alone with Gulappan, Sona suddenly felt desperately shy. "I have a question for you." She pulled the pendant out of her shirt and showed him. "Do you recognize this?"

Gulappan's eyes widened. "Where did you get that?"

"From home," Sona said. "It was my mother's. I never knew her, but her name was Lia."

Gulappan's brow furrowed. "But it cannot be. My wife and child were both lost to Goldstorm Fever."

Sona took a breath. "I only recently learned my true parentage. I'm half-Devan. My mother, Lia, was Malechian. She died of Goldstorm Fever the day I was born. But I survived, and was raised by my uncle, Bar Kalpani, as his own daughter."

"Truly?" Gulappan asked, his eyes widening with wonder. "You—you were raised by Bar Kalpani?" He paced back and forth and ran his hands over his face.

"Yes," Sona said. "So . . . it's true, then? You are my father, Gupil?"

Gulappan stopped pacing. He stood in front of Sona, reached for her hands, and held them gently as he looked at her with new eyes. "Yes," he said softly. "That is the necklace I gave my wife, Lia, long ago. I had it made and painted the enamel myself. It contains the symbols of both of our nations, in harmony with each other. Back in a time when we believed that Devan or Malech, we could have a life together." Sadness and wonder fought on his scarred face. "If only I had known that you lived!"

Gulappan let go of one hand and touched Sona's cheek gingerly, like she was a mirage that might disappear. "I loved your mother more than anything, and we were so happy to be married. But then new laws were passed by the Malechs, and we had to hide with your uncle and aunt. I couldn't work outside the farm, could barely show my face in public. But we were going to have a baby, and I held on to that hope. Once you were born, I wanted to take us far away from Devia to a place where we could live as free people." His face fell. "But when that terrible Goldstorm struck, and Lia became so ill . . . I knew the only hope of saving her was to seek help from my mother, reluctant though I was to ask her.

"So against Bar's advice, ignoring his pleas, I went out into the storm. I tried to follow the road to the village, but I couldn't see my own hand in front of my face. Then a gust came through, like a wave on the ocean . . . and that's the last thing I remember, until I awoke in the middle of nowhere. I could barely move, could barely talk. I had Golddust burns everywhere. Each breath was like inhaling fire. I had no idea how much time had passed, but I knew for sure that I'd failed, that my wife and unborn child had perished. I dragged myself along, practically crawling, until I found myself at the Genla.

"I fell in, and I could barely keep afloat because I was so weak. All I could think of was that it would be a blessing to join Lia and our babe in the afterlife." He swallowed. "But I was found by some of the Genpur villagers, half-drowned and raving."

"Yaami?" Sona asked.

Gulappan nodded. "She wasn't Pitarau yet. But she had also suffered a great loss. Malechian soldiers had recently killed her husband. We had . . . shared grief. And so Yaami and I formed a friendship. The villagers nursed me back to health and gave me something to live for. I became Gulappan, striking fear into the hearts of Malechs wherever I could and stealing back the gems that were the reason why they continued to pillage our country and rule over our people. And Yaami provided transportation to Bhoominath and beyond. Together, we started the Free Devia movement, and convinced others to join us. We used the symbol from the pendant as the symbol of our cause."

"But why didn't you seek out your mother?" Sona asked. "She would have told you I was alive. She saved me from illness when I was a newborn, and she's been my ayah since then. She helped raise me since my mother was gone. If you'd come back . . ."

Gulappan dropped her hands and shook his head. "I hadn't spoken to my mother since before I married Lia. Ma was against the marriage, against the idea that Devans and Malechs should lead lives together. And when I went through Kanthpur in disguise a few months after the Goldstorm, I was told that both Lia and Bar's wife had died. I didn't know that the baby had survived. Not many other than your grandmother and Lia's family knew that Lia had been pregnant, so no one spoke of it. And I couldn't bear to face your grandmother. She had been right: all my hopes had resulted in disaster. I didn't want to witness my mother's disappointment, or even worse, her pity. So I thought it would be better if she believed I was dead. In my heart, I was no longer Gupil, but someone else, someone whose mission in life was to undo some of the damage that the Malechs wrought. Now that I know what I've missed, it is my greatest regret. Oh, Sona, can you forgive me?" Gulappan put his hand on her shoulder.

Sona thought carefully. "I grew up not knowing the truth. But I also grew up happy, and safe." She rested her forehead against her father's. "I wish I'd known you for longer. And I'm sorry for all you've been through, how lonely you must have been. But now we've found each other after all."

He drew back and put his hand on her head in a blessing, like Ayah used to do. "I'm so grateful to have found you. Whatever happens after this, I will always work to make the world better for you."

Sona embraced him again. She had found the father who had given everything years ago to try to save her, who worked his entire life to act on his beliefs. She loved the father who raised her, but she loved the father she'd discovered, as well.

She couldn't imagine what her family would look like after this. First, they had to complete their quest. And then, she could bring her father home.

Raag appeared in the doorway with Willa.

"And Raag, in case you haven't guessed, is Ayah's grandson, your sister Ashvi's son."

A strange look came over Gulappan's face. A beat later, it was gone. "Nephew!" he cried. "Come here!"

Raag ran to Gulappan, but instead of hugging, they clapped each other on the shoulders. "I found some berries," Raag said. "Are you hungry?"

"Do you even have to ask?" Gulappan said.

If the Gray Ghost was hungry, Sona thought, then perhaps soon, they could keep going with their mission.

The children made Gulappan rest in the cave for the remainder of the day while they prepared their packs and saddlebags for the next morning. "You are riding Willa," Sona said to Gulappan, who merely inclined his head. He was not going to argue with her instructions now.

The next day, they packed up everything and Gulappan climbed onto Willa. They bundled up against the drifting Gold-dust and started their trek farther into the mountains.

But even after they had walked and climbed for hours, the snow-capped Meru stayed far away. Sometimes it seemed like they had found paths that had been marked by people, but these often dead-ended at a cliffside or circled back upon themselves.

"I swear we passed that same boulder three times already!" Raag exclaimed. "It's like these paths were created to confound travelers."

"Maybe they were," Gulappan said, scratching his newly grown beard. "What do you think we should do?"

"Do you think the Hawk is out there, somewhere?" Sona asked.

Raag looked at Sona. "You're going to make me sing again, aren't you?"

They sat and had a midday meal tucked into a flat area on the mountainside. After they'd finished, Raag sang the Song of the Hawk. Sona's heart leaped at the last two verses:

> *The mountain's looming silently*
> *The river rushes through,*
> *The day is dawning violently,*
> *Oh where, oh Hawk, are you?*

> *For Devia has need, my friend,*
> *Of hearts both strong and true.*
> *Before the world comes to an end*
> *I call, oh Hawk, to you!*

Sona waited for the returning tune to fill the air, to show them the way to the Hawk, the Air gem, the top of Mount Meru. But all she heard was Raag's voice, echoing back.

The travelers sat together for some time, listening.

"It didn't work," Sona said. "I think the Hawk might truly be gone forever."

Gulappan sighed and clenched his jaw. "We will finish our quest. We're still going to find Bhoomi's Crown."

The travelers kept trekking for the rest of the day, but they got no closer to Mount Meru. Willa was being particularly ornery, and kept refusing to move forward, even with hooli fruit bribes. Each step they took seemed to be against her will. Finally, they gave up, made a fire, and spread out their mats for the night.

"We've got to try something different tomorrow, or we'll never make it," Gulappan said.

"I don't know what else to try," Sona said. "But I agree that today was a waste of time."

"At least we learned what's not working," Raag put in.

"Yes, everything we know how to do isn't working," Gulappan replied with a scowl.

"So maybe tomorrow we try what we don't know how to do," Raag said.

"What does that mean?" Sona asked.

"Let's go to sleep," Raag said. "Things usually look better in the morning."

"I'll take first watch," Gulappan said.

But Gulappan stayed up all night to watch alone, and Sona opened her eyes after a good night's sleep to find Raag arguing with him.

"You should have woken me, Uncle. You're still recovering from your injury and need the rest."

Gulappan shook his head. "I sit on the pony all day, while you two are walking on your own feet. You needed the rest." But he looked particularly exhausted.

The next day was the same story with Willa, who seemed even more stubborn than the day before, huffing and stomping her feet so much that Gulappan got down off her back. "Maybe I'm too much for her to carry in these mountains," he said. "I can walk."

Swara ran in circles, clearly enjoying the brisk mountain air.

But Willa still refused to move from her spot. She snorted and tossed her head.

Raag rolled his eyes, but Sona spoke to Willa tenderly. "What is it, girl? What's wrong?" She examined her hooves, took off her saddle to look at her back, scrutinized every inch of the pony, but other than the hard bump of a white scar on her forehead, there was nothing wrong with her—at least not physically. Willa kept huffing and turning to a path that led downhill.

"Maybe we should let her lead us," Raag said finally.

"What?" Sona asked.

Raag shrugged. "She led me to water, and to an area with trees for firewood. Oh, and to those berries I brought the other day. Maybe she knows where she's going?"

Sona looked at Gulappan. "It's as good an idea as any other we've had recently," he said.

So Sona let go of Willa's lead and told her, "Help us, Willa girl. Help us find the place we're looking for. Help us get to Mount Meru."

And Willa turned around and trotted downhill, back the way they had come.

They followed the pony down, down, down. It was painful to retrace all the progress they'd made the day before, and Sona feared that Willa was trying to lead them out of the mountains, trying to get them home to Tirna somehow. The pony whinnied and started to pick up speed. "Willa," Sona called.

Then Willa turned suddenly and went over the side of the path.

Shyena, the Hawk

The Hawk is far-seeing, fast, and free.

Her song soars through the sky, promising freedom to all: leaf and water, sun and wind, beasts and people and land.

Her wings lift hopes, promising joy, pushing away sorrow and bitterness.

She loves the man who stalks her. He is human, she is animal. They are friends, both part of Devia, both part of Bhoomi's grace.

She does not fear him. But he covets her strength, her beauty, her freedom.

He takes a long talon and hurls it through the air. It spears her through the heart and grounds her. Never again shall she soar above the mountains.

As her Devan blood drains from her, she thinks of the egg in her nest, one that has not yet hatched. And she cries out to Bhoomi to punish the one who has committed such evil.

Her wings are stilled forever.

But in her heart, there lies a seed, a seed that may be used someday to set free what has been bound.

37

The Ruin

"Willa!" Sona called. "WILLA!" She ran to where the pony had disappeared and braced herself to see her friend broken below.

But instead, she found Willa trotting down a steep path into a green valley in the middle of the gray mountains. Here, whatever Golddust was left from the storm seemed to have blown away.

"Raag! Gulappan! Willa found something! Swara, come," Sona cried.

The children helped Gulappan make his way down carefully as Swara ran ahead to catch up with Willa. Once they entered the valley proper, Willa stopped and began munching on fresh grass, and Swara rolled on her back with abandon.

Raag let out an exasperated breath. "I don't know if she got us any closer to Mount Meru, but Willa certainly got to her favorite meal."

They passed a rushing river with clear, cold water, and stopped to take a drink and refill their water jugs. The air was warm and sweet in the valley, so different from the harsh mountain wind. In the distance, Sona spotted something she'd never expected to see in the mountains: a whillet field. The stalks were straggly and bent and had gone to seed, but there was no mistaking what they were.

Sona took Willa's lead and called Swara to her as they passed mounds of rubble that dotted the area periodically.

"I wonder what these were for," Raag said.

Gulappan stopped to examine one of the stones. "They were houses, I think," he said. "Of the people who once lived here. The people of Paravat."

Goose bumps erupted on Sona's skin as they walked along a central path in the middle of the ruined houses, and she got an eerie flash of Kanthpur, its orderly lanes and sturdy homes. She wondered what had caused these people to disappear. Her heart squeezed as she thought of Ayah, sleeping in her bed, waiting for them to return.

Up ahead, a steep cliff of rock rose before them. They kept walking, and as they drew closer, they saw that etched into the stone was a circle—the sacred circle of Devia, with a symbol for each of the five sacred beasts on the outside and a design in the middle that included all of the symbols. Sona's pulse raced. "This must be something important," she said.

Raag pushed against the stone with his hand, and it didn't budge. But a crack appeared in the stone—a crack that went straight up from the ground, over the top of the sacred circle, then straight down again to the ground.

"A door!" Sona said.

The three travelers pushed on the slab of stone but couldn't move it.

"What's the point of a door that no one can open?" Raag said, scratching his head.

"There must be a password of some kind," Gulappan said. "Devia," he said to the door.

Nothing happened.

"Bhoomi," said Raag.

Then Raag and Gulappan tried all kinds of words and phrases in Old Devan, none of which Sona understood. But it didn't matter. The door stayed shut.

"We're missing something," Sona said.

"Yes, yes, yes," Raag said. "A song, right? I don't know any songs for opening doors. Do you?" he asked Gulappan, who shook his head.

"Oh!" Sona gasped. "What about the beginning to all our songs?"

Raag took a breath and nodded.

You are because we are. We are because you are. We call to you in love, Sona and Raag sang.

And the cracks around the circle widened until the door swung in as if on hinges.

"This is how to get to Mount Meru!" Sona said. She called Swara to heel and pulled on Willa's lead as she stepped up to the musty darkness. "Ready?"

"Wouldn't it be better to leave Willa here, where there's plenty of grass? It might be dangerous inside the mountain," Raag said.

Sona rounded on him. "Why are you always trying to leave Willa behind? She's the one who found this valley in the first place!"

Raag put his hands up. "I'm not trying to leave her behind. I just . . . it's dark in there. She might misstep."

"Well then, we'd better bring torches, hadn't we? Willa's the one carrying them, in case you didn't notice. Why don't you light one?"

After some fumbling, they all lit torches and entered the passage. Sona was glad that Swara didn't run ahead like usual and instead stayed close to her side. As far as the torchlight reached, they saw gray stone—stone floors, stone walls, stone ceiling arching above them.

The passage climbed up steeply. After ten minutes, Gulappan muttered, "So much stone. I could use a little of the air that Paravat is so famous for."

After another half an hour of climbing up, the travelers blinked as they entered a large chamber with curved walls and a ceiling open to the sky. It took a few moments for them to acclimate themselves to the sudden flood of daylight.

"That's more like it," Gulappan said.

"Are we in the chamber with Bhoomi's Crown?" Raag asked.

"I don't think we're high enough yet," Gulappan said.

They went to the center of the room, where a line, glinting silver in the sunlight, was etched into the ground in a circle. In its center, above the symbol containing all the sacred animals, was a slim stone column with a small bowl at the top.

"This looks like a temple," Sona said.

"It must be an Air Temple," Gulappan agreed.

"But we don't have an Air gem. No one does," Raag said.

"I'll bet this place could tell us a story," Gulappan said.

Willa nosed Sona's hand, and she petted her tenderly as they moved toward the pillar holding the stone bowl. Sona noticed something lying at its base.

It was a piece of stone, flat and rectangular like a book. And on it was a carving: a nest with an egg, high on a mountain cliff, then a hawk in flight, then the hawk speared through the heart with an arrow. Then the swirl of a storm. Then gemstones, dwindling in number. Then dozens of figures of people, small and large, lying on the ground. Then several triangles in a row. And finally, the nest with the egg on the mountaintop, repeated once more.

"It depicts the death of Shyena, the Hawk," Raag said. "It looks like—it's possible that someone from Paravat killed her. And then the gemstones disappeared. And then—why are the people on the ground?"

"It doesn't matter," Gulappan said hoarsely. "They're gone. They're all gone."

Sona peered at him; she wasn't sure he meant just the people of Paravat.

"I'd never heard that the people of Paravat were the ones who killed the Hawk," Raag said. "And why is the nest repeated twice? And what do those triangles mean?"

Gulappan shook his head in dismissal. "It doesn't matter. The sacred Air gem is gone. We need to keep going," Gulappan said. "We need to finish this. Sona, keep Swara close."

Sona was taken aback by Gulappan's dismissive attitude. But then she noticed how he limped to the opposite end of the chamber, where the passage continued.

"I think his wound is bothering him again," she whispered to Raag.

"All the more reason to finish our quest quickly," Raag replied.

They continued up the passage that led, weaving back and forth, up Mount Meru.

38

The Knife

The passage climbed steeply upward—so steeply that they had to stop frequently to rest and drink water. Gulappan's limp became more pronounced, and he grunted in pain with almost every step.

"You should stay here," Sona said. "We can go up and see, and then come back to you."

"I'll be fine. I said I would be with you until the end, and I meant it," Gulappan ground out.

"You could ride Willa again," Raag suggested.

"I can make my own way," Gulappan insisted.

"By Bhoomi's breath," Raag exclaimed. "Swara! Look at you!"

Sona turned to look at Swara, who had hung back to help Gulappan. Every inch of her fur was golden now, and she had grown even larger. She had become the Wolf.

"She's no longer that pup I rescued," Sona said. "Maybe it's the air of this mountain?"

"I'm grateful for her. For all of you," Gulappan said. He held on to Swara's scruff, and she bore some of his weight.

And so they continued to climb up and up and up. Sona and

Raag each put a hand on Willa's flank, and the pony was sure-footed and tireless. It felt like time had stopped, and they climbed for what felt like hours, or possibly days. They paused from time to time for Gulappan to rest, but Sona and Raag found they needed no food or water.

After long stretches of dark pathway, the flames of their torches began to flicker like fresh air was reaching them. Sona picked up her pace. They needed to get the amrita for Ayah; Sona hoped they weren't already too late. And if they could play their part in saving Devia from the Malechs who oppressed it, from the Gold-storms that destroyed so much, then they would do that as well.

Even though they didn't have the Air gem.

And they had no idea what the Sixth Beast might be, or how to call it.

Finally, they reached a narrow rounded archway that opened to the sky.

In front of them was a large circular stone platform that floated above the clouds. At one end was a sheer cliff wall that went up to the very top of the mountain. And in the center of the platform, there appeared to be a fountain made of the same gray stone that they saw throughout Paravat.

"How are we supposed to get there?" Sona asked.

"That jump has to be at least ten feet," Raag said.

"There has to be a way," Gulappan said. "The Hawk could fly, but the people of Paravat could not."

Swara pushed past Sona and sniffed at the floor of the archway.

Then she stepped out into the air like she was strolling on a road in Tirna.

"Swara!" Sona cried.

But Swara did not fall. She appeared to be walking on thin air.

"There's a path!" Raag said.

And under Swara's paws, they could make out a narrow path, made of clear stone or crystal, just wide enough for one person (or one Wolf) to cross at a time. Swara didn't seem to mind the dizzying drop to the mountain below on either side. She scampered across and ran to sniff at the fountain in the center of the platform.

"Maybe that's where we'll get the amrita," Sona said.

"I'll go look," Gulappan said. He limped onto the nearly invisible path, and Sona held her breath with his every step. But he made it across safely, stepped out onto the platform, and joined Swara at the fountain.

"It's dry," he said.

"There must be some way to get it flowing again," Sona said.

Gulappan bent down to sweep away some dust from the floor. "Look," he said.

He had uncovered a golden line in the floor, a line that curved around the edge of the whole platform in a circle. He brushed away more dust, and Sona could see the symbol of the Tiger with a small indentation in the center.

"Do you have the gems?" Gulappan asked.

"Yes," Sona said, reaching for Willa's saddlebag. But the pouch holding the gems was not near the top. "Hold on, it must have shifted." Sona reached in farther and groped.

"How about your tanpura, Raag?" Gulappan called.

"Yes, it's in my pack," Raag said as he pulled it out. "Oh. I've broken a string."

"Take your time, both of you. In the meantime, I'll try to clean off the floor, so we know where to put everything."

Sona finally found the small pouch holding the gems. But the string that held the bag closed had become tightly knotted. "How did this happen?" Sona asked. "I certainly didn't tie knots like this."

"No hurry," Gulappan said. "We've taken this long to get here; a few more minutes won't matter." But his voice sounded strained.

Raag was fiddling with his instrument. "I've got the old string off. Now to get the new string on, then tune it," he said.

Sona took a deep breath and tried to calm her irritation while Gulappan limped around the platform. "Wait for us, Gulappan. We can do the sweeping."

"Let me do something useful while I can," Gulappan said hoarsely. "And Swara is here with me."

Willa snorted and moved, and Sona dropped the pouch with the gems. "Willa!" she cried, annoyed. "What's gotten into you?" she said, picking up the pouch once more.

Willa whinnied and shook her head.

"Come here, Swara," Gulappan called to her, his voice rasping.

Willa continued to neigh and snort.

"What's gotten into you, Willa?" Sona asked. She was down to the last two knots.

"Almost there," Raag said. "New string is on, now I just have to tune it."

Gulappan had uncovered the entirety of the circle: it featured all the sacred animals of Devia, spaced around the central fountain.

"Bhoomi's Crown," he croaked. "This is it."

"I'm coming," Sona said. "Just one last knot."

"Me, too," Raag said. "This string is almost right."

Willa flattened her ears and rolled her eyes.

"It's all right, girl," Sona soothed. "We're not making you go out there."

Gulappan stood near the sign of the Wolf. He was leaning on Swara. "Whatever happens, you must complete your mission. Even if it's—even if it's without me. Promise me you will," he said. He looked as weathered as the stone of the mountain, and his face had a gray cast to it.

A chill went up Sona's spine. She thought his leg was healed. Was he ill again?

"We'll sing to Swara and ask her for the Earth gem. We'll place the four gems we have here and figure out how to get the amrita for Ayah. Then we'll search the world for the Air gem if we need to," Sona said.

"Together," Raag said.

Gulappan collapsed to the floor near the far edge of the platform. "We'll see about that," he said. "The Hawk is gone forever; there is no Air gem in this world. We have reached the end." Swara whined. She leaned against him, as if to lend him strength.

"We do what we can now," Raag said. "Then we'll go forward together."

Willa wouldn't stop whinnying. She sounded more and more desperate, until finally she was screaming.

Sona undid the final knot. "It's all right, Willa," she said, reaching for Willa's lead.

Swara's cry pierced the air. Sona forgot about the gems and looked to see what had happened.

Swara let out the terrible cry of an injured animal once more, and once more again. She fell to the floor at Gulappan's feet and whimpered. A pool of dark liquid grew underneath her.

Sona screamed.

Gulappan lumbered to his feet, and in his hand he held the Air Blade, its silver tip dripping blood. "It will be over soon," he said. "And Devia will be saved."

Urka, the Wolf

A wolf is loyalty, a heart that beats with the earth. She loves the members of her pack more than anything.

First, there was the girl. The girl healed her when she was hurt, after she lost her mother. The girl gave her food, and shelter, and love. She gave the wolf a name—Swara. The girl kept her safe and taught her how to be in the world.

Next, there was the pony. The wolf knew that this one did not smell like the others. But she carried Swara, and took her to many strange places, and became one of the pack.

Then there was the boy. The boy was cautious at first, but then showed that he liked to run and laugh. He tried to make Swara go away with him alone, and Swara was sad. But then he changed his mind, and the pack was united again.

Next came the man. The man was a surprise, but the girl and the boy loved him, so the wolf loved him as well. The man was full of sorrow and anger, and Swara understood that this was because he thought he had lost everything.

The pack roamed over land and water, in the desert and the mountains, and Swara was proud and happy. There was a place they were trying to get to, and Swara could smell it, could hear it. She tried to help them, for the most important thing was to help members of her pack. She was afraid of nothing, because she had her pack with her.

But then the man she loved pulled a fang of metal and hurt Swara. She didn't know what she had done wrong. She whined in apology, but it was too late.

As her Devan blood soaks the stone, Swara sends her thoughts to the girl. She has loved her from the start, she loves her now, and she will love her always.

And the Wolf leaves behind a seed, a seed of faithfulness that even death cannot destroy.

39

The Last Goldstorm

"No!" Sona screamed. "What have you done?" She ran across the narrow pathway, heedless of the treacherous drop to the mountain below. She shoved Gulappan away from Swara, and he gave way easily, dropping the Air Blade and holding his hands up. Swara stayed very still on the ground, as if any movement might increase her agony.

Swara had lain at Gulappan's feet, had put her head on his chest to help him when he was ill, had literally held him up during the climb up the mountain. And this was how he repaid her.

Raag ran out to join Sona.

Sona knelt in front of Swara, and the Wolf's golden eyes shone with pain. She whimpered and flicked her tongue out to kiss Sona's hand as the pool of blood underneath her grew larger.

"I had to do it, Sona," Gulappan said, his face full of anguish. He looked like a ghost, like he could fade into the air.

"*We do not have to take, when we can ask.* You said that yourself, before. She would have given us the gem." Sona sobbed. "You didn't have to do this." She tried to put pressure on the wounds in Swara's chest, but the blood poured out like a red river.

"I did," Gulappan said. His mouth trembled, and tears streamed down his face. "We do not have all the stones. We cannot fulfill the prophecy. But this way, Devia will be safe."

"How can Devia be safe without any of its sacred beasts? You're not making any sense!" Sona could barely see through her tears.

"Think about it, Sona. Whenever a sacred beast and all its children die, *all its gems disappear.* It happened centuries ago in Paravat, and happened in recent months in Vanam, and Sindhu, and now Khila. All that remains is Tirna. And once Swara is gone, the Earth gems will disappear, too. Once all the gems are gone, the Malechs won't care about Devia anymore," Gulappan continued. "They will leave, once and for all."

"You're just like the Hunter!" Sona cried. "You don't care what horrible thing you have to do to get what you want."

"We trusted you!" Raag cried. "I thought you were a hero. But heroes don't betray their friends."

Gulappan shook his head. "I never said I was a hero. And I take no pleasure in doing this. But it's the way it must be. The Malechs must be stopped. Now the King of Malechia will not care about Devia, for its most valuable treasures will be gone. The Malechs will leave, and the land will finally be at peace."

Sona thought of what Gulappan had said: *Whatever happens after this, I will always work to make the world better for you.* This couldn't be the only way. Killing Swara couldn't make the world better.

Swara whimpered again, more weakly this time. "No, Swara," Sona whispered. "Don't leave me. I need to save you."

"There's no saving her now," Gulappan said. "She's suffering. Let me put her out of her misery. Then we can get the Earth gem.

Come, my daughter, move aside, and let's make this quick for her."
He bent to pick up the Air Blade once again.

"No! Do not call me *daughter*!" Sona thought of her kind and thoughtful father on their farm in Tirna, the one who cared for his animals and indulged her love of strays. She flung herself to cover Swara's body. "If you want to stab her again, you're going to have to go through me!"

Gulappan shook his head. "I don't need to. She's going to die of her wounds, but will suffer longer this way. I love you, Sona. I'm doing this for you and Raag. For all the children of Devia who need to be free of Malechian rule."

"This isn't love!" Sona cried. The pool of blood grew larger, and Sona's tears fell to mingle with it.

"Love means sacrifice," Gulappan said, his face full of weariness and pain.

"Not sacrificing someone else!" Raag yelled, gripping Sona's arm and putting his other hand on Swara.

Swara closed her eyes and grew still.

"Swara!" Sona cried. "Don't go, Swara. Not after all this time. We need to get you home," she said.

"It's over, Sona. Now let's get that gem." Gulappan advanced on them.

"Stay away from her!" Sona screamed. "She's still breathing!"

"Let me do what must be done," Gulappan said gently.

"No! I won't! I can't!" Sona cried, her entire body quaking. "Help us! Someone help us, please!"

A vicious wind blew in flakes of gold. And on the wind was a cry, a lament that went on and on.

Sona understood what she'd been hearing in the Goldstorms.

She understood the anger and sorrow in the wind. "That is the sound of Bhoomi's wrath. Do you hear her?"

"Ahh!" Raag cried, covering his ears.

The cold wind blew, bringing a tempest of Golddust, and Gulappan staggered as if he'd been struck. "I am ready to accept my punishment," he cried, coughing and choking.

Raag hunched over and tightened his grip on Sona's arm.

Gulappan fell to his knees, crying out as Golddust swirled around him.

Sona welcomed the burning of the Golddust. She welcomed the pain in her hands, her face, her lungs, her soul. She hoped Gulappan felt the same. He might be her real father, but after what he had done, she hoped he choked on the storm he had caused. Sona's rage churned through her like a cyclone. She finally understood how Bhoomi felt. If Swara died, Sona wanted everything to end with her. She wanted the whole world to burn.

Sona felt for Swara's breath as everything fell apart around them. She held her hand to Swara's mouth and felt something small and hard land in her palm. Sona choked on her sobs.

She heard a note, a clear tone. Swara's tone. And it was fading. "Please," she whispered. "Please help me save her."

Swara's chest grew still, and her last ringing note faded into the screaming of the storm.

Blinded by Golddust and grief, Sona bowed her head over Swara's body and howled. The Sixth Beast had not come. The fountain yielded no amrita. And Swara was gone.

Raag squeezed her hand. "Sona! We can still try! Where are the gems?"

"I don't know," Sona said, choking on the words. "I don't care."

40

The Answer

Sona was the keening on the wind. She was Bhoomi's sorrow and rage that knew no bounds. She was Devia, that had suffered for so long, and was now coming to an end.

But then Sona heard something, something that was not the wind or the Golddust or the cries of her companions.

It was a song. A song that called to a creature that had not been seen in centuries. *Oh where, oh Hawk, are you?* it asked.

The wind howled and screamed, and Sona screamed with it.

But then, she heard an answer.

She lifted her head. She couldn't see anything, but there was music that came from somewhere else, a response to the call of Raag's song. And it was growing louder.

Sona shook her head. It couldn't be.

But Raag kept singing, and the reply kept coming.

Sona remembered who and where she was. Raag couldn't hear the song, but she could. "Raag!" she cried. "Keep singing! It's here! The Hawk is here!"

Raag kept playing. Squinting through Golddust, Sona saw Willa's face at the entrance to the chamber, staring at her with calm blue eyes. And next to her sat Raag, playing his tanpura and singing as if the world depended on it.

Perhaps it did.

Sona tilted her head to try to understand where the answering song was coming from. It was above her, somehow. But what was above this platform, which was at the top of the world? And what Hawk could fly through this Goldstorm?

Then she remembered the stone tablet they'd seen in the abandoned Air Temple. "There's a nest!" Sona cried. She stood and staggered toward the back of the platform, where the cliff stood, the one that led to the very top of the mountain. The nest must be there, and inside it would be an egg. An egg with a Hawk inside it, answering Raag's song.

Sona put a foot against the gray stone of the mountain and reached up to grab a handhold as the wind whistled and screamed. She hoisted herself up and took another step. She reached again but couldn't find another handhold. She leaped, hoping she'd grab something, but her hand found nothing but smooth stone. She lost her grip and fell, landing painfully on her feet.

Raag kept singing, and the Hawk's musical answer kept coming without pause.

Sona had to try again.

Sona managed three steps up the wall before she fell again. "Keep singing!" she cried to Raag. She took one, two, three, four, five steps up the wall. But then she fell once more, crashing to the platform and banging her knee.

Sona squinted at the cliff wall. She didn't know if she could scale it. But she had to keep trying. And she had to succeed, before the Goldstorm took its toll on all of them.

Sona began again. She imagined she was climbing up to the loft in the barn, chasing after her brothers. She leaped from spot to spot, hoping to find a rock to hold on to, hoping to find a place to step.

And she did, step by step. She kept listening for the Hawk's song, faintly audible despite the howling wind, kept letting it lead her forward to the next hold. Because of the Golddust, she couldn't tell where she was or how far she had to go. She just kept reaching up.

Suddenly, Sona's hand found no more wall. She stretched up and gripped, her palms scraping. Using all her strength, she pulled herself up over the edge of the cliff.

Sona wiped her bleeding hands on her pants and stood. The top of the mountain was no larger than the mat she had slept on during the journey. And there at her feet, at the very top of Mount Meru, was a nest that looked large enough for Sona to lie in herself. And in the nest sat a single golden egg.

The egg was the size of a grown chicken. It was rocking and shaking, and Sona thought it was not just from the wind. There was a Hawk inside, singing to Raag, trying to get out.

It couldn't hatch in the middle of the storm, exposed to Golddust and the vicious wind. Sona had to get it to safety.

She carefully lifted the egg. And where her hands touched its smooth, warm surface, they no longer stung from the Golddust.

Sona tucked the egg into the crook of her left arm and eased herself down over the edge.

Going down was even harder than going up. Sona had to trust her instincts. The trick was to not look how far she had to go, but to concentrate on just the next space she had to land. She inched her way down, step by step by step. With her one free hand, she sought new holds and held on to each rock tightly, while gingerly cradling the egg in the other. She had to keep the egg secure but not crush it. The palm clutching the rock of the cliff began to bleed again, and her arm trembled from the strain. Bracing both feet and leaning against the rock wall, she carefully switched the egg to her other arm. Her injured palm cooled, and her uninjured palm gripped a new rock. She took another step down. And another.

She slipped.

Clutching the egg, she fell.

The wind howled, and Sona braced herself for the pain that was coming.

Something grabbed her waist, and she stopped falling. Sona hung, suspended, with the egg still gripped in her arm.

"Raag?" she cried.

But she could hear that Raag was still inside the chamber, was still singing the Song of the Hawk.

"I've got you," Gulappan said, his voice straining. "Try to regain your grip."

Every instinct told her to push him away. He had betrayed them. He had killed Swara.

But she needed to save the egg.

Sona reached out her right hand but couldn't get ahold of the rock. She tried again. She kicked out a boot and found a foothold.

"Good," Gulappan said. "Keep going."

Sona yearned to scream at him that she didn't need his help. But she didn't want to waste her breath.

Sona kept reaching with one hand and both feet and made her way down the cliff. Her arm holding the egg felt painless, but every other muscle screamed. The Golddust blew, and Sona's skin burned, but she kept going. It seemed to take forever. And Gulappan didn't let go. His arm stayed around her, guiding her to footholds and grips. Each step brought the egg closer to safety.

Sona's right foot slipped. Then her left. She dangled by her arm for a few seconds until it lost its grip as well. Gulappan grasped her tight across her waist and tried to hold on. But then his hand slipped, and he cried out in pain.

Sona hugged the egg and closed her eyes as they crashed to the ground.

41

The Final Creature

All the wind was knocked out of Sona's chest. She tasted the iron tang of blood in her mouth. The egg had tumbled a few feet in front of her.

Sona moved her legs. She moved her arms. She shook her head. Nothing hurt too much. She scrambled to get up and hurried to the egg.

It was unharmed! She held it to her chest.

She turned and saw Gulappan.

He lay on the ground, his leg bent at an unnatural angle below him. "Sona," he gasped. There was a trickle of blood at the side of his mouth. "Are you all right?"

Sona nodded. "You're hurt."

"Don't worry about me," he rasped. "The egg?"

Sona nodded again.

"Go, then," he said. She could barely hear him above the screaming of the wind. "I can die now knowing I've helped you all I could."

Sona needed to get the egg out of the storm, back to Raag. But she hesitated. She didn't want to leave him—just recently, she'd been so overjoyed to find him. Then she glanced to where Swara's body lay, dark and still.

"Go, Sona," Gulappan said. "My body is broken. I will never leave this mountain. Go, and help the Hawk, and get the final gemstone. You can do it. You can save your grandmother. You can save everyone."

Sona turned to look at Raag, who beckoned to her as he sang. Still, she hesitated.

"I heard the music . . . while you were climbing down . . . I heard the Hawk answer Raag's song, and I realized," Gulappan coughed. "I shouldn't have lost faith . . . I shouldn't have allowed despair to overcome me. I became no better than the Hunter. I shouldn't have hurt Swara, who trusted me, who gave me nothing but love. But I had lost so much, and I couldn't hold on to hope. I needed to make the world better for you in the only way I knew. I don't expect you to understand. What I did was unforgivable."

Sona closed her eyes. Her heart felt like it had been pierced by an Air Blade. She tried to untangle her emotions. Only recently, she'd learned she'd lost her father and mother. For a day, she'd gained a father back. Before the betrayal.

"Sona, I know I can't make up for what I did. But for what it's worth, I'm sorry." More blood trickled from Gulappan's mouth, and he didn't have the strength to wipe it away.

Sona blinked furiously. She hated what Gulappan had done. But then she remembered: *It is not people who are good or bad. It is our actions.*

Gulappan had done a terrible thing.

But he'd done good, too, many times over. And he had just sacrificed himself to save the egg of the Hawk. What did Sona know of how many years he had suffered, how lonely and lost he had been?

"It's not my place to forgive you. But I will remember the good that you've done," Sona said.

"Thank you," Gulappan whispered. "Now go, Sona, my daughter. Do what you are meant to do. Leave me and save Devia. Save it for all the children who need you. I don't deserve to see it, but I'll rest easier knowing Devia's fate is in your hands."

And he closed his eyes and spoke no more.

Sona still didn't want to leave him. Her breath coming in short bursts, she turned away, hugging the egg to her, and walked through the Goldstorm on trembling legs, across the narrow pathway, and back to the chamber where Raag was waiting.

She brought the egg to Raag and laid it carefully on the ground in front of him.

Raag kept singing, kept calling the Hawk.

Sona joined her quavering voice with his, and once again felt hope and love shine through during a Goldstorm.

The egg cracked from the inside, and a golden beak poked out, then a fuzzy golden head. The baby Hawk had amber eyes that reminded her of Swara, and Sona smiled through her grief and exhaustion. She reached out to touch its downy feathers.

They sang the song one more time. The Hawk opened its mouth, and Sona reached out her hand again, and felt something small and hard drop into it. *We do not have to take, when we can ask.* It was more than that. These wonderful creatures gave freely. They, not the gems, were the greatest treasures in Devia.

As they finished the last refrain, Sona looked at Raag. "You didn't give up on me. Not even when I'd given up on myself."

"You didn't give up on me when you could have," Raag said. "I'm just returning the favor."

Sona held the Air gem out to Raag. "Come on," she said.

Raag played one more ringing note on his tanpura, then set it down. Willa snorted as Sona grasped the bag with the remaining gems and finally undid the last blasted knot. "Watch over the Hawk, Willa," Sona said.

The Goldstorm picked up its pace. Sona felt that it had grown immensely—perhaps it had grown to cover the entire country. She grasped Raag's hand. "This is it," she said. "Our final chance. Devia's final chance."

"Whatever happens," Raag said, "we'll face it together."

The children walked carefully across the suspended pathway and onto the platform again. As the storm swirled around them, and the keening on the wind rose, they made their way to the circle, clasped their hands, and bowed.

"*We are because you are. You are because we are. We sing to you in love*," they both said to Bhoomi.

"In honor of Vyaghra, the Tiger." Raag placed the bright green Leaf gem in the hollow near the Tiger's symbol.

They walked farther. "In honor of Mahseer, the Fish." Sona placed the blue Water gem and thought of Mahseer's majesty.

"In honor of Sarpa, the Snake." Raag placed the red Fire gem.

"In honor of Vrka, the Wolf," Sona said. She put the black Earth gem down gently, not far from where Swara lay, and fresh tears sprung to her eyes.

"In honor of Shyena, the Hawk," they both said as they placed the clear Air gem in the final spot.

Sona and Raag held hands and stood before the fountain, but it was still dry, as dry as the Goldstorm that swirled around them.

"We've gathered all the stones and placed them in Bhoomi's Crown." Raag's voice sounded far away as he shouted through the wind. "Why has nothing changed?"

Sona shook her head. Then she said, "Maybe we have to call the Sixth Beast?"

"But what is the Sixth Beast?" Raag yelled above the wind.

Sona didn't know.

The tempest swirled, and the children stood, unable to move, unable to think of what else to do.

Could they have come this far, only to fail?

But then Sona heard a melody—a gentle melody that she'd been hearing for weeks, the melody that promised love, and peace. Forgiveness. She thought it had been part of Swara's song. She thought she'd never hear it again. But Swara was gone; it was not her song.

And Sona finally understood. Her body sprinkled with goose bumps. How had she not realized all along? She looked across the path to the chamber where her friend stayed, waiting for her.

"Come on, Willa girl," she sang.

❧ 42 ❧

The Song

The song grew louder.

"Why are you calling Willa?" Raag asked, trying to shield his face from the Golddust. "She won't fit on that walkway."

"You'll see," Sona said.

Suddenly the Golddust in front of them parted, and the children saw something large flying toward them, something black and orange, red and blue and white. It landed in front of them, and even amid the Golddust, the creature shone with its own light. Her coat was shaggy, gold-and-black striped, like the Tiger's. Her tail was scaled like the Fish's, and her blue eyes had turned amber, like the Wolf's. From her flanks sprang enormous golden wings—the wings of the Hawk. And on her head was a single golden horn—a horn like the Snake's.

"The Sixth Beast," Raag said, his eyes widening in wonder.

"She's been with us all along," Sona said. "And that horn is not meant to hurt, but to heal—to play music."

"Well," Raag said, "I guess that broken-down pony was something special, after all. And I guess we are the Beast Singer—together." He laid a hand on the Beast's shaggy flank.

Sona nodded. "Because of us, the Sixth Beast has traveled with us all across Devia. We saw her worth when others did not. We've helped her, and now she's going to help us, help the whole country. That's how all healing begins. With respect. With kindness. With love." She laid her cheek against the unicorn's neck.

"You're right," Raag said. "The Sixth Beast chose you—someone who's not fully Devan. That means something. I wonder if we can make other people realize that, too."

Sona turned to the unicorn. "As our grandmother taught us, we do not take, when we can ask. Please, Willa," Sona said, "please sing your song."

Willa played a song that spread from the mountain outward. The children stood with their arms around each other, listening as golden light connected them and the Beast. All their hurts were healed, and they felt refreshed. The song made them want to laugh and cry, to dance and be still. The song made them want to sing, and it made them want to be silent. Most of all, it made them think.

Sona thought of all the things she'd taken for granted growing up—safety, shelter, food, family—and how this had been denied to so many in Devia. She'd started on the path to correcting that. But she was determined to do more. Her power was in caring—for Devans and Malechs, people and animals.

Raag also looked like he was lost in memories, but he straightened his back. "We'll keep working," he said. "Whatever happens here is just the beginning of what we have to do."

The Goldstorm stopped swirling around them, and the Golddust flew up, up into the air to disappear into the waiting blue sky, where a golden Hawk circled.

Willa walked around Bhoomi's Crown. She reached down with her soft mouth and gathered the gemstones, one by one.

One by one, she dropped each gem into the empty fountain: Earth, Leaf, Water, Fire, and Air. Then she stomped her foot next to the fountain, and it started to bubble forth with clear, cold water. The Sixth Beast was all the sacred beasts together. And so were the people of Devia.

"Thank you, Ekashaggra," Sona said. She looked at Raag, and they both spoke together: "We are because you are. You are because we are. We call to you in love. We seek amrita not for ourselves, but for another."

And for a moment, the water from the spring turned multicolored, as bright as Purvi's dresses, as bright as Devia. And then it turned golden as Golddust. Sona held out a jug and collected some amrita—enough for a mouthful.

Then Sona and Raag stepped to the edge of Bhoomi's Crown and looked out over Devia. Their beautiful country spread out before them: the blue-gray mountain range, the desert that stretched like a golden blanket, the colored spires of Bhoominath, the broad riverlands and leafy jungle, and, sweetest of all, the dark earth of Tirna.

Sona looked back toward Swara's body. "Raag!" she cried. "Where's Swara?"

Ekashaggra

She landed in the world, lost and hurt.

She was here to do something. But what, she did not know.

She wandered the land. Creatures frightened her. No one helped, though she was wounded.

Until the girl found her. The girl spoke to her softly, laid a gentle hand on her, brought her to a place that was warm and dry and safe. She fed her with her own hands, brought her hay and oats and sweet fruit.

The girl gave her a name and showed her what it was to be loved.

They formed a family, the girl and the pup. Then the boy and the man.

They traveled across farmland and water, city and desert.

She saw death, saw the wounds death left in the world. She felt the Mother rage and weep.

They came to the mountains, and Willa remembered where they had to go. She led the family there.

But despair grew in the man.

And at the very top of the mountain, his despair turned to desperation. Willa tried to warn the rest of the family.

But her little sister went with the man, and he killed her.

The girl was filled with rage and despair, like the Mother.

But then the boy sang a song. A song with an answer. And the girl found her hope again, and so did Willa.

They returned the gems, and Willa remembered her name—her original name. She remembered who she was.

She was Ekashaggra. The last Golden Beast. And she was Willa, part of a family.

She was all the Beasts, and none of them. She was fierce, and fluid, and free. She was loyal. She was transformed. She had never been lost; she had always been home. With the Mother. With these two children.

She asked the Mother to rage no longer. She gathered the gems once more, to restore what had been lost.

The Golden Fountain flowed again.

But how to heal the land?

Willa remembered why she was. She recognized her power.

She played her horn.

She sang the truth.

43

The Journey Back

Sona and Raag brought Gulappan's body inside, shrouded him in his gray clothes, and covered him with the gray stones of the mountain.

To Bhoomi you go, Sona sang. *She has loved from the start, she will love till the end.*

To Bhoomi you go. May she give you peace, Raag sang.

It hurt Sona to think that they couldn't say the same over Swara's body, but it was nowhere to be found.

Then it was time to go home.

They removed Willa's saddle and bridle, took off her saddle-bags, and repacked what they could carry. Willa led them on the climb down Mount Meru to the abandoned mountain village, then farther down to the base of the mountains.

Sona brushed Willa one last time, and Willa huffed and nosed Sona's hand.

"Thank you, Willa," Sona said. "Thank you for everything."

Willa snorted softly.

"I'm going to miss you," Sona said. She hugged Willa around

the neck. "You probably have important things to do. But feel free to come and visit whenever you like."

"Here's one last gift," Raag said. And he held out a hooli fruit.

Sona laughed as Willa dispatched it in three bites.

Then with one last toss of her head, the unicorn ran a few steps into the desert. And then she flew.

The children watched until she shrank into a slender line, high in the sky.

"Now what?" Raag asked.

"Now I guess we walk across the desert again? We'd better refill all our water jugs first," Sona said.

"Why couldn't Willa have offered us a ride?" Raag asked.

"I think she had more work to do," Sona said. But she missed her.

As they stopped at a stream in the foothills of the mountains, the children saw a narrow shadow coming toward them across the sand. And then they saw square black sails.

"I know better than to try to stow away again," Raag murmured. "But do you think we can ask them for a ride?"

Sona shrugged. "I'm sure they'll say no, but maybe they'll feel sorry for two kids at the edge of the desert."

The Sun Ship came to a stop, and they hurried to meet it.

Sona gasped when she saw the first person climbing down the long rope ladder.

"Father?"

Bar Kalpani jumped off the ladder and ran to her. "Sona," he cried. "Thank goodness. I've traveled all of Devia to find you."

And Sona fell into the arms of the man who raised her, the man she would always think of as her father.

"You're safe," he murmured over and over as she inhaled his

familiar scent of sandalwood and pipe smoke. "Just as I hoped and dreamed you were."

"But how did you find us?" Sona asked.

"I've been looking for you since you disappeared in that Gold-storm. I was frantic, thinking I'd lost you just as I'd told you the truth. And we were stuck with that Hunter under our roof for four more days." His mouth curled in distaste.

"I'm sorry," Sona said. "I didn't intend to leave the house when I did. But then the Hunter came sniffing around, and I was afraid he'd find Swara—the wolf cub I'd rescued. She had golden ears."

Father's eyes widened. "Now I finally understand what you were carrying in your sweater that night." He shook his head. "And I thought it was another kitten."

"I couldn't let him kill her like he'd killed her mother," Sona said. "Do you understand?"

"I do," Father said. "Although a note would have been helpful. Even when you left Ayah's house."

Sona nodded. "We didn't want the Hunter to be able to follow us. But he did anyway."

Father looked around in alarm.

"He's not here," Sona said. "Not anymore. But tell us, is Ayah still alive?"

"As of a week ago, when I left, she was," Father said. "She was unconscious, but her fever had gone, and she was still breathing."

Sona looked at Raag and sighed with relief.

"After I got your letter, and with the Hunter long gone, I knew I had to venture out to look for you. Ashvi didn't know where you'd run, but she had an idea of whom you might turn to for help.

"When I pressed her, she finally told me you might have sought out Yaami in Genpur, but that I wouldn't be allowed there because I'm a Malech. So I made sure your brothers had everything in hand on the farm, and set out the next day. I thought you might be traveling the country as a Devan girl." He winked at Sona. "I found passage on a boat heading upstream on the Kaveri. I heard that the Hunter had been there, and the Great Fish had been killed, and a Devan boat had been present when it happened. So I kept going, to Bhoominath."

"You looked for us there?" Sona asked.

Father nodded. "It's a big city, though, and I had no idea where to even start. But then I thought about where you might be able to stay with a pony, and I visited the Great Temple. I dressed as a Devan and learned you had stayed there. But they didn't know anything about where you were going."

"So how did you get here?"

"I thought about how you would want to save Ayah more than anything. And I knew of the legend of Mount Meru."

"You did?" Sona asked.

He nodded. "Ayah told me the story of the amrita when she used it to save your life as a baby. I wasn't sure I believed her, but I saw that it worked. I learned from her. I missed her. I missed you."

"Oh, Father, I missed you, too," Sona said, and fell into his arms once again.

"So I took this Sun Ship here," Father said into her hair.

Sona pulled back. "How in the world did you afford that?"

"Don't tell me you stowed away," Raag said.

Father laughed. "Not a chance." Then his face grew more serious. "I sold my earring," he said. "The one with the Earth stone in it. And your brothers gave me theirs, so I sold those, too."

Sona gasped. "But those are family heirlooms," she said.

Father shook his head. "I've been thinking a lot about heirlooms and history. And it seems to me that it's wrong for one group of people to be insulting their friends and neighbors and family by their very appearance. I think we all need to stop paying so much attention to people's ears, and more attention to their hearts, and their actions."

Sona pressed her face to her father's chest.

"Come here, son." Father reached out his other arm and pulled Raag into his embrace.

Eventually, Sona and Raag pulled away, and Father wiped his eyes. "Something fundamental has changed. There was a terrible Goldstorm that stretched over the desert on my way here. I thought this was the end—the end of the whole country. It seemed impossible that we'd survive a storm of that size. I thought I'd never see you again."

Sona nodded. "We felt that way, too." She thought about Swara, and some of the joy and relief she'd been feeling started to drain away.

"But then the storm faded, like fog on a warm morning. And then there was that song."

Sona gaped. "You heard it, too?"

Father nodded. "I'll never forget it. I've never heard anything like it. It made me see things more clearly than I ever have. I'm going to make some big changes when we get home—including making sure that Darshan and all the Devan farmers get their fair share of land. I've been afraid for too long, worried that I'd lose you, lose our way of life." He reached out to stroke Sona's cheek. "I think it's time we all faced the truth of the consequences of our actions."

"That's something I can agree with," Raag said. "I'd love to help."

Father smiled. "Of course you can help. We're kin, after all." He glanced back at the Sun Ship. "You've clearly done wondrous things on your quest. I can't wait to hear all about it. You can tell me on the way home, if that's all right?"

Sona thought of the gems secure in Bhoomi's Crown, of Willa flying away, of the amrita in her pack. "Yes," she said. "Please."

Raag nodded.

Father put an arm around each of them as they walked back to the ship.

When they reached the deck, they were greeted by the leathery-skinned captain, the same one whose ship Raag had tried to stow away on. "Turning around again so soon? Ah, I see why," she said to Father. "Turns out *this* was the treasure you were searching for."

"The only treasure worth having," Father said with a smile.

"In that case, let me offer you a free ride back," said the captain. She furrowed her brow. "It's the least I can do, after a life chasing coins and gems."

Raag, Sona, and her father didn't stay long in Bhoominath, which appeared to be in turmoil, with Devans and Malechs rushing about. But they did pay a visit to the Great Temple, where a girl in a dress that swirled with colors was supervising a group of smaller children handing out food. "Sona and Raag! I knew you'd return!" She ran to hug them both.

"Purvi! We're so glad to see that you're all right!" Sona said. She stepped back to gaze at her. "We heard there was a fire."

Purvi nodded gravely. "Four people died," she said. "Lars, and three children. Shilpa, Ven, and I managed to bring everyone else to safety. So"—she said, looking behind them—"is Gulappan with you?"

Sona spoke carefully. "He helped us get all the way to Mount Meru. He saved us more than once . . . but then he was terribly hurt." She paused. "Unfortunately, he won't be coming back." She wanted to let Purvi hold on to the best of him.

Purvi's face fell. "It's not going to be easy without him, but our dream of Devans and Malechs living together in harmony is one step closer to coming true. After the fire, there was a huge protest in the streets, and so many people, Devan and Malech, joined in. And we were all singing! It got people thinking. We're demanding equal Devan representation on the City Council."

Sona grinned. "That's amazing!"

"It was just the beginning," Purvi said. "Yesterday, there was a song that seemed to come from the sky!"

Sona and Raag looked at each other and nodded.

"It made me think about all we've been doing with the Free Devia movement: proud of what we've done, excited to work even harder. But it seemed to have a very different effect on many others."

"What do you mean?" Sona asked.

"At least half the Malechian soldiers and magistrates in Bhoominath threw down their swords!"

"What?" Raag asked.

"It's true," Purvi said. "Some of them came here to the Great Temple and gave money to the priestesses to help the poor of the city. See?"

Sona looked to where Purvi pointed and saw a long line of what looked to be soldiers, helmets off, giving bags of coins to priestesses.

"But why—"

"There's more. The City Council voted unanimously not to follow the King's terrible law about mixed marriages and children. Those who don't agree are gearing up to leave the country. There's so much to be done now. There are many who want to find a way to live together in harmony. Will you stay and help us?"

"This is amazing! We'll come back to see you someday," Raag said. "But we have work to do, too."

"Yes," said Sona. "Work we must do at home."

The travelers caught a boat heading downriver and stopped at Genpur only long enough to tell Yaami what had happened. Revati was delighted to see Sona and Raag, but clearly disappointed that Swara was not with them.

"We know you succeeded," Yaami said. "For the rivers have returned to normal. After Mahseer was killed, many children grew ill"—she put her arm around Revati—"but now they have recovered. But who is this with you?"

"This is Bar Kalpani," Sona said, leaning against him. "My father."

Yaami raised her eyebrows.

"You can't tell a person's heart from the color of their ears," Raag said, showing his own.

As Yaami looked from one child to the other, several expressions flitted across her face. Sona took Raag's hand as she waited to see how Yaami would react.

Yaami showed her palms in the sign of friendship, and Sona and Raag took one each. "It's been an interesting time," Yaami said. "A time for reflection. A time to see that perhaps the enmities of the past need not be sustained. I knew you would do great things, Sona and Raag. It's why I sent Gulappan to you—to help you."

"He did," Sona said. "And he died bravely, still trying to help us." She swallowed the lump in her throat.

"To Bhoomi he goes," Yaami said. "May he find peace with her."

"He had tasted so much bitterness, but he was hopeful in the end," Raag said, glancing at Sona. "He wanted Devans and Malechs to find a way forward together."

"It's time to let go of anger and hatred, and work to make Devia a place for everyone," Sona said.

"Wisdom from Janaki Pitarau, I'm sure," Yaami said.

"Wisdom from Bhoomi herself," Sona said. "All of Bhoomi's blessings start with respect and kindness, even when it's difficult. Especially when it's difficult."

Sona put her arm around Revati. "Revati was right, after all. The Sixth Beast isn't ferocious or fearsome. It's not meant to threaten or frighten." She thought hard to capture what she felt. "It's about seeing the good in everything, no matter how humble. And it's about forgiveness and healing."

And Sona and Raag told the Sindhus about the Sixth Beast, so they could spread the word.

$\backsim$ 44 $\backsim$

Home Again

Two days later, the travelers finally arrived at the town of Kanthpur and hastened to a familiar house with a dark brown carved wooden door. At their knock, Ashvi flung the door open, grabbed Raag, and held him fiercely.

"I'm sorry I left without telling you, Ma. But I'm back, and I'm not going anywhere for a while. I missed you."

Ashvi smiled through tears. "I have so much to tell you, Raag. So much I should have told you years ago. I thought I'd lost my chance to do so."

Sona found to her shock that in the house were her brothers, and Darshan, and many others, Malechian and Devan, together.

Sona made her way through the crowd. "How is Ayah?"

Ashvi shook her head slowly. "She is awake, but she barely has the strength to talk. I fear her time is near."

"Not if we have anything to say about it," Raag said.

"Everyone, come with us to Janaki Pitarau's room," Sona said.

And they all piled into the room, where a villager was sitting with Ayah, lying so still. Her face was thin, her skin gray, her breathing shallow.

Ayah opened her eyes and smiled at them. "Pautri, dauhitra," she whispered. "You have returned."

"Yes, Ayah," Sona said. "And we've brought something for you."

"Join hands, everyone," Raag said.

Sona and Raag placed their hands on Ayah's chest, and then reached out to Ashvi and Father, until everyone was linked together. Sona poured the mouthful of amrita into Ayah's mouth.

And then they all sang the words, in Old Devan and the Common Tongue: *We are because you are. You are because we are. We call to you in love.* A golden light glowed in their chests and hands and formed a globe that filled the room. Devan and Malech, they were all connected—to each other, and to the beautiful land they lived in.

The music swelled as if it could heal the whole world.

At the end of the song, Ayah sat up. The color had returned to her face.

Sona and Raag embraced her. "Oh, Ayah," Sona said. "We missed you so much. But we remembered all that you'd taught us, and that's how we succeeded."

"We've been on quite a journey," Raag said. "One that should be captured in a song. But perhaps you'd like to eat first?"

"Oh! I am hungry," Ayah said. "Let us all sit and eat together. You can tell us your story. You can sing us your song." She swung her legs over the side of the bed, and they all went outside together.

As food was brought and shared among everyone, Karn came to Sona and squeezed her tight. "We brought the rest of the harvest in together—Devans and Malechs."

"And we told the soldiers who didn't like it to stuff it," Ran said with a smile. "If they didn't agree to share with the Devans, we wouldn't share food with them. But many were happy to help."

"Many Malechs are leaving the country," Lal said. "But those of us who love Devia are staying. We want to choose our own leaders, and no longer answer to any king."

"We have a lot of work to do, figuring out how to live together, as equals," Darshan said. "But we've made a start. And now we have a chance to figure it out together."

"We will," Sona said, reaching for Raag's hand. "We must."

Sona and her family stayed in Kanthpur that night, eating and drinking, talking and singing until everyone in the village knew what had happened on their adventure. They mourned those who had been lost, including all those who had fallen to violence, and the children and Lars in Bhoominath. They spoke of Sona's mother, Lia, and Gupil, a son of Kanthpur. And Gulappan, the Gray Ghost. And they celebrated all that had been saved. They sang their praises to the trees, the water, the fire, the air, and the earth. They sang of the animals, small and great. They sang to Bhoomi and the other gods, and they were filled with joy.

The next morning, Sona took leave of Raag, Ayah, and Ashvi, promising to return the next day. She went with her father and brothers to their farm. Sona's first stop was the barn, where she said hello to the horses and the cows. She looked at Willa's empty stall and sighed.

But then a wolf's howl rang through the air, and Sona's heart started to race.

A clear, bell-like tone came from near the door to the barn. Sona turned.

Standing there was Swara, whole and healed and golden. She was Vrka, the Wolf. She grinned at Sona, and her golden eyes sparked with joy. And coming from her was a song of loyalty, of deep roots in the earth, of a friend who would never give up.

Sona knelt and opened her arms, and Swara bounded to her. Sona hugged her friend and felt her heart beating, strong and steady. Swara looked at Sona for a long moment.

"So you're back!" Sona exclaimed. "Willa did her job well, I see. And let me guess: the other Golden Beasts live again?"

Swara panted happily and kissed Sona's face.

Sona pressed her forehead to the Wolf's. "I love you, Swara. Visit anytime you like. Be free."

And after giving Sona one last look, Swara ran off into the fields and woods of Tirna.

As Sona stood again, she heard the song of the earth, the song of Bhoomi: gentle and loving, patient, kind, and forgiving. The songs of leaves and water, of air and fire, of all the beasts and all the people harmonized to fill their golden land.

Suddenly, she heard the whine of a small creature.

Sona searched the stall, and in a pile of hay, she found a small bundle of dark fur. She picked up the little cat, who mewled and licked her hand.

"It's okay, little one," Sona said as she held the creature to her. "You're home."

Devia, YK 721, Year 241 of the Devan Fourth Age
꙳ 2 months after Sona and Raag's return ꙳

I write to you, Minister, from my own heart and conscience.

The Devans have been telling us we've been wrong for nearly two centuries . . . but we were willfully blind to the truth. Why would we treat other people this way, when we would not treat our own mothers, brothers, and daughters like this? Why have we made the color of one's ears the only thing we could see?

The answer is simple: greed.

I have already publicly acknowledged the many mistakes of the Malechian regime in Devia. I have asked for forgiveness from the Devan people, although some things can never be forgiven. Still, we are making reparations, in coins and in deeds.

I am spending my last days here helping to organize the transition to full Devan rule. I know the King will seek to punish me. To punish all of us. But it doesn't matter.

If you had experienced what we have—a moment of such clarity that does not allow us to lie to the world, nor, more importantly, to ourselves, any longer—you would understand my decision.

I encourage you to look to your own heart and see what you find there.

Farewell,

Taj Zamani

THE NEW SONG

Come in, my friend, and rest awhile.
Sit down, I welcome you.
With open hands and honest smile,
I will sing you true.

I'll sing to you of Devia,
Our land so sweet and fair,
Our golden land of Devia,
Where music fills the air.

Two hundred years, the Malechs stayed
Two hundred years of rule
Until they looked into their hearts
And found them harsh and cruel.

For Sona, Raag, and the Golden Beasts
Have set our country free
But it will take work to make this land
All that it ought to be.

Now Devia has need, my friend,
Of hearts both strong and true,
With wrongs to right, and hearts to mend,
I call, my friend, on you.

Acknowledgments

In this book, my first otherworld fantasy, I tried to tackle the complex and complicated topic of colonialism and its consequences for a middle grade audience. I wanted readers to sit in the uncomfortable space where right and wrong isn't always clear and good people sometimes make bad choices.

My wonderful agent and friend, Brent Taylor, has always encouraged me to write whatever my heart tells me. He believed in this book from the beginning and read an early draft of it just because he wanted to. Brent, thank you for trusting me to tell the stories I need to tell.

Alexandra Cooper didn't bat an eye about taking on this book, even though it was a departure from the realistic verse novels that we had previously worked on together. She took my rough (in the truest sense of the word) draft and helped me shape the story into the fantasy adventure I wanted it to be. I am indebted to Alex for her thoughtful reading, editorial discernment, and incredibly detailed (sixteen pages, single spaced!) notes. Alex, thank you for your friendship and for gently coaxing the best from my writing.

I am forever grateful to Rosemary Brosnan, her vision for Quill

Tree Books, and her commitment to allowing diverse authors to share their stories with the world. Many thanks to the whole Quill Tree team—including Allison Weintraub, assistant editor; Shona McCarthy, production editor; and Vivian Lee, copy editor. Thanks also to Mark Rifkin, Celeste Knudsen, Danielle McClelland, Melissa Cicchitelli, Sabrina Abballe and marketing, Abby Dommert and publicity, Patty Rosati and the School & Library marketing team, and Kerry Moynagh and the sales team.

Kathy Lam designed the incredible cover, the typography, and the interior elements, and made the pages of this book sing. Nidhi Naroth's cover art is the stuff of fantasy dreams, capturing the energy and the urgency of this story in the most stunning way. And Abrian Curington's gorgeous, detailed map makes Devia feel like a real country.

I couldn't write anything without my incredible critique partners, who read and commented and helped me find my way through this story and others: Theresa Milstein, Lisa Rogers, Donna Woelke, Jenn DeLeon, Desmond Hall, Susan Tan, and Katie Bayerl. Thank you also to my wonderful author friends Chris Baron and Josh Levy, who share my love of fantasy.

I'm so lucky that the people I love most in the world always lift me up with their affection and belief and give me the motivation and ability to create. Lou, Joe, and Mira, you are the ones who make everything possible. An avid fantasy reader, Mira spent many a long walk talking over the plot of this book with me, and her input on early chapters was crucial. Mira, thank you for sharing your imagination and insight. I hope this story makes you proud.

Finally, I must thank you, reader, for going on this journey with me and Sona and for trusting me with your time, imagination, and heart. I hope you enjoyed this adventure. I hope it made you think. I hope this story helps bring people together in love and understanding, and inspires you to tell your own stories.